APH
T

ANDREW
VAILLENCOURT

Aphrodite's Tears

The Fixer: Book Four
by Andrew Vaillencourt

APHRODITE'S TEARS
First edition. February 13, 2018.
Copyright © 2018 Andrew Vaillencourt.
ISBN: 978-1976957529
Written by Andrew Vaillencourt.

Also by Andrew Vaillencourt

The Fixer

Ordnance
Hell Follows
Hammers and Nails
Aphrodite's Tears
Escalante

See more at www.AndrewVaillencourt.com

Table of Contents

Chapter One

Roland Tankowicz was once again in a bad mood.

Astute chroniclers of the man's emotional states might point out that he was often in a bad mood. Brave souls, possessed of courage in excess of intelligence, might go so far as to opine that all of his moods seemed to fall on a spectrum that ranged between 'mild irritation' and 'homicidal fury.' They would not be wrong, but this was a special case.

Specifically, his irritated state was wholly the responsibility of external actors, and not a function of his more general grouchiness.

"I'll give you that one for free." His voice could be likened to the sound of a giant piece of industrial machinery as he growled the words through the evening rain. "The next one of you to try that shit is going to die screaming."

The objects of his ire found themselves at an emotional and strategic crossroads. The seven young men dressed in black coveralls and hoods paused in mute wonder, minds boggling at what they had just witnessed and wishing with ardent furor that they had the time to engage in a conference to discuss it. In silent agreement, the men deduced that they did not, in fact, have this kind of time. Instead they gaped in slack-jawed stupidity, each waiting for another to do something brilliant or perhaps burst into some kind of spontaneous and effective action.

Roland sighed. It was a sad testament to his existence that the easiest way to tell if folks were new in town was to observe the type of weapons they employed in their inevitable attempt to kill him. This felt like the sort of thing that said a lot more about his life and his choices than anything else, though this was a probably not the best time to reflect upon it.

For instance, this stalwart crew of bravos was quite obviously not a local group. This was clear to Roland because he now sported eight neat little five-millimeter holes in his shirt. It was new shirt and it was unique in that it was a nice dress shirt that he actually liked. Tailored to fit his bizarre proportions, the garment resided well within the twin categories of 'stylish' and 'expensive.' Or it *had* until a group of black-clad fools decided to make an attempt upon his life, at least. It was now ruined, and somebody was going to have to account for that to Lucia. Roland was a brave man who had seen violent action on twenty different planets, and he was not volunteering for that dangerous duty. Acceding to tactical necessity, the big man decided that one of these poor, stupid, soon-to-be-maimed morons was going to be the one to do it.

His volunteer materialized in the form of frantic incoming bead fire from a dark shadow at the end of the alley. There was a disturbing constant in these interactions that remained a perennial mystery to the big man. A distressing proportion of these cagey killers and criminals, upon seeing exactly how inadequate small-arms fire was when applied to battling Roland, seemed convinced that employing more of the same would make a difference. Objectively speaking, there was no way that shooting Roland ten times or a hundred times was going to be any more effective than shooting him once. It simply did not matter. Roland's skin was impervious to small arms, and his shirt could not get any more ruined than it already was. With a resigned sigh, Roland ignored the frenzied hail of hypersonic projectiles and charged.

Roland's size often led folks into the hasty assumption that he must be slow. This was an entirely understandable mistake for those unfamiliar with the man to make. Six inches shy of eight feet tall and as wide as a small car, moving with any kind of speed would necessitate strength and agility far in excess of what a reasonable person might think feasible for a man of such stature. If that same (likely doomed) individual knew that Roland weighed nearly a thousand pounds, he could be justifiably relied upon to dismiss the thought of so large a person covering a distance of say, thirty feet, in one half of one second.

While the misapprehension might be entirely understandable, the person was likely to die horribly all the same. This hypothetical miscreant, being not so hypothetical in the wet alleyways of this particular Dockside Friday night, might have six friends with him as well. They would be no help to him, which would make him sad during the all-too-brief moment of clarity he enjoyed before Roland hit him.

Roland's hand struck the coverall-clad attacker in the chest. At the last instant, he opened his fist to strike with his palm. As an afterthought, he pulled the blow so as to not shatter the man's ribs or sternum. Instead of a gruesome and instant death, the unfortunate thug accelerated from a standstill to approximately thirty miles per hour in the space of about an eighth of a second. The breath left his lungs with a whoosh and his feet separated from the ground with so much violence that he left his boots behind.

Off into the mist and drizzle the man flew, until the unforgiving stoicism of a concrete wall arrested his flight and he crumpled to the street with a sloppy splash. His hood had slipped from his head during his transit, and a clue as to his origins became abruptly visible. Others may not have seen it, considering the rain and darkness, but Roland's night vision was far better than average. The sight of it made him regret sparing the man's life, though this was an oversight he could rectify later if he wanted to.

The big man straightened, rolling his shoulders back and cocking his head from side to side as if it was stiff and needed a stretch. It did not, but Roland was not above showboating just a little. These men were about to pay the full admission price for their attempt on his life, and Roland figured they were thus entitled to the whole production.

"Somebody," he growled, "is going to have to answer for my ruined shirt." He turned to assess the remaining six men. They stood in the alleyway, hunched against the slick walls with guns in their shaking hands. Their black workman's coveralls were soddened and clinging to their bodies, black hoods pulled low to cast deep shadows over their faces. Roland needed very little light to see, so the effect was wasted on him. It was yet another deficiency in what should have been a textbook hit, if not for a single fatal flaw in the execution. These obviously professional killers had thought they were hunting a man. Their weapons were concealable yet lethal. They had picked an ambush point that was private and had only one exit. They had struck with accurate fire from more than one direction. If Roland had been anything other than what he was, it would have been a perfect assassination. Roland, however, was

9

exactly what he had been made to be. Thus, it followed that the little squad of hitters was about to suffer a slew of career-ending injuries.

The location of the ambush, selected so carefully to keep the ambush-ee from escaping, now served the same purpose against the ambushers. There was only one way out of the alley, and Roland was blocking it. Charitable individuals might choose this moment to point out that this situation was entirely unfair. There was no way this squad of assassins could have known that their target was the sole surviving member of a top-secret warfighter enhancement project. They could not know that his whole body was constructed of exotic techno-organic bone and muscle analogs driven by the same power cell used in large military vehicles. No one had told them that his skin was thickly armored, or that his neurological processes were greatly accelerated by the millions of nanomachines that swam around his manufactured body.

Roland was a technological juggernaut birthed by the darkest corners of the industrial-military complex, manipulated and enslaved by a secret cabal of corrupt military and business leaders, and subsequently discarded when his existence became a liability to the government. Roland did not like to discuss such things, and the Planetary Council would have him imprisoned or destroyed if he did, so it was unsurprising that a bunch of lightly armed killers of indeterminate origin found themselves ignorant of their own inadequacies.

Bereft of any other course of action, the remaining men opened fire in unison with their sidearms. Beads streaked across the alley in a fusillade not unlike the one their unconscious compatriot had just attempted. The shiny black shadows, slick with the rain, lit up like orange flashbulbs as the incandescent trails of ceramic beads lanced through the raindrops and bounced off Roland's chest with showers of sparks and the hiss of steam. The rest of his shirt began to tear away in smoking bits as a hundred direct hits abraded the cloth from his body. It exposed the flat black color of his dermal armor mesh, and the darkness of it sank his form even deeper into the shadows.

Roland shrugged out of the rags and leapt forward. The assassins scattered as he lunged, but they were far too slow. He caught a black-clad foe in each hand on his first pass, and sent each into the walls with far more force than was strictly necessary. Bodies thwacked against masonry with wet thuds and the dull pops of snapping bones. Roland was supposed to be pulling his punches these days, and the changes that had come to Dockside in the last few months were encouraging him to adhere to a lighter touch than in previous decades. However, he had a hunch about this crew, and if he was right, a few of them dying this night would leave the universe better off for his trouble.

More beads exploded against his back. A few remaining assassins had slipped in behind him and were emptying their magazines at close range. The enterprising killers were seeking out weak points, with rounds striking him in the back of the head, his knees, and the creases of his shoulders. Roland spun a half turn and saw three men posted in solid shooting posture, methodically dumping ammo into him with professional accuracy and rhythm. They were close, so Roland stomped on the ground between the clustered group as hard as he could. A foot like a piledriver, driven by leg muscles that could drag sixty tons from the floor and backed by nearly a thousand pounds of mass, drove into the asphalt. The street lurched as a circle of radiating cracks darted away from Roland's boot and nearby puddles erupted into geysers of water vapor. The shooters lost their footing because the ground itself heaved violently beneath them and both men crashed to deck in a tangle of limbs.

The last man still standing decided to take his chances with escape and bolted for the mouth of the alley. Roland could not have this, so he scooped one of the fallen shooters from the puddling crater into a monstrous hand. With the flick of a thick wrist, the remorseless giant hurled the screaming man at his fleeing partner.

The two full-grown men collided at speed, one flying through the air, and the other running with singular focus. Their heads smacked together like coconuts and the sound of it communicated to Roland that he may have hurled his missile with a touch too much energy. Neither projectile nor target moved once they came to a halt on the ground, and the poor lighting and the rain made it impossible to determine if the growing puddles beneath them were water or blood. Roland assumed it was blood, which was generally a safe assumption under the circumstances.

The alleyway, so recently alive with the lights and sounds of a pitched battle, went dark and quiet once again. The dull white noise of accelerating rainfall muffled the distant groans of dying men, and for a minute Roland simply stood with his head cocked to one side. With his auditory gain turned up as high as he could, the big cyborg simply listened. It took a moment to filter out all the other sounds of the rainy Dockside night, but one by one he eliminated them and was left with nothing besides the breathing of his victims and the shuffling of those still capable of some small degree of movement. Soon, he heard a small whine and the immobile onyx statue became a darting black wraith. He scooped the first man he had downed from the ground and flipped him to his back, revealing a small explosive device clutched in a desperate fist.

The man's face, pale and drawn with pain from any number of horrible injuries, wore a small sanctimonious expression as their eyes met. That look changed to confusion when he saw neither fear nor shock in Roland's. Thick fingers closed around the clutched grenade in the limp hands of the semiconscious man. The massive black paw engulfed the smaller hands, preventing the killer from releasing the spoon and triggering the device.

Roland leaned in to put his face very close and grinned. "We figured you guys would show up eventually. Now, in a second I'm going to release that pin so you can blow yourself up. Before you go, I want you die knowing that this little thing," he squeezed the hand, cracking finger bones against the grenade they held, "won't even scratch my paint."

Roland hoisted the man aloft, still trapping the explosive in a balled fist. He marched his gurgling captive over to a recycling container and keyed the lid open. The injured man, suddenly realizing what was happening, began to lurch and gasp, unperturbed by how much his thrashing aggravated his already serious injuries. The gasps took on a desperate, terrified wheezing tone when Roland lifted the man over the dumpster and held him there, dangling by his own mangled hand. Roland's other hand closed around his neck and with a ruthless, merciless twist, the pitiless cyborg tore his doomed victim's arm from his shoulder. A spray of arterial blood followed, and the heaving gasps of pain morphed into a tortured scream that for a moment drowned out the rain itself. Eyes bulging, the bleeding man could only stare in abject horror at the leaking nub of his own arm as shock and blood loss began to close the door on his cognitive faculties.

Roland dropped the maimed man into the recycling container and tossed the removed limb on top of him.

"Welcome to Dockside, pal."

Then Roland closed the lid with a metallic bang and stepped away. Six seconds later the grenade went off and the heavy metal lid of the dumpster cartwheeled forty feet into the air propelled by a gout of yellow flame and a noise like a thunderclap. It crashed to the pavement with a wet clang and Roland nodded in approval. Then he turned to the other downed men to assess and clean up his mess. Of the remaining six, four were dead, one would not last long, and another looked like he might survive long enough to give some good intel. Or he would not give good intel and likely not survive at all. The choice would be his to make.

The big man sighed, keyed his comm to Lucia's channel, and pinged her. She answered quickly.

"Roland! Where the hell are you? You're late!" Lucia did not like to be kept waiting.

"Sorry, Lucy. Not going to make it tonight. Something has come up."

There was a long pause. "How many dead and who's crew was it this time?"

"Five dead, two badly wounded, one likely survivor."

"Okay," she responded, "I'm sending one of Rodney's clean-up crews..."

"No!" he almost shouted. "No regular crews. Send me Manny and Mindy. We'll clean this one in-house."

"Roland..." Lucia's voice had that 'tell-me-what-the-hell-is-going-on' tone to it. It was a dangerous tone, delivered by a dangerous woman.

He interrupted her. "Better warn Manny, Lucy. The Red Hats are here."

This pause was longer than the last.

"Oh, shit. Dammit. Timing really sucks on this. Okay. We are on our way."

Roland closed the channel with a sigh. Then he turned to the only surviving man uninjured enough to be useful to him. He was still unconscious, and a cursory examination made it clear that at a minimum he had a severe concussion. If the extra bends in his right leg were any indicator, it did not appear likely it was going to support his weight for a very long time either. Other than that, his breathing was regular and his pulse was fine. One could be forgiven for assuming this meant the man had been 'lucky.' Roland soon put the lie to that erroneous assumption.

"Well, my little friend," Roland growled at his oblivious foe. "We have about twenty minutes before my back-up arrives and Lucia makes me play in a nice, enlightened manner with you." Basketball-sized shoulders slumped, "Let's just see what I can get out of you before they get here, shall we?"

Chapter Two

Lucia Ribiero took one look at Roland's disheveled appearance and threw him an irritated chuff.

"Now you know why I never bought nice clothes before," he responded to her glare with a sheepish shrug.

"This is getting re-goddamn-diculous." Her irritation was legitimate, but the half-life of clothing in his line of business had always been brutally short and there had been no reason to believe that improving the quality of his wardrobe would alter this. All the same, she did not want the big man to start dressing like a hobo again.

She gave up on chastising him for the premature destruction of yet another pricey suit, and turned her attention to the carnage in the alley. Broken bodies and the charred remains of a recycling unit were strewn about in a random pattern, while greasy streaks of mixed blood and rainwater swirled across the pavement to pool in crimson eddies. A dark eyebrow rose over a pretty brown eye as the astute woman began to piece together the events of Roland's evening. Her brain, home to millions of nanomachines not unlike Roland's, began to work backwards from the available evidence to assemble various scenarios. Soon, she had narrowed the possibilities down to eight or nine most-likely versions and she huffed again with consternation at the implications.

Lucia's father had been one of the scientists who had built Roland, and then part of the renegade group that had freed him from government slavery. She had grown up blissfully unaware of this, for obvious reasons. She had always thought her father was just a successful biotechnologist with a couple dozen lucrative patents to his name. As an adult, she was content to be the vice-president of a beverage company and enjoyed a lifestyle that would be the envy of anyone from outside the posh Uptown districts. This carefully crafted existence crumbled abruptly when her father got kidnapped by a giant corporation bent upon bringing Roland's technology back to the military. That was when her own augmentations asserted themselves, revealing a nervous system and brain almost entirely rebuilt with cutting edge nanotech. Lucia, they found, had the fastest reflexes in the galaxy with agility, balance, and proprioception to match it. The machines drove her own bone and muscle cells to the limits of their genetic potential as well. Underneath the tailored suits of the successful executive was the body and brain of a superhuman. Once she had started turning over rocks in the seedier zones of the New Boston Megalopolis, more than one large and strong man had learned to his chagrin that the lean one-hundred-and-thirty-pound woman was as strong as he was. Over a four-day period of frantic running and gunning, the career businesswoman had morphed into a fantastic field operative. After a whole year of missions, battles, and scheming had passed, those machines had further adapted and refined her skills to a razor's edge of professional competence.

"They were hunting you, huh?" She tossed the question to her oversized partner.

"They thought they were," he corrected. "I picked them up on The Drag back by Farragut's. I let them herd me over here, just to see what they were up to. I figured they were moving me somewhere quiet to go for a takedown, and since I didn't want to wake the neighbors either..." He shrugged with a small smile, "... I thought I'd go ahead and use their own cleverness against them."

"You missed at least two of them, I think," she shot back.

"I know," he agreed. "I spotted one scout, but he never engaged. I thought there might be an officer of some kind out there. If there was, he never showed himself either."

Roland had learned in their time together that the most impressive of Lucia's abilities was not her speed or strength. It wasn't her marksmanship or martial arts prowess either, though both were suitably impressive. As good as Lucia was in a fight, the galaxy was full of augmented humans who were fast or strong or skilled in the arts of war. It was Lucia's ability to process numerous data streams and trains of thought simultaneously that made her truly unique. When she focused, and when she kept her anxieties in check, she possessed a positively inhuman quantity of parallel processing ability.

She was employing it now, and Roland could see her face twitch as she put it all together. She had figured out that the hit squad would have had a scout and a leader from their numbers and how they had maneuvered him into the alley. The condition of the recycler and the distribution of debris and gore told her that there had been an explosive in play. She found no craters or gouges in the surrounding walls, and this told her that there had been no large-caliber weapons used and that the men had not missed when they fired.

"Professional group," she said out loud. "No misses and no signs of wild fire. One of them had a bomb or something, in case they needed a fail-safe." She looked again at the red smears on the walls, showing up as dark stained areas washed in ragged streaks by rivulets of rain water from overhead gutters. "You lose your temper a bit, dear?"

Roland looked at his feet. "When I realized they were Red Hats, I may have overdone it a little, yeah." He looked up. "I'd apologize, but I'm not really all that sorry."

"I hear ya, big guy." She smirked at him. "I'm not going to give you to hard a time about that. We got a talker?"

Roland gestured to a lone figure, sitting up against the wall and staring at them with a vacant, heavy-lidded gaze. "He's not real chatty, yet. I think he's warming up to me, though."

"Mindy will be here in a minute, then he'll probably open right up." Lucia seemed to take delight in the thought of that, which made Roland nervous. He decided to change the subject.

"How'd Manny take it?"

"Fine. More resigned than anything. He's coming with Mindy."

Roland shook his head. "This is going to be very interesting."

Lucia winced at the thought of Mindy's interrogation methods. "I'm just glad I haven't had dinner yet."

"Sorry I ruined date night." Roland actually was sorry about that. He had only ever dated one person in thirty years, so he took his responsibilities in this regard very seriously. Then another thought hit him. "You haven't eaten yet? When did you last eat something?"

Lucia's body burned through energy at several times the normal rate. Keeping her adequately fed was a fairly daunting process, and the consequences of her getting hungry could be dire for any person fool enough to get between her and her next meal.

17

"I'll be fine, Roland." She flicked the magenta streak of rain-soaked hair stuck to her forehead away from her eyes. It sat in stark contrast to her otherwise brunette pixie cut. Roland liked the way the rain was soaking her clothes to her body, faithfully portraying her athletic physique in contrasting blue and black shirt and pants. One year in, and the giant cyborg was still completely at a loss as to why a woman of her beauty, taste, wealth, and intelligence would ever slum it with a glorified goon like him. For whatever reason, he was not the sort of man who was going to spoil a good thing by asking too many stupid existential questions about it. Roland was more than happy to leave the deeper ruminations on love and relationships to the poets and philosophers and just trust that Lucia knew what she was doing. Lord knew he did not, so it was good that at least one of them felt confident.

"What do we have so far?" Lucia pulled his attention from her body and back to business.

"Very little. It's a good-sized team, so this was not a scouting mission. They knew Manny would be here and that he was with me. They had enough intel to try and hit me first, but like most folks who aren't from around here they underestimated my capabilities."

"We have a leak?" Lucia wondered aloud.

Roland frowned. The expression clouded his already heavy-browed face in even deeper shadow, and cast his likeness in competing streaks of darkness and light under the inconsistent illumination of the alley. "I don't know. It took them a good six months to find him. That's not so fast that it rules out regular old hunting." He rubbed his face with a giant gloved hand. "I'd hate to think we have a leak."

The alleyway lit up in that moment, harsh horizontally directed light burning everything into either stark illumination or blackest shadow. Lucia covered her eyes and squinted into the pair of blazing headlamps casting their garish beams into the tiny space. "Looks like Mindy and Manny are here."

She registered the hiss and click of doors swinging open and then slamming closed again. Two silhouettes obstructed the beams of light and Lucia removed her shielding hand when the searing radiance of the headlights swung backward and away from her eyes. When her night vision returned, she could see a young man of medium build standing at the entrance of the alley. He was

18

aggressively average in stature. Neither big nor small. Not tall, yet not exactly short, either. His face was a deep tan and smooth, and he wore his black hair long and tied back. He was dressed simply in blue dungarees and a brown jacket. A satchel hung diagonally across his chest, and Lucia knew that it was filled with exotic electronics and other tools of his trade.

Next to the young man stood a tiny blond woman. She was as pale as the man was dark, and her shape was as striking as his was average. The little woman had squeezed shapely legs into black pants so tight as to appear painful and her prodigious chest was barely contained by four brave buttons manfully holding a too-small dress shirt closed against the intense pressure.

The young man's face was cast in a bronze rictus of tight-jawed apprehension, and the woman was leering irreverently down the alley toward Lucia and Roland. The little blond spoke first as the pair walked into the rain-slick shadows. "Hey, Boss! Roland kill a bunch of people again?"

Lucia gave the woman a look that communicated quite clearly that her humor was ill-timed. "Mindy, this is one of those times when a wise little assassin would stop talking."

The goofy visage evaporated at this and the small woman had the good sense to affect an air of sheepishness. "Got it. Sorry, Boss."

Lucia turned to the young man, now staring with distant rage and transparent sadness at the bodies strewn about the street. "Manny? You okay, Manny?"

"Yeah," the dark-skinned youth said quietly. "I always knew they'd come. Usually I'd have moved on before they got to me, so I never had to see them. Feels weird to look at them now."

"Anybody you recognize?" Lucia was not sure this was a question she wanted an answer to, though she asked it out of necessity.

"No. But it's been a few years since I was home."

Roland spoke up. "Well, looks like it may be time to go visit. Are you ready for that?"

Manny shrugged. "Who knows? Is that the type of thing anyone is ever ready for?"

Mindy took a chance on speaking, and for a change, she kept a respectful tone. "Let's sort out exactly who they are and how they got here without us knowing first, huh? If we are talking about taking the fight to them, then we need to do this right."

"You're the expert on this stuff," Roland conceded. "I was never much of a hunter."

"First, we pull IDs," Mindy instructed, and Manny waved a dismissive hand at her.

"There won't be any. These aren't Dockside hoods or even registered hunters. These are Balisongs."

When the women showed nothing more than confusion at this proclamation, and Roland supplied the necessary details. "The Red Hats call their in-house death squads 'Balisongs.'" When this did not seem to clear things up, he explained further. "A balisong is a kind of knife, made to look like a woman's hand fan when closed. It opens to reveal a blade. It was a popular assassin's tool in the far east and Polynesia a long time ago.

Lucia looked askance at her large partner. "Each morning you wake up and can't remember where you put your shoes the night before, yet somehow you have memorized the history of every weapon ever used by humans?"

Roland shrugged. "Limited storage. I save my memory for the important stuff, obviously."

"Like ancient weapons?"

"Don't knock it, kids. I killed a heavy armature with a war-hammer once."

"I was there," Mindy pointed out. "That was weird to watch."

Manny chose this moment to pipe up. "There won't be any ID on them, and their fingerprints will have been burned off. We'll need retinal images or DNA to identify them. Even so, if they are free-birth Venusians with no previous criminal records, then there will be no records of that stuff either."

Mindy wrinkled her nose. "What are the chances of them being free-birth Venusians with no records?"

"Pretty damn good, to be honest." Manny shook his head and said with gravity, "Balisongs are a carefully chosen group."

"All right," Lucia threw her hands up in defeat. "Let's get what info we can and clean up this mess. I can only assume that someone from Rodney's crew will be sniffing around soon. I'd like for there to be no way for anyone to tell that a terrorist hit squad was here. We'll take this one..." she tossed a disgusted look over at the wounded terrorist, still swaying and groaning against the wall, "...back with us for interrogation."

A brisk search of the dead men confirmed Manny's suspicions. Mindy took retinal scans and DNA from each of them just in case, and then the team confiscated all of the crimson skull caps the assassins had worn. Roland scanned them for augmentations, but as they had all suspected, there were none to be found.

With the search complete, the team hustled the nearly-unconscious Red Hat survivor into a waiting ground transport and headed back to their office. Roland stayed behind to await whoever came to investigate the gunfight.

He did not have to wait long. The red lights of the transport had barely faded into the greasy darkness of the rainy streets when the splish-splashing of several pairs of boots clomped over to his alley. Roland was leaning casually against the wall with his arms crossed, and the approaching group of men met his laconic stare with expressions of frustrated incredulity. There were four of them, ranging in size from medium to nearly as big as Roland. All were dressed in shabby, ill-fitting suits with worn overcoats, and none of them looked comfortable wearing either. The changes to Dockside had come quickly, and so much of the newly-organized street muscle was still adjusting to the new paradigm. Dressing like professionals did not come naturally to this cohort. Roland could sympathize, since he didn't like wearing suits, either.

"Evening boys," he drawled.

The largest of the group sighed heavily in his direction. Rain pooled and ran off of his wide-brimmed hat in determined streams as he spoke. "Jesus goddamn Christ, Tank. What the hell happened here?"

Roland waved his arms to indicate the carnage. "Bunch of foreigners tried to take me down with bead pistols. Now they're dead."

"Foreigners?"

"They look local to you?" Roland answered the question with a question.

The man leaned over and scowled at one of the bodies in the alley. "They look like hamburger, Tank. You ever consider leaving one alive for questioning?"

"I wasn't feeling talkative. Whoever sent them will get the message just as clear this way."

"And here I heard you had gone soft." He looked around at the mangled bodies and ruined faces of Roland's deceased enemies and shrugged. "Sure as fuck don't look soft to me..." he grumbled under his breath.

"I'm all kinds of reformed now. Can't you tell?" Roland was not big on jokes, and the man in the hat could not tell if he was supposed to take that comment seriously or not.

He decided to ignore it. "Christ, what am I going to tell the cops?"

That was another new element of the Dockside cultural landscape. The end of the turf wars with The Combine and The Brokerage meant that the local police were once again attempting to assert themselves in this little quarter of the New Boston Megalopolis. For the last several decades, the police had been very much an afterthought down by the Docks. Now without the big dollars of giant crime syndicates keeping them at bay, the boys in blue were more inclined to act like they were a real constabulary and not just another gang these days. This was a welcome shift for Roland, though it did not sit so well with the local crime bosses. Roland knew it would all get sorted out, and that it remained supremely unlikely Dockside would ever get a real police presence. He was simply happy to have any improvements he could get.

"Tell them that a bunch of hitters from out of town came after me. Probably because I have more enemies than you have crabs. If they want to come talk to me they know where to find me."

"The boss ain't gonna like this, Tank," the man said with a look of deep apprehension.

Roland grunted a laugh. "I don't give two shits what your boss will and won't like. Tell The Dwarf to stay the fuck out of my way if he doesn't want to deal with it."

The man in the hat decided to ignore that, too. He addressed his men instead. "All right. Strip 'em of anything interesting and then one of you call this in." He turned to the big cyborg, still leaning against the wall with his arms crossed over his bare chest. "You sticking around for the cops, Tank?"

"Nope. Figured you guys could handle it. Tell 'em where to find me if they want my statement."

"They won't," the man replied with conviction. "I'll take care of it."

"Thanks."

Sometimes it was good to be The Fixer.

Chapter Three

T he captured Red Hat Balisong regained consciousness abruptly.

His senses swam into focus with a jolt and he lurched in an inadvertent spasm that sent electric shocks of intense pain through his right leg and most of his right arm. He gasped in agony and then went very still. Instinct told him that the pain would be less if he did not move, and a moment later his instincts turned out to be correct. The white-hot spikes of hurt subsided into shadows of their previous magnitudes and the small man once again began breathing in slow and shallow breaths. He took a pause to assess his surroundings, and as his memories began to organize themselves the injured assassin began to realize that his situation was dire indeed.

They had failed abysmally in bringing down the faithless traitor's bodyguard, and that alone was as dismal a thought as the man had ever had. Even worse than that, the loss of an entire squad of Balisongs and his own capture served to compound the disaster into a true catastrophe. He was not concerned for himself, such as it was. Despite the undeniable certainty that he would be tortured for information, the man was not so inclined to dread it. This had always been a risk of his profession, and his calling to the cause would keep his resolve as firm and focused as it needed to be. He would give them nothing willingly, and what little they eventually wrenched from him would be nigh unto useless to them anyway. He took a moment to assess his surroundings. He was lying on the floor of a dark room. There was carpeting beneath him, and the sound of rain tapping a determined staccato rhythm on a window could be heard. He did not know if it was day or night, as the window in question had obviously been dialed opaque. He was unbound, which surprised him. Then again, he was currently broken in enough places that restraints would be superfluous. He found himself alert and not at all groggy, which was also bizarre considering the nature of his evening's calamities. He did not have time to sort out the reasons for this. Escape was more important.

Carefully, he shifted and writhed to a sitting position. His injuries reminded him with each movement of all the places he was broken. It was a depressingly large number, but the pain was merely a distraction. His relationship with pain went deeper than many marriages, and it would take much more than some broken bones to stop him from attempting escape.

"Comfortable?" a voice inquired politely.

The assassin's eyes darted around the darkened room in search of the speaker. His eyes were still adjusting to the lack of light, and all he could make out were a few shifting shadows in the oppressive gloom of his prison. He squinted at a dark silhouette, configured in a vaguely manlike shape as it rose from a chair and moved toward him. The assassin showed no fear. This was a simple thing to achieve since he felt no fear. Apprehension, perhaps, and a sadness that his mission was a failure and his life was at its end. Neither of those amounted to fear, though. With a resolve born in the grueling crucible of fanaticism, the Balisong prepared to meet death with a snarl of defiance.

He was robbed of his chance for such theatrics when the figure calmly reached over and turned up the lights. Illumination filled the room, making the injured killer wince and squint. When his eyes at last adjusted, he could see two people sharing the room with him. One was an obscenely dressed blond woman and the other, he realized, was the feckless traitor he had been sent to kill. The boy's tan face was set in a featureless mask. He was hiding something. It was obvious the boy was crushing an expression that was trying to make itself plain on his face. He had hunted dozens of men across dozens of planets, and he knew when a mark was legitimately stoic and when a young terrified boy was putting on a brave face. The urge to taunt the little turncoat was strong, but something about the expression on the woman's face told him to forbear. He could recognize his own species and that person was not to be trifled with under the best of circumstances. Instead, he cut to the chase and preempted the boy's attempt at interrogation.

"You already know that you won't get anything from me. Why are you bothering with all this, boy?"

The young man's jaw flexed, tightening the tendons in his neck in an involuntary reaction to the assassin's voice. The Balisong relaxed, knowing he was already in the boy's head. "Just kill me. It won't matter. More will come. Have you told your friends that? Have you told them that the Red Hats have marked them all? Have you explained that our blades are sharp and unrelenting?" He shifted his injured body and sighed, "Oh, little boy. How many more will die for your betrayal? How many good and faithful soldiers of the cause will it take? You should turn yourself in and return to face the judgment of your brothers and sisters." He pointed to the woman in the room. "You will have her blood on your soul as well if you do not."

Manuel Richardson scowled at that comment as if he did not understand it. He looked over at the woman and clarified, "You know what? I don't think he knows who you are, Mindy." He turned back to the injured assassin and explained this oversight. "The Balisongs are very into an ascetic lifestyle. Lots of isolation and meditation and stuff."

The woman stood up from where she was sitting and walked over to look more closely at the wounded man. She leaned over and scowled into his face. The Balisong met her gaze without flinching, a smug smirk twisting his lips ever so slightly. Mindy smiled right back.

When she spoke, it was to Manny and not their captive. "That explains why their hit was so sloppy. They always this unprepared or is this a special thing?"

The Balisong frowned at the affront to his professional pride, and Manny did not let him retort.

"They don't operate outside of Venus too often. I figure these guys were just so damn successful back home they assumed that New Boston would be no different." The boy cocked an eyebrow at his prisoner, "That sound about right?"

The Balisong ignored the question. "We always get our man, traitor. You will be no different."

"That's sort of the thing," Manny said with a rueful shake of the head. "You do always get your man. I explained that to Mindy, here," he jerked a thumb at the top-heavy woman, "and she kind of pointed out that she is not, in fact, a man."

"Definitely feels like a loophole," Mindy agreed.

26

The Balisong scowled. He knew Richardson was scared, and he knew the boy was a runner at heart. He could see the urge to flee written all over the little traitor's face. However, instead of backing down Manuel was trading barbs with him as if he was in total control. Something was keeping him from bolting now, and the assassin began to suspect what it was.

"And so it is behind the skirts of this..." the Balisong sneered, "...tramp you're hiding, then?"

Mindy's eyebrows began to climb at the insult, though her posture remained relaxed as the Venusian guffawed. "Little Manny, you have betrayed your family, left your mother weeping and shamed your father's house. Hookers from the planet of fascist oppressors will not save you from the death you so richly deserve."

"Hey!" Manny snapped. "Mind your language, buddy. Mindy may be a tramp, but she is totally not a hooker!"

"I'm not from Earth, either," she pointed out.

The assassin leaned back against the wall, wincing only slightly as broken bones ground against each other. A disappointed look split his face when he spoke again. "You are brave now because you have friends to protect you. You have that big fixer and this brazen slut to help you and suddenly you are better than your family?"

"I'm an orphan." It was the first thing Manny had said that rang of true conviction, and the Balisong raised an eyebrow at the proclamation. "You animals were never my family. You tried to kill me as soon as I stopped helping you murder babies and old men."

"Is it murder to kill those who take what is yours? Those who would steal your very home?" It came out as snarl, twisted by a lifetime of hatred and the lessons taught by fanatics. Manny had heard it before and he recognized it now for what it was.

"Yeah. I knew you'd say that, and I don't really care." He rubbed his forehead in a bizarre show of weariness. "Do you know why you are still alive, oh brave Balisong?" Manny sneered the name.

"You think you will interrogate me, of course." The assassin appeared quite confident and unconcerned with this potentiality.

"Not really," Mindy shrugged, earning a small smile from Manny.

"She's right," the young man concurred. "We already know as much as we are going to at this point. You could tell us where the rest of your squad is holed up, but they'll have already moved on.

You could tell me who sent you, but I already know. You might even have information on the best way to avoid you guys in the future." His shoulders rose and fell in a big expressive shrug. "Honestly? We don't fucking care. So, the good news for you is that you get to live. The bad news is that you get to be a message to your masters."

"You see," Mindy interrupted, "that big doofus you shot up tonight? He has some history with you guys. It's old history, but he's not really the kind of guy who lets stuff go, if you get what I mean." She winked. "He really wants an excuse to just go hop a ship to Venus and finish up a job he started about thirty damn years ago."

Manny chuckled, and the Balisong could not help but notice that all signs of fear or apprehension had left the boy's body language. "You really don't want that," the young man admonished his prisoner. "Seriously. If you care for any of your 'family' you would be doing everything you could think of to stop Roland from coming to Venus."

Mindy gave a sad little pout. "But you're too stupid to realize that, aren't you? Look at you, with your stupid smug face and your silly fanatic's confidence." She looked over to her partner with a defeated eye roll. "Seriously, right now this dipshit is sitting there with a mess of broken bones thinking that we are the ones who don't get it. Ugh!"

Her hand went to her hip where she rested the palm against the hilt of a black dagger. "We're wasting our time, Manny. I think I'm just gonna kill him."

Manny held up a hand to calm her. "Easy, Mindy. The boss wants us to play this one calm." He turned back to the prisoner. "We were going to toss you back on a ship to Venus. Obviously, that won't work because you are a stupid zealot who will just try to complete your mission anyway. Then you will be as dead as the rest of your team." The young man winced, "Man, was I really as bad as you when I was younger? It all sounds so stupid now. Anyway. We need you to deliver a message, and we were kind of struggling with how to get that message back to the Red Hats in a way even a mind-wiped fanatic like you couldn't screw up."

The Balisong stiffened. This was not going the way he thought it would. Everything was wrong, and he could not figure out why. There was no way he was going to go back to the domes with his mission incomplete and he would die in this room before he would ever consent to be a messenger for this traitor. His captors had just said as much, so he could not understand why they were even having this conversation.

"So, we decided," Richardson continued, "to turn you over to the cops. We figure the InfoNet aggregators will lose their minds over a Red Hat death-squad operating this close to Uptown."

"Gateways is gonna blow a gasket, too," Mindy added. "You were five blocks from the Guts, man. Twelve docking towers moving billions of creds a day in goods and services, and you dinks ran an unauthorized hit not two miles away from them!" She shook her head again. "Morons! Do you know how many millions of creds have been spent by Gateways to keep the Docks clear of threats over the last two decades? Do you know how many people have *died*?" She laughed in the man's face. It was harsh and mean. That laugh rang with pure, undiluted condescension and it stung the assassin's pride to hear it. "You colossal dipshit, entire criminal *empires* were crushed over shit like this! Man, if I was a group of reviled terrorists -ah 'freedom fighters'- I mean, well I'd just hate to have a giant mega-corp breathing down my neck."

Manny affected an air of mock concern. "You're totally right, Mindy. I bet the Planetary Council might even get involved. That would really complicate things back under the domes. They might even send the Expeditionary Forces back over there."

"That's true. Wow! If I worked for the Red Hats, I'd be really worried about my little operation getting exposed like that, so far from home and all."

Manny chuckled in agreement and gave the Balisong a hard look. "We know you are a free-birth Venusian, but after tonight, you will have a record. Obviously, your career as a Balisong is over, and if you don't want your whole Earthside operation exposed, you will deliver our little message to your handlers."

The injured assassin was now beginning to understand his predicament. He was in a unique position, and not one he had been trained for. He could handle the pain of torture, and he was not afraid of death or dying. Even though every fiber of his being was screaming at him to resist, the part of him that could still think logically knew that this instinct was more likely to hurt the Red Hats than help. The traitor was not wrong. Being turned over to the New

Boston Police would be a disaster. Naturally he would be disavowed, but the research they had done on the big fixer had indicated that he did have the ear of Gateways. That research had failed to prepare them for his physical capabilities, sadly, but his business operations were well-known at least.

He tried to play it tough. "And what, exactly, is this message I am to deliver? That a dead man sends his regards? Perhaps you want me to tell them that little Manny the sackless traitor and his pet stripper want us to go away? It doesn't work like that, boy, you know as much."

Manny gave the man a look that was a cross between disbelief and pity. "You really don't know who she is, do you?"

"She looks like a common whore to me."

Manuel sighed again. "Wow. Was I this bad, too? Please tell me I wasn't this bad." He gestured to the blond woman, "This is Mindy. She is currently the top-ranked assassin with the Hunter's Lodge for all systems. You're an assassin, so can I assume you know what that means?"

He did, but he decided not to respond. This did not faze Manny at all.

"She killed the Pirate King with a knife, buddy. She broke Iron Sven Paulsen's arm, and she has a kill count of..." he looked at her.

"One hundred and sixty-three," she responded without inflection.

"Thank you," Manny said, then looked back to the prisoner. "I know you don't give a shit about that. I know you think that you are the baddest thing alive. I don't care about any of it, myself. You, on the other hand, need to think about what happens to your leaders. What happens to Craddock and Hardesty if the most successful assassin in all of space decides to target them?"

As Manny had predicted, the Balisong was not impressed. "Please. We have dealt with many assassins. One more will not frighten them."

"Yeah, yeah, yeah. You are all very brave and awesome. Whatever. Don't care. Here's the thing. I'm done running."

The tanned youth leaned in very close to the man who had been sent to kill him. There was iron in his voice, and he spoke slowly and with great conviction. "Your message is this: Stay away from Dockside. Stay off of Earth. The Red Hats are done with Manuel Richardson."

The injured assassin sneered and opened his mouth to speak. He was cut off by Manny, who grabbed him by the throat with a grip curiously strong and fingers that felt like steel. His injuries screamed in fresh protest and an abbreviated gurgle of pain swept past his lips. With a strength that felt incongruous to the young man's small frame, the killer was thrust back against the wall with a bone-jarring thud. He nearly passed out as another thunderclap of agony wracked his body.

A snarl that did not sound at all like a confused young boy fleeing the terror of his youth erupted from the chest of Manuel Richardson. "Otherwise, you piece of shit, Manuel Richardson will be done with them."

Chapter Four

"**Y**ou all right?"

Mindy fired the question to Manny as they left the interrogation room. Most of the time it was a supply closet in the back of their office. For tonight at least, the small dark space was an interrogation room. The young man, who a moment ago had been the very picture of resolve and conviction in the face of his enemy, did not look so strong now. His brave façade had melted like spring snowfall as soon as the door closed behind him, and this left him looking pale and pained.

"That was... uh..." he faltered, shaking his head, "...harder than I thought it would be."

"Well, you did great. I think he is going to send just the message we want him to."

They passed into the main office, which was little more than a converted storefront looking out onto The Drag. The rain still fell in stubborn drips outside, even as they watched through the large front window the purple gloom of encroaching dawn paint the streets in sloppy blue brush strokes. Long shadows were stretching from the parked cars and signs, the inky blue pools of darkness teasing Dockside with the promise of sunlight. Manny stared out the window for a protracted moment, just watching it happen. He had grown up under the artificial light of colony domes and space stations, so the transitions of natural sunrise and sunset still gave him pause. He was fascinated by the cleansing brightness of a dawn, and how the entire spectrum of color could be dragged through a single place while the night surrendered to the inevitability of daytime.

"It was... strange." Manny moved to a chair in front of a desk and sat down with a heavy sigh. "Talking to him was strange. I thought it would have been more... intense?" He scowled, and a map of deep lines aged his face by decades for a moment. "Is intense the word? I don't know. I just thought there would be more... argh!"

"Shouting?" Mindy supplied helpfully.

"Yes, shouting." His head bobbed in agreement. "I figured that he would be more angry. Like he hated me or something. I mean, he was here to kill me and all, yet it seemed like he didn't give two shits about me either way."

"He didn't give two shits about you, Manny." Mindy sat down at another desk and looked at her hands. "When I left home, part of me was sure that they would all be sorry for pushing me away. I thought that me not being there would show them that they had been wrong. Because if they really cared about me, they would be sad when I left." She slowly looked up and met Manny's eyes. "It didn't feel all that great when I realized that if they didn't care enough to make me want to stay, they wouldn't be all that sad to see me go."

"So much for 'family,' huh?" The young man's voice was bitter, his words crisp and angry. "Twenty goddamn years they called me son and brother. They told me I was part of something special, and that no one would ever love me like they did." Manny's voice was beginning to shake. "When I ran, I knew they would feel betrayed. Can you believe I actually felt guilty? They tried to murder me in my sleep, and *I felt guilty for leaving them!* God, I am such a fucking moron."

"You're not a moron, Manny. You were a kid. They lied to you, and manipulated you."

"Do you know what sucks the most?"

"Yes," Mindy sighed, even though Manny wasn't really listening.

"If they had ever loved me, then they should have hated me for leaving. They should be mad right? They should be fucking furious!" It certainly sounded to Mindy like Manny was. She did not interrupt him. "But what happens when they catch up to me? It's just some unfinished goddamn business. I'm an account to be settled and nothing more. They never loved me. How do I fucking process that? My entire goddamn life is a stupid lie. They must have thought it was so funny, too." His eyes, tear-filled, had taken on a faraway look. "Look at the stupid little kid. Ha ha ha. Let's see what we can make him do. Can we make him into a murderer? Why not? He's stupid and sad and scared, he'll do anything if we just pretend to love him, right?"

Manny could not hold back what was coming. He hated the weakness of it, but his tears ran unchecked and his voice cracked into sobs.

"Why didn't they love me? I was just a little kid! I didn't want to be a... what they made me into." He could not bring himself to say the word. "I was scared and lonely and instead of helping me they tricked me into hurting people."

He looked up at Mindy and what she saw nearly broke her heart. It was easy to forget that Manuel was only twenty-four, and that he had only lived outside the domes of Venus for a couple of years. His entire universe had been the Red Hats for his whole life, and he had been far too young when he realized this universe was no more than a horrible fiction perpetuated to control him and use him. Mindy saw the terrible truth in that moment, and while she was not of a particularly maternal nature, the stark reality of it filled her with the deep animosity of a mother bear.

He was still that little boy. He was still scared and lonely, desperate for somebody to love him yet too afraid to ever let that happen. She knew the feeling all too well.

"Do you know why I left Gethsemane?"

Manny looked up at the non-sequitur. "What?"

"Do you know why I left my home?"

Manny looked confused. "No?"

She leaned back in her chair and settled into her tale. "I fell in love. It was the stupid teenage kind of infatuation. Not real love. But when you are fifteen, you don't know the difference. She was my best friend too, and I lived for her attention and approval. I never told her I was in love with her, of course. Homosexuality is a felony crime on Gethsemane, and I wasn't sure she felt the same way at first." A slow, sad moue crept across the little blond's face. "Turns out she did not. When I finally confessed my sinful desires-" Mindy rolled her eyes at that, "-she immediately ran off to report me."

She stared hard at Manny. "My best friend, Manny. A girl I had known my whole life. A person I trusted and who I had shared all me secrets with. Poof! Just turned on me."

"And you loved her..." Manny added.

34

"Yup. As much as I knew how to love at the time, anyway. Honestly, that wasn't even the kicker. What really sucked? My mom, my dad, my eight siblings all turned on me, too. I became an instant pariah. The only time they discussed me was to decide if my transgression warranted life in prison, or just five years in a church-approved re-education facility."

"Shit," was Manny's eloquent reply.

"Yup. It's no middle-of-the-night death squad, but it was still a pretty shitty thing to do to a teenager, right?" She shook her head. "I felt exactly the way you did when I left. Like somehow I was the one who was wrong or bad. Like maybe I was hurting them and not the other way around. Just like you, though, it turns out that me leaving was perfectly fine with them. Not a one of them gave a single shit about it because I was a dirty sinning lesbo and good riddance to me. Eventually, I ended up having the same epiphany you are having right now, Manny-boy, the one where you figure out that those people never really gave a shit about you and that nobody loved you the way you thought they did. It fucked me up pretty bad and well, let's just say that my chosen career may have something to do with how I decided to process all that." She gave him a big wink, as if the trauma of a horrific childhood driving a young girl to become a professional killer was somehow funny. "But then something happened to me, and this part is really important, so listen carefully."

Manny's eyes were dry now, and he awaited her wisdom with a child's anticipation.

"I met somebody who actually did gave a shit about me."

"Mack?" Manny asked with a sly smile.

"Hell yes," Mindy agreed emphatically. "Mack was the first person I'd ever met who didn't want to either fuck me or kill me. He respected me and loved me and we took care of each other for more than a decade. He never put a hand on me and he never asked for anything in return for it, either. He was just a great man and a great friend. One guy like that is worth more than every piece-of-shit bigot on Gethsemane combined. One guy, Manny. Just one guy in a whole universe of dipshits, and everything changed. Those people back on Gethsemane? Or the assholes on Venus? Those people ain't shit. They never were and they ain't never gonna be. You don't owe them anything, least of all your happiness. The galaxy is a big place and it is full of awesome folks. Just because you didn't know that before doesn't mean that it isn't so. Go find those people and hang out with them."

She wagged a finger at him. "Just don't be like Roland and wait thirty freakin' years to do it. His story is more fucked up than either of ours, and we are all just lucky he likes to brood into beer instead of throwing temper tantrums."

"But it's the same story, isn't it? He loved the Army. They told him he was a soldier, and they made him think he was a superhero."

"Then they used him to kill anyone they didn't like." Mindy shrugged. "Yup. It's an old story, and way too damn common, too. They told me I was special and chosen by God, Manny. All they really wanted was to own my body." She looked at the youth, and her expression was a soft, sad thing. "They told you were a freedom fighter after all, but they really just wanted a terrorist."

"Shit." Manny leaned forward in his chair and rested his elbows on his thighs. His face fell into a pensive frown, fading blue light from the street casting his features in melancholy shadows. "That is some really heavy shit, you know? I tried so hard to be hard, you know? I know I have to keep it all together, but..." he trailed off, not knowing how to say what he wanted to say, or how to ask for what he needed. "You had Mack, and Roland found Lucia. I guess that gives me hope that maybe I'm not, you know..."

"Unlovable?" Mindy said, eyebrow arched.

"Makes me sound like a bit of a wimp when you just say it like that," Manny grumbled. "But that's the word for it, I guess."

"You're not unlovable, kid. Just unlucky. But stick with us, and I think you will find your place just fine. I think the big guy has taken a shine to you, after all. He does plan on going to Venus to deal with your former 'family,' right?"

"Is he doing it for me? Or does he just want to punish the Red Hats for blowing most of his body up?"

A sheepish frown flashed across her pretty features. "I'd say a little of both? I think he mostly let go of that stuff a long time ago, though. Lucia has been good for him, I think."

"She's been good for you, too." Now it was Manny's turn to be insightful.

"I'd call you a liar, but you ain't wrong. She's something special all right. She'll be good for you as well, if you are smart enough to stick around."

The young man pulled his left sleeve back, revealing the smooth white features of a prosthetic arm. The limb had no exposed joints, and muscles eerily analogous to human tissue rolled and flexed beneath the alabaster dermal mesh. "I think I have to! Her dad's the only one who knows how to work on this thing." He wiggled his fingers in an intricate pattern. "It's crazy how much it feels like my real arm."

"Roland's whole body is made of that stuff, Manny. Remember that. Doctor Don is the best biotech nerd in the whole damn galaxy. What he has done to fix my neuro shit has been just crazy. No headaches or nothing anymore. I guess the implants self-adjust now, which is just about the weirdest feeling in the world, I might add."

"You ever get the impression maybe he is enjoying tinkering with all of us?"

The blond head ducked in agreement. "You noticed that, too? I think he missed it. Refusing to work on military stuff took him out of the game. I don't think that ever suited him. Now he has his favorite contraption, his daughter, and the two of us to work on and I think he may be having just a little too much fun with it."

"He could make billions if he wanted to..." Manny started to say, and Mindy cut him off.

"He'll never do it. Too much guilt over what happened to Roland and his squad. That guy is never going to let his tech out of the bottle again. Not even for the civilian market. Too much risk of the military contractors reverse-engineering it."

Manny waggled his fingers at the little killer. "Are you sure? He giggled like a schoolgirl the whole time he was making this thing. He neither slept nor ate for three weeks." Then to himself, "This thing is just... crazy cool..."

Mindy chuckled at a young man's childlike wonder over a new toy. "The man loves his work. Don't knock it."

The two sat in silence for a moment, processing everything they had just shared in quiet reflection while the sun completed its ascent over the horizon. Outside their window, The Drag lit up with red and orange glee as the sun finally claimed victory over the night's rains. The pallid gray streets were showing the first signs of life just as the colors melted from blue into orange and a small army of day shift dock workers filed onto the sidewalks. Hundreds of booted feet commenced their daily march toward The Guts and a solid eight hours' worth of work unloading shuttles. Coffees clutched in tired hands and eyes drooping with the lingering weight of determined sleep, the masses shuffled across the office window in bleary-eyed ignorance of the previous night's adventures and the emotional trauma of a young man carrying a head full of demons.

Manny broke the silence first. "I suppose we should send that Balisong back to Venus, now, huh?"

"Probably about that time, yeah," Mindy concurred.

"Should we have told him about the crate?"

Mindy grinned at that. "Nah. Let it be a surprise."

He nodded at that, then cocked his head an angle and said, "I'm really glad you convinced Roland to use a full-sized crate. I don't think that guy was going to fit into the one he picked."

"That was the point, Manny-boy."

"Oh, I get it. But, yeesh!" He shuddered. "Roland makes me nervous sometimes."

Manny," Mindy admonished, "if you were smart, Roland would make   you   nervous   *all*   the   time."

Chapter Five

"We still need to find those last two Balisongs."

Roland did not like loose ends, and the Balisong team leader and scout were still skulking around somewhere. Shipping their prisoner back to Venus in a livestock crate would send the message they intended, but that did not do anything meaningful for the immediate tactical situation. The team addressed the issue over lunch after they had all managed a few hours' sleep.

"Those critters are stupid hard to hunt," Mindy complained. "They don't have augmentations, they only use hard creds, and they apparently don't need to eat or sleep."

Manny answered her unasked questions. "They will sleep outside and they will eat whatever they can steal or catch. They know how most assassins get caught and they simply avoid anything that can be traceable. They were born under the domes, and not in any hospitals, so there are no records of birth or DNA on file. These are ghosts, Mindy. It's an intentional thing." He shrugged and gave her a lopsided grimace. "Look on the bright side. There's a good chance they'll take a crack at me before another team arrives. We'll get our chance, then."

"So, you don't think they will take our 'message' seriously, huh?" Roland snorted, "Figures."

"Oh, come on, Mr. Tankowicz." Manuel looked askance at the big cyborg. "These are zealots. They've been told since they day they were born that they are the deadliest, most elite assassins in the galaxy. They train all day, every day of their lives. The leaders of the Red Hats keep them in the dark and tell them only what they need to hear so they will be fearless and dedicated to the cause. I'm guessing they have already decided that you just got lucky."

"Are they that good?" It was Lucia now, her brow scrunched while her brain calculated outcomes.

"Most of the time, yeah. They really are crazy good. They train a lot with very simple weapons, which means they can strike literally anywhere. Sneaking a smart gun into a building is hard. Getting a sharpened piece of metal through is pretty easy by comparison. Generally they don't get augmentations and they don't operate outside of Venus very often. They are ghosts."

"That tracks," Roland agreed. "The guns they used on me were pretty common around here. Easily acquired if you've got hard creds to burn. They did not miss, either."

"Yup," Manny nodded. "They like to pick up whatever is available in an area. They are real big on flexibility and adaptation."

"Fine. What do you think the last two will do, Manny?" Lucia wanted more data for her brain to crunch.

"They had to be watching, so I doubt it will be pistols in alleyways next time. What's weird is that went for Roland first. They are usually more single-minded."

"I'm a harder target. They wanted me off the table. It was worth tipping you off to their presence if it meant not having to fight with me on my terms later. What is interesting to me is how badly they underestimated me. You don't need to be very good at intel to know that's a bad call. Hell, you can ask anyone in this town and they'll tell you not to bother shooting me with the little stuff."

Mindy frowned at that statement. "Right. Now imagine a group of newcomers popping over to Dockside and asking the local hoods about the best thing to shoot Tank Tankowicz with. How long before that news finds its way back to us?" She turned to Lucia, "I thought you said he was supposed to be pretty smart?"

The brunette came to the defense of her paramour. "He is smart. Just not very good at things that don't involve beer or fighting."

"Everything involves beer or fighting," Roland grumbled. "Everything that matters, anyway."

Lucia flipped the magenta stripe of hair away from her eyes and steered them all back to business. "What will they do, then?"

Manny held out his hands, palms facing upward. "If they saw what happened in that alley, I'm guessing they wait for another team. They are fanatics sure, but they are fanatics about mission success, not dying in glorious service to the cause, if you know what I mean."

Roland harrumphed his response to that. "Venus is still a hundred million miles away, so if they took the fastest ship available..."

"They won't," Manny interjected. "Too expensive, too public."

"...that gives another thirty hours at a minimum before another squad arrives."

"Call it forty," Manny said. "They really won't be on a fast boat. They'll come on something small, slow and with the kind of crew that doesn't ask a lot of questions."

"But in the meantime," Lucia reminded them, "the remaining two will probably make at least one attempt to kill Manny."

Manny's head nodded in sad agreement. "Yeah. That sounds about right for them. I should probably go to ground. These are the kind of guys who will get you if you move around too much, no matter how clever you think you are." He smiled at the group. "Or how tough your co-workers are."

Roland leaned back, dragging a groan of protest from his chair as his nearly half-ton of mass shifted. "I'm not real fond of waiting around for hitters to show up, personally. I'd rather go kick down some doors and take the fight to them."

"Imagine that," was Mindy's sarcastic response to this revelation.

"The tricky part is going to be the 'how' of taking the fight to them," the big man continued as if he had not heard her. "It's not like we can just drop me on Venus and have me storm the domes. Even if that was a fight I could win, it doesn't really fix the problem. Unless I kill every Red Hat and Red Hat sympathizer, all I'm really doing is escalating the scale of the conflict. If we do this the wrong way, folks? The problem just gets worse."

Lucia gave him a playful slap on the arm. "Ever the soldier, Roland. Always thinking with your guns. Not every solution needs to be a military one. The Red Hats are terrorists. They use violence against civilians to in pursuit of a political goal."

"And I use violence against them to make them stop." Roland was a very linear thinker when it came to terrorists.

Lucia sighed and shook her head at him. "But it won't make them stop. If that was the case, the troubles would have ended decades ago. This is not a case of an army trying to seize and hold ground, this is about breaking the political will of their opposition."

"Fine. I get that. But how does that help us persuade them to leave Manny alone? Unless he's been holding out on us about having an uncle on the Planetary Council, it's not like he has any political capital to spend."

"That's true. We will just need to bring in somebody who does have a stake in the game."

"Like who? I mean, I assume you have a plan already here, but I'm just not seeing it."

"What would happen if a certain oversized military cyborg went ahead and found a Red Hat Enclave on Venus?"

Manny, being the expert, supplied the answer. "If it's outside the colony domes, the Republican Unification Corps would swoop in to clear it out. But lots of Enclaves are deep in the colony domes. No RUC out there. They can only legally operate outside of them."

"What's keeping the RUC out of the colonies?" Mindy's face betrayed complete confusion.

"The biggest reason to ever go to Venus," Manny stated, "is the collecting of sulfur compounds and easily-mined iron. Otherwise, Venus wouldn't have anyone on it. It's a fiery shithole. At first, there were only the big factory domes and the giant atmospheric collector things. There were some dormitories for workers and stuff like that. But it was pretty much just industry on Venus for decades. When ore mining was banned on Earth, those industries ramped up really fast and whole boatloads of workers were needed on Venus. The big companies built these huge Colony domes to house all the commerce and infrastructure a huge workforce would need. The factories are stuck in the areas with the best resources, but the colonies are built in the areas that are less inhospitable. I mean, for Venus anyway. The whole damn planet is inhospitable."

"The point," Roland grumbled, "is that the life support for a dome can only handle so many people. Security personnel cost money, they don't produce it. So, the factories have little to no security because they are still run by businesses, while the colonies have bunches of security because they are a sovereign state with taxes and elections and that sort of thing."

"That doesn't make sense," Lucia said. "Aren't the factories more important?"

"They don't teach this in history classes on Earth?" Manny seemed genuinely hurt by this.

"Not in business school," was the clipped response.

Manny conceded that point by filling her in as best he could. "The old miners didn't like all the new colonists. They thought that the corporations were invading their homes. The Planetary Council didn't care, so the 'native' Venusians tried to secede from Earth's governance."

Roland's voice took on a wistful air when he spoke. "I was deployed for that. Fighting was nasty. It was all indoors and close-quarters. Dangerous stuff."

"We lost the fights." Manny spoke as if he was there, even though he was just a baby at the time. "But we won the secession in the end." He shrugged, "Well. Mostly. The council agreed to let the Colonies self-govern, while the factories and collection domes stayed with the corporations and under Planetary Council jurisdiction. It was the best deal they could make, I guess. That's the entire crux of the troubles. A lot of folks are okay with the deal, but there is a large number of factory workers and miners who don't want to be under the Council. They want to be part of the free Venus."

"And this is why they blow up hospitals?" Mindy's disgust was transparent.

Roland helped her understand. "When you live in poverty under a bubble, isolated and neglected, abandoned by the folks you thought would help you, it's not particularly hard to get to real bad place in your own head."

"Preach it, Mr. Tankowicz," Manny nodded emphatically. "A lot of the miners were fine with the deal. A lot more felt betrayed. Like they had been ignored and sacrificed. When things got violent, the Council created the RUC to restore order." The young man's head shook, heavy with sadness. "It was awful. Armed soldiers walking the corridors demanding to see identification, intimidating innocent people and treating everyone like second-class citizens. I don't care what they say, the RUC really was an occupation force. Maybe it wasn't supposed to be. I can understand that now. But in practice?" He scoffed, "Hah. Tell it to the men they beat up or the girls they molested. I was raised to believe that if the RUC ever got me they would torture and murder me, and I believed it."

Roland was forced to agree with that. "I know plenty of RUC. They are not the best and brightest. Venus is a shit post, and lots of divisions use it as a dumping ground for their worst soldiers."

"Not to mention all the freebooters the corporations hire for security," Manny added. "We couldn't tell soldiers from thugs growing up. They all looked and acted the same. My people told us that the Council poisoned our water and stole our children in their sleep. Anything bad that ever happened was the fault of the fascist oppressors, and everything would be perfect if they were done away with. They made us hate the people who didn't agree with us, too. Called them traitors and whores to the corporations." There was still real anger in his words when he looked up at the group, "I know I was lied to, but I also know what I saw with my own eyes. The RUC did treat us like shit, and The Council never did anything to help us. I'm not proud of the Red Hats. I'm not okay with what they do but..." he shrugged, defiant. "...I get it."

"They come by their anger honestly," Roland agreed, placating the young man. "It was an ugly situation made uglier by the incompetence of bureaucrats and the violence of a small group of zealots on both sides."

"Isn't that always the way of it?" Lucia added softly. Then she brought the conversation back on topic. "If we dig up one of these Enclaves in the Council-controlled areas, the RUC swoops in and cleans house, right?"

"Yes," Manny nodded back. "It's not uncommon."

"What if we find one in the colonies?"

Manny equivocated. "Depends on the dome. Some take that shit very seriously and stomp on it hard. Others are more... sympathetic... to the cause. There might be a couple of show trials and some hand waving at those ones."

Lucia had taken on a detached, faraway expression. Her brain was working hard, processing information and aligning strings of causality. "We need a threat." She whispered this. "A threat so terrifying to the Red Hats that they abandon their hunt for Manny. We need both a carrot and a stick."

"No," Roland interrupted. "I know how this goes. What we need is to hit them with a stick as a warning, and then show them we have a bigger stick if they don't behave."

44

She gave a knowing nod. "That's probably more accurate. It just sounds so ominous when you say it like that. How's this sound, Manny?" She shifted her gaze to the young man. "A two-pronged attack. You and I go to Venus and dig up an Enclave somewhere in one of these sympathetic colonies. Roland and Mindy go and hit the factory groups like the very wrath of God himself. Roland will break stuff and Mindy will start dropping leaders and key personnel. When the Hats are really good and angry, we threaten to expose a sympathetic dome to the Planetary Council."

Manny's face was writ large with confusion. "What will that do?"

"Roland?" Lucia raised an eyebrow to the big man.

"If the Council thinks that Free Venus is aiding or abetting the Red Hats, they'll send the Expeditionary Force."

"Oh shit," Manny said softly.

"Oh shit, indeed," the big cyborg agreed. To Mindy he explained, "There is a reason the Red Hats don't operate much outside of the Domes. The Expeditionary Force is that reason. As long as the problems are on Venus, and only Venusians get hurt, nobody on the Council cares much. If it starts to look like Free Venus is actively supporting terrorists against Council interests? Yeah, there'll be some consequences for that."

This time it was Mindy who looked aghast. "Y'all are planning to start a civil war just to help Manny?" She tossed Manny a crooked smile. "Told you they were good friends to have!"

"We are going to *threaten* to start a civil war," Lucia amended. "Manny says they are zealous to the cause, not vengeance."

"They are also corrupt and cowardly," the young man added, the bitterness tinging his words unmistakable. "They act like it's about freedom and justice, but I think they forgot about that shit a long time ago. Don't get me wrong, there are a lot of true believers in the Hats, still. Especially in the rank and file. On the other hand, I think most of the leaders are just angry murderers and opportunists these days. They are killing because they are angry at the RUC and the colonists and everything else is just an excuse." He sighed, "It all feels so stupid now that I've been away from it a while. The RUC arrests a sympathizer, and then makes a bunch of new Red Hats out of his family and friends. Red Hats kill some RUC, and so they crack down on the homes and businesses looking for them, which just makes more Red Hats. Nothing changes and nothing improves, and the cycle has been going on so damn long that it is sustaining itself at this point."

"Growing up sucks," Mindy said helpfully.

"How would you know?" Manny fired back with a laugh.

"Do you think the plan will work?" Lucia asked.

"Hard to say," Manny said, turning back to Lucia. "It ought to. Nobody in the Red Hats wants the Expeditionary Force on Venus."

"Good," Lucia nodded. "Step one is to snag those last two Balisongs. Then we get to take a trip to Venus."

"I hate Venus," Manny and Roland said in unison.

Chapter Six

They decided to keep Manny at the office. His apartment in Big Woo was just too hard to secure, and the team wanted to stay in a central location. Roland and Lucia took shifts watching him while Mindy hunted. If anyone was going to be successful in a stalk against highly trained assassins, it would be another highly trained assassin.

Mindy's pursuit was dogged, though her quarry was canny. She nearly had them twice, but both times the cagey killers eluded her with mere moments to spare. Despite their best attempts to keep things quiet, all of Dockside knew that Roland and his crew were out hunting, and the stream of tips and snitches kept the Balisongs from settling into any sort of comfortable rhythm. This assistance was not born of any sort of civic pride or altruistic desire to be helpful. Every crook in Dockside wanted Roland to owe a favor, and nobody wanted Roland to think they had been less than helpful. Despite the softening of his image, Roland's reputation was still a terrible thing.

Manny's initial estimates proved to be good, as it was approximately forty-eight hours later that the Venusian assassins made their second attempt. The attack came as no surprise at all to the team of fixers. The first team had slipped into Dockside unnoticed, simply because no one had been looking for them. With the whole town alerted to something being amiss however, it was just not possible to maneuver a team of out-of-town hitters without somebody seeing it. The nine Balisongs had been spotted within minutes of arriving, and a rabbits' warren of information channels buzzed and chirped with the news at speeds defying rational explanation. As it stood, Roland and his group had more than four hours' notice to prepare for their guests, and they did not waste any of it.

"Tangos in the perimeter," Mindy's voice rang clear and tight over the comm. Perched atop the building that housed their office, her bionic eyes could see the body heat of the assassins as they crept through the darkness. She graciously allocated a small degree of professional approval to how silent their movements were. Even her enhanced ears could not pick their footsteps out of the background noise of the city.

"Quantity?" Roland responded.

"I have eyes on nine hitters. Looks like two more hanging back in overwatch down the block."

"Can you engage the two in overwatch without alerting the rest?"

"Easily."

"Then engage. We'll handle the troops. Try not to wake the neighbors. Good hunting."

"Roger that," she said with finality, then leapt from her alcove onto an adjacent rooftop.

Roland closed the channel to let Mindy work, then turned to Lucia and Manny. They had dialed the office window opaque and fortified the door to prevent easy access. The building had no basement and since life was not an old action movie, the ventilation system remained far too small to let anything human sized in. This left the front door the only way inside that did not include breaching a wall. If the killers chose so boisterous a tactic, there was nothing to be done about it, so no special effort was made to counteract such.

Manny's warnings about the resourcefulness of the Balisongs were not hyperbolic. Absent an obvious way in, the clever killers attempted to flush their prey out. Happenstance prevented the technique from being successful, but it was a clever enough tactic all the same.

Forewarned of the attack, Roland had chosen to wear his helmet. This was not something he often did when working in Dockside. The skull-faced head covering was an overt indication of his cybernetic origins, and his was a brand built upon mystery. Despite their poor performance in executing the first attempt, Roland respected the Balisongs enough to assume they would be better prepared for the second. His face and head carried far less armor than his body, and the helmet effectively eliminated that liability. The helmet came in two pieces. The first a black skull cap and the second a silver-white faceplate that loosely resembled a metallic mouthless skull's face. It

48

was alien and angular and more than a little cartoonish, yet effective in its dual purposes of protecting his head and terrifying his foes.

It also contained a suite of various sensors, communications gear, and augmented reality displays. It was his helmet that first detected the subtle introduction of halothane gas to the ventilation system. A warning chime clanged softly in his ears and his HUD blinked a text warning at the corner of his vision.

"Shit," he growled. "Manny, Lucia, head to the back room. They're pumping gas in somehow. I'll kill the ventilation and try to draw them out."

He stomped over to the environmental controls and closed all the vents while Manny and Lucia secured themselves in the storage room. He set the system to recirculate and hoped the filters would be adequate to scrub the air. Modern Uptown buildings would have scrubbed it automatically, but this was Dockside, and there was not a whole of 'modern' anything going around. Data on the gas began to scroll across his HUD, and relayed helpful information to Manny and Lucia. "This stuff is heavier than air, so stand on something. Also, keep away from the vents for a few minutes." He scowled under his faceplate. Halothane was a crude and old-fashioned anesthetic. There were several more effective and more modern incapacitating agents they could have employed. Upon further consideration it occurred to Roland that there was no need to incapacitate them at all. The Balisongs were here to kill, so he was hard pressed to figure out why they had not simply pumped the air full of poison.

This train of thought answered the question for him. His building may be old, and it may not have modern equipment, but even a cheap ventilator could recognize deadly poisons.

The realization twisted his lips into a wan grimace. *They picked something out of date and only mildly toxic. They knew that my system would probably not notice it. Clever bastards.* His helmet sensors were designed to keep him alive on foreign planets with radically different atmospheres. These were sensitive in the extreme, and this had saved them from an otherwise devilishly clever move. Roland was relieved that the trick had not worked, yet irritated that it was luck that had prevented its success. Soldiers who relied on luck often found it to be a fickle ally.

There was good news at least. Using a mild anesthetic gas told a story about their enemy's tactics. The assassins did not care whether the halothane killed the group or merely incapacitated them. It was just the opening salvo. Roland conceded that it was a smart play, though it also betrayed their next likely move. There was really only one tactical reason to try to slow them down or knock them out as a first step.

He called back to the back room. "Get ready, they are going to come through the front door."

"I'm standing on a chair in a storage closet, Roland." Lucia sounded just a touch shrill and more than a little irritated. "What exactly does 'get ready' look like in this situation?"

"Have your gun out," he suggested.

"Thank goodness you were here to tell me that." Roland could hear the eye roll in her sarcastic tone, and wisely chose to not respond. He was sweeping the front with infrared and double checking the magazine in his large custom-made machine pistol. Capable of indexing four separate load-outs simultaneously, Roland had decided not to load 'Durendal' with exotic munitions. Flechettes were likely to over-penetrate and high-explosive rounds were an obvious no-go for close-quarters indoor work. All four slots of the modular magazine were thus charged with fifty-caliber ceramic beads.

Through the grayed-out front window, Roland's helmet sensors began to trace the silhouettes of moving men in ephemeral red and orange shadows. A further testimony to the professional competence of the Balisongs, it seemed that this group was wearing thermal camouflage. While probably more than adequate to prevent detection by a police drone or a satellite, the men were far too close to Roland's sensors for the garments to hide all their body heat. The man-shaped blobs flicked and swirled in his HUD as small traces of heat slipped past their shrouds. Four red and orange wraiths sidled up to the door and aligned themselves to either side. A fifth settled in front and began to gesture and manipulate something against the metal panel.

Since this was obviously a breaching charge of some kind, and Roland was not interested in having his own door blown into his face, he pre-empted the maneuver with a level of force and violence that he felt was appropriate to the nature of the threat.

At speeds nearing twenty times the speed of sound, hypervelocity beads would incandesce from atmospheric friction and deliver massive amounts of heat and kinetic energy to soft targets. Normally, these small projectiles did a poor job of penetrating hardened surfaces. They were more prone to cracking and ricochets when they struck something rigid and hard because they were typically small and light.

Roland's beads were neither small nor light, relatively speaking. Durendal roared to life with a yellow blossom of fire and the crack of hypersonic projectiles. Half an inch in diameter, the heavy munitions blasted through the door with ear-shattering explosions of light and shrapnel. Not every bead fully penetrated, of course, but this did little to reduce the overwhelming lethality of the barrage. The hits turned the area in front of the door into a horizontal wind of ceramic and metal fragments hurtling at several times the speed of sound. The resulting maelstrom flayed the flesh from the man at the door away from his bones and churned the top half of his body into pink mist and flying gobbets of chunky meat. Through the platter-sized hole his burst had created, Roland saw what remained of the Balisong stagger and crumple to the sidewalk with a wet splat.

"Contact!" he shouted into the general comm channel. "Engaging!"

"No shit." Roland heard Manny's dry retort but did not acknowledge it. He was already moving to the door to have at the rest of the men in the street. The Balisongs had the good sense to have brought heavier weapons this time. Whereas previously they had employed small easily-concealed pistols, for this attempt several carbines and bullpup flechette rifles were present.

Four weapons chattered to life as the big cyborg cleared the threshold, and it was only through excellent muzzle control and well-honed trigger discipline that the assassins did not shoot each other in the crossfire.

Beads and flechettes both cut through his shirt and bounced harmlessly off the thick expanse of armored skin underneath. The guns were powerful enough to crack or penetrate most commercially available mid-level body armor, but against Roland's hide they may as well have been throwing spitballs. Durendal answered with window-shaking booms and crimson explosions of gore as the half-ton war machine methodically drilled the assassins with projectiles better suited to bringing down vehicles than they were to killing lightly-armored men. A dedicated pragmatist, Roland did not believe that 'overkill' was a thing. As far as he was concerned, there was only 'dead' and 'not dead.' The giant machine pistol gripped in his oversized fist was designed to ensure his enemies fell into the former category and not the latter.

The assassins were skilled and athletic, and they kept the gun battle going for almost fifteen seconds. The faster ones managed to secure what they thought was cover behind a ride-sharing kiosk, only to find that Roland's beads chewed through the thin metal and plastic shack as if it was made of cardboard. It was impossible to score clean hits, so Roland did not try for cleanliness. He flicked the selector to full-auto and sandblasted the defenseless kiosk into perforated shrapnel with a twenty-round burst. The black-clad men posted in shooting positions inside were thrown to the street as if struck by a car. They writhed and gurgled like landed fish as they died, but Roland did not spare the time to watch. He was scanning the street and surrounding buildings for the rest of the Balisongs. A total of five black-clad men were gasping and moaning in puddles of their own congealing blood around him, and that left four unaccounted for.

A flechette screamed from the far side of the darkened street and sent a lightning bold of fiery pain across Roland's chest. It was large, and carrying a considerable quantity of velocity. In the protracted instant between the impact and his reaction to it, Roland decided that it was likely designed to take out lightly armored targets at a very long distance. As far as man-portable rifles went, this could justifiably be considered a powerful weapon. It was also probably the biggest gun the Venusians could get their hands on in Dockside without alerting Roland's informants.

Sadly for the Balisongs, it was wholly inadequate for the task of bringing down Roland. Despite its power, the flechette did not penetrate very deep into the cyborg's dermal armor. The tungsten and aluminum spike threw burning orange shards in a flaming corona when it tore itself to pieces trying to puncture his left pectoral. Failing in this, the round scorched a ragged stripe across his chest spending its energy against the surface of his skin. The resulting wound was an ugly smoking tear in his skin, but it was neither deep nor dangerous, so Roland did not care. His helmet had pinpointed the shooter's location and Durendal was already sending fire back toward the shooter.

The sniper's nest was four floors up in an old commercial building. The edifice was currently home to several small businesses providing services for longshoremen and shipping concerns, so Roland was confident that the hail of high-powered gunfire would not find any civilian targets this time of night. The window and surrounding wall disappeared in explosions of shattered glass and dust, obscuring his view of the shooters, but the shots had served their purpose. The bolt clicked home on an empty chamber after only a second or so and the lumbering war machine dropped the mag with a practiced flick of a large black finger. A new magazine slammed home a fraction of a second later and the bolt automatically cycled a new bead into battery.

The big man sprinted for the building, booted feat churning and cracking asphalt with each thundering footfall. With a grunt of effort, he planted a foot hard and leapt as high as he could. Despite his staggering physical prowess, Roland could not leap four stories straight up. Nor did he want to in this case. He crashed through a second-floor window and tumbled into a wide lobby. Spun askew by the impact with the side of the building, Roland's landing was an ungainly tangle of flailing and crashing limbs. Lack of grace notwithstanding, he found his footing quickly. Without pausing, the massive man rolled to his feet and sprinted toward the stairwell. The door to the second-floor landing exploded in a shower of sparks and the crash of shattered masonry when Roland's shoulder struck it. The giant remained blind to the destruction and was climbing stairs before the last pieces of detritus had fallen to the deck. As he suspected would happen, Roland encountered the sharpshooter team coming down. Like all good snipers, this pair had made their shot and started to move. What they had not accounted for was the speed with which Roland could move. The two men probably thought they would have plenty of time to get down and move to a different firing position, and this error proved to be fatal.

When the shooters realized Roland was below them on the stairs, they tried to turn and retreat back up. A twenty-round burst from Durendal ended this escape when it filled the stairs with a shrieking hail of shrapnel and death. The Balisongs hurled themselves back onto the third-floor landing for cover while they waited for the storm to pass. Roland used this time to ascend the last flight between himself and his prey. He caught them trying to flee back to the fourth floor, and a single blow from his right fist sent the spotter into a cinder block wall, against which his skull cracked open like a rotten egg.

The shooter was not lucky enough to die so quickly. A hand the size of a serving tray closed over his head and raised him kicking and screaming from the floor. The assassin gave a spirited defense despite being outclassed, but his protestations ended when that hand spun his world upside down and drove him to the floor. A voice, filtered and synthetic, growled from behind the death's head mask of his target and spoke with menace so pure and unfiltered that even this trained killer felt the icy tendrils of fear crawl up his spine.

"That makes seven. Now where are the last two?"

Chapter Seven

T he last two members of the team of assassins waited.

Everything up to this point had been a distraction, a ruse. It was sleight of hand and misdirection all designed to pull the treacherous little boy's team of protectors away from the building so Killam Grimes could get to him. His was a position of high honor in this operation. Many of his brothers would die tonight, and all for the sole purpose of getting him close to their prey. It would fall upon him to ensure that their sacrifices would not be in vain. His partner shared in this honor, but it was obvious who was the better warrior. The man crouched next to him in the deepest shadows of the night-lit street had only one purpose. He was to draw fire and distract any final guardians so Killam could get close and do what must be done. It was a thing Killam could do better than any other.

When the giant man sped off to engage the snipers, they made their move. Like slithering shadows, the two men snaked across the street, deftly avoiding the circular pools of blue-white illumination cast by the streetlights. Their feet were silent, their movements invisible. The pair of assassins moved to the destroyed front door of the office and paused a moment to listen and wait. When no sounds came from the dim shadows, and there was no indication of life or movement inside, each glanced to the other. In silent, wordless agreement, the men flitted through the portal on silent feet and separated to disappear once again into opposite corners of the unlit office.

Dark eyes flicked back and forth behind black balaclava masks. Details of their surroundings filtered in slowly, the indistinct shapes of furniture and other office fixtures fading into position as their vision adjusted. The space appeared empty, though these were not men so easily fooled as all that. There was no other path in or out of this office and they had seen their prey enter. The boy was here, and his big bodyguard was otherwise engaged. Now they would finish the job and honor the sacrifices their brothers had made to get them this far.

With a hand signal, one of the two alluded to the presence of a door at the back of the office. Their recon indicated that this was likely a storage closet and instinct told both it was an excellent place to hide and defend. Assuming their quarry was competent and intelligent, it made sense that they might be in there. With subtle nods of affirmation, the assassins moved. Ever wary, the men approached the door using extreme caution and an intense scrutiny that seemed incongruous to so banal a task as crossing a room. Killam had seen far too many random events conspire to thwart a kill to ever take anything for granted. They might hope that the gas had rendered the enemy unconscious, and they might want for the target to be alone. Training dictated that hope and want were the enemies of a good plan, so these two were having none of either.

Their caution proved to be warranted, which the men discovered to their dismay a moment later. From under a desk rolled an amorphous blob of darkness. The crushing silence of the office was then shattered by the report and flash of a CZ-105 flechette pistol. Killam's partner yelped and lurched to the side like a man poleaxed. His body slammed into a wall tearing a gasp of surprise and pain from his lips. Then the wounded assassin slid heavily to the floor, leaving a bloody smear down the beige wall.

The other assassin did not hesitate; rather he had already begun his attack even as his partner fell. Killam's pistol barked in response, his muzzle lighting the room in white flashes of man-made lightning. His reflexes were good, and his marksmanship unerring. Two 5mm beads exploded against the back of the dark blob, each burst of orange fire illuminating the grimacing face of a pretty brunette. The mission briefing flashed through his memory and he identified his opponent as one of the traitor's other associates. They had precious little information on that one, though her full set of armor and the weapon in her hand very clearly defined her role in this fight. She spun with a speed that beggared belief and her answering fire knifed through the empty air where the Killam had been standing. The man was not there, as he was already charging for the back room where he was certain his target was hiding.

An office chair clattered across the floor to tangle his legs in the midst of his headlong flight and the killer tumbled. The woman was upon him before he could right himself and a savage brawl was thus engaged.

Killam Grimes was one of the finest assassins in all of Venus. He had been trained from birth to be the ultimate killer, and his unarmed combat skills were the envy of his whole unit. Why this woman had chosen to close for a fistfight when she could have just shot him, he could not say. Neither did he care, because Killam considered himself to be a fighter without equal. A charitable observer might forgive the man the hubris of this assessment, as he proved worthy of the grade under most conditions. This was not like most conditions, and Grimes found himself fighting an opponent every bit his match and then some.

His strikes were fast and coordinated. He wove complex patterns of punches and kicks the way a composer wove entire symphonies from individual instruments. He was savage efficiency itself, a whirling and darting maestro of pugilistic virtuosity. Grimes loved to fight, and he was good at it. He grinned at the primal ferocity and intimacy of this close-quarters battle, and kept his attacks coming without pause.

After a few frenzied heartbeats of this, the man realized something was wrong. His blows always landed just a hair too late, or missed their marks entirely. Their scouting had alerted him to the woman's preference for using PC-10 gauntlets, and he had planned accordingly for that. His insulated coverall prevented a crippling electric shock from rendering him immobile, but did little to prevent the heavy knuckledusters from bruising and scratching him with every landed punch. It felt like a sledgehammer to the guts each time the fists made contact and no quantity of training or fitness was going to make that feel better. The woman was preposterously fast, and her footwork and timing belied many hours of training and no small quantity of natural talent.

His right hook was blocked and the follow up straight left was slipped. He managed to twist away from a left hook to his body with enough time to turn a punishing punch into a glancing miss, but was too late to avoid a low kick that swept him from his feet. Only superb athleticism kept Grimes from losing the fight in that instant. He bounced to his feet as soon as his buttocks touched the carpet and a booted foot stomped the ground not six inches from where his groin would have been.

He flung himself backwards to avoid a head kick and crashed against a desk. His hand fell on something solid and he grasped and hurled the object in one motion on instinct. A terminal monitor flew at the face of his enemy, who caught it easily and cast it aside without a second look. Then she was on him again and Killam fell under a hail of punches and elbows that came far too fast for him to do more than weather the storm. The man who had never lost a fight in his life found himself overwhelmed by a barrage of precision strikes that found the gaps in his defense as if it was not even there. On the happenstance he actually parried a hit, he found it was merely a feint to open his guard for some other blow, and the harder he tried to protect his bruised body the more the damned woman hurt it. He scrambled for distance and found himself abandoning offense all together, trying desperately to prevent a knockout punch from ending his mission.

His rescue came when the staccato sounds of a pistol fire broke the woman's rhythm and the telltale flashes of ceramic beads exploding against body armor marred his vision. He took advantage of the distraction to send a front kick to the woman's gut, pushing her away. She ignored him and turned to address his wounded partner, who was still trying in vain to cycle his useless pistol at the armor-clad warrior woman. Grimes did not hesitate. He drew a vibroblade from his belt and leapt for the closet door.

Killam conceded the woman was far too fast, far too skilled, and far too well armored for him to defeat. This shamed him, and the only way to restore his honor would be to complete the mission despite being thoroughly outclassed. Whispering an apology to his downed brothers, Grimes drove his blade through the storeroom door latch and kicked the flimsy metal partition into the space beyond. He did not have much time, he knew. The woman would be on him in a second or two. He could feel it. He hurtled through the aperture and swung his blade with wild abandon, desperate in his hope to score a hit on this traitor who let women and foreigners fight his battles. The blade was impossibly sharp and lethal. It would slice or stab through most materials with ease and it rent flesh like so much wet tissue paper. He needed only the tiniest slice to open a fatal wound in his victims, and he cast his arm in a wide arc in the hope the edge might make contact.

His wrist struck something hard and unforgiving, and what felt like a vise closed around his weapon hand. The blade slipped from numbed fingers as the bones of his wrist ground against each other, and in the dim purple gloom of the closet Killam saw the silhouette of his target. The boy was holding his wrist in his left hand, and for the life of him Killam could not comprehend the horrific strength of that grip. Fortunately, Killam did not need to understand, and so he acted.

A booted foot snapped upward and into the traitor's guts, doubling the boy over and tearing a gurgling whoosh of expelled air from his lungs. The grip on the assassin's wrist loosened and Grimes yanked his injured arm free. Seizing the opportunity, the Balisong leapt on the stumbling boy as he fell. Gritting his teeth at the pain in his arm, he forced the traitor's chin up and exposed the throat of the struggling boy. His left arm ascended, poised for a killing strike. Before the fist could fall, Grimes was jerked backwards off his target and hurled with preternatural strength back into the main office where he struck a chair and crashed to the floor.

He was back to his feet in an instant, but despair had already begun the inexorable trek from the pit of his guts to the front of his mind. He again faced the terrifying armored woman in hand-to-hand combat and he knew in the deepest part of his blackened heart that he could not beat her. All his great skill, and all the years of brutal training would amount to naught, and he was going to fail in his mission. His thoughts went to the explosives strapped to his vest, but they were crude by necessity and his target was in another room. He held little hope that the blast would kill the boy, and he instantly regretted not trying it when he was in there. His confidence in his own martial prowess had gotten the better of him, and this shame burned his guts like liquid fire.

Killam Grimes resolved himself to get back to the closet and complete the mission at any cost. Having no illusions about what that would take, the trained killer feinted a series of punches at the woman's head. As he expected, she parried or dodged easily, and her return strike came at a speed he simply could not compete with. The counter right hand spun him to the left and robbed him of his balance. Instead of recovering his equilibrium he allowed himself to fall past the woman, where he rolled to his feet and sprinted for the closet without looking back. His hand went to his pocket and searched for the dead-man switch to his suicide vest, and panic set in when he realized it was not there.

He was just clearing the doorway when something struck him from behind with incredible power and hurled him into the back of the closet. His head bounced off a shelf of office supplies, and a jagged cut poured blood from his forehead over his eyes in a sheet of warm red liquid. Killam's legs went limp and he careened to the carpet in a clumsy pile of limbs whereupon a torrent of plummeting supplies pelted his bleeding skull. With desperate zealot's strength, the assassin rolled and tried in vain to rise. Rough hands tossed him back to the carpet and shoved him to his back.

The armored woman stood over him, with a booted foot across his throat, and the traitor stood next her, a strange mask of anger and sadness on his face. The youth's hand rose from his side, and Killam saw the black box with his bomb trigger clutched in lean fingers.

"Lose something?" The boy's voice was dry and tired.

"Fuck you, traitor! We will never stop! All of your—"

A fist like a metal cudgel struck the sputtering assassin in the mouth and drove the back of his head against the floor. Blood-smeared eyes rolled back in his head and then closed as the raving killer lost his tenuous battle with unconsciousness.

Lucia looked over to the young man and put a hand on his shoulder. "Nice punch, Manny."

"It's a good arm," he agreed. "Let's get him tied up before we have to smack him around some more."

A voluminous black shadow was blocking the door to the street when they emerged from the storage closet, and Lucia tossed a nod at the shadowy figure. "Get yours?"

The response was deep and guttural. "Yeah, got them all. Mindy check in yet?"

"Right behind you, old man," came Mindy's squeaky voice. Roland stepped aside and let the street lights illuminate the tiny blond. She was standing in the street, with two unmoving bodies trussed behind her like game animals.

Lucia raised an eyebrow at the bizarre picture. "Can I assume that those two are not dead, since you bothered to drag them back?"

"Either that or I am going to have the carcasses mounted as trophies," Mindy said with a non-committal shrug, as if such a thing was entirely plausible and not at all psychotic. Manny's face paled at the implication.

Roland was disinclined toward levity this soon after a fight, and irritation colored his inflection accordingly. "Let's get these assholes secured and debriefed. Maybe they talk, maybe they don't, but it's obvious that a trip to Venus is unavoidable at this point. I'd just as soon have these guys handled before we leave." The big man harrumphed, "I am inclined to let The Dwarf have them. It'll be interesting to see how the new trade association president deals with foreign terrorists running operations in Dockside."

Lucia looked delighted. "You want to get Rodney to pay us to 'fix' this, don't you? What a shrewd business move, Roland!" She reached up and gave his cheek a gentle pat. "My little boy is growing up!"

"I'm   learning,"   he   growled   back.

Chapter Eight

The three captured Balisongs were not particularly helpful. Not on purpose anyway. Once Rodney "The Dwarf" McDowell found out that Venusian terrorists were running unsanctioned operations in Dockside, some experts in the field of information extraction were called in. Lucia had no stomach for interrogations. Watching people pump a man full of psychotropic drugs and then manipulate the resulting hallucinations was the sort of dark entertainment that still turned her stomach. Even more so when one considered just how little useful information the team of assassins gave them for all the effort and expense.

Manny had warned them that might be the case, but prudence dictated an attempt needed to be made all the same. Killam Grimes put up the most resistance, as he was as pure a zealot as the Red Hats had ever produced. His love of cause and home was nearly enough to stymie the interrogators and their various pharmacological tools, yet in the end his mind broke and the information began to flow from even his hardened lips. The two team leaders, on the other hand, proved surprisingly easy to break. So much so that Roland suspected they were not all that committed to resisting. This seemed to magnify Manny's cynicism even more.

The young scout and Roland had elected to spare Lucia the gory details and perused the information alone at Roland's favorite watering hole, The Smoking Wreck. Anticipating Manny's demeanor and Roland's likely reaction to the prospect of dealing with the people who had blown most of his organic mass from his body, Mindy had declined to attend this session as well. This left the two grouchy men to their own devices and company.

Roland had not chosen this bar just because it stocked good beer. He was a well-known fixture in The Wreck and he knew he could have a quiet and private conversation here without fear. The owner and bartender, a man named Marty Mudd, was also a four-year veteran of the Venusian secession. He lent his considerable knowledge of both fighting in the domes and his talent for invective-laced understatement to the cause.

Marty, as was his way, minced few words when it came to the Red Hats. "Of course they broke easy. It's all bullshit to them. It's people like the kid here and Grimes who they need to be true believers."

"It's a hard lesson, Manny," Roland concurred. "Old men start wars that young men have to finish. Those pricks broke easy because they didn't care enough to fight."

"They did not seem all that choked up about losing eight 'brothers' either." Manny made the quotation marks around the word 'brothers' audible with a sneer of transparent derision.

"Of course not," Roland shrugged. "Why would they? There are always more angry young folk under the domes to fill the ranks."

"I feel like such an ass." Manny was taking all of this hard, but this was not an opportune time for him to become maudlin. In a rare instance of social awareness, Roland caught on to this and deftly changed the subject.

"They gave us enough. We know where to start looking for the cell running these ops, so we will be able to hit the ground running. That's going to be important."

"Yeah. I suppose it is," the young man agreed. He scanned through the report from The Dwarf's interrogators with a wary eye. "I only know some of these names, and few personally. Craddock and I go way back. His people practically raised me. He is a fairly popular leader, and he reports to Hardesty. Well, loosely anyway. There is very little in the way of formal structure to the cells." His eyes flicked across the list of names for another second, and he continued. "It looks like they are operating out of The Colander, which makes some sense."

Marty's face twisted into a comical wince. "The goddamn Colander, huh?" He flipped the taps back and started to fill a pair of large beer mugs. His grizzled face swung side to side as his head shook in obvious disapproval. "I did sixty days in that shithole. The whole damn place was built in pieces, by a bunch of different mining companies, over several decades each. There is no sense to any of the layout in the older sections. It's huge and all that, and if you get lost in the lower levels, you ain't never getting found." Two mugs of light amber brew clunked down in front of them and Marty rested his elbows on the pitted wooden bar top. Narrow eyes squinted through the craggy brows of his scarred tanned-leather features. "We lost a squad down under the refractory section. Took us a week to find them, even with the comms working."

"Perfect place for a terrorist cell to hide," Manny agreed. "I've been to the bottom levels, and you aren't wrong, Mr. Mudd. Most of the original industrial domes are like that."

"Yeah," the bartender grunted. "But those others might only be half the size of The Colander. The fucker is what? Ten miles across?"

"And a thousand feet tall," Manny added. "All told, we are looking at more than five hundred square miles to cover, if we include all the vertical decks." The tan youth sipped his beer and raised his eyebrows in appreciation. Marty stocked the best brew in Dockside, and Manny was unused to the quality. "But they'll be in the bottom two levels, so realistically, we are only looking at about a quarter of that, I'd guess."

"One-hundred-and-twenty-five square miles of unmapped industrial space and abandoned maintenance tunnels? That sounds all kinds of easy, then!" Marty snorted and started to pull himself a mug. "I hope you can narrow it down more than that, son."

"I sure can." Manny seemed to be warming up to the conversation. Even though Roland and Marty had been on the opposite side of the fight he had been born into, at least they had been there. A much-younger Roland slogged his way through the brutal fighting on Venus for ninety days before a Red Hat booby trap had nearly killed him, starting him on his path to Project: Golem and his own personal tragedies. Ten years prior to that, Marty had finished his two full tours as well, equaling more than three years deployed under the domes. Considering the population's mortality rate and rampant expatriation, a three-year residency made the gnarled veteran sergeant a native as far as Manny was concerned. To a young man torn from his home and hunted by the people he had called family, sitting in the presence of these men who had seen so many of the same things he had was nice. It was not the same as talking to old friends, but when you are far from home, any reminder of how things used to be was comforting. The domes were a unique paradigm in the expanding sphere of human influence, and Manny had never really acclimated to life outside of them. Only those who had been there truly understood the byzantine cultural entanglements that grew from living on a planet where the surface temperature could melt lead and acid fell from the sky every day.

Once Anson Gates had opened up travel lanes to more hospitable worlds, the need to colonize hellish rocks like Venus disappeared virtually overnight. Much like Enceladus, only its proximity to Earth and abundant resources kept the mining stations working at all. If gate fees and shuttle speeds ever improved significantly, Venus was likely to be abandoned by the corporations altogether. Manny was starting to think that would be a good thing for all involved.

The scout was snapped back to the conversation by the bartender's grunted assent. "I bet you can, kid." Marty nodded his approval over a big swig of something dark and foamy.

Manny began to build a diorama out of random bar ware as he explained. "Okay. So you've got the main dome, right?" He pantomimed a hemisphere over an aluminum napkin holder flanked by a stack of coasters and a tray of mixed nuts. "In the middle you have all the power generation and environmental stuff." He pointed to the napkin dispenser before continuing. "On the North side of that are the atmospheric condensers that pull all those VOCs from the air."

"You mean the nuts?" Roland asked as he grabbed a cashew and popped it into his mouth.

"Yup. The nuts. That area runs deep under the surface where the collection tanks are. RUC are heavy there because that's what makes all the damn money."

He gestured to the stacked coasters. "Over here we have the refractory and refinery. This is where all that stuff was processed. As Mr. Mudd pointed out—"

Marty interrupted him, "Stop calling me 'Mr. Mudd.' Feels weird. Like my dad is here or something."

"—Sorry, uh, sir."

Marty rolled his eyes. "Don't call me sir, either. I work for a living."

"Right. Marty. Like you said, the refractory is old and mostly abandoned. The refinery is in a different dome now, and processing has mostly moved off-world or to more controlled domes to prevent the Red Hats from sabotaging it. It's an equipment graveyard and a bunch of unused space now, and man, can you hide a lot of shit in there."

Roland nodded. "You figure that's where we will find Hardesty and Craddock?"

"I'd bet we find Craddock. Hardesty moves around a lot. He's as close to a leader as the Red Hats are ever going to get. Hardesty also has a semi-legitimate face, so skulking in abandoned tunnels is not really his style, if you get what I mean."

"What the hell is 'semi-legitimate?'" The old bartender chuckled into his beer glass. "That like when you are a complete shit-heel but also hold elected office?"

"Hardesty is president of the Venusian Labor Conclave. Even though RUC knows he's a Red Hat booster, they can't do much directly unless they want a full-on rebellion again. Most of the workers don't realize it, but he is probably playing both sides. No one who knows can do anything about it because he holds the keys to so many factions." Manny shook his head in frustration. "I was a damn good scout, and I'll tell you right now I *know* Hardesty is playing the Red Hats just as hard as he is the RUC. I once reconned a RUC admin facility and found that Hardesty was using the Conclave to pressure OmniCorp into bringing in more security. All to cover his own smuggling operations." He threw a hand in the air. "When I brought that up, you'd have thought I'd insulted Craddock's mom. Then there was my reluctance to bomb a children's hospital. That really sealed my fate."

The bartender coughed. "Those hardcore types don't really take it well when you ask questions that don't play with their dogma, kid. Everybody knows that." Roland thought perhaps this admonition could have been delivered with more tact, but Marty Mudd was not a nurturer.

"Nobody told me," Manny shrugged.

"Wait," the big man interrupted, "this Hardesty guy is playing his own people?"

"Yeah," Manny shrugged again. "But that kind of crap is practically a cliché in the factory domes. It's just most Red Hats are so caught up in their own bullshit they don't realize it can happen to them."

"There's Lucia's political angle right there." The big cyborg grew very thoughtful. "We don't have to expose a dome as sympathizers, we can just incriminate Hardesty. We let him know we can burn him with the Hats, and I bet he will find a way to let Manny off the hook."

"He is a weasel," Manny concurred.

"They always are, kid." Marty wasn't smiling when he said it. "But if he's a smart little weasel, it won't be no picnic catching him in the act. And like you said, it will need to be real damn convincing if all his true-believers are gonna accept it."

"True," Roland added, "if he thinks our dirt is weak, he may just roll the dice. Can you prove any of it?"

Manny bobbed his head from side to side, as if weighing his options. "Probably, if we can get me back into Hardesty's records. I know where to look for the dirt, and if we get enough out it might scare him off." He thought some more, using a long swig of beer to buy time. "He's a coward for sure, but a powerful one. If not for what they think I know, I'd be a relatively small fry to them." His face cracked into a feral leer. "Man, did I hurt Craddock's pride when I started to resist their..." Manny seemed to lose the word he was looking for. His eyes narrowed when he found it. "... influence." Then he finished his thought as if nothing had happened, "Hardesty won't care one way or the other, as long as he doesn't get exposed. It's Craddock we have to worry about. I'm guessing he took my escape very personally."

Roland asked, "Won't he just do what Hardesty tells him to?"

Manny shrugged and looked into his beer. "Probably," he said, not sounding very sure of it. "It depends on how angry he is. Hardesty doesn't rule the Red Hats. We're talking about mid-sized groups made up of smaller cells. Everybody communicates, and some groups and cells are more influential than others, but there is no clear chain of command. Hardesty has more influence than anyone else in the Hats, but that doesn't mean Craddock will obey him blindly. I wouldn't be surprised if Craddock has his own game going on, either. He comes off like a true believer, but he is greedy as all hell, too."

"Sheesh," Marty grumped. "What a fucking nightmare."

"Hey man, I grew up in that nightmare." Manny winked at the pair of old soldiers. "At least with you guys here, I don't feel like the most messed up guy in the room anymore."

"Speak for yourself, kid." Marty grabbed the mugs and turned back to the taps. His hands flicked the handles with the ease of endless repetition. "I turned out just fine. Just because this big ape," he jerked a thumb at the sour-faced cyborg, "got himself all messed up doesn't mean we all did."

Roland scoffed at the ribbing and returned fire. "How many confirmed kills you get over there, Marty?"

"Only thirty-one confirmed. Fifty-seven probable. Hard to keep track in the darker spots."

"And how many guns you got under that bar, Marty?"

"Right now?"

"No, Marty, yesterday." The big man rolled his eyes. "Of course, right now!"

"Six." The man seemed genuinely confused, as if keeping a veritable arsenal at arm's length at all times was entirely normal behavior.

"You sleep with any of those guns?" Roland already knew the answer, but this dance was for Manny's benefit.

Marty still sounded confused. "Of course not. These are bar guns, not bedroom guns. What kind of barbarian brings workplace weapons to the bedroom?" He looked at Manny, incredulity writ large on his grizzled features and pointed at Roland. "Bar guns in the bedroom? Can you believe this guy?"

Now Manny was lost. "What is the difference?"

"Workplace guns are bigger, kid. No big deal if I gouge the bar a little bit or shoot the walls here. Bedroom guns need to be smaller because ladies like nice sheets and curtains. Those are pricey. Also, interior walls are thinner, too. Don't want to wreck the living room shooting someone in the bedroom."

Two pairs of eyebrows rose at this response, and Manny could not stop himself from asking, "Are there 'living-room guns,' too?"

"Obviously. Who has time to run to the bedroom for a gun if you are sitting in your favorite armchair watching a holo?"

"And the kitchen?" Manny took a long pull on his beer to hide his burgeoning laughter.

68

"Nobody, and I mean nobody, would be stupid enough to fuck with me when I'm in the kitchen. I have something real special in there just in case, though."

Manny spat beer at the plain unvarnished sincerity of Marty's response. Roland finally made his point with a sarcastic pat on the bartender's shoulder.

"Sure, Marty. You turned out completely normal. Certainly no lingering issues following you around."

Manny joined the fun, and it felt good. "Nope. No paranoia or hyper-vigilance with this guy!"

Finally realizing what was happening, Marty tossed both men a rude gesture. "Ah, fuck you both. Just for that, you can actually pay for your beers tonight, smart guy."

"Put in on my tab," Roland raised his glass and Manny clunked his against it with a chuckle.

For the next two hours, Manny and Marty proceeded to get roaring drunk. Marty told stories of his time on Venus that Roland suspected were only moderately exaggerated. Manny peppered his tales with insights from the other side of the conflict, often filling in the gaps of Marty's understanding with poignant and usually humorous anecdotes. Roland, being biomechanically incapable of getting drunk on beer, sat and encouraged them to ever higher levels of boisterous revelry. He knew that this sort of interaction was important for Manny, and he knew better than anyone why. The boy was hurting, and for the first time in a long time Roland understood that hurt. He was not a man prone to empathy, yet something inside the thousand-pound war machine wanted desperately for that scared young man to get past this, to grow beyond the monster his own people had tried to make him.

Upon reflection, the reason for this was obvious. Roland had never been very big on reflection.

Chapter Nine

T he Colander was a descriptive moniker, and unironic. The first of the great industrial complexes to be constructed on Venus, the yellowing dome was peppered with ten thousand tiny holes and as many weeping cracks. Seventy-five years of boiling sulfuric acid rain wore away the shielded surface as quickly as it could be repaired, and teams of drones supervised by cyborgs stalked the dome in constant search for the next failure point. It was a holding action at best. Men and women who plied trades near the weeping skin were forever at the mercy of "Aphrodite's Tears." These wayward drips of hot acid migrated through the tiny gaps as saturated steam condensed into liquid sulfuric acid in the crawlspaces and structures of the dome. A single drop of the stuff could meander along joists and other surfaces, coalesce into a globule, then fall and burn unsuspecting skin like liquid fire. No person who lived or worked in The Colander for any period of time escaped the tears, and many wore the resulting scars as a perverse badge of honor.

Though far more agreeable than the thousand-degree daytime with its corrosive downpours, inside The Colander was not what Alasdair Craddock would call paradise, either. The exhaust fans were continuously breaking down, and the liquid helium cooling system was prone to random flights of whimsical malaise. On a good day, the temperature could be as comfortable as eighty-two degrees Fahrenheit. A bad day was the sort of torture that could drive a man to want to go for a walk outside. Furthermore, no amount of filtration and recycling was going to eliminate the smell of sulfur, gear oil, and machinery that permeated the air. One might get used to it after a while, but it only took a brief trip to one of the newer domes for a man to realize just how much the average Venusian laborer could stink.

Craddock was acutely aware of this as he had just returned from Caelestus. The shining silver capital city of Free Venus was as modern as anything on the planet, and tax dollars invested in creature comforts had done much to make that place deceptively hospitable. Returning to The Colander was like stepping from Elysium to Tartarus, made even more poignant for the pervasive stench of brimstone. The short man stepped from the surface crawler hatch and hopped down to the deck of the cargo bay at ground level. It took a moment for his eyes to adjust to the deep shadows and weak illumination of the cavernous room, and another dejected comparison with the capital city became unavoidable.

Everywhere that Caelestus was bright, The Colander was dark. Most of the original lighting in the lower sections had died decades ago. No one had wanted the expense of upgrading it, so lines of emergency lighting were strung up along grimy corridors like dirty yellow Christmas lights. The yawing darkness of the cargo bay was just barely beaten back by a few anemic high-bay luminaires casting their weak blue-white rays against the walls and floors. Heavy lidded eyes looked at these splashes of light and could not help but think it all just a pathetic anachronism. He sneered at the shapeless darkness, watching it encroach upon the pools of soft light like a hungry fog. It looked to his tired mind as if the very night itself was using the lighter patches as bait to catch unsuspecting fools tempted by the illusion of brightness.

Craddock had days when the mere thought of looking at something without squinting was luxurious enough a prospect to justify so dramatic an impression. Already he felt his face scrunching, the pale skin of his cheeks tightening, the familiar moleish peering squint of the Venusian laborer twisting his otherwise unremarkable features. He hated it all so much.

To be fair, his mood may have been artificially dampened by exterior influences. Losing two teams of Balisongs was the type of setback that drove a man in his position to new and interesting heights of frustration. No traitorous little turncoat was worth that many quality men and women, but that traitorous little turncoat knew things that had Hardesty breathing down Craddock's neck in a most annoying fashion. The predicament caused by Manuel Richardson's stubborn refusal to die had grown from a minor inconvenience to a full-blown crisis in just a few days.

71

"Good evening, Alasdair," said a thin man in green coveralls as Craddock stomped past. "We got word from New Boston."

"Well?" Craddock tried not to sound irritated. It was not Sully's fault any of his was happening, and snapping at his second-in-command would not be conducive to finding solutions. He tried to keep his tone businesslike, but his follow up of, "Out with it, then!" came out with more bite than was strictly called for.

Sully, who was an otherwise competent commander, was distinctly terrified of his boss, and this fear turned his response into a nervous stammer. "They, uh... the local community leader guy, or whatever he is. He's uh, pretty pissed. He has Killam, Percy, and Laslow."

"And?"

"And, uh..." Sully looked afraid to speak, but Craddock's frantic gesturing edged him forward. "They say that they're sending a 'fixer' to settle this. Whatever that means."

Craddock stopped just shy of the exit. He turned to Sully with a look of bemused expectation. "A fixer? Like, a local hood who does mob negotiations?"

"Yeah. I... Uh... I guess. Yeah."

"Christ on a fucking cracker. I got two dead teams of Balisongs, and some streetwise mutt from Earth is sending his local muscle over here to do what? *Scold* me?"

Sully offered only a blank stare in response. Craddock rubbed his eyes with palm already sweating in the cloying warmth of the poorly ventilated cargo bay. "Well, do we know anything about this fixer? Is he coming here to pick a fight? Or is this just a courtesy visit to chastise me for not hiring local muscle?" The man was acutely aware of how intensely local unions could defend their shops and territories. If this was just a case of him having to make nice with a shop steward, then he could stomach a sit-down over it.

"I can't imagine, uh, that this guy would be sending, like, a hitter or nothing, right?" Craddock could not tell if Sully was trying to convince his boss or himself of this. Either way, he was doing a poor job of it.

"Goddamnit, Sully. The universe is chock full of shit you can't imagine. I bump into three things you can't imagine before I take my morning shit. As matter of fact, my morning shit probably has things in it you can't imagine."

Sully did not deserve his wrath, and Craddock instantly regretted the outburst. "Ah, fuck it, Sully. This ain't your fault either way. Maybe if I ate a piece fruit every now and then my shit wouldn't be so interesting, eh?" Turning his rant into humor seemed to work, because the looking of creeping terror on Sully's face shifted into a goofy grin at the crass joke.

"Too much rich food in Caelestus, Boss?"

"Damn straight."

Craddock needed answers. He motioned for Sully to walk with him as he crossed into the access tunnel. The heat was worse in there, with nowhere to rise the air was thick and moist with the stink of sulfur and machine oil. "Seriously, though. If this is just a union thing, no big deal, right? I'll apologize and transfer some creds. But who knows what is going on with these Dockside pricks, anymore? God, I miss the fucking Combine." He tossed his head in a rueful shake, "Imagine ever saying that? At least with those crusty old mobsters you knew where you stood. You knew the goddamn rules."

"Yeah," Sully agreed. Then he squinted at his leader. "But wasn't, ah, one of those... uh... rules that you had to stay the hell out of Dockside?"

Craddock stopped walking and turned to his man. His head was cocked at an odd angle and something in his eyes told Sully that perhaps his input had been ill-timed. "Well thank you, Sully. Thank you so much for pointing out this thing that I already knew."

"Just, uh... saying. We should, uhm, you know... be kinda careful around those guys. They are kinda touchy, I guess. Maybe it wasn't the Combine with that rule, but you know, the Dockside rackets."

"I really wanna be pissed at you Sully. But dammit, you're probably right."

"Happens sometimes." Sully's face took on a look of competing chagrin and pride.

Craddock turned and resumed walking in silence. The corridor was wide enough for small vehicles to pass each other, and enough lights had been strung back and forth across the high ceiling to keep the worst of the muddy shadows at bay. His footfalls echoed through the otherwise empty hall and tapped a brisk tattoo as his short legs worked hard to cover the half mile to the barracks. Sully followed quietly, his longer legs keeping easy pace with his stocky leader's strides.

The pair stopped at a heavy steel hatch built into the tunnel wall. The door was equipped with an intimidating locking bar and a control panel. Craddock pressed a series of numbers on the control pad and a blinking red light flashed over to solid red for a few seconds. Then it resumed flashing. Craddock sighed in frustration and looked at the taller man next to him. Sully did not notice for a moment, then jumped as if smacked when he realized the man was waiting on him.

"Sorry, Alasdair. We had to change the codes when we found out the first team had been taken."

Slender fingers punched a different series of numbers. Then a pop and a whirring noise followed, and the bar slid back, freeing the door.

"Dammit, Sully. You could have told me before I made an ass of myself just now."

"Forgot. It's been kind of busy around here while you were gone."

The pair crossed the raised threshold and passed into a smaller, more brightly lit corridor. The dirty yellow and brown walls of the tunnel shifted to slab-gray steel panels with white lights at regular intervals. It was cooler in here, to Craddock's supreme relief, and the stink of sulfur was one full standard deviation better than in the cargo bay. He picked up speed as he moved, as if proximity to his own office and bed drove him harder the closer he got to them.

"Anything I need to know about?"

He did not turn to address this question to his subordinate, though he could hear Sully's shrug in his voice. "RUC, uh... swept Warrentown and The Quad. They grabbed a few of the boys on random minor shit."

"Like what?"

"Uh... a couple of the boys had some guns. Mostly old smoke-poles, but uh... One or two good bead pistols, too."

"Well, shit," Craddock groused as he walked. "Decent hardware is hard to get."

"Yeah," Sully agreed eloquently. "Sean thinks they are just, uh... shaking folks down again. They're still too dumb or too scared to go too far below the refractories though. The main armory is still safe."

"Did someone from Earth squawk about the Balisongs?"

Sully shook his head. "Sean doesn't think so. He's been on all the wavelengths and the uh... only guys yelling about it is that Dockside guy sending the fixer."

"Hmph," grunted Craddock. "Looks like they are trying to keep the official bulls away from this, too. Good on them. Nice to see that some of the old rules still apply."

With a sigh of relief, Craddock at last found himself at the door to his office and quarters. He keyed his personal code into the lock without thinking, and Sully had not changed this one at least. Thus, he was spared the embarrassment of not being able to access his own space. The door ground open with a screech, and Craddock stalked into the room. With an expressive grunt of purest satisfaction, he promptly and unceremoniously crumpled into an old stuffed chair.

As leader of the local Red Hat enclave, Craddock's quarters were positively opulent by Colander standards. A square room nearly twenty feet on a side with an attached sleeping compartment large enough for a queen-size bed constituted the height of luxury for those who made their homes in the aging complex. Having his own un-shared bathroom complete with a shower stall, cemented these quarters as the sanctum of a very important man. Craddock had killed the previous occupant and he was certain that the next tenant would need to duplicate this feat to remove him.

"Sully?" He breathed lazily, eyes closed with pleasure.

"Yeah, Boss?"

"If you were to go to my fridge and grab us a couple of beers, I would be eternally fucking grateful."

Sully's eyes widened. "Real beer?"

"Yup. It's been that kind of week."

The rangy man fairly skipped over to the small refrigerator across the room and yanked it open. He grabbed two cans of thin lager and rushed back to Craddock's side. He offered the reclining man a can with an excited, "Here ya go, Boss!"

The men clanked their cans together in comradely fashion and both tipped their treasures back for a long pull. Against the elevated temperature of the recycled air, the flood of frigid liquid raced down Craddock's throat like the swollen flood of an arctic river. It was sweet, savory, and bitter all at once, and a small groan of ecstasy rumbled from his barrel chest. A single can of honest-to-goodness beer cost as much as many Venusian laborers made in a week, and Craddock pulled fully a third of his in one decadent gulp.

"Ahhhhhhhh," he sighed. "That is the stuff right there."

Sully was trying manfully to not chug his. It might be months before he ever tasted real beer again, and Craddock could see the man forcing himself to sip slowly. "Oh, drink up, Sully. Times are a-changin' around here. Soon we'll be able to afford all the beer we want."

"Really?" The taller man seemed confused but hopeful.

"I gotta go have a sit-down with Hardesty, and we got to perish this Richardson kid on the quick. But yeah. It's going to be real different around here real soon."

"What's going on?"

Craddock shifted in his chair and stretched his short legs. Riding in a ground crawler for eleven hours was murder on his knees. When he was comfortable he looked back up to his partner. "Hardesty has some big shit show in the works with the RUC. He says he can get the Hats access to the nav pylons."

Sully's eyes widened more for this than they had for the beer. "You mean...?"

"Yup. We get a shot at taking over shipping and receiving. The corps will have to deal with us after that or no more iron and VOCs. I went over to Caelestus to make sure that we'll still be able to move food and supplies in after that. Hardesty's smugglers will keep us fed while we strangle all those corporate whores in their sleep."

Sully gulped, then swigged his beer with gusto. His eyes glistened wetly in the cool white light of Craddock's apartment and his jaw flexed. Anticipation and trepidation warred across the pitted terrain of his face, and his mind tried to make sense of the potential consequences of this new development.

"This is gonna be real big, Alasdair."

Craddock chuckled at the naked vapidity of so grievous an understatement.

"Big?" He drained the last of his beer. "Sully, this is bigger than big. This is it. We are about to get a chance at breaking the hold those corps have on us. The Council's gotta try to help the bastards, but they sure as fuck don't care about us. The RUC will get pulled as soon as the corps give up and stop screeching. Hardesty is going to use the union to force the companies to the table, and he says he's got a council member in his pocket, to boot."

"What, uh... what about the other domes?"

"Hardesty says the union will keep them in line. Plus, he's got some super-big investor backing him now. He can afford all kinds of political favors I guess."

"When?"

Craddock sighed, "Yeah, well, that's the damn trick isn't it? Apparently, our little lost lamb has some shit on Hardesty. If he pops that data at the wrong moment, apparently all the crap falls apart."

"What kind of shit?" Sully frowned. "What could a kid uh... have that would affect a swinger like Hardesty that much?"

"Fucked if I know, but it has him all sorts of worked up. I already spent two teams of Balisongs on him and he ain't handled yet. It sure looks like somebody else thinks he's important too."

"If two squads couldn't uh... get it done, what else can we do?"

Craddock peered into the bottom of his vacant beer can, wishing it was not so damnably empty. "I dunno, Sully. Maybe we can hire local muscle or call it in to the Lodge." This put a deep scowl on his face. "Imagine that... the Red Hats using the goddamn Lodge for a kill. I'd never live it down." He tossed the can into a waiting recycler and pressed his palms into his face. He rubbed his cheeks briskly for a few seconds than brought his palms down on his thighs with a slap. "Well, I suppose we hear what this damn 'fixer' has to say about it first."

"Can't hurt," Sully agreed. "When does he get here?"

"According to this Dwarf guy, there will be no mistaking it when he gets here. Whatever that means."

Chapter Ten

Mirth was not a thing that came quickly or easily to Roland Tankowicz. One could blame the horrors of his past or the violence of his present for this, but that would be a cop out. Roland was born a grumpy baby, grew up as a grouchy kid, went through an extended phase as a sullen teenager, and then evolved into a strapping young soldier with a personality modeled after his least favorite drill instructor. All of this occurred before his conversion into a towering technological juggernaut, and thus could not be attributed to that. Of course, getting enslaved and manipulated by his own people was the catalyst that had allowed him to blossom from a normal everyday kind of hardcase into the full-blown cynical curmudgeon that the Dockside locals had learned to know and fear.

But for one brilliant star-crossed moment in time, the slab-faced old cyborg had all he could do to restrain full-blown guffaws from escaping his mouth.

Roland, Manny, Lucia and Mindy found themselves on a thirty-seven-hour shuttle ride to Venus. They had selected a cargo craft and not a passenger ship to hide their arrival from any Red Hats that may be watching the passenger manifests. The quartet had taken to the cargo bay for some exercise and distraction, since the dingy industrial space ship had none of the amenities of a commercial passenger vessel. Spending thirty-seven minutes with Mindy tended to be about as much as Roland could handle even when he had booze and holos to distract him. With no such items available, he had boarded the ship convinced that he was going to have a terrible time of it. He was wrong in this assumption. Not because Mindy had suddenly matured and stopped annoying him, rather because she had elected to take this time to continue training Manny in the arts martial. Roland had seen enough of Manny in action to know that the kid was tough, brave, and resourceful. What he lacked was not talent, but training. Mindy had taken it upon herself to correct this deficiency, and after several weeks things were going about as well as could be expected.

"Dammit, Manny!" Mindy squeaked. "Keep your hands up! Stop letting them dip when you are about to throw a punch!"

"I swear I'm not!" the tanned youth whined back, rubbing a bruised cheek. His blue foam sparring gloves lay on the deck where he had dropped them after receiving an educational rap in the face from the tiny blond.

"Every time you throw the right hand, you let the left drop and then I punch you on that cheek. If you hand was where it was supposed to be, I'd be bruising your hand, not your ugly face!"

Manny waggled alabaster bionic fingers at her. "This one doesn't bruise. Mindy."

"All the more reason to use it correctly, then."

Mindy was not being very fair to her pupil. Roland could see that Manny was actually doing fine. His momentarily lapsed guard was a brief twitch of his hand, and it would take a very fast opponent indeed to capitalize on it. Mindy was superhumanly fast, and what was the briefest flinch to Manny was a gaping chasm of opportunity to her. Lucia had seen it as well, and she could not help but poke fun at the pair.

Lucia said coyly, "Here, Manny. Let me show you what she means."

She walked over to the center of the room and stood in front of Mindy. "What Mindy is saying is that when you begin to chamber the right hand, your left shoulder rotates out of line, which causes your elbow to dip, and opens up your face." She pantomimed the movement slowly, exaggerating the steps to show the mechanics. "If you chamber the punch by rotating your hips instead of your shoulders, you can line up behind the punch without dropping your guard." She demonstrated what she was talking about, smoothly twisting her right hip back to align her right fist for an overhand punch. Her shoulders indexed naturally to her hips and her left hand rotated with the torso, without moving from its defensive position.

Mindy watched, head nodding in appreciation and wearing a look that bordered upon leering. Then she looked at Manny. "Yeah. What she said. Do that."

Manny sighed, "Thanks, Coach," and rolled his eyes. He practiced rotating his hips to position himself a few times, searching awkwardly for the rhythm of it. Then he fired some mock punches from various angles, shuffling his feet to keep his body square to his imaginary opponent. Roland allowed a small amused expression to crease his face.

"Kid's got potential," he called to the group. "Lucia should be his coach, though. Mindy, you don't have the head for instruction."

"What's that supposed to mean?" Mindy huffed back.

"It means Lucia trained for thirty years with some of the best coaches and trainers in the solar system. Based on how you move, I'd say you learned by sparring with mercs. You got by because you have a lot of natural talent." He held up a placating hand to forestall the incoming invective. "You're damn good Mindy. One of the best I've seen. But you're all talent. You don't even know why you're so good, so how are you going to explain it to a kid like Manny? All Lucia has to do is teach Manny all the drills and skills she went through when she learned. She probably remembers them all perfectly."

Lucia nodded, "I still train twice a week when I'm in town."

"See?" Roland pointed to Manny. "He doesn't have your natural skills, and he doesn't have any speed or strength augmentations, either. He needs to learn the way regular folk do."

Mindy put her hands on her hips and thrust her chin toward Roland, "So you think Lucia can do a better job than me? Even though I have way more fighting experience than she does?"

"Yes."

Manny was starting to catch on, and one corner of his mouth turned up. "He's right, you know. You have the wrong kind of experience, Mindy. Besides, we all know Lucia is a way better fighter than you are."

Mindy whirled on him, "What? No way!" She spun back to Lucia, "You don't think that, do you?"

Lucia smiled a slow, predatory smile.

"You do think that, huh?"

Lucia bent slowly and picked up Manny's discarded gloves. She winked to Roland and began to tug them over her hands.

"Ooooohhhhhh shit!" Manny chuckled. "This is gonna be awesome." He quickly backed away from the women.

"All right, then!" Mindy fairly growled it. "Time to try the boss lady on for size!"

This is where the big cyborg began to feel the first pangs of what he would later describe as 'amusement.' To his practiced eye, the match-up was intriguing. He had not been lying when he described Mindy's skills. She was an excellent hand-to-hand fighter. That was not in question. She was born to it, however. She would have been an amazing athlete in any arena. Mindy had a natural grace and an instinct for movement that could not be taught. Training with assassins and mercenaries had taken that talent and built layers of skills and techniques onto it, and the result was the top-rated assassin in the whole Hunter's Lodge.

Lucia, on the other hand, was extremely well trained. While she lacked Mindy's natural abilities, Lucia had the benefit of high-cost instructors and the time and luxury to master the intricacies of hand-to-hand fighting over many years. She still trained regularly with her old coach, Rodrigo. The ancient teacher was an ex-pro fighter who had molded several champions in his years and had amassed the kind of intimate knowledge only extended decades of experience could garner a man. Rodrigo had forgotten more about fighting than the average mercenary could teach anyone.

The two women squared off in the center of the cargo hold. Though it was full of crates and containers, the pair had a square of open area approximately thirty feet on a side to work with.

"Sure you want to do this, Boss?" Mindy chuckled and bounced on the balls of her feet. Her chest, bulbous and straining the seams of her undersized athletic top, jiggled and gyrated in hypnotic waves. Lucia was glad she was not a heterosexual male, because fighting with those things in plain sight would have been a very daunting prospect otherwise. The iridescent pink shorts were not any less a distraction, not only for their brevity, but for the burning fluorescent hue of them.

Lucia beamed back, "You dressed yourself for this, Mindy. I don't think my choices are really the ones in question here."

"Them's fightin' words, lady," Mindy snarled playfully at the barb.

Lucia settled into a relaxed orthodox boxing stance, and Mindy bounced lightly on the balls of her feet.

"Ding, ding!" Manny cried, signaling the start of the bout.

Mindy darted at Lucia, her left hand snapping through the air in a lightning jab. Lucia cocked her head to slip the punch and fired an answering right at her opponent's head. The shot landed flush on Mindy's cheek and Lucia stepped back to wink at Manny.

"See, Manny. She does it too. It's a common mistake."

Manny chuckled, and Roland's grin crept another few degrees upward. Mindy stuck her tongue out at the men and returned to the attack. She anticipated Lucia's jab and turned to catch the hit against her gloves. Turning slightly, she shot a low kick toward the inside of Lucia's left knee. Lucia simply stepped back and dropped an overhand right over Mindy's guard. It scored a grazing blow against the chin, and Mindy spun back with graceful sweep of her hips to resume a more defensive posture.

"Did it again, Mindy."

"It wouldn't work if you didn't have those crazy reflexes," she pouted.

"If you didn't have modified bones and muscles, that shot would have knocked you over." Lucia shrugged, "We all work with what we got."

Physically, Mindy was much stronger than Lucia, and despite the size difference, she was a good forty pounds heavier due to her reinforced bones and muscles. Mindy was right about Lucia's reflexes, and despite significant speed enhancements of her own, the little blond killer was having a hard time dealing with the preternatural speed of her opponent.

Roland watched Lucia carefully. They had been adjusting her nanomachines lately to address some issues with Lucia's brain chemistry. The clever little 'bots did an excellent job of correcting for her various neurological issues, including her acute anxiety. Subsequently, they had found that too much enhancement was altering her personality and cognition in ways that were unexpected. Unchecked adaptation by the machines was affecting her natural sense of empathy and danger avoidance, and firmware upgrades had been added to account for this. This had cost her some speed and re-introduced aspects of her anxiety issues, and several versions of the new firmware were still being tested. Mindy was fast enough to really push Lucia's limits, and the ensuing exchange of blows revealed a Lucia Ribiero still moving and thinking with blinding alacrity. Roland wondered if Lucia had asked her father for another adjustment after the attack on the office. He scowled at the thought. Her duel with the assassins must have put her off. It looked like she had cranked her speed back up a notch from a few weeks ago.

Otherwise, Lucia's technique was perfect. Footwork, hand position, transitions and combinations were crisp and all in accordance with solid fundamentals. She was not some flashy fighter, no silly spinning moves or acrobatics. She eschewed high-risk gambits and pressed her opponent's defenses with a solid, workmanlike progression of combinations and flawless footwork. It was counterintuitive, but Lucia needed to treat the diminutive assassin as if she was a larger and stronger opponent, because frankly, that's what she was.

Mindy was considerably wilder. She relied on her strength and durability augmentations to keep her in the fight and she stalked Lucia like a hungry wolf. She bounced, she flitted, and she leapt in wild cavorting attacks. Mindy showed Lucia serious consideration, and did not hold back much. While not using her full strength, her punches and kicks were sent with enough force to make Lucia behave like she was in a real fight or suffer painful consequences. She respected Lucia enough to give her the full treatment, and Lucia was hard pressed to maintain her assault because more often than not, she needed to avoid hits rather than block or parry.

Roland nodded in approval. Mindy was starting to figure Lucia out. The clever killer was trying to force an opening because Lucia was obviously not going to give her one. Lucia's training was too good, her tactics too evolved for her to make any slips on her own. Thanks to her extensive biotech, Mindy could afford to take risks when Lucia could not. Her strategy seemed less wild now that Roland knew what she was doing.

Mindy fired a flurry of punches, each swing flowing into the next in an attempt to pry a hole into the other woman's guard. They came with brutal power, forcing Lucia to slip and dodge which kept her from countering. After the fourth strike sailed past Lucia's nose, Mindy dropped her hips and dived for a low tackle.

Roland again grunted approval. It was a good play. Lucia was primarily a muay thai-style kickboxer, and a double-leg takedown attempt was good way to counteract Lucia's impeccable striking.

Lucia threw her legs back and drove her hip into Mindy's shoulder. It was a textbook sprawl and it would have worked but for

83

Mindy's superhuman strength. Enhanced muscles kept pushing, though, and Lucia was nearly swept from the floor entirely. Thinking quickly, Lucia locked a front headlock on Mindy and sat down hard. Mindy went from a head-first tackle to a forward tumble. Using her legs and Mindy's own forward drive, Lucia kicked the little blond over her body and kept rolling to land on top of Mindy's chest.

Roland barked a guffaw at the smooth transition. Judo had been his first fighting style and a flawless *sumi gaeshi* was still a thing of beauty to him. To see Lucia do it to Mindy warmed the cockles of his giant bionic organic fluid pump.

Mindy looked confused. The whole transition had happened so quickly she wasn't entirely sure what had happened. Lucia did not afford her the time to recover, and began raining punches down on Mindy's face. She kept them playful for safety's sake. Her own impressive musculature, while not superhuman, was more than strong enough to ruin Mindy's looks if she wasn't careful. Mindy bucked and heaved, compromising Lucia's balance and snagging one of her descending arms. She tried to drag Lucia off to the side, but Lucia switched to a two-handed death grip on Mindy's elbow and spun until her body was perpendicular to Mindy's. Swinging one leg around, Lucia trapped the arm between her knees and leaned back. She arched her hips against the bony little joint and stretched the limb as straight as it would go.

With a laugh Mindy relaxed and tapped Lucia's thigh rapidly.

"Dammit, Boss, you got it."

Lucia let go immediately and both women sat up with grins on their faces. Sweat ran freely from Lucia's forehead, and she wiped it absently with a sleeve. "You didn't want to try to get out of that? Wasn't sure I had it tight enough."

The blond killer shrugged. "I have enough extra strength to give it a shot. Maybe. I think. Maybe I could've busted out, maybe not. You had it good enough that it wasn't worth a ruined elbow trying, though. You've been rolling with the big guy, haven't you?"

"He's too big. I did some jujitsu years ago, and I have been working again to brush it up."

"The extra leverage is nice when you're fighting augmented guys," Mindy agreed.

"What the hell just happened?" Manny sounded confused, impressed, and terrified all at once. "That was the craziest shit I've ever seen."

Mindy turned to look at Manny, and because she was still sitting on the floor, her expansive cleavage was displayed prominently. The young man wanted so badly to be more mature and stoic, but his eyes went where they willed, and Mindy snapped her fingers to get his attention back.

"Hey. Up here, buddy!" Manny snapped his gaze back to her face. Chagrined at his lack of discipline though not embarrassed enough to give her the victory, he smirked at her. "You picked the outfit, Mindy. Don't blame me for looking."

"Roland doesn't look."

"Roland better not," Lucia acknowledged.

"Mr. Tankowicz is a robot," Manny quipped. "Doesn't count."

Roland answered the question. "Lucia wasn't strong enough to hurt Mindy, and Mindy couldn't get a hand on Lucia. Mindy tried to take the fight somewhere Lucia's speed was less effective and where her strength was more applicable."

"The ground," Mindy supplied, unnecessarily.

"Right," Roland continued. "But Lucia caught on just in time and turned the tables. No amount of strength was going to save Mindy if she got her elbow dislocated."

Mindy nodded. "I used that same arm bar on Sven Paulsen, too. Irony sucks."

"What's important, Manny, is did you learn anything?"

"Yeah. Don't fuck with Lucia or Mindy."

"Clever boy," Roland replied, chuckling.

Chapter Eleven

T heir arrival on Venus was as unobtrusive as they could make it.

They skipped the tourist and commuter terminals and unloaded themselves as cargo at one of the distribution centers. The hard part from there was going to be infiltrating The Colander without tipping off their prey. They discussed their options while unloading their luggage into the small cargo dock.

"I could always just walk there," Roland opined. "This is sort of exactly why I was built. It's only fourteen miles, and the weather isn't so bad right now."

Lucia rolled her eyes. "It's nine-hundred degrees out there. It's not actually raining acid at this moment, but it might at any time. I don't think we brought the right kind of raincoat for that kind of stroll, big guy."

"You're right," he acknowledged with a wince. "It would ruin my clothes. In the old days we had special BDUs for this crap."

Mindy chuckled. "I'm just picturing the look on their faces when old metal-butt here shows up naked and grumpy, banging on the door, and yelling 'let me in!'"

That drew a laugh from Manny, which relived everyone. The young man had become progressively more withdrawn the closer they got to Venus. He looked ten years older now, and not just because he was apprehensive. They had extended his dark hair until it flowed past his collar, and a local body shop had altered his facial features enough to make him look slightly different. They did not have the time to get him a total reconstruction, so only some minor dermal implants had been used. It would be enough to stymie facial recognition systems and people who did not know him well, but such subtle changes were not likely to fool anyone who had been close to him.

"Manny," Lucia snapped, her tone authoritative, "Roland and Mindy don't have to be all that sneaky. Craddock is expecting them, thanks to Rodney. Can you get us to The Colander more quietly?"

"There are ways," he said with a nod. "They are not fun, but there are ways."

Mindy laughed, "She shares a room with Roland, kid. I think she can handle 'not fun.'"

"I'm fun," Roland protested dryly. No one looked convinced, and he let the matter drop.

"Okay," Manny sighed. "Roland and Mindy, you two can just buy passage on a crawler if you don't care about Craddock's spies telling him you're coming. Lucia, you and I will have to take the tunnels."

Lucia's eyes squinted into narrow slits of apprehension. "I suppose I can assume that these tunnels are not well lit, clean, and smelling of the autumn breezes?"

"They are not."

"So you and I get fourteen miles of hot, smelly, grimy tunnels while Roland and Mindy get to ride in an air-conditioned vehicle?"

Manny shrugged. "The air-conditioning in the crawlers sucks, if it makes you feel better."

"It does not."

"Well, Boss, you have a good time in there. Old Ironsides and me are off to go buy us a ticket on the next crawler."

"Keep comms encrypted," Roland grumbled. "Minimal communication. Emergencies only. We will rendezvous at the rally point in six hours. Is that enough time, Manny?"

"Oh yes. Part of the tunnels have a tram system. It's for supplies, but it I know how to catch a ride for most of the way."

"Good." Roland shrugged a brown sport jacket over his shoulders. It settled in place, obscuring his leather shoulder holster and the massive machine pistol under his left armpit. This completed his outfit which consisted of gray pants and black boots with a white collared shirt. Atop his bald head, a brown flat cap in Donegal wool sat square and straight, aligned to his brow with military precision. On anyone else, it would be a smart, businesslike ensemble. Nothing about it should have attracted any undue attention whatsoever. Still, to Lucia's perennial dismay, such attempts at sartorial sophistication on Roland always ended up looking like some jokester had taught a large gorilla to wear people clothes.

Mindy, as usual, wore her favorite blue jumpsuit. Owing to Mindy's penchant for employing sex appeal as a weapon, the jumpsuit hugged her curves with a faithfulness that bordered upon scandalous. Her physical attributes, when crammed into the suit, were unavoidably and prominently on display. The genius of the outfit was that it was so much more than a tawdry distraction. The dense weave was proof against most commercially available pistols and small arms, and a complex system of nanotubes allowed the high-tech garment to provide compression and reinforcement against cuts and broken bones. Various pharmaceuticals could be administered as needed by the rudimentary AI that operated those systems, and as whole the jumpsuit would keep her alive and fighting all by itself if things got hairy.

This time Mindy had decided to cover herself a little more modestly than normal. She slipped a pair of black pants, ironically only slightly looser than her jumpsuit, over the sleek blue armor. Roland could not be sure, but he suspected she may have even zipped the front up an inch or two higher than usual. It was hard to tell, and he was not inclined to get caught looking, so he let it drop. Mindy was as far from modest as a person could get and still remain in this plane of reality, so Roland was not fooled. Most of the time she was perfectly happy to flaunt her good looks and she enjoyed the consternation of males who caught sight of her body. It was all an act, and the tiny blond was a professional first and foremost. When she wanted men to look, they looked. Conversely, she had no issues covering it all up if that was the best plan.

A thin brown jacket went over her torso, covering the long dagger strapped to her back. Roland noticed that the well-endowed woman could not bring herself to button it. Some things just were not in her nature. Roland admitted to himself that as far as he could tell, it did appear Mindy was trying to attract less attention than usual on this part of the run. It would have to do.

Roland concurred with her assessment that the crawler ride over to The Colander was not the best time to court undue scrutiny. They were going to be conspicuous enough considering his dimensions and her obvious good looks. The big cyborg was sure that when it served her purposes, that zipper would descend as low as necessary to ensure the gawking attentions of whoever she was manipulating. If he could find fault with the method, he would, however Mindy's eyes recorded video and her ears were wired for sound. Her chest was simply there to ensure that her subject faced the cameras, and Roland would be damned if it did not work more often than not.

Lucia had worn simple black fatigues, snug yet flexible. Her PC-10 gauntlets were strapped to her arms and her CZ-105 flechette pistol rode on her right hip underneath her dark gray over-shirt. Her armor plates stayed in her backpack however, as the temperature in the cargo pod was already over ninety degrees and the possibility of receiving incoming fire in this place seemed remote.

Manny called to her, "Okay, Boss. You ready?" Manny was wearing blue dungarees, black T-shirt, and a simple gray ultra-lightweight jacket. Over his shoulder was slung his satchel, which Lucia knew was full of all manner of electronics dedicated to the art and science of infiltration. Lucia had seen Manuel treat high-end security like a mildly interesting distraction and penetrate restricted zones without breaking a sweat. Just looking at his green bag reminded Lucia that she needed to change all of her passwords and update the security procedures at the office. A guy like Manny would not even consider it a challenge to break into their systems.

With a nod to Mindy and a smile for Roland, Lucia left with Manny for the back of the cargo pod.

"Just follow me," Manny instructed. "And try to look bored."

They passed through a large door to a central command center, bustling with men and women in dirty coveralls barking into comms or scowling at DataPads. Lucia tensed, and then remembered Manny's instructions. She tried to affect a look of bland irritation as she followed the younger man.

Manny led her to a corridor across from the receiver's office and the pair strode casually down the passage until they stopped at a small metal hatch marked "maintenance." Lucia could not understand how they simply walked past all the staff and workers milling about completely unnoticed and unmolested. She knew it was probably silly, but all the holos and old books had led her to believe that this sort of activity had more sneaking and stalking to it. She felt she was at least entitled to a disguise or perhaps knocking out a sentry. Just walking across a few rooms and accessing a corridor with a blank look on her face felt anticlimactic, as if she had been robbed of an adventure. Manny shrugged when she asked about it.

"People come and go through here all the time. If you just look like you know where you are going, no one will bother you. It's not like this place is super secure or anything. If we had tried to get to the receiver, or maybe tried to access another cargo pod we might have had some trouble. But just walking over here?" He snorted, "Pshhht. Nobody cares. They all have their own shit to do." Then he pointed to the maintenance hatch and bobbed his head. "Now, getting through here? That will be more fun."

"What does 'fun' mean?"

"It means I need a handprint for the biometrics. That means I need a maintenance guy." On cue, a tired-looking man in red coveralls rounded the corner and began to stroll down the hall with the telltale unhurried gait of man trying very hard to avoid real work. "Watch this!" The boy seemed excited. This made Lucia nervous for some reason.

Manny walked up to the man with giant grin on his face and called out," Hey! I know you!"

The worker looked up, simultaneously irritated and confused. Manny stuck his left hand out and presented it to the bewildered man and waited with a big stupid look of expectation on his face. The maintenance man slowly extended his hand and grasped Manny's. "I, uh. How are you man?" The question was delivered without confidence. Lucia watched the workman's face as his mind tried in vain to place the name or face of his beaming new friend.

"Doing great man! How long have you been here?" Manny kept a firm grip and pumped the hand vigorously, looking exactly like a person excited to see an old buddy.

"Couple years now. Uh... where are you at these days?"

"They got me running sulfites out at The Colander. Shit work but the raise was nice. It was great to see you! Gotta run!" Manny released the trapped worker who took the opportunity to escape down the hall at a pace far more determined than the one he had used to enter it. The young scout sauntered back to Lucia with a wide grin and casually placed his left palm against the scanner. The panel buzzed happily, and the hatch swung inward with a hiss.

"After you, Boss," he said politely.

Lucia cast a sideways look at the boy as she ducked her head through the opening. "You've been hanging out with my father again, haven't you?"

Manny waggled his bionic fingers at her. "Your old man loves his biotech, Boss. He and I have been playing with the nanomachines in my arm. This thing has so many cool tricks right now..." His voice trailed off and he shook his head wistfully. "...Lots of potential is what I'm saying."

They moved into a poorly-lit tunnel. Silver pipes and conduits ran in horizontal stripes along the walls and control panels blinked various messages to the unfortunate souls who found it their task to monitor such things. The air was hot enough to steal Lucia's breath for moment while her lungs adjusted. Then Manny gestured for her to follow him. "Come on. It's a bit of a walk to the freight shuttles."

"How'd you get my dad to modify your arm? He swore off weapons decades ago."

Manny looked over his shoulder and gave her a wink. "No weapons, Boss. Just tech. That trick I just did was just the hand's sensors reading that guy's biometrics while I shook his hand, the same way the scanner was going to. Then, the nanomachines duplicated what the real scanner wanted to see. Basically, I copied his palm."

"So, my dad is getting around his own principles by making infiltration tech instead of military tech." She gave her head a wry shake. "He must really miss it."

"He fixed Mindy's reflexes, too. Well, as much as they can be fixed, anyway. He's not real fond of the commercially available stuff out there, is he?"

"Did he use the phrase 'amateur-hour bullshit' when talking about it?"

"Yeah." Manny laughed, which took some of the weight from his face. "He swears a lot when he drinks."

"Boy, you don't even know the half of it."

"But he is real smart. He's been teaching me about the arm, how it works, how the nanobots work, stuff like that. I've even written some of my own firmware. It's crazy stuff."

Lucia's eyebrows climbed her forehead. "Really? You understand it all?"

91

"Not the theoretical parts, and some of the machine language is beyond me. But the mechanics of it, sure. Machines are easy. It's all the neuro stuff that gets a little too complicated for me."

Manny stopped in front of another hatch. It was a big black metal rectangle, ringed with rivets and held in place by a large sliding bar. A single panel sat on its face, and an old style alphanumeric keypad was illuminated in weak blue light.

"Now this," Manny spoke as if giving a lesson, "is a little different. No biometrics, no beamed codes. Just an old-fashioned combination lock."

His left hand came up, and he placed his palm over the keys without touching them. Then his hand drifted across each key, lightly brushing the panels as it passed. Suddenly, his right hand came up in a melodramatic flourish, and the left hand rapidly tapped a series of buttons. "Have at you!" he barked, and the fingers pecked keys faster than the eye could follow. The young man simply stood there a moment, right arm outstretched behind himself and his left thrust forward. It was comical, the young man posed like a lunging fencer while his bionic fingers pattered away at the keypad.

Finally, after about three seconds of this ridiculous performance, the keyboard flashed from blue to green and the bar retracted with a clang.

"Voila!" he crowed, and the door opened. "A four-digit code, with no repeated numbers, and four worn keys on the pad, equals twenty-four potential codes." He stepped beside the opening and bowed deeply to Lucia. "Your chariot awaits, milady."

"You are having way too much fun, kid."

"This is what I do, Boss. The only thing I'm good at."

Beyond the hatch was a maintenance platform that looked out into yet another tunnel. This one was wider, with a set of two-rail mag-lev tracks running down its center. The twin rails converged with distance, highlighted in dirty yellow neon as they disappeared into the darkness of the tunnel. Lucia's gaze wandered upward, and found suspended from gantries overhead rectangular containers of unadorned gray metal as big as aerocars. She gave her partner a look of incredulity, and Manny indicated, to her chagrin, that one of these would be their transportation.

"It's either these or walk the whole way..."

"You sure now how to treat a lady," she sighed, even as Manny was already tapping at another control panel. A few practiced keystrokes later, one gantry surged to life with a whir of electric motors and the screech of poorly maintained actuators. The closest big freight car surged and lurched sideways, then clanged into position over the track. With a ponderous heave, the ominous steel box dropped smoothly into position and the smell of ionized air hit them accompanied by the crackle of charged electromagnets. Several track lights faded into life around the freight car, limning the edges with soft yellow light.

"After you, ma'am," Manny said.

Lucia stepped to the edge of the walkway and leapt lightly to the lip of the open-topped bin. She alighted on its edge, turned back to her partner, and gracefully back-flipped inside.

"Now who's showing off?" Manny asked with a huff. Displaying far less grace and a mere fraction of Lucia' agility he scrambled over the side and fell to the floor with a crash. Lucia helped him up with a chuckle.

"Ready to go to The Colander, Boss?"

"I positively tingle with anticipation, Manuel."

"Well, remember you said that when we get there. Now hold onto something. These things weren't made to carry people, so they tend to—"

The words were torn away by the heave of acceleration as the car bolted   forward   without   warning.

Chapter Twelve

Roland and Mindy were more comfortable than Lucia and Manny, at least. The Material Sciences Corporation surface crawler had a dedicated passenger deck with comfortable seating for Mindy, and a sizable cargo compartment for Roland. His was not a frame destined for regular seating.

Manny's assessment of the air conditioning inside had been accurate, however. The interior of the house-sized vehicle was ninety degrees Fahrenheit, and the little blond assassin perspired with wanton excess. Roland felt nothing, of course. His skin was laminated with large areas of Peltier-effect crystalline sheets, and these sections would recycle any accumulated heat into electricity. Under normal Earth conditions, this was a miniscule trickle charge that amounted to little more than a fraction of a percentage point of his normal every day operations. On fiery Venus, his skin could generate enough power to walk him around rather comfortably. Thus, having been built for just this sort of thing, Roland could operate more or less normally at any temperature below the melting and ignition points of his surface armor. If he was wearing his helmet, that was just under eighteen-hundred degrees. Without his helmet, he was limited to about two-hundred-and-fifty, which he allowed was not too shabby. Either way, a warm stuffy cargo bay was nowhere near any of his thresholds for discomfort, and he sat out the ride in stoic silence.

Stoicism was never Mindy's style, and she complained vociferously upon their arrival at The Colander.

"Holeee jeeeeezis, Roland!" she whined when they stepped into the marginally cooler air of the passenger reception area. "I feel like my tits are floating! How do people live here?"

"They get used to it. They also are not wearing two layers of clothing." He waved a hand to the people around them. Most wore only the thinnest of garments, and exposed skin was the norm. Exotic, dry-weave textiles were in abundance, and most folks glistened with a sheen of sweat that defied all attempts to wipe it away. "You should have some sort of cooling built into that suit if you're going to do that kind of thing here."

"I've looked into it. Too bulky. I need to keep it thin and light if I want to wear it under street clothes."

"Then you're going to sweat," he said with a shrug. "Deal with it."

She shrugged back. "Armor trumps comfort every time."

Roland nodded in rare agreement with her. "That is a fact."

They stepped out into a wide concourse. The high-ceilinged area reeked of stale sweat, gear oil, and the mélange of various different foodstuffs. Hundreds of people milled around them, shuffling from crawlers to security checkpoints like intoxicated ants. Many stopped at a long row of vendors purveying food and supplies to weary travelers before ambling over to the long security checkpoint lines. Roland took a moment to simply observe the reception area. His height put him firmly above the heads of most of the people crowding through the turnstiles, and he took some care to watch the process. It appeared an extremely basic procedure. Once disembarked, travelers would proceed to the checkpoint and have identification verified and bags checked for contraband by scowling RUC soldiers behind reinforced clear panels. Those warranting extra scrutiny would pass over a floor scanner and be interviewed by bored and marginally competent staff before being waved on or detained. It was all fairly standard procedure for any place that had a terrorism problem. He recognized it for what it was: The security was as much pure theater as effective prevention. Skilled smugglers would have already figured out how to circumvent the process, and only the most inept would ever get caught by such flimsy measures. The production, however, gave people the illusion that their government was working on the problem, and served as an effective first-level deterrent for the most mundane forms of smuggling and terrorism.

In very short order, his practiced eye found the two men, who had almost certainly been sent to watch for their arrival, leaning against a food stall just past the checkpoint. They were robust individuals, but otherwise nondescript. Their long jackets were out of place in the steamy heat of the concourse, and gave them away as muscle better than a lighted holographic sign. It was far too hot to wear anything like that unless you were concealing something, and he suspected the dirty brown outerwear was covering a weapon or three. Roland found their location and position to be the more interesting aspect of their presence. He figured Craddock's people would have tried to make contact before the checkpoint, to prevent any issues with admissions and to placate Rodney. This pair of hoods were on the far side of the gates, watching with bored expressions on their faces and pretending to not be watching at all. He nudged Mindy.

"See the scouts?"

"Yeah, they're not real subtle, are they?"

"See anything interesting about them?"

She snorted, "Either they haven't made us yet or they want to see if we can get through security on our own." She paused. "That's kind of a dick move, seeing as we are here in an official capacity."

"These are terrorists, and they are isolated from the rest of galaxy. They don't play by any rules you are used to."

"But you are used to them?"

"I've killed a lot of terrorists in my day." He sounded rather satisfied about that, Mindy noted. Then he took on an instructor's tone. It was such an automatic shift from his usual brusqueness that Mindy wondered if he even knew he was doing it. "When you are dealing with crooks and governments, greed forces people to play by some sort of rules, if only to maximize profits while minimizing risks. With terrorist groups, the regular troops are almost entirely fanatics. They don't care about profit or risk. So they don't care about rules. For this op to work, we need to get to the leadership, which is usually far less fanatical and far more risk-averse than their foot soldiers."

"Right," she sighed. "So this Craddock asshole might want to make sure he doesn't have problems with Dockside because it will hurt his lifestyle, but those dopes over there could care less because we represent the fascist oppressors?"

"Bingo," Roland grunted. "Worse, Craddock has to make it look like he's also a fanatic or his minions will turn on him. So he is going to fuck with us just as much as he thinks he can get away with without causing a ruckus."

"Oh, goody. How much shit do we have to put up with before we demonstrate our disapproval?" She sounded hopeful. Mindy was capable of infinite patience and forbearance when pursuing a target, though she did not enjoy it.

"We'll play it by ear."

"Your ear or mine?"

"Mine, Mindy. Your ears are way too sensitive."

"From you, Roland? That stings." She affected a pout, and it was a very good one. Roland allowed that more than one man had probably suffered palpitations at the sight of that pout. He was entirely unaffected however, and the pout became a frustrated frown. "You are seriously no goddamn fun, Ironsides."

"That is a fact," he agreed. "Let's go."

They approached the first turnstile with an affected nonchalance. To a degree, Roland could afford to be relaxed. The scanners would certainly ping all his extensive bodywork, there was simply no way around that. If anyone here showed enough initiative to check on his augmentations, they would find themselves having a very uncomfortable conversation with the UEDF. This would bother the RUC far more than it would Roland.

His only concern was that if found, they would almost certainly want to confiscate Durendal, and that would make the big cyborg very grouchy.

Mindy's challenges were much more immediate. She was a famous assassin with more than a few unregistered augmentations. Outside of the wealthier urban zones of Council space, this was not an issue. Operating this close to Earth in an area with very real internal problems was a markedly different situation. If she got caught, she was looking at a long stretch at the penal colony on Titan.

Manny had taken care of it all. Or at least, he had said as much. He modified Mindy's bodysuit to spoof only her registered mods and hide the others. Mindy had seen Manny's work in action before, and she knew he was good, but she would be lying if she claimed to be entirely at ease with trusting to that. She was a professional assassin, and she knew fooling high-end scanners was not a task easily accomplished. Manuel had shrugged her concerns off with the confidence of a skilled tradesman and the irreverence of youth.

97

"I wouldn't try to walk into a secure military research facility or anything, but the leftover surplus shit they have on Venus?" Manny had snorted derisively, "They won't see anything I don't tell them to."

Getting Roland's gun through was even easier. Manny's test scan had pinged so many military exemptions for Roland that he simply added a weapons exemption to the rest of the list. It was a fake, but the RUC would have to scroll through several dozen legitimate exemptions before encountering the counterfeit. As a retired member of the Expeditionary Force, this would arouse virtually no suspicion on Venus. Manny had made one final, very important point. "Hell, the RUC will probably love having an ex EF guy around. I bet they treat you like royalty." He sounded bitter when he said it, and Roland had to stifle a small internal wince. Manny had not fought in the secession, but living through the troubles meant the war had never really ended for him.

Roland stepped up first, in the hopes that Manny's impression about RUC regard for the Expeditionary Force was accurate. Such good will might help smooth things over if things went poorly for Mindy. When Roland clumped up to the window, an RUC sergeant took one look at the nearly eight-foot monster and rolled his eyes. "Christ. Step on the pad, please."

Roland complied, standing patiently on the scanner pad while the security AI interfaced with his internal bionics and scanned him for weapons. The sergeant's eyes bulged at the results, and he looked to Roland with competing awe and fear.

"Ah... welcome to Venus, sir. Would you like to check your weapon with us?"

Roland tried to put on a friendly face, which was not helping. "I'm a corporal, Sergeant, I call you 'sir,' not the other way around. And I'll hold onto my weapon if that won't cause a problem."

The non-com seemed conflicted, though he was not brave enough to push the matter. "Right, Corporal. Of course. I'll just make a note of that. Been a while?"

Roland sighed, the man seemed intent on small talk. "I did a run here during the war."

"You back here for a visit, then? Or business?" It was a standard question for the RUC to ask any visitor. However Venus was not a popular tourist destination, and any business Roland had here was likely to make the constabulary nervous.

Roland's practiced lie came easily. "I'd rather not say. If you want, have the watch officer check exemption 125-A, Sergeant. It will clear things up for everyone. I won't lie, Sarge. There's going to be a lot of paperwork if you do. It's all above our pay grade, know what I mean?"

The sergeant's jaw worked in a tight chewing motion while he pondered this, then he blanched some more when the implications became apparent. "Sorry, Corporal. Just doing my job, you know."

"And doing it well, sergeant. But you understand if I can't say much."

"Of course!" The sergeant stood to attention and scribbled some notes onto his DataPad with a stylus, "And be advised that the RUC will be available to render any assistance you may need."

"I never doubted it. Please extend the same courtesy to the contractor as well."

"Contractor?"

Roland pointed to Mindy, still waiting her turn. The sergeant's face flushed crimson when he saw her, and Roland noted that at some point her zipper had plummeted several inches. He realized, with sudden clarity, that there were not a lot of women who looked like Mindy walking around The Colander. The appearance of so much appetizingly sculpted flesh looked to be a serious shock, and the sergeant's reaction to her décolletage was predictably flustered.

"Do I stand right here?" Mindy purred, dragging her drawl out to its most disarming cadence. She glided over to the pad, somehow managing to make all the muscles in her thighs and buttocks wiggle at the same time. It looked complicated to Roland, and he assumed she had to practice it. She stopped on the scanner and clasped her hands behind her back. It was a casual pose that only incidentally thrust her chest out even further. Roland could swear he heard the zipper scream in protest at the increased pressure, but that may have been his imagination. She beamed a girlish leer to the sergeant, who simply gaped for a moment like a moron.

"Eyes up, Sergeant," Roland barked, breaking the man's trance. The non-com jolted and flushed even more, which Roland would not have thought possible up to that point.

"Right! Sorry!"

He scanned Mindy and gave the readout only a cursory examination. Roland imagined that the scan of her body would get printed out and studied in more intimate detail later. For now, at least, the man's embarrassment ensured there would be no trouble passing the checkpoint.

"You are all set, Corporal. Enjoy your stay." Then he leaned in and winked, as if he and Roland shared some intimate secret. A dirty finger pointed to his name tag. "And just look for Sergeant Cummings if you need anything off record or off the books." He gave Roland a comradely clap on the arm, and then winced as the armored skin stung his fingers. "Happy hunting," he whispered.

"Thank you, Sarge," Roland replied and quickly moved away from the checkpoint. When they were well past it and heading into an area of food stalls, Roland had to ask, "Does that shit work every time?"

Mindy chuckled, "You would be amazed at how well it works. You boys are all the same." Her zipper had re-ascended to a more demure position, though the jiggle in her walk remained.

"That's really kind of depressing," he lamented as much to himself as to her.

"Every so often I find a guy who doesn't get rattled by 'em. For instance, Mack never looked, and you don't get all googly-eyed, either."

Roland knew why. "Discipline and focus. Also, Mack and I both figured out that you were fucking with us. Being manipulated pisses guys like us off, and neither of us were ever going to let that happen."

"Sounds right. The old 'wiggle and shake' never worked on Pike, either." She shuddered, "And that guy was not subtle about pointing it out, you know. That guy knew how to make a girl feel real damn stupid for trying, I tell you what. I cried every time he looked at me for a week afterward."

"You tried it on Chris Pike?" Roland was impressed at either her confidence or her stupidity. He could not decide which.

She sighed, and nodded slowly at the memory. "Yeah. Turns out he's seen a lot of nice racks in his day. He was not impressed."

"So it mostly works on idiots, is what you're really saying," he amended his earlier assessment.

"Yup. But then again, most men are idiots when it comes to sex," she countered.

"Fair point."

"So tell me, mister 'focus and discipline,' how exactly did the daughter of your creator catch your eye, then?"

Roland stopped walking and turned to her. "She didn't. I caught hers, I guess. You need to remember I had been out of that game for a very long time. I didn't even know I was playing until I had already lost." He sighed and started walking again, "But she didn't try to manipulate me, at least. I scared her at first, I think. Even that didn't last long, though. She was too smart, too tough. Once she decided she was interested, it was all over, really. Hell, I tried to stop her, and that only made it worse."

"Is that the only battle you've ever lost?"

"No. But it's my favorite."

Mindy punched him in the gut, "Careful, Ironsides. People are going to think you've gone soft talking like that."

"Ask your knuckles how soft I am," he responded without humor.

Mindy scowled and have her bruised hand a surreptitious squeeze. "Right."

"Now let's just focus on the two bozos over there." He indicated Craddock's scouts. "Should we let them follow us or go confront them?"

"You're asking me what to do?"

Roland nodded. "This cloak and dagger bullshit is your wheelhouse. I mostly break stuff."

"They made us yet?"

Roland squinted at the men, standing about fifty feet away. They were pretending to be engrossed in conversation, but their eyes kept darting to the large and conspicuous cyborg moving through the crowd. "Maybe. They keep looking at me, but that may just be my size."

"Since we don't really know how to find Craddock without Manny, I think you should go over and have a nice chat. Low level hoods seem to respond well to your style of charm. Might as well keep me as unknown a quantity as possible for now. I'll break off and hide in the crowd while you go talk to them. Let's see what shakes loose while I move to drop them if needed."

"You're a devious little lady, Mindy. I'll give you that."

Mindy's country girl accent flared back to life, "Why, Mr. Tankowicz, I declare! That sounded like a compliment."

His tone came out gruff, but Mindy could tell his heart was not in it.

"Yeah, well it wasn't, you yellow-headed psycho."

Chapter Thirteen

It was not false modesty that had driven Roland to seek Mindy's insight. His callsign had been 'Breach' and this was a descriptive moniker, not an ironic one. He had been designed and built to breach fortifications, and he was configured for that task to the exclusion of most others. Unlike other members of his original squad, he had no augmentations for stealth beyond his ability to shift the color of his surface armor. His training had been focused entirely on heavy weapons, demolition, close-quarters battle, and small-unit tactics. When Mindy told him to go and talk to the men, he had no deep strategic insights about how to effect such a conversation in a manner that furthered their aims. He had been a fixer for a long time though, and he supposed that at this point in his career there was no real point in trying to out think his opponents.

He had the presence of mind to continue his amble in nonchalant fashion. The pair of scouts held their posts, content to do a poor job of clandestine observation as the big man let the river of people moving through the concourse move him along. When Roland was about ten feet from the stall Craddock's men were using for a prop, he turned and stepped across the lanes of ambling passengers. His sudden move upset more than a few of the walkers, scattering some carts and drawing shouts of dismay and anger. The protests died early when the irate people saw the dimensions of their antagonist, and most scuttled off mumbling imprecations they hoped the large man would not actually hear.

The scouts froze, eyes bulging at the giant now standing directly in front of them.

"Afternoon, boys," Roland growled in a manner not at all friendly. "I need to see Craddock."

The men said nothing, their faces hanging slack as brains not selected for their horsepower struggled to send words to mouths still agape with confusion and generous dollop of fear.

Roland dealt with a lot of street-level hoods in his business. He understood that terrorists were not the exact same species as mobsters. Even so, when it came to interactions with the street-level operators, the differences between the groups would be academic at best. If one substituted 'greed' with 'zeal,' then there was little difference at all. He could assume these two were motivated by their love for the cause and not the desire for a quick credit, and other than that he expected their capabilities and behavior to be somewhat predictable. Thus, he spared them little concern or courtesy.

"You guys deaf? Craddock. Now."

The taller of the two finally managed to access the language center of his brain, and his mouth began to cycle up and down as he stammered his words. "You're the fixer?"

Ever the conversationalist, Roland's response oozed sarcasm like a leaky grease barrel. "No. I'm the stripper for your mom's birthday party." The taller man scowled as if confused by this answer. Roland imagined him checking his mental calendar to see if he had in fact, missed his mother's birthday somehow. The big fixer closed his eyes and swallowed his frustration with how poorly this was going. Back home, he would have already hurt one of these two just to make a point. But he was not at home, and so he forced himself to clarify. His irritation was palpable, yet he answered the question more explicitly so as not to further bewilder the scouts.

"Of fucking course I'm the fixer. At least I am when I'm fixing things, anyway. When I'm stuck dealing with brain-dead hench-pricks like you two geniuses?" He folded arms like ship cables across a chest wider than both men combined, "...I'm more often the 'breaker,' if you catch my meaning."

Educational shortcomings notwithstanding, the men appeared to catch his meaning perfectly well because the speaker bobbed his head up and down enthusiastically. "He's expecting you."

"I know he is. Now are you two PhDs going to stand there all day or take me to him?"

"Yeah. Just ah, let me call it in," said the second man, finally speaking.

"Please do," Roland sighed.

A quick comm call was thus engaged, and the taller man looked to Roland when it was completed. "Okay, Craddock is waiting in Refractory Nine." The man paused, shuffling nervously and looking sideways at his partner. His partner looked back, and his own face betrayed apprehension bordering upon panic. "He wants us to make sure you're uhm..." The voice trailed off, as if whatever he was trying to say was too terrible to bear.

Roland supplied the answer with a laugh. "Unarmed?"

"Yeah," the taller one mumbled, unable to meet Roland's eyes.

"Not going to happen. I'm carrying on a military exemption. If you morons get caught with my piece, we'll all hang. Tell Craddock I'll keep my weapons, and he can bring anything he thinks will make him feel safe. I won't mind."

Another whispered comm call was made and Roland waited in amused silence. With a subtle series of palm presses and eye movements, he turned his auditory gain up to hear the conversation. The man at the other end, who he presumed was Craddock, was less than thrilled with Roland's conditions. But, as Roland knew he would, the man acquiesced to the terms with a burst of profanity and an angry click.

With a shrug, the taller man gestured to the fixer and grunted, "Okay. Follow us."

The three of them moved through a winding series of tunnels. Before too long Roland was completely disoriented. He was savvy enough to understand that their meandering path was specifically constructed to get him lost, and he could not fault the Red Hats for this caution. It did not bother him either way. Mindy would be following and marking the trail somehow, so he did not care. Mindy annoyed him, but he could not deny it was nice to work with competent professionals.

The hallways and concourses got progressively smaller and dimmer as the group descended. Roland's eyes were not bionic, but they were augmented with gene therapy and he saw in dim light as well as many people could in bright, so the dank yellow illumination and the muddy shadows it created did not bother him. Mindy could see both infrared and ultraviolet, so he did not suspect she would struggle either. His nose found new stimulus as well. The smell of sulfur and hydrocarbons grew stronger, while the air grew cooler and drier once they descended below ground level.

105

It was as if The Colander had two distinct biomes. The surface levels were cleaner and at least lit as well as possible. The nominally commercial nature of this dome meant that services and amenities, though rustic and intermittent, could be acquired there. However Roland noticed that once the main level was above you, conditions grew ever more squalid. Much of what he saw was abandoned industrial space re-purposed for dormitories and essential worker's supplies. With a jolt of mixed surprise and sadness, Roland noticed the people below were different as well. The folks he saw were hunched and tired-looking. They squinted into the dark as they walked, and their feet shuffled rather than stepped. A lifetime of living in tight quarters and bad light had made them cautious when they walked, and the shambling gait cast them in the mold of mole-eyed subterranean creatures. Above, the stalls had been reasonably well-lit and clean, serving travelers and businesspeople what supplies and goods they may need to accomplish their on-site business. Engineers, scientists, accountants, and other well-paid professionals filtered through the Venusian industrial dorms constantly after all. Roland began to grasp that there were two distinct classes of people in The Colander. His eyes flicked to the weary faces of the lower-level denizens, and his lip curled in disgust. These hunched masses were not businessmen or travelers. These were the permanent residents of The Colander, banished to the underworld where the nicer things in life were not reserved for them. He was reminded of what he had said to Manny earlier that week; for all their despicable behavior, the Red Hats came by their anger honestly.

That's how they kept their movement alive over the decades, he mused quietly to himself. *Every day they are reminded of how much better other people have it. When they get mad and lash out, the companies retaliate with the RUC. Every day the corporations and the RUC breed new Red Hats down here simply by trying to stop them.*

It was a pattern he understood very well. He had seen it in a dozen operations on a dozen worlds. Once the two sides start hurting each other, the cycle of retaliation becomes self-sustaining. The RUC was mandated to stop the terrorism, but every terrorist they killed or imprisoned bred three more of them, even thirstier for vengeance. It would have been bad enough if the RUC had been a disciplined, professional force that never exceeded their mandate. Simple observation of his surroundings confirmed that no quantity of mental contortion could believably make this case. Making things even worse was the deep partisan divide amongst the Venusians themselves. The Red Hats were not universally loved or supported, even within the industrial domes. Many Venusian laborers were perfectly happy to not be part of Free Venus, and were content with corporate employment and council governance. Corporate work could be very high-paying and offered a lot of advancement opportunities for the right kind of person. It was not hard to see how a lot of Venusian laborers would not want the higher taxes and lower social mobility living in a free dome would bring.

Roland gave up on trying to sort it all out. In the Army, his officers would refer to this as a 'quagmire' and his sergeant would have called it a 'cluster-fuck.' Both assessments seemed far too weak a description for the pure unmitigated maelstrom that was Venusian partisan politics. Roland was not here to solve the troubles, and so he put it out of his mind.

Eventually, his guides brought him to a hatch barely large enough for a man to pass through. One of the men tapped a code into the panel and the door swung open, revealing a large open chamber. Roland peered through the narrow opening and saw that a table and chairs had been set up, and that a barrel-chested man sat there. The man was flanked by two armatures, hulking gray mechanical anthropoids with tiny human heads. Both models were identical Erberhaus Incorporated Stahlkorpers, light-framed industrial models modified for Venus. Each cyborg had a pair of cylindrical tanks mounted to their backs for the large supplemental liquid-helium cooling systems that would enable the men to work outside the domes for several hours before having to come back inside. These two had not been modified for combat, he noted with relief. While not a high-end model, the Stahlkorper was designed for harsh environments and that meant they would be tenacious and durable all the same.

Craddock, who Roland assumed was the man at the table, probably felt this pair of metal guardians constituted a very impressive show of force. It was an understandable position for him to take. Stahlkorpers had multiple redundant systems to keep them running in bad situations and would be immune to virtually any form of side-arm or smaller rifle. In a place where most weapons were smuggled in or home-made, the two looming guards would be as close to invulnerable as made no difference. Roland, however, was not impressed. A couple of laborers in light armatures presented little more than the opportunity for some exercise to him, and he let this conceit show as he wormed his not-inconsiderable bulk through the narrow opening.

After sliding his shoulders through sideways, he stepped over the sill and uncoiled to his full height. Craddock's eyes widened, and his guards shifted with a whir of motors and the metallic clank of steel feet on decking. Roland had a sneaking suspicion that the guards had never met anyone taller than they were outside of another cyborg. Roland's stature and nominally human appearance was putting them at a loss, and he like that.

"Mr. Craddock, I presume?" Roland kept his tone even and polite. Craddock, to his credit, recovered from his surprise quickly and waved to chair across from the table himself. "Ah, you must the fixer. Please, have a seat."

Roland looked at the flimsy metal seat and shook his head. "Roland Tankowicz, and I think I'll stand, just the same."

"Suit yourself, pal. Straight to business, then? I understand one of our internal problems has wandered into your boss's territory. I want to apologize or—"

Roland interrupted him, "I do not have a boss, Mr. Craddock. I have a client."

Craddock's heavy brows furrowed, "Right. Okay. Whatever. Your client is mad because we ran a hit in Dockside. Right?"

Roland nodded and said nothing. It was an old trick. The less he spoke, the more Craddock would.

"Right. We didn't mean to cause no trouble with that. It's totally an internal thing that spilled over the lip, you get me?"

Roland nodded again. Craddock furrowed even more. "So- uh, I guess I just need to know what's going to make your client happy again."

Roland was committed to one good-faith attempt to actually negotiate. "There is to be no Red Hat activity in Dockside, Mr. Craddock. The territory is in a very transitional state right now, and having your kind of trouble there is inviting the Council and Gateways to interfere. It's unacceptable to my client."

One side of Craddock's mouth turned in a small snicker. "That's kind of an issue, then. We have an... asset... in Dockside we need to retrieve, if you understand my meaning."

"Is this asset a defector from the cause?"

Craddock's face went blank, then he leaned back in his chair and crossed his arms over his chest. He looked at Roland through narrowed eyes. "You have a very good intelligence network, buddy."

"You have no idea, Craddock. Can I assume that is a 'yes?'"

"And if it is?"

"You are going to have to let this one go. We have rules in Dockside. If this asset had broken any of those rules, he'd be yours for the taking. He did not, and Dockside is a free trade zone now. As long as he follows the rules, you will need to leave him alone or go through channels to get him."

Craddock's expression did not change. "I'd heard about that. We got rules in the Red Hats too, buddy. He broke them. What about those?"

"Outside of Dockside and Big Woo, the Guilds don't much care," he said with shrug. "But the free trade zone is to be respected. I'm here to shut this down so I'll be truthful, Craddock. Nobody in the Dockside rackets really cares about your asset, but the Trade Association is very keen for an opportunity to demonstrate to the whole system what happens to folks that don't respect the free trade zone."

"And they sent a single guy onto my turf to make that point?" He hissed, "Feels risky to me."

Roland cracked his favorite smile. It was an ugly and terrifying sneer. "A few thousand years ago, the leader of a besieged city-state sent to Sparta, a place of great soldiers, to ask for help. The Spartans obliged him by sending a single warrior."

"Feels like pretty shitty help to me."

Craddock was not warming to the tale, Roland noted.

"It was sufficient."

Craddock leaned forward again, eyes beginning to show the first hints of anger. "Are you here to fix this or pick a fight, Tankowicz? Because you don't look like no Spartan to me, and unless my math is shit, you are one oversized prick against two cyborg armatures right now. Maybe you should watch your tone a little?"

"I was sent here to either resolve the issue or make an example of your organization. My clients are equally happy with either outcome, so it's really up to you and me. Personally? I don't really want to fight."

Craddock must have misunderstood this for back-pedaling, because his retort was smug to the point of brash. "And what if I do? I like my odds pretty good right now, Mister Spartan. Maybe the Hats want to send a message, too. How about that?"

"One of the rules we have on Earth is 'safe passage.' It means when folks like us agree to a sit-down, we promise not to try and kill each other. I am extending that courtesy to you so we can talk frankly. I'd advise you to return the favor and abstain from threats against my person."

"I think I see your problem, Tankowicz. You've lost track of where you are. We ain't on Earth right now, pal. You are playing by my rules, asshole, so listen up." The thick man stood, as if the extra height made any difference when compared to Roland. "We need to round up that traitor, and we intend to do exactly that. If your fucked up little Trade Association wants me to jump through some hoops first, fine. But one way or another, the piece of shit is mine. If that doesn't work for you, I can have the boys here drop you outside to think about it for a while."

The two cyborg guards stepped forward on this remark, lending the looming presence of their mechanical might to the threat. Roland, who would later admit that perhaps his good-faith attempt at negotiation had not been as sincere as it should have been, lunged for them. The Stahlkorpers had no chance of matching Roland's speed, and even before their eyes had registered his movements, the towering Dockside fixer had each by the forearm.

With a jerk that all but split the seams of his jacket, Roland brought the two together in a thunderclap of colliding metal bodies. Another flick of thickly muscled arms then hurled both wobbling men face-first to the floor. Almost as soon as they struck, hands like vises closed over their helium tank harnesses and the bewildered guards found themselves yanked from the deck. One managed to utter a startled cry of pain and fear before being tossed into a wall hard enough to dent the thick metal. His head, not being encased in any sort of helmet, bounced off the unforgiving surface and the man slumped unmoving to the floor without further incident. The other

110

guard gasped in terror when his opponent's now-free hand closed like a docking clamp over the left elbow joint of his armature. This slight hesitation cost him dearly, because a moment later that elbow was a twisted shattered mess and the corresponding arm a useless dead weight hanging from his shoulder. Another merciless, savage, contemptuous yank from Roland and the arm was torn free of the chassis completely. The still sparking appendage stayed clutched in a gloved fist while Roland kicked the wounded man's legs from underneath him. The guard slumped down and stayed there, eyes stretched wide with shock and fear, panic holding him immobile.

"Stay down, boy," Roland grumbled unnecessarily, and turned to address   Craddock.   "Now,   where   were   we?"

Chapter Fourteen

T he ride was smooth enough, at least. Floating on a cushion of pure magnetic force, the freight car did not bounce or bash its way through the largely unilluminated tunnel leading to The Colander. It did, however, sway and lean quite a bit. Lucia's augmentations would keep her from suffering the indignity of motion sickness, but at three minutes into the ride Manny was looking very green around the gills.

The young scout saw her look of concern and he gave her thin smile.

"I always hated these things," he admitted.

"Not exactly a comfortable way to travel, are they?" she agreed.

It was obvious the tunnels and cars had not been built to carry people. The temperature inside was over one hundred degrees and the air reeked of oil and solvents. There was almost no light, with tiny glowing emergency diodes spaced every fifty feet preventing total blackness and doing little else. Lucia felt like she was being boiled alive in her clothes, and the immodest dress of the native Venusians began to make a lot more sense with every passing minute. Her gauntlets were akin to close personal friends at this point, and while she loved them dearly, they were torture to wear right now. She kept them on out of a sense of prudence and no more than that. Their snug fit, armored panels, and sturdy construction felt like liabilities and not assets at the moment.

"It's only a nine-minute ride to the transfer station, Boss," Manny assured her. "It will be cooler there."

Lucia nodded. "Then what?"

"Well..." Manny seemed reluctant to say what that was.

"Manny..." There was a warning in her tone.

"We will need to get out of the car before it docks. An inspector will want to see the cargo I spoofed into the manifest to get the car to run at all. If he finds us, there will be a problem."

"How do we get out of a moving car, Manny?"

"We're going to have to jump."

Lucia peeked over the side of the car. The emergency lights whisked by like orange lasers and Lucia's heart leapt.

"Manny..." The warning tone was back, and stronger this time.

"It will start braking early enough. It's not so bad, I promise!" He nodded in manner he hoped was comforting. "I told the system that the payload was very heavy, and since it won't want to throw a hundred tons of cargo through the terminal at forty miles per hour it will start to slow us down very soon!"

As predicted, the car began to slow with ratcheting lurches well before their destination. Manny's artful deception about the cargo mass confused the unsophisticated software and the car over-braked to nearly a halt before adjusting to a smoother deceleration. Manny and Lucia leapt from the rocking container when it was barely moving and dropped to the floor of the tunnel without incident.

"Now," Manny instructed, "we need to sneak into the transfer station and get into The Quad to see an old friend. After that, we go to our camp in Warrentown."

He read the confusion on her face and explained, "Warrentown is the area under the old main refractory. In the old days it was a bunch of machinery rooms and lab stations and other support areas for it. After the big refractory was abandoned, Venusians started to carve out dorms and businesses in there. It's just a bunch of re-purposed compartments connected by open spaces, like a rabbit warren." He sniffed, "Hence the name."

"Got it. How do we get in?"

"There will be a receiver at the transfer station we will have to get by, and then it's just a matter of slipping into The Quad. It's not terribly secure once we get past the transfer station."

They crept along the tunnel, hugging the walls for safety. In a few hundred yards, Lucia began to notice the oppressive darkness becoming brighter. The dirty glowing emergency lights became more frequent, and soon Lucia could see her path quite easily.

Before long, the low tunnel opened from a narrow serpentine track into a cavernous cargo bay. A platform built into the side of the

113

tunnel extended metal decking out over the track and positioned an operator station directly above the cargo car they had previously exited. A single man stood at that station, staring down into an empty freight bin and washing his control panel down with a furious scowl.

Manny signaled for a halt when they were still fifty yards away and well hidden in the deep shadows of the cargo bay entrance. He leaned in to whisper to Lucia.

"There are scanners and cameras on the receiving deck. We need to stay as close to this wall as possible to avoid them. When we get to the platform, you wait at the maintenance ladder. I'll disable the surveillance stuff and pull the guard away so you can get past him. When I give you the signal, climb up and get across the receiving office as fast as you can. There is a back door that leads out into a hallway. Take a left down that hallway and there will be some restrooms on your right. Wait for me there."

Lucia had a million questions as to how Manny would accomplish these feats, but she had seen him in action enough times to know that he was very good at this sort of thing and she should trust him.

Per his instructions, she kept herself deeply shadowed as she sidled up to a worn metal ladder ascending from the track level to the receiver's platform. Lucia could not see the man on top, though she could hear the irritated grumblings as he attempted to reconcile the empty container before him with a manifest for a hundred tons of trade goods.

Manny stayed in the tunnel entrance and watched her. It was too dark to follow all her movements, but once she made it to the ladder he could make her out as a deeper pool of blackness against the rusty orange canvas of the receiving dock. When he was sure she was in position, he rolled his left sleeve past his elbow and looked down at the inside of his forearm. He tapped his left thumb to his fingertips in a coded pattern, and his wrist lit up with a small projected control panel. The smooth white surface of his arm danced with the blinking display, a softly glowing series of options and settings played along his inner arm in a parade of information and controls.

He swiped back and forth, moving through menus and selecting options until he found the systems he wanted. He allowed himself the tiniest instant of self-satisfaction as he did this. Doctor Ribiero had been both pleased and proud of how Manny had learned to configure his prosthetics' systems. While certainly no biotechnologist, the young man had shown the old scientist just how much Venusian ingenuity and a head for engineering could take a person with no access to higher education.

Manny clenched his fist tightly for six seconds, closing the menus and turning off the display. Then he opened his hand and pointed his fingers at the receiving platform. Sighting the control console and the still-swearing receiver firmly between his pointer finger and his pinky, Manny slowly pressed his middle and ring fingers into his palm.

An invisible, silent, and undetectable electromagnetic pulse shot from his hand in an expanding cone. To keep the pulse from affecting other systems, Manny had selected as tight a spread as the tiny emitter could manage. Even with this precaution, the wave of energy washed over the whole platform. A geyser of white sparks spurted from the console with a snap loud enough to be heard all the way over by Manny. The shrieked curses of the receiver carried much further. The lanky man clawed at his ear, and it took a moment for Manny to realize he was trying to remove his comm's earpiece. The young scout winced at how excruciating it would be to have the tiny little capacitor in the thing rupture while still in place.

The observed effect of just such an occurrence seemed to coincide with his suspicions. Screeching another shouted expletive, the man fled the platform and ran wailing into the office. Manny could not see him after that, but he believed the receiver would not stop running until he made it all the way to the infirmary. Manny could not fault the man for his singe-minded pursuit of medical attention.

"Go!" he said into his own comm, hoping against hope that his EMP had not damaged Lucia's.

"Moving," she replied, and Manny breathed a sigh of relief. The black-clad woman went up the ladder like a caffeinated squirrel. It seemed as if she was in zero-G and the mere act of touching the rungs hurled her upward rather than her hands and feet pulling on the rungs.

Her feet struck the deck lightly and Lucia was across the platform before her partner had even heaved himself into a run across the tracks. But run he did, and with all the speed he could

115

muster. The consoles and equipment on the platform that had not been damaged by the pulse would reboot in mere minutes, and Manuel Richardson was not as fleet of foot as Lucia Ribiero. He hit the ladder at a dead run and scrambled up the rungs at a pace embarrassingly slow compared to the woman's. He was breathing hard when he hit the door to the hall, keeping his pace fast as he scampered down the corridor. He burst through the bathroom door and slid to a halt inside.

Lucia was standing over the crumpled form of a man. She looked up at Manny and held up her hands. "You sent me into the men's room, Manny."

"Right," he shook his head. "Right. Men's room. Shit."

"He's not dead, and I don't think he got a look at me. I was moving close to top speed and I caught him turning. He won't be out long, though..." The form was already stirring. "...And I'd rather not hit him again. Might do permanent damage."

Manny reached into his satchel on reflex and rummaged around. His hand came out a moment later with a hypo and two ampules. "What do you think he weighs?" he asked absently.

"Call it two hundred pounds?" Lucia replied with a shrug. "How the hell should I know?"

"Close enough, anyway." Manny was focused on the hypo. He slid both smooth plastic capsules into the contoured grip of the cylindrical applicator, then twisted the base to seal them and pressurize the chamber. Satisfied, he stepped over to the groaning man, flipped the safety cover off the applicator pad, and placed the device against the meat of the fallen worker's thigh.

With a hiss, a small needle sprang from the device and enough piperidine to keep the man asleep for hours was injected. The fallen man groaned, then sighed. His muscles lost all tension and his already prone body sank even further into the floor. Manny checked pulse and breathing to ensure he had not overdosed the poor slob, then snapped the hypo closed. He returned it to his bag and huffed, "Right. That's managed. He won't wake up for long time and he won't remember shit when he does. We need to go, though. That spontaneous EMP and a drugged worker means our infiltration will be suspected sooner rather than later. Too much coincidence, I think. We need to be deep into The Quad before they decide to look for us."

116

Lucia gestured to the door. "Let's move then."

They left the men's restroom quietly. While not necessarily in a secure location, they certainly were not employees and really had no business being there. With no easy answers for how these strangely dressed folks had arrived in the receiving section, the pair expended no small quantity of effort escaping unseen. Several times, they had to duck down hallways or hide in closets to avoid detection. Yet other than these few tense moments, the duo cleared receiving without further incident.

Once out of receiving, Manny ushered Lucia to a wide double door that looked as if made from recycled plastic. She was no expert in things industrial, but she had a strong feeling that this passage had been carved from a wall to create a shortcut between receiving and the other areas. The aperture had been cut cleanly, and she could see that it had been done after the wall went up. She asked Manny about this and he nodded in the affirmative.

"You'll see a lot more of that after we get down to The Quad. Years ago, these areas were crammed with machinery and work stations, and the hallways were designed to accommodate the work flow of the refractory process. Products moved from one area to the next and the hallways followed. With the machines removed, there was no real reason to have the passages wander all over the place, and people started cutting through the walls to make moving around easier."

"Makes sense," Lucia replied. She had seen brewing and bottling operations in her old job and they followed the same pattern. Efficient task management and smooth production flow dictated the design, not convenience.

Manny led her to a smaller door and he cranked the handle to release the bar. Beyond it was an ugly gray metal stairwell, poorly lit and stinking of sulfur. Lucia winced and Manny gestured grandly to the darkness beyond.

"Let's head down to The Quad, ma'am."

"I am positively a-flutter with anticipation, kid."

Manny shook his head. "Don't poke fun, this was my home. I used to think The Quad was the greatest place in the universe when I was a kid."

After a short descent, an identically ugly door yielded to Manny's attentions and Lucia stepped through. On the other side she was nearly overwhelmed by a wave of sights, sounds, most strongly of all, smells.

The Quad, Lucia quickly realized, was a proper noun. She stood on a metal grated deck that led to a rusted staircase. The door had opened to a catwalk perhaps thirty feet above the floor of a wide, cavernous space hundreds of yards on a side. Her eyes could not take it all in at first, packed as it was with stimuli so bizarre and frenetic she simply did not have a paradigm to compare it to. Despite its size, the landscape was crammed wall-to-wall with a stippled morass of human activity. Dirty brown lanes and paths spread out before her like cracks in a dry riverbed. The lines ran like ant tunnels, twisting between hundreds of stalls, ramshackle buildings, and other rough-looking structures. Strings of lights in a nauseating array of sizes and colors wound like spiderwebs from tall poles erected at regular intervals. The shadows seemed to fall in every direction, and the colors of clothing and surfaces shifted and blurred as a hundred different frequencies of light competed for dominance. The giant space was both bright enough to sting the eyes yet dark enough to hide shadows so black they seemed to swallow photons. What one saw simply depended upon where one stood and where one looked.

Her vantage point gave her a panoramic view of the teeming floor. There were long strips of neon in garish shades highlighting purveyors of goods and services, as well as crude holograms depicting dancing girls or foaming beverages. Fuzzy blue-green titans engaged in a pitched battle in the air over one corner. This startled Lucia at first, and then she saw that men were fighting bare-handed in a cage that had been erected behind a building advertising blood sports. A small yet bloodthirsty crowd cheered and jeered for their favorites while a holographic projector broadcast the bout fifty feet above them all. The sound was a physical thing, a wall of rumbling white noise pockmarked with the jangling chimes of a slot machine or the pulsing music of a cantina. Shouts of vendors, cries of hawkers, and the raucous banter of thousands of rough men and women pressed on Lucia's ears like a heavy blanket, both hot and oppressive.

She wanted to take a deep breath, to calm her screaming nerves. It was impossible. The humid air assaulted her nose and tried to crush her lungs with the aromas of strange food, unwashed bodies, and the ever-present taint of sulfur. Lucia's eyes watered and her heart raced. The familiar creeping dread of her anxiety began to claw its way from her guts and sink icy claws into her throat. She forced it back down with will alone and turned to Manny. She said nothing, not trusting her voice, and he only beamed back at her and said.

"Told you it was amazing."

Chapter Fifteen

Craddock stared up at the big New Boston fixer.

The big New Boston fixer looked down at Craddock.

Neither blinked, neither flinched. The air in the room was electric with tension while each player affected an air of calm repose, betraying no weakness.

The silence was broken by the crackle of a capacitor popping. Blue sparks spewed from the twisted metal arm still gripped in Roland's gloved fist. Craddock winced at the sudden noise and Roland grunted in annoyance. Craddock used the interruption to speak.

"They build fixers real different Earthside, I guess."

Roland exhaled a grumbling growl. "Your problem is that you keep thinking you're dealing with a fixer." The big man waved the bulky arm of the Stahlkorper in front of the other man. Then gripped it in both hands. With a twist and a pull, he yanked the metal limb in half, sending more sparks and metal fragments all over the room. "I'm THE fixer." He groaned inwardly at the melodrama of that, and was thankful Lucia had not been present for it. He loved her dearly, but she would have teased him without mercy over the macho posturing. But men like Craddock were driven by passion, and this made them susceptible to drama.

To his credit, the stocky terrorist did not rise to the bait. Craddock twirled an index finger in a circle and rolled his eyes, "Well whoop-dee-doo big man. You're THE fixer. I'm both surprised and impressed that the Dockside boys have the juice to send..." He sneered waved his hand at Roland dismissively, "Whatever the fuck you are. But thumping two of my boys don't change much of what I have to say."

Roland smiled again. He was arguably the worst smiler in space, and his facial expression conveyed neither mirth nor satisfaction.

"Well, that's just stupid. Obviously, it does. You brought two of you best hitters in here to intimidate me." He gave a big expressive shrug. "I hope you now understand that a couple of low-dollar work-mechs don't amount to much more than my morning calisthenics."

Craddock looked like he was about to interrupt, but Roland cut him off. "I know that Venus has a lot of armatures, Craddock. I know they all belong to your little union, too. I get it. You got a hundred of these guys, and some meaner ones on top of it. The point, Mr. Craddock, is that the Dockside Trade Association paid my astronomically exorbitant rates because they knew you would try to push me around and they wanted me to push back. We've done that bit. If you like, that part of this interaction can end here and now. Or, you can push back some more, and see what happens." Roland folded his arms across his chest and tilted his head to the smaller man, indicating that he was finished with a sardonic, "Your call."

"You got a lot of nerve, asshole."

"I could kill you right now, Craddock. No one could stop me. So, yeah, I guess you could say nerve comes easy to me."

Craddock's face flashed with anger, but he clamped down on it before it could make his situation worse. His reply came through gritted teeth. "You kill me, pal, you die on Venus."

Roland laughed. It was a harsh, humorless sound. "I DID die on Venus, Craddock. Once. I'll give you one guess as to how that little misadventure happened, too. Here's a fucking hint: Crimson headware." Craddock's eyebrows rose slightly at this, and Roland's tone darkened. "What you should be very worried about, you piece of shit, is whether I'm here on business or if I'm here to return the favor."

"Is that why you're in here, pal? You got bad blood with the Hats and now you wanna get some payback? That ain't a great way to play fixer."

"Truthfully?" Roland shook his head. "I don't give a fuck about you guys and your bullshit revolution."

Craddock bristled at the dismissive tone, but kept his cool all the same. "Hard to tell by looking around, buddy." He gestured to the injured men still on the floor. "That felt excessive."

"Like I said, Craddock. That was a warning about trying to push me."

"Message received. But we still need our boy back. It's important to us. So let's talk." The stocky man shifted back into his chair. "What if we paid you to bring him back? A show of good faith and cooperation between the Red Hats and the Dockside..." He scowled and waved an impatient hand in the air, "...whatever the fuck they are now."

"The Trade Association cannot afford to be seen cooperating with the Red Hats. We literally live in the shadow of the Planetary Council. There can be no 'good faith' anything with known terrorists."

"We are not terrorists!" Craddock blurted. A diatribe seemed forthcoming, and since he was in no mood for it, Roland cut the man off.

"Spare me, Craddock. No one outside of your little hellhole here is buying into your freedom fighter message. Too many dead innocents on your resume. You're either too dumb to catch on or too fanatical to back down, so I'll spell this out for you. I am convinced that the higher levels of your little group are not after this runner because of a perceived betrayal. Your latest attempts to bring him in have 'desperation' written all over them. Just like your little play at intimidation here does. Everything about this farce tells me you shits are scared, and we can guess why." Thanks to Manny, Roland was well aware of why the Red Hats were so keen to bring their former scout back in, but he was not quite ready to play that card just yet. "Now, as we speak I have people digging into your little runaway. Once we find out what it is he knows that has you guys so worked up, we are can do one of two things with that information." He held up a thick index finger. "We can do nothing with it, because we don't give a fuck." A second finger extended, "Or we can turn that information over to the Planetary Council because you couldn't be bothered to play by the rules, and thought you could push me around."

Roland watched Craddock's face, eager to see how close to home his dart had struck. The man's jaw flexed, and his eyes twitched ever so slightly. *Pretty close, I'd wager.* Roland nodded in silent approval. The minuscule tell confirmed that Craddock knew Manny held sensitive information, and that meant Craddock was probably in on whatever it was Hardesty had going. To his credit, the terrorist spoke evenly, betraying none of this with his voice. "Pal, you gotta be the worst fixer in the whole goddamn galaxy. You don't know shit about what people do and don't know. Threatening to bring the Council in won't make anyone around here eager to work with you, either." He blew a big expressive sigh. "But fuck it. This shit is turning into a giant fucking headache so I'll run what you have to say up the flagpole with the other groups. It'll take a week or so, and you can use that time to pull your head out of your ass and stop acting like you know what the fuck you're talking about."

"I'll do my best," Roland said affably.

"Right." The man did not sound convinced of this. "You go ahead and just keep your fucking head down while you are here. This ain't your precious Dockside, pal. Venus can be real dangerous for uppity pricks who think they are hot shit."

"I know it," Roland said with mock severity. "Just look at what happened to these two punks." He pointed to the silent Stahlkorpers. "I bet they woke up this morning thinking they were pretty hot shit, themselves."

"There are worse things than armatures on Venus, fixer. I'm trying to warn you nicely, here. Accidents happen in The Colander all the time. We got huge vats of acid, big crucibles of molten metal, heavy industrial shit. It's a dangerous place for tourists. Even big cyborg tourists. It could take a month for anyone to even notice you're gone. They may never find your body."

The big man was impressed with the temerity of his adversary. Despite being completely outclassed, the grouchy terrorist was still trying to intimidate him. Roland spared a moment's reflection for all the places he had been that had been as dangerous or more than Venus, and laughed right in Craddock's sputtering face. "I'll be careful. You've got your one week."

For a brief moment, Roland considered extending his hand to the man, but then thought better of it. To think a perfunctory handshake could color what had just occurred as a meeting, and not the first exchange of warning shots in what was likely to be a long and bloody battle, was a level of self-delusion in which Roland was not inclined to indulge. Instead, he straightened, nodded to the seething Craddock and his trembling cronies, and turned his back to them all. He would have preferred to sweep out of the room with calm elegance betraying his supreme confidence, but he realized he still had to navigate the tiny hatch. There was no viable method for him to choreograph an artful exit while cramming his bulk through the undersized opening, but he did his best to look regal in the attempt. He assumed he had failed, but it was the thought that counted.

His two guides were waiting for him just outside. If their eyes were any indication, they were as close to panic as one could get without spontaneous defecation. Roland allowed himself a moment of internal approval. His theatrics in the meeting had been over the top and dramatic to a fault, but the effect was exactly what he hoped it would be. These two would be telling tales of what happened here to everybody they met, mixing the most important ingredient of Roland's recipe for success into the mission.

Fear is contagious, he mused. *And in a place like this, it spreads faster than typhoid.* In a few hours, everyone in The Colander would be buzzing and talking about one thing and one thing only: the giant fixer from Earth who came in and shook down Alasdair Craddock. Manny and Lucia might never even get noticed as long as he kept his profile high enough. Picking fights and making a lot of noise was very much within Roland's skill set, and the captive audience of The Colander should make this task rather simple.

He gestured to the trembling flunkies, startling them out of wide-eyed paralysis. "You morons want to lead back up to ground level now? Or should I find my own way?"

The taller man stammered an unintelligible reply, but Roland got the gist of it and followed the retreating man down the hall. In their haste to be rid of their terrifying charge the guides forgot to meander the route and took what appeared to be a direct path to the surface. With far more speed than it took to get down, Roland was back and standing outside the reception zone again. His minders vanished like so much vapor as soon as he was back in front of the stall, and the big man could not help but surrender to a wave of smug satisfaction at his afternoon's work.

"Don't you just look like the cat that ate the canary, Ironsides." Mindy sidled up beside him.

"Won't lie. That was fun. Felt like the old days."

"As far as negotiations go, that was pretty shitty work."

Roland started to walk toward a food vendor. The stall smelled of burned meat and some kind of salty-sweet sauce. He could not identify it, but it smelled good enough and he was hungry. He ordered four of the stuffed pastry being sold there and crammed the first into his mouth. He offered one to Mindy, who declined with an expression that was rather unambiguous about her opinion of Venusian street-meat. He shrugged and swallowed his mouthful of food, pleasantly surprised at how good it was. "Wasn't really trying to negotiate. Wanted him mad, and I wanted people to talk. So I pissed him off and gave everybody something to talk about." He switched gears on her. "How was recon? You find anything interesting?"

Her tone went very businesslike. "This place is crawling with cyborgs, Roland. I've never seen so many armatures in one place before."

"Get out to Enceladus sometime," he replied with an unimpressed toss of his shoulders. "Dangerous work out here means lots of walking wounded. Good clients for armature companies. Looks to me like the Erberhaus marketing department has an office on site. They specialize in low-cost hostile-environment armatures. Craddock didn't mind bringing two Stahlkorpers to a meeting, so I'm guessing they're thick on the ground here."

"Yeah, well I saw a couple of those big quadropod things, too. You know the ones that look like big green centaurs?"

"Erberhaus?"

"Yeah."

"How big?"

"Bigger than you, not as big as the bastard you smashed in Quinzy."

"EisinStier mediums. Cheap but tough." He winced as he recalled the specifics of that model. "Small power plant, but great heat shielding and redundant actuators. They aren't the strongest or fastest rigs for the money, but they are designed to get the shit kicked out of them and keep running."

"Whatever, they had two of them just moving tanks of stuff around down there. I also counted about thirty lights of various types. Lots of those ugly-ass Erberhaus tin men, a bunch of little AutoCat BobCats, too." Her face twisted. "But get this. I saw at least three Shikomi Kanos down there." Those she knew well. Her former partner and best friend had worn a Kano.

"Kanos, huh?" Roland looked impressed. "Those will bear watching. A Kano is a damned expensive rig for Venus. What do you bet those are plants for Hardesty?"

"My thoughts exactly. You could get three BobCats for the cost of a single Kano."

"And five Stahlkorpers." Roland agreed. "Somebody paid for a bunch pricey rigs, anyway. You spot any heavies?"

She shook her head. "Not live, but I found cradles for four. Two AutoCat and two Erberhaus stations with all the tools."

"At least no Shikomi heavies, then. That's a relief. They are all probably outside. With supplemental helium tanks, those things will have enough cooling to ride out the heat for a few hours."

Mindy looked very concerned. "If these guys are all in the union, we could be in serious shit, Roland. That is a lot of heavy metal walking around. I ain't saying you can't whup a lot of ass, but..." Her voice trailed off and her eyebrow rose. "It's a lot of very big bad guys."

"I get you. But the mediums and heavies won't fit on the upper levels. And the lights can't keep up with me, not even the Kanos. As long as we play a nice, careful, strategic game we will be fine."

Her expression did not broadcast hope. "Well that's just a huge relief, buddy."

Roland bit down on another pasty and ignored her sarcasm. "We need to regroup with Lucia and Manny. You figured out how to get to the rendezvous without being followed?"

"We're being followed now, Ironsides," she drawled. "It's more of a matter of losing the tail than it is of avoiding it."

"That's your angle, lady. I only know one way of dealing with nosy hoods who want to follow me around, and Lucia says I'm not supposed to kill people over that stuff anymore."

"Just start walking that way," she sighed, pointing down the concourse to a network of corridors. "I'll handle the tail."

Chapter Sixteen

Walking through The Quad was one of the most stressful experiences of Lucia Ribiero's life, and she had raided a pirate ship once. Manny hustled through the masses of people as if they were not even there. Lucia was bumped and jostled constantly as she tried to keep up with the darting scout. Hands brushed her body, strange feet tangled with hers, and the dull roar of voices and music pressed on her skull with an unrelenting wall of sound. She forced her sense of time to dilate so she could steal a breath between steps and hopefully dodge the next invasion of her personal space.

A hand closed over her wrist, and she looked up to see Manny yanking her into a gray building. It was one of the larger structures in The Quad, and she could see it had been made from the sturdy metal panels that delineated the industrial spaces. Despite the recycled nature of its materials, the structure had been assembled carefully and by skilled workers. Lines were straight, walls were plumb, and floors were level. The whole façade managed to be both neat and ramshackle at the same time. Lucia realized that this juxtaposition was a key component to the jarring personality of The Quad. Obviously, everything down here was either a hand-me-down or scrap. While most slums wore this shame on their sleeves, it appeared that Venusian laborers were committed to doing the best work they could with the skills of their hands and the materials available. She could respect that.

"Come on," Manny called. "We need to find someone. It's going to be a little weird in here. Just keep your head down and let me do the talking, okay?"

Stepping through the door, Lucia observed what appeared to be a tavern of some sort. Growing up in Uptown, Lucia had few opportunities to experience seedy dive bars. Even after relocating to Dockside, she avoided the rough pubs that catered to the longshoremen and spacers. The Smoking Wreck was about as bad as she could handle and places like Hideaway actively turned her stomach. This establishment was easily the strangest she had ever been in. Tables in varying sizes and configurations littered the wide-open floor, and what was ostensibly a bar lined the back wall. Tubes of light in obnoxious colors crisscrossed the ceiling, most pulsing in patterns that accompanied the thrumming of terrible music. The music, omnipresent and indistinct, thumped from hidden speakers. It was a talentless and tuneless heartbeat that was more felt in the guts than it was heard with the ears.

On a raised platform, a woman danced provocatively wearing little more than a fake smile and twisted tubes of neon light. She was young and reasonably attractive, but her eyes were tired and heavy. Her dancing was competent, yet uninspired and unconvincing. All the elements were present, but off just ever so slightly. Feet stepped and hands waved, hips gyrated and shoulders swayed, all accomplished in a manner superficially sexual. It still looked listless, though. It was as if the dancer was only pantomiming the steps, moving in a pattern repeated so often it had burned a track into her brain and worn grooves into the stage floor. In front of the lethargic woman, a row of unkempt men howled and slid cred chits into tip slots as she worked each one with a feigned smile poorly concealing a bored expression of professional disinterest. Lucia thought it odd that the men were so enthusiastic about a woman so obviously not invested. *It's all such a bland fiction, and who would pay for that?* She answered her own question a moment later. *Lonely people would.* It was one of the strangest and saddest things Lucia had ever seen. A perverted music box ornament twirling in mechanical rote to a song played with neither skill nor joy.

Manny, oblivious to Lucia's distraction, walked straight to the bar and sat down on a rough plastic stool. Lucia was surprised at how relieved she was to sit next to him. Put off by the spectacle on stage and slick with her own sweat, the frazzled woman was more than ready for the temporary relief of a cold beverage. The bartender, a hard-looking older woman who had probably been beautiful once, walked over and placed stained menus in front of them.

"Thirsty?" she droned. Her blue eyes were narrow and lined, and her lips were thin. She was tall and lean in a manner oddly athletic.

Despite her humble surroundings, the woman held her chin with an almost imperious tilt.

Manny looked directly in her face and grinned. "I'll have the special, Ellie."

"We don't do specials here," the woman said, sounding annoyed. But then she stopped and squinted at the younger man. The eyes widened in recognition for the briefest second, then returned to their normal width before anyone could notice. "Two specials," she said loud enough for anyone to hear and then walked away from the bar to disappear into the kitchen.

"Come on," Manny said to Lucia. He slid from the stool and shrugged his satchel on. He looked at his confused partner and gestured for her to follow.

Lucia spared herself a moment of regret for the unpurchased drink, but then chided herself for the weakness. She was on-mission right now, and she supposed she could at least pretend to be a professional. With a sigh she stood and followed Manny back outside and around to an alley. The space between the tavern and the structure next to it was barely thirty inches wide, yet somehow it was clogged with trash and hid at least one intoxicated man. The rumpled figure lay face down in a pile of discarded food containers and old crates, snoring without shame into his arm. Manny and Lucia stepped over the unconscious man and slipped further into the alleyway.

The garish photonic cacophony that was lighting in the main thoroughfare disappeared within ten feet of the alley's entrance. Shadows swallowed everything as the dull gray of walls refused to reflect light any deeper into the gap. Lucia strained her eyes, and could still make out most major obstacles when they finally stopped at a nondescript service door. Many punched a code into a panel and frowned when nothing happened. His frown deepened into a scowl, then he passed his left hand over the buttons and repeated his rapid-fire code entry trick from earlier. In eight seconds the latch finally yielded with an audible click and Manny nodded in satisfaction.

With a shove, the door swung inward, completely silent on well-oiled hinges. Manny stepped through and beckoned for Lucia to follow. She did, and found herself in a dim foyer. From there, Manny led her into a larger room with a table and chairs set up at the center. A narrow counter ran along one side, and a decrepit coffee station stood defiant at one end of it.

"Have a seat, Boss." Manny waved dismissively to the table. "I'll make some coffee."

"Exactly where the hell are we?" Lucia asked.

"Somewhere Manuel should be very far away from," a voice answered from the doorway.

Lucia looked up to see the woman from the bar scowling at them, hands on hips and face locked in a glare both disapproving and scared.

Manny's face was more serene, and his answer had iron in it. "I can't run forever, Ellie. It's time to end this." He turned to Lucia. "Lucia, this is Ellie Connelly, the best smuggler, trader, madame, fence, and coin-changer in all of Venus."

Lucia stood and offered her hand to the woman, who stared at it for a moment before giving it a perfunctory shake. She then turned away from Lucia without a word and started in on Manny with a scolding tone.

"You should have gone to the frontier. You could have gotten away from them."

"No I couldn't. I know things. Things they can't ever let get out. I didn't realize it at the time, but it's a lot bigger than Craddock's ego or the glory of the Cause."

"So you came back?" The woman was becoming shrill. "To do what? Fight them? You stupid child! You are not a fighter, Manuel! You are a sneaker, a planner, a tinkerer! You are one lost little boy all alone against those... those... *animals*! They will kill you and laugh about it when they are done!"

"I've changed, Ellie." Manny punctuated this by yanking the sleeve from his left arm and holding the smooth white prosthetic up for her to see. "And I'm not alone anymore."

The woman, who Lucia had deduced was an old acquaintance of Manny's, looked wide-eyed at the exotic technology of the limb and then to Lucia in her expensive armor. "Oh you poor stupid boy," she whispered. "What have you done?"

"I've come back to make this right, Ellie. Craddock needs to know he can't hound me anymore, and I am not the child who ran away five years ago."

Ellie shook her head, a sad rueful motion, then turned to Lucia. "And who is this Lucia to you, that she is so eager to die helping?"

Lucia's eyebrows rose at the woman's dismissive tone, yet she held her tongue. This was Manny's play and she was content to let him have it.

"Lucia is a fixer, and my employer."

"So she is this fixer from Dockside everyone is talking about?" Then Ellie frowned and dismissed that notion. "No, the word is that one is a big bald male. Apparently big enough to put down two of Craddock's metal men bare-handed, from what the lads are all-flutter about it."

Manny winced, "That would be Lucia's partner. He's... special. Two of those jerks wouldn't give him much trouble."

Lucia spoke up for the first time, a deep uncomfortable groan in her voice. "Please tell me he didn't kill anyone?"

"Your partner walks into a meeting with Alasdair Craddock, fights with two cyborg thugs, and your concern is how many of them he may have killed?"

"If you ever meet him, you will understand," Lucia responded dryly.

Dark hair bounced as the older woman threw her hands up in defeat. "He did not kill anyone, but the lads on the decks are suitably terrified, all the same."

"That was probably his goal all along," Lucia sighed. "His negotiation tactics are not particularly sophisticated."

"Ellie," Manny interrupted. "I had to come back. There's so much I wish I could tell you, so many reasons I have to do this. But I don't want you to know all the things I know."

"So now you're here, filled with secrets and bringing allies from far away to fight with you." Her eyes tilted downward, and suddenly she looked very tired. "You stubborn fool. What those lads did to you was horrible, but it's what they do to everyone. I tried to keep you away from them, but you wouldn't listen to me then. Even though those bastards proved me right, and I told you to run far away and never come back, you still can't bring yourself to listen to sense! It seems nothing has changed on that front."

Ellie looked like she was going to cry. "This goddamn rock ruins everything! Everything! I thought maybe, just maybe, little Manuel had gotten away. You just couldn't let an old woman think she had saved just one person before they got ruined, could you?" A big wet tear traced a muddy line down her cheek. "I guess I should have known better."

"I'm not ruined Ellie." Manny stepped over to wrap the crying woman in a big hug. "And before I'm done, Craddock and Hardesty will know it, too."

"Oh, my little Manuel," she sniffled. "It's too big now. You can't beat them."

"I probably can't." He smiled, giving the woman another squeeze. "But *we* can. Lucia and her partner have handled things like this before." Lucia winced slightly at the fib. She and Roland had certainly tackled some suitably impressive opponents, but this job was a markedly different animal than their usual fare. No one caught the minor tic.

"We will need help, all the same," Manny added.

Ellie straightened, "So you didn't just come here to visit a sad old woman? You want me to help you in your fool's errand against Craddock?" This seemed to put the woman back on her heels. "I still have to live here, Manuel. If Craddock finds out I'm helping you, I'll not survive it."

Lucia interjected, and her voice came out as either resigned or confident, depending on how well one knew the speaker. "I'll be honest, Ms. Connelly. We don't know the political landscape here very well. But if I know Roland, it is likely going to be Craddock who doesn't survive."

"That's all well and good for you," Ellie retorted, "But what about the rest of us? There will be reprisals."

"There are always reprisals, Ellie." The ferocity in Manny's voice shocked Lucia. "It's always fucking reprisals on Venus! The RUC, the Council, the Red Hats? All of them and their goddamn reprisals! Nobody does shit because of *reprisals!*" His bionic fist struck the table hard enough to crack it. "Well, this time Manuel Richardson is the reprisal. I've been wandering the system for five years wondering what was wrong with me, when all along it was them. The goddamn Red Hats and this place are what's wrong, not me and not you, Ellie. Somebody needs to do something about that."

"So you have come back to help us, now? Five years away and suddenly little Manuel knows how to fix all our problems? You're going to save poor, helpless, backward Venus with a metal arm and your new friends? Gods above, you are still a just child, aren't you?"

"No, Ellie. I'm not here to fix Venus. Only Venus can fix Venus. But I've learned something from Lucia and Roland. Sometimes the solution to a problem isn't about fixing things."

"It's about breaking them," Lucia finished for him.

Manny picked the thread back up. "That's exactly it. I know I can't fix the Red Hats, or the RUC, or the Council. But I do know that with this team, and a little help from you, that we can break Craddock and Hardesty. The rest will be up to those who choose to lead afterward."

"Are you talking about me?" Ellie was not all the way past her anger and frustration yet, and the question came out laced with bitterness.

"They'll follow you, Ellie. I did. You are the only one they all trust."

The woman, Lucia noticed, had a very eccentric temper. She could go from crying to scolding to boiling rage and all the way back with little to no transition.

"How the hell are you going to put that on me now?" Dark eyes blazed, and small hands pushed at the young man holding her. "You're gone for five years, and you come back stuffed with lofty notions about taking on the Red Hats. That's stupid enough for you, Manuel. But to tell me I am going to have to pick up your mess when you are done with us is some serious bullshit!"

Manny held onto her, his hands on her narrow shoulders. "It's either this, or spend my whole life running. If I don't face this, I'm turning my back on everyone here and giving the victory to the same men who tried to kill me because I didn't want to bomb a hospital filled with kids." Suddenly, it was Manny who was angry. "You think I should run away and save myself? That's not saving myself, Ellie! That's losing myself. The Red Hats take *children* and teach them to kill *other children!* Fuck free Venus, and fuck their great cause." He jabbed a finger in Lucia's direction for emphasis. "Her partner is right. If I don't beat this when I have the means, if I don't bury this demon? Then I am condemning another generation to my own personal hell. If I win, no other kid has to grow up like me. If I run away?" He shrugged. "Then sweet Ellie Connelly will always have another 'little Manuel' to try and save."

Lucia had a strange moment of clarity, and spoke without thinking. "That girl out there. The dancer?"

Ellie replied with a biting look, defensive and maternal. "What about her?"

"Are you saving her? Is that what 'saved' looks like on Venus?"

Lucia thought that Ellie would try to hit her when her face cast itself in a mask of feral hatred. It was a fleeting thing, flashing for only an instant, then vanishing as quickly as it had appeared. "There are worse things than that stage, young lady," Ellie cautioned. There might have been menace there, or sadness. It was hard to say which, and she suspected the truth of it lived somewhere in the middle.

Lucia did not want to hurt Ellie, but a point had to be made. "I believe you. I also believe there is much better. Of course, that naked girl onstage getting leered at by a bunch of drunk men will never know that. Not unless things change here."

Ellie Connelly did not move or speak for a long, painful interlude. Her face was a moving picture show, portraying an entire spectrum of emotions in stark relief across features worn with age and sorrow. Both Lucia and Manny simply let her have the moment. Then the young man finally dropped his hands to his sides and walked over to a waiting chair. He slumped into it with a heavy thud and sighed. "You can't save us all, Ellie. Not if we won't save ourselves."

Chapter Seventeen

T o say that Alasdair Craddock was furious would have been an unforgivable understatement. The beefy man stood shivering with barely constrained rage before his office terminal. The long lined face of Lincoln Hardesty stared back at him from the screen, wearing a look of bland irritation.

"You didn't see him, Lincoln!" Craddock blustered. "Something fucked up is going on for them to send..." he waved his hands in frustration, "...whatever the fuck he is here."

"What, is he some kind of augmented guy, maybe an armature or something? You must have a hundred armatures down there. So what's the big deal?"

Craddock wiped his face with a sweaty palm. "You aren't getting me. Yeah, I got lots of mounted metal heads down here. I got armatures coming out my ass, Link. I know armatures as well as you know underage whores. I figured that Dwarf clown was going to send some sort of hitter, sure. So I bring two of the lads with me, right?"

"We covered this, Al."

"Yeah, but you ain't hearing me. This big bald fuck scraps two of my boys in Stahlies with one hand a piece, and he doesn't even rip his jacket doing it."

"So? Bring three guys next time."

"Goddamn it, Link! Pay the fuck attention! Taking two Stahlkorpers ain't impossible. A Kano could do it. That ain't the point. What you should be as pissed off as me about is that this guy bent them into pretzels and he wasn't mounted to shit." Craddock held a palm up to the screen to stop Hardesty's dismissive retort. "Yeah, yeah. Maybe a guy can throw a suit over some of that high-end exotic voodoo the military likes and still look all right. That kind of shit don't fool me, Link. I know the look, I know the walk, I know the feel of it. This was something else, and it all stinks like shit to me. I've lost two teams of Balisongs, and I get reports that some big augmented bastard and a couple of broads are the ones who put them down. Then I get this giant cyborg of seriously fishy origins thumping Stahlkorpers two at a time in my goddamn office. This shit don't sound like coincidence to me, and nobody wants to tell me nothing about it!" Craddock leaned into the monitor. "So I ask again, Link: exactly what the fuck have you brought down on us?"

"I never figured you for a man who would turn belly up and whimper over some dirtside muscle just because things got a little scary."

Craddock made an eloquent and emphatic gesture at the man on his screen. "Oh fuck off, Link. That macho bullshit might work on the other guys, but I know you too well to fall for it. I asked a question and I'm still waiting for the answer. What the hell are you into that we gotta throw Balisongs at a runaway, and causes Earth bosses to send high-end mystery hitters at us?"

On the screen, Hardesty's face twisted into a placating mask of beneficence. "I'm into all the same things you are, Al. Just more of them and bigger. I figure some of my smuggling operations have probably pissed off the Dockside crews. With their whole new trade system going on, we got to figure they are looking to flex a little on us. If only to make a damn point."

"Yeah, well it looks like they are flexing more than a little. And that still doesn't explain why I'm bleeding assassins over a damn runaway."

Hardesty's smile faltered for a moment, and then fell away completely when he saw that Craddock was watching intently. "That little runner of yours was our best scout, Al. He has seen a lot of very sensitive information. How long before he gets desperate and starts to sell that information?"

"Link, we've had all kinds of runners over the years. You and I both know how the Red Hat life breaks people. We like to make examples of 'em to keep everyone in line, but we have never chased one this hard before." Craddock leaned back, eyes narrowed. "I've never seen one get you this rattled, neither. I don't get spooked just because something don't smell right, but I get irritated when my partners hold out on me. I've known Manuel since he was five goddamn years old. He ain't selling shit to no one. He left because he got squeamish, not because he stopped believing in the cause."

"He left because you tried to kill him, Al."

"No, Link, *you* tried to kill him. That was your call, and I was never on board with it. I'd have worked him a little longer before going that route, personally. Losing a guy like him was wasteful. I figured he has some shit on you, and you not wanting to tell me what it is means it's probably shit I ain't gonna like."

"He has shit on all of us," Hardesty sounded like a man beginning to lose his temper. "He broke into the RUC garrison and walked out with all their personnel files. He stole the hard copies from the Material Sciences Corporation main offices. He had his fingers in every major operation we've done for the last fifteen years. You will find yourself mining ice in an Enceladus work camp for the rest of your life if that boy starts talking. You should be as keen as I am to bring him down." What he left out of this list was the damning OmniCorp files Manny had seen. Craddock did not ever need to know what was in those.

"Yeah, yeah. I get that part. What has me sweating and cranky is the stink of bullshit coming off you over this kid. Now, it's obvious you aren't going to level with me. You never have on anything else, so why should this be different?" That last part was almost an aside, but Hardesty took his meaning all too well. Theirs was not a relationship built upon trust or respect. The narrow-faced man let it slide as Craddock continued. "I'm all the way in on this one because you say you can get me the nav pylons. But I'm warning you, Link. If this starts to stink too much..." His head shook side to side, teeth clenched. "Like maybe I'm being offered as a sacrificial lamb or some shit? Then you and I are gonna have a serious problem."

"Relax, Al. Nobody is getting sacrificed. There is really, really, big stuff going down, and when it's all shaken out you are going to have your crack at the nav pylons. But a whole bunch of other shit is going to be shaking out at the same time, and you can't know about all of it. The stupid kid can hurt this. He probably doesn't realize it, but he has seen things that are a big problem for us all. My other partners really want him handled. They got deep pockets, Al, and so I'm going to deliver on that."

Craddock was not satisfied with this answer, this much was obvious. Irritation was written across his features in strokes of conflicting anger and suspicion. In a few tense seconds, expedience proved victorious over trepidation. Though not pleased, he resigned himself to being placated. Such was his desire to secure the nav pylons.

"Fine. Keep it to yourself, then. But that still doesn't solve the problem with this fixer freak. He says Manuel is to be left alone because we broke some of their rules, and they need to make an example of it. I know you and your buddies need him dead, but is it worth going to war with Dockside? We unload shit there too, you know."

Hardesty seemed happy for the change of subject, and his response was dismissive. "I'll contact this Dwarf character and see what can be done. In the meantime, just keep an eye on Richardson and don't move on him until we know what we are dealing with. Where is the boy now?"

Craddock's eyes flicked, a subtle show of chagrin. "Nobody fucking knows, Link. You knew him in the old days, too. If this kid wants to be invisible, he's fucking invisible. We only see him when he moves or fucks up. After the last run, he went silent again. So now we are stuck waiting for him to pop up on the radar. He might still be on Earth, or he might be halfway to Galapagos by now."

Hardesty shook his head. "Dammit. But you are right about that kid. No one will find him unless he wants to be found. At least running silent is almost as good as dead as far as our plans are concerned." His eyes darted back to Craddock's. "But dead is still the preferred outcome."

"What do I do with the fixer? He ain't gonna sit on his hands and wait for us."

"Is Grimes awake yet?"

The stocky man sighed. "Not yet. He rode in that crate for almost sixty hours. He was pretty messed up. Docs say he'll be up and running in a day or two though."

"Have Grimes take a look at this fixer. See if he recognizes him from the Dockside operation."

Bushy eyebrows rose. "You think it's the same guy?"

"Like you said, Al, it doesn't feel like coincidence."

"I hadn't thought of that," Craddock admitted. "If Manny is hooked up with this fucker..."

"His message was very clear," Hardesty prompted. "Richardson *did* say he would come after us if we did not back off."

"That little piece of shit," Craddock fumed. "He's here, isn't he?"

"Don't get ahead of yourself, Al. We don't know any of that for sure."

"Link," Craddock's voice had a hint of warning to it. "That would mean the Dockside crews are in on this, too. The big bastard wasn't lying. They really are trying to make an example out of us."

Hardesty nodded. "That sure seems likely. Their whole Trade Association is a brand new thing. They have no reputation and no history. If they can back us down, they are going to look a lot stronger than before."

"Fuck!" A meaty fist struck the desk, causing a worn DataPad to jump and clatter. "We really don't need this hassle right now! Now we can't back off Manny even if we wanted to. Shit! If he really is here, right now? Do you realize how bad that is?"

This seemed to confuse Hardesty. "We're trying to kill the little shit. I figure that makes things easier, not harder, Al."

"Link." Craddock sounded tired. "Why is it so important to kill him?"

"Because he knows things that can upset lots of people's plans. We covered this already."

"And how does a twenty-four-year-old punk know all these dangerous things?"

Hardesty frowned. "Because he is a kickass scout and infiltrator, and we used him to steal information from important people. I fail to see how..."

Craddock interrupted, "And if he is here, wondering why we want him so badly, what do you suppose he will be doing with his time?"

There was a long, pregnant pause as the older man processed this line of questioning. "Aw, crap," was his final, eloquent response.

"Yeah," Craddock agreed with a curt nod. "You better lock all your shit down as tight as you can, because it ain't Alasdair Craddock he'll be looking to expose. He already has enough to burn me anytime he wants to. He hasn't done it because he already figured out that you are the problem, not me. Whatever your game is, Link, this kid will want to know the details so he can use them to fuck you over. And when Manuel Richardson wants to know something?" The stocky man held his palms up in a gesture of futility. "Ain't nobody figured out how to stop him from finding it out."

"Well now, Alasdair," Hardesty sighed. "Now you know why we need him dead so urgently."

"I still don't know shit, Link. But you gotta help me here. I need passenger logs for the last week. I need security logs, too. Fuck it, I got to have cargo manifests on top of it all, because the little prick likes to hide as cargo when he sneaks around."

"Do you have any idea how much cargo moves between the domes every day?"

It was a stupid question. Craddock knew exactly how enormous a task he had just put on Hardesty. His response conveyed exactly how much sympathy he had in reserve for the older man. "This is your fuck-up, Link. Sorry if it means you'll have to do some actual work to fix it."

"Richardson won't be on any logs, you know that."

"Yeah, but he ain't working alone. The Balisongs talked about a couple of women with the fixer back in Dockside. If this really is the same guy, then I want to know who they are and if they are here, too. This fixer also said he had a military exemption, so somebody's got to get that information from the RUC. I don't have that kind of juice. So you gotta do that too, Link."

"Fine," Hardesty sounded tired and irritated at having to get his hands dirty, but Craddock did not care. "I will run this mess to the ground for you, Link, but you and I are due for a reckoning soon."

"I'll read you in on everything as soon as I can, Al. Trust me. We've known each other for a long time. I would not expose you to anything that could harm our relationship."

"Yeah. Sure. Whatever. Get me that intel and get your house in order before Manny breaks in. And believe me, he'll get in. So just make sure there is nothing for him to find when he does.

"Of course." Hardesty nodded his agreement. "Alasdair?"

"Yeah, Link?"

"Big things are coming. Things that will secure the future for Free Venus. I need you to know that no matter what happens, I am loyal to the cause and we will live to see a Free Venus. Together."

"That's real nice to hear, Link. Get me that intel and we'll talk again tomorrow."

Craddock cut the connection, leaving Lincoln Hardesty staring at a blank screen. Gnarled fingers sporting neatly manicured nails wiped a face lined with age and stress. With a deep sigh he looked out through his penthouse window, overlooking the capital city of Free Venus. It was well into the city's night cycle, and the dome lights had been lowered to minimum to help with sleep patterns. But Caelestus never really slept, and a sprawling metropolis of steel and light spread out below him. Ten thousand blinking dots pulsed like the synapses of an overworked brain, streaks of light darting across the blackness to disappear like the fleeting thoughts of a child's fancy. There was a beauty in it all, but Lincoln Hardesty had lost the taste for it.

He sighed again, and swung his gaze back to his terminal. Fingers tapped against the controls, coding instructions to underlings and sending missives to allies. Craddock would get his information, though the harder items would be costly to acquire. More difficult would be managing the surly terrorist's suspicions. Craddock did not rise to his current position by being stupid or reckless. The man had a devilish cunning and preternatural instincts for trouble. He was a useful and powerful ally. Though like any well-trained-yet-vicious animal, he could be very dangerous to work with all the same. The situation was far too precarious for his liking. The boy was unaware of what was he was holding, that much was obvious. As long as he never figured it out, things would be fine.

However, if the spineless little turncoat put the pieces together, it would spell disaster for Hardesty and the Red Hats alike. The lie to Craddock had been more painful than he thought it would be, but Hardesty had long ago outgrown his zeal for a Free Venus. If Venus truly wanted to be free, it would be. Too many of the rank and file were satisfied with Council leadership, and without unity, the industrial domes would never be free of that yoke. The Troubles had been very profitable for Lincoln Hardesty, however. Thus his participation in the conflict had increased even as his convictions weakened over the years. The irony was not lost on him.

Sometimes, when he was deep into his drinks or caught in a rare moment of reflection, Lincoln Hardesty would feel a great pang of guilt and sadness over this. There was something comforting and cleansing about the absolute unwavering dedication to an ideal. It kept things like guilt and responsibility from weighing a man down, and allowed him to become a creature of pure purpose. Great things could be accomplished when a person spared no thought or effort for anything but the goal. Tantalizing as it was, it was a conceit restricted to the underdeveloped mind. Nothing that simplistic could survive scrutiny or logic. When Hardesty could no longer hold back the encroaching doubts of a maturing worldview, he was forced to abandon those ideals for more practical goals. Still, he envied those who could hold onto the singular drive of a pure zealot. He missed the simplicity of it all. But then he would sober up and realize that he had no desire to trade his current situation for that of a Red Hat.

To emphasize this point to himself, Hardesty pinged the concierge for a nice steak dinner that cost more than a Venusian laborer made in a week, then scheduled his favorite prostitute for an after-dinner appointment. Craddock would handle Manuel Richardson and the fixer, so there was no need to get too upset about it. Despite his own greed, that man still had more than a little fanatic left in him. An honest opportunity to take the nav pylons would keep him focused for a while yet, so Hardesty would let him have as much rope as he asked for.

It was a very calm and detached Lincoln Hardesty who answered the gentle chime of his door. Dinner had arrived and there was no sense in letting an expensive meal get cold, after all.

Chapter Eighteen

Roland and Mindy met up with Manny and Lucia in an unused supply depot. It was little more than a large closet with steel shelving along bare gray walls, with a small attached office. Manny insisted that the dark space had been unused for decades, and the level of dust and accumulated grime sticking to every surface supported this assertion. The Colander was riddled with such spaces below the old refractories. At the peak of production, the giant dome had been crammed full of workers and equipment. Work crews would be hot-bunking and every space living and breathing with the noise and activity of three-shift production schedules. Times had changed on the fiery orange planet, and the intervening decades had been unkind to the aging facility. Once refining moved to more modern facilities or off-world, many places exactly like this one had simply been abandoned to the ravages of time. The door, closed and locked decades before, yielded to Manny's ministrations with some small protest. Yet it opened all the same, and the team set up camp inside it for their clandestine stay on Venus.

Lucia found the adjustment to be more difficult than she thought it was going to be. Despite her career change in the last year, her sensibilities were still those of a rich Uptown girl. She had been on camping trips before, and she assumed campaigning on Venus would something like that. Upon reflection, this was a patently stupid assumption. Camping with her college friends had involved a very nice sleeping pod, decent food, comfortable clothes, and no small quantity of alcohol. Here on Venus, she had none of those things. Their hidden base camp, abandoned as it was, was nowhere near any area with reliable cooling. The metal cube had to be close to one hundred degrees, and there was no cool night breeze wafting down from Cadillac Mountain inside. What she had now was the omnipresent sticky heat of poorly conditioned air surreptitiously borrowed from other more comfortable areas. It was enough to keep them from boiling in their own juices, while also woefully inadequate for comfort. The atmosphere, unfiltered and stale, was redolent of sulfur, oil, and sweat. Where was the soothing aroma of Douglas Fir and Jack pine trees? Instead of a luxurious and expensive sleeping pod, she had a bedroll of simple textiles. Not that anyone would be needing blankets to sleep in the stifling heat. On the whole, this was nothing like camping, and the discomfort was needling at her mood. She couldn't even complain to anyone. Roland did not perceive hot, cold, humidity or pain the way others did, so he was likely as comfortable as he ever was. Even if that was not the case he had been a special forces soldier before his conversion, so she suspected he had slept in places far worse than this either way. It occurred to her that Roland may have slept in a place *exactly* like this one during his three-month deployment here thirty years ago.

Manny had been born and raised in these domes. He was home, and did not look to be at all uncomfortable setting up his own bedroll and checking his equipment. He had removed his jacket and outer shirt, and he was not even sweating at the moment. It felt like a personal insult.

Lucia knew that Mindy would not complain either. She was a famous assassin, mercenary, and bounty hunter. Her professional pride would never allow her to admit to so paltry a weakness as physical discomfort. She expected the killer to gripe a little bit, just for the jokes. However, when push came to shove, Mindy was a pro.

So with an internal sigh of epic proportions, Lucia resolved herself to suffering in silence. She tried not to groan with disgust as she peeled the PC-10 gantlets from her arms, rivers of greasy sweat flowing from inside as they slid off her slick skin. Her jacket was next, and after a moment's consideration for modesty, her outer shirt as well. Her undershirt was plastered to her body, and the wetness cooled her skin once the air was able to touch it. While it was not a look she would have chosen for herself, she had to concede that based upon what she had seen of most Venusian dress, she would fit right in looking like this. At least the thin shirt was a deep navy blue, and thus it did not reveal anything that might get Manny killed by Roland for the crime of looking. He was still a young man, and internal discipline was new to him.

144

The cyborg and the assassin were late. In hindsight, this should have come as no surprise to anyone. Even with a solid location fix, navigating the labyrinth of tunnels and ad hoc passageways beneath the refractory level was the sort of quest that would have given Lewis and Clark the fits. The additional necessity of constantly discouraging tails while meandering through The Colander slowed an already arduous trip to a frustrating crawl.

Roland, being impossible to conceal, would have to walk far out ahead of Mindy, where he would inevitably pick up a follower intent upon broadcasting his destination to Craddock. Mindy would then remove the tail in a manner both painful and humiliating. The tiny blond assassin demonstrated remarkable creativity and a disconcerting level of glee with this part of the job. On Roland's strict instructions, none of these individuals died for her efforts. What was certain was all of Craddock's men would carry the shame of Mindy's ministrations for long years afterward.

Eventually, the pair did arrive at the designated location, and Lucia greeted them both with a look both concerned and irritated. "You guys okay? Where have you been?"

"Had to lose a bunch of Craddock's guys. Slowed us down." Roland saw the expression on Lucia's face and he answered the silent question there. "No fatalities."

"Thank God," she breathed. "Everybody is buzzing about your meeting with Craddock. Just couldn't restrain yourself, could you?" If her tone was a touch disapproving, she hid it well.

"I needed to draw attention. Mindy was doing recon while I was in there, so I figured it was prudent to be distracting."

"It worked," Mindy added. "I was able to go all over without anyone paying me any attention at all."

Mindy had begun to peel layers of sweaty clothing off, eventually arriving at her blue armored jumpsuit. This she unzipped and opened, fanning herself with the lapel and only incidentally making Manny choke and stumble.

"I bet," Manny snorted when he had recovered his balance and his dignity. "Putting Craddock on his heels is a big thing down here. He likes to parade his metal men around like his own personal army. Most folk on these levels are pretty scared of them."

Many abruptly lost his train of thought because Mindy had begun drying her cleavage with a towel.

"Cut it out, Mindy, you'll give Manny a heart attack," Lucia chided the half-naked assassin. At least Mindy was as uncomfortable as she was. Somehow, knowing that Mindy shared her misery made things just a little more bearable. Then she addressed the matter at hand "You mean cyborg armatures? Are they a problem here?" Lucia had seen Roland handle cyborgs before, and barring the really big and nasty ones, they never seemed too much of an issue.

Manny realized that Lucia had not spent much time below the refractory level yet. "Venus has a lot of armatures, Boss. A whole lot. Second only to Enceladus."

Understanding broke across Lucia's features. With understanding came waves of probabilities. She had never seen more than one or two armatures in one place before, and the ramifications of operating in this environment suddenly manifested in her mind as a thousand variable outcomes. A normal person would just shake their heads at this and sort it out one step at a time. Lucia, however, had nearly infinite parallel processing power and her brain immediately began to imagine and calculate all the branching possibilities.

The rest of her team recognized the change in her demeanor and held their collective breaths. She was either going to come out of the spell with a highly complex analysis of their situation, or the exercise would devolve into a panic attack. Since the recalibration of her nanomachines had become necessary, it was very much a toss-up as to which it would be.

Mindy had learned to feed Lucia productive information and encourage solution-based thinking when this occurred, so she rattled off information about numbers, makes, models and configurations of what she had seen while Roland was dealing with Craddock. Lucia's voice was tight and clipped while she asked relevant questions and sought clarification as needed. The bulging muscles in her neck and jaw made it obvious she was working against encroaching panic, but it also looked like she was winning the fight.

Roland hated to see her struggle like this, especially when he knew that a few firmware updates from her father could kill her anxiety completely. It was a tantalizing solution, an easy fix to take away all of her fear. This would come with a price however, and nobody was ready for Lucia's personality to devolve into an emotionless difference engine. The correct balance between biotechnical assistance and her natural personality had proven very elusive up to this point, and this made it hard for Lucia to experience a normal existence. She was determined to master her mind and her machines nonetheless, so Roland supported her efforts wholeheartedly. It was a thing he had more than a little experience with, and together they were unique in the galaxy. Though their origins could not have been more different, the pure randomness of happenstance had put the same demon in their heads and pulled them together to fight it. The old soldier respected fighters, and he knew there were many different kinds of fight. This one was hers and hers alone. There was an odd poetry in this. A symmetry Roland lacked the soul and emotion to truly explore. He saw it and appreciated it for what it was, and that was the best he could do for now. It was enough.

On this occasion Lucia was victorious over her demon, and after a moment her face relaxed. "Okay. It looks like those of us who can't bench-press a third-world country are going to need to tread lightly down here. Roland, I can't tell one armature from another. Can my CZ punch through these things or am I whistling Dixie?"

"Avoid the chest and limbs. Those are all going to be reinforced. Your flechettes might get through, but they won't have enough energy to do much after that. Shooting the helium tanks will be dramatic though it won't hurt them unless they are outside when you do it." The big man shrugged. "I'd aim for the face if I were you. The Stahlkorpers and Bobcats will have next to no armor there. Don't waste your ammo on a Kano."

Mindy slapped her Sasori dagger affectionately. "I don't mind tussling with the little ones. Unless these guys have boosted reflexes they'll never get a paw on me. After that, they are just big ol' tomato cans if you are prepared for them. At least I brought a proper can opener."

Manuel, having grown up and lived on Venus most of his life, offered his insights. "Hit them with the gloves, Boss. The Stahlkorpers have virtually no protection from EM stuff. It's just not a thing that they come with. If you aim for the left side of the chest, you can probably cause the whole chassis to reboot. That's a ninety-second window where the guy will be completely immobile. Anywhere else is still going to hurt like hell and probably scramble the control signals. Bobcats are a better rig, but if you hit them in the head, they'll probably reboot, too. Probably."

"And the Kanos?"

"Avoid them."

Lucia nodded, sending rivulets of sweat streaking down her neck and over her collarbones. "Are the Kanos that good?"

Mindy answered this one. "Mack had to sign a seven-year contract to get his. It's a very nice rig, Lucia. The most advanced light chassis you can get without going for military hardware."

"So how the hell are there high-end rigs like that on this rock?" Lucia wondered aloud. Then she added, "No offense, Manny."

"None taken, Boss." Manny waved a hand dismissively and continued. "It's weird to me too. There were no Kanos in The Colander when I left five years ago."

Roland's rejoinder came laced with disbelief. "Somebody paid a lot of money to drop some serious tech down here. For what? Material handling? I call bullshit on that."

Manny spoke for them all. "I don't like it."

"Are they Craddock's or Hardesty's? Or maybe someone else's?" Roland asked the group. "Ideas?"

Manny looked up at Roland, eyes narrow. "No way to know unless..."

"You think I should go pick one up?"

Manny shrugged, "Can you handle a Kano by yourself without scrapping it?"

Roland looked insulted. "I beat Grim Roper with my bare hands, kid."

The young man stared back with blank features. "Who's Grim Roper?"

Lucia groaned. "Long story, Manny. Some other time. As for taking a Kano in for questioning? That feels like a very bad idea. Like maybe we'd be tipping our hands really early if we did that. I'd prefer a more measured approach for now. Are you making a run at Craddock's records soon, Manny?"

"Yes. Ellie is setting up my opportunity right now."

"Good. Try to either establish if those things are his, or eliminate him as suspect."

"That will depend on how good his records are, Boss. I might find nothing."

Lucia tried to blow the magenta stripe of hair away from her eye. The stubborn streak remained plastered to her forehead with sweat, so she flicked it back with an angry jab of her finger instead. "We can always send Roland out if it's inconclusive. Just trying to avoid that drama for now."

"Right. Got it."

Lucia turned to Mindy. "You are still on recon, Mindy. I want you to stick to these Kanos like a blister. My gut says something is not right with them being here. Find out what you can." Then as an afterthought, "And Jesus, Mindy, put those away!"

The little blond bobbed her head and zipped her suit up a fraction of an inch. Making men hyperventilate was one of her favorite games, but it was just too hot for anyone to find it funny right now.

"Sorry Boss, I'm just really cooking in here."

"That suit can't be comfortable." Lucia thought about how she had felt wearing her gauntlets. She could imagine the blue jumpsuit must be a thousand times worse. "Why don't you change out of it?"

"Armor trumps comfort every time, lady."

"You sound like Roland."

Mindy scrunched her nose in an adorable frown. "No need to be insulting!"

Roland interrupted. "I'll go up and scout the RUC records. It sounds like these chumps will give me whatever I want, just to look helpful and kiss ass with the Expeditionary Force. Might was well see who pushed the permits through if I can. I've got nothing else to do until Craddock calls for another meeting, anyway."

"Perfect," Lucia said. "As for me?" The corner of her mouth turned ever so slightly upward. "I'm going to go meet Mr. Hardesty."

Chapter Nineteen

As the Alasdair Craddock meeting had lent itself to Roland's crude tactics, it was universally agreed that meeting Lincoln Hardesty would be better accomplished with Lucia's more polished style. Manny knew the man's proclivities well enough to recommend taking Mindy. Hardesty was a man of appetites, and his penchant for stacked blonds was a known factor. When informed of her role, Mindy's eyes narrowed and her face contorted into one of the most delightfully predatory grins Roland had ever seen. Making men do stupid things was her second-favorite hobby, and the opportunity to make Lincoln Hardesty look the fool warmed Mindy's soul in a manner best not elaborated upon.

Manny's task was simple enough for the experienced infiltrator. Break into Craddock's records and steal everything not locked down. Special attention was to be paid to finding out who or what was financing high-end armatures for the low-rent denizens of the dome, but any good dirt would serve their purposes.

Roland's role was more nuanced than he preferred. His formula since beginning his career as a fixer had always been fairly predictable. The steps were well-practiced and followed the same pattern for the most part:

Go talk to guy.

Guy chooses not to listen.

Hurt guy.

Guy listens.

Sometimes the order got mixed up. Sometimes a piece would be skipped or repeated. Nevertheless, for as long as he had adhered to this four-step dance he had enjoyed universal success. This time was different. He needed to go up to the RUC garrison and charm his way into their records. In all his years, the big cyborg had been called many things by many people. People had called him 'Breach,'

'Tank,' 'Corporal,' and a host of other names that polite company would never allow for. However, in his whole life no one had ever called him 'charming,' or any other word or words synonymous with it.

On the surface, his task was a simple thing, but every step on this path came with staggering consequences for failure.

He walked up to the RUC office at the security checkpoint, and asked the PFC at the desk to get him Sergeant Cummings. He assembled his features into the best, most comradely façade he knew how to do. Lucia had coached him on his demeanor, and Manny had explained how to use body language and inflection to disarm someone's suspicions. Ever the soldier, Roland had listened faithfully and executed all of their instructions to the best of his limited ability. When the private fled his station as if Satan himself had poked him in the ass with a pitchfork, Roland knew that his instructors would not be pleased with his performance.

The familiar face of Cummings appeared in the doorway and Roland straightened. Again he beamed his most disarming expression at the man. Cummings just looked confused.

"You all right, man? You look like you're about to puke."

Roland stopped trying to smile. "Must be the food here, Sergeant."

"It'll do it to ya," Cummings agreed. "What can I help you with, Corporal?"

Roland cast an evaluating eye over the PFC and the general bustle of the security office before responding. "Is there somewhere we can talk, uh, securely?"

The Sergeant's eyebrows rose an inch at that. "Sure. Let me just grab my jacket."

He left the office to return a few seconds later, throwing his black and tan uniform jacket over his gun belt and fastening the buttons. Okay. Let's go get some lunch." Turning to the Private he added, "Sign me out, Wally."

It was three in the afternoon, local time. Roland chose to not argue with the man over the timing of his meal. He simply followed Sergeant Cummings as the noncom pushed through the reception area crowds until they got off the main concourse. Down a few corridors and through a couple of too-small doorways, Roland found himself in a small commercial promenade catering almost

151

exclusively to eateries. These were all noticeably cleaner and nicer than the food vendors on the concourse, and Roland noted the conspicuous absence of shuffle-footed Venusian laborers winding through the halls leading to each restaurant. Cummings led him up to a place with a bright green holographic sign blinking "McAlpine's" and flashing an animated workman swinging a pickaxe. "In here, Corporal. Best lunch in The Colander and plenty of privacy to boot."

Roland stooped through the door and clumped into the restaurant. It was easily the nicest and cleanest place he had seen in The Colander so far. Tables were metal painted to look like wood, and the bar along the back wall was smooth and polished stainless steel. The afternoon crowd was thin. A few older men sat at the bar grumbling to each other and drinking amber liquid from faux-crystal glasses. At one table a couple of women sat talking loudly, cackling like witches as a raucous liquid lunch trespassed into the mid-afternoon hours.

Roland and the sergeant found a booth near the back. The bench looked like it had a reasonable chance of supporting his weight, so he sat. The table had to be pushed back to give him some more room, but this proved to be no challenge, either. Cummings settled in across from him.

"What's on your mind, Corporal?"

"This place secure?"

"Absolutely," Cummings said with confidence. "Bob McAlpine ain't going to let any morlocks in here."

"Morlocks?" The reference confused Roland.

"You know," Cummings said with a sideways wink, "...morlocks."

Roland did not know. This was written plainly across his face. Cummings sighed. "You have been gone a while. I am referring to those lesser inhabitants here who live in dark places and don't get out much. Like in that old book about the time machine."

"Ahhhhh." Comprehension came, and disgust followed it. "I get it. You know, in that story the Morlocks eat the surface dwellers."

"They do? Huh. Weird book." Apparently, Sergeant Cummings was not big on irony. He dismissed the cognitive dissonance with a wave of his hand and pushed ahead. "Look, the Red Hats have a lot of support here in The Colander. So nicer places like this don't let any of the laborers or union guys in because they don't get along with all the, uh... 'surface dwellers,' if you get my meaning. Folks need a safe place to eat, y'know. Bob McAlpine has some connections, so the Hats leave this place alone. Plus, hitting the restaurant district is bad for everybody, even them. It's safe and quiet enough here."

The big fixer began to assemble the pieces of the puzzle. "I see. He keeps the undesirables out and pays off the Hats to prevent reprisals."

Cummings winced, "We try not to say it that way, Corporal."

Roland let it drop. Sociological debate was one of his least favorite things. In truth, hearing Cummings casually dismiss a whole class of people as monsters from an old story was putting him in the kind of mood that usually resulted in a fatality. Since that would not be helpful to his current mission, prudence compelled him to give the Sergeant a pass this time.

"Fine. What I need to talk to you about is something I noticed down below the refractory level."

"You went all the way done there by yourself?"

"I brought the contractor, too."

Cummings' eyes widened, "Oh yeah. Her."

"Anyway," Roland's reservoir of social grace was dangerously low at this point. "We noticed at least three Shikomi Heavy Industries Kano-type armatures down there."

"Yeah?" The sergeant's response clearly indicated that he did not understand.

"That doesn't seem weird to you? A couple of hot-rod armatures walking around with bargain-basement Erberhaus gear?"

The waitress showed up at this moment, and Cummings was granted a moment to consider his answer while lunch orders were recorded. When the pretty redhead had left the table, he turned back to Roland wearing an expression of curiosity and confusion. "We get a whole lot of armatures down there, Corporal. Most of us don't really pay attention as long as the paperwork is in order. I don't remember any Kanos coming through, but I don't work every shift, either."

Something about his answer did not ring as entirely truthful. It felt like Cummings was dodging the question rather than answering it. Roland tried very hard to keep the frown from his face. "But their paperwork had to be in order, right? To get armatures down there, I mean."

It was obvious Cummings did not like the direction the conversation was going. The man was making an effort to appear nonchalant, but he was shifting in his seat and his eyes had starting darting around with a furtive, nervous twitch. It was a behavior Roland had seen in a thousand street-level hoods and hustlers. The man was lying and Roland knew it.

"Well, yeah. The forms have gotta be straight, because the RUC keeps track of all armatures in The Colander."

Roland now suspected that this was not the case. He lived in one of the busiest and most profitable smuggling hubs in known space, and he knew how contraband moved. He was not a subtle man, and being circumspect was not his style. "Jesus Christ, Cummings. How many of these things are getting by you guys?"

"What?"

"Sergeant, don't pull my chain. I'm on the clock, here, and this ain't my first rodeo. I don't really give a fuck what side hustle you guys are running, I just need to know who is bringing in those Kanos."

Cummings, sweating openly now, refused to let go of his poorly constructed veneer. "What do you mean, Corporal?"

Roland heaved a mighty sigh. He hated this part. The part where the stupid hood pretended that Roland was more stupid than he was, necessitating an adjustment in their operating dynamic. It was wasted time really. Once the strategic situation changed, a smart soldier adapted to it. Doubling down on a losing strategy only made you lose faster and harder. Roland was now nearly one-hundred percent certain that the RUC was taking bribes to allow certain things through with minimal scrutiny or none at all. It was common knowledge Venus was a shit posting, and the men and women who found themselves assigned to the RUC were usually there as a punishment for multiple screw ups. It stood to reason that Sergeant Cummings was a multiple-offense screw-up. None of these conclusions were the result of advanced intelligence or preternatural intuition. It was very basic logic and not at all complicated. The sweating non-com before him was a living, trembling testimony to the temerity of tiny minds.

"Sergeant?"

"Yeah?"

"How many exemptions do I carry?"

"Like, forty, I think?"

"How were those designated?"

"Mostly classified," Cummings seemed alternately confused and nervous. This was Roland's goal.

"Do you think that the UEDF sent me here with a classified contractor and three dozen top-secret exemptions to bust your little smuggling racket?"

"I don't really know what..."

Roland cut him off. "I have infiltrated the refractory level already, smacked around two of Craddock's thugs, and I have a machine gun big enough to drop a tank strapped to me right now." He leaned forward, letting his physical presence dominate the space between them. "I am not the guy you send to ferret out greedy non-coms at a border station, Sergeant. That's like killing an ant with a grenade. You understand?"

Cummings nodded. His head jerked up and down, as if his brain had forgotten how to move his muscles properly.

"I need to know who is sending million-credit muscle to the Red Hats, Cummings. There are two ways for me to acquire this information right now. One of them involves you enjoying a lengthy stay in Leavenworth, the other does not. Pick one."

Sergeant Cummings seemed to deflate in his seat, shrinking two sizes in as many seconds. "We don't know."

Roland raised an eyebrow. "You don't know?"

Cummings rested his head in his hands and rubbed his face wearily. "We don't know who sent the Kanos. Not really, anyway. It's all coded transfers. They don't even use credits. It's all back-channel transactions using a dozen different currencies. Even we get our kickbacks in Markers, not creds."

That revelation increased the intensity or the big man's frown by several degrees. "You take Markers? That is seriously volatile shit, Cummings."

"Most of the guys are gamblers anyway," he said back with a shrug. "Markers are like lottery tickets to us. They might be worth ten creds today, or a thousand tomorrow."

"So you guys are taking bribes in highly unstable pseudo-currency from unknown sources, and none of you thought maybe it would be a good idea to check on it?"

The sergeant's crestfallen face indicated quite clearly that this was in fact the case. Roland's sneer hit the browbeaten man like a cudgel. Cummings responded with all the conviction of a whipped dog. "It fucking sucks here, Corporal. We all just want to leave and go home. The pay is shit, the work is shit, the booze is shit, and it's a million goddamn degrees all the time. Some mystery jerk shows up with the chance for a big payout, and all he wants is to get some basic items inside without a hassle? Most of us are going to go for it. It ain't even technically contraband. No guns or drugs or nothing. Just some armatures, a couple of operatives that scanned clean anyway, and some communications gear that isn't even illegal."

"You got a list?"

Cummings turned white when he realized what Roland was asking. "You can't be serious, man."

"Do I look like the kind of guy that makes jokes?"

"You don't understand. These guys'll kill us. We aren't stupid..."

Roland doubted that statement very much, but he abstained from commenting.

"...we know this is some sort of crazy Red Hat shake up. Some weird shit is going down with Craddock and Hardesty. If you shake this tree, we could all get killed!"

Roland was not a sympathetic person. "Shouldn't have climbed the tree, then. You get me everything you have, and I'll go do my job. I may even tell the UEDF that instead of taking bribes and facilitating the operations of terrorists, you were gathering all this intel on your own. That's the kind of initiative that can make a career, Sergeant."

Roland was playing the man's greed and stupidity simultaneously. It seemed to be a winning formula, as demonstrated by a noticeable shift in demeanor from abject terror to deep thought. The possibility of career advancement and reassignment was definitely attractive to the corrupt soldier. Naturally, Cummings' career would not survive this operation under any circumstances. Roland would see to that personally. Whether or not Cummings himself survived was still very much a nebulous quantity at this point, such was the big man's disgust. The sergeant did not need to know that part.

"So you need what? Transaction records? Not much to work with there. No banks, no brokers. Just Markers shifting through anonymous digital exchanges. I can get you scans, points of entry, and ship manifests, though. We got IDs on the pilots and what we think are a couple of intelligence assets, but I'd bet you a million credits their all spoofed anyway."

"What about equipment?"

"Yeah, we got all that info somewhere. None of it was really interesting stuff. High-end communications gear, mostly. One big shipment of construction 'bots."

"Somebody going to build something?"

Cummings shook his head. "Probably a small dome to hide their communications gear in. It ain't illegal to put up a dome outside of Free Venus. Criminal types do it all the time. This rock is a great place to hide shit because looking for anything out there is a pain in the ass. Most of us figured a rival organization was setting up a spying ring to get at the Red Hats. Might even be the Free Venus folks from Caelestus. Most of those guys hate the Hats, but it's too politically dangerous to say it out loud."

"You'd think they'd at least bring you guys in on that kind of op," Roland speculated.

"They don't trust us." Cummings sounded miffed by this, as if his own actions were not directly responsible for the offending sentiment. This was not a man who understood or appreciated irony.

"Imagine that," Roland said without inflection. "Get me that info. I'll come by tomorrow to pick it up." The big fixer stood, lunch all but forgotten. His hunger was insufficient to overcome his antipathy to the thought of sharing a meal with the dirty official. Dropping enough hard cred chits to the table to cover the ordered food, he gave the man a scowl conveying levels of threat and menace sufficient to cow the hardest of men. "Be thorough, Sergeant. A guy might get suspicious of something important got left out."

"Of course, Corporal," Cummings responded. "Anything to help out the Expeditionary Force."

"Right," Roland grumbled back. He did not sound convinced.

157

Chapter Twenty

The ride to Caelestus was uneventful. Lucia booked a first-class seat on a pogo plane and enjoyed real air conditioning for the first time since landing on Venus. If it had not felt so wonderful, the pure pleasure of it would have embarrassed her. The rest of the team would be sweating it out in The Colander while she spent the day in relative luxury. The pogo would rocket them above Venus's roiling yellow atmosphere where it would traverse the several hundred miles between The Colander and the Capitol city far above the satanic heat and corrosive acid. After a graceful arc, the narrow vessel would descend like a lawn dart over the shining silver of the Caelestus city dome before depositing itself neatly on a pad by the main intake doors.

Her first-class ticket ensured a minimum of hassle with intake, which was most of the justification she had posited for the expense. The decadent comfort of a seventy-degree cabin with a comfortable acceleration couch was entirely incidental. After a gentle touchdown, the concierge escorted her from the G-Pod and led her to the first-class tunnel. Soft music played as she walked down the clean white corridor, and Lucia settled into the stream of well-to-do business folk and their retinues as they shuffled in a slow-moving river to the main dome of Venus Caelestus.

Having been to and experienced The Quad, and hearing the stories of Caelestus from Manny and Ellie Connelly, Lucia had expected something like Uptown New Boston. She had anticipated bright whites, clean streets, shining towers and antiseptic surfaces. The first thing Lucia noticed was that while Venus Caelestus was entire orders of magnitude cleaner than anywhere in The Colander, it was no Uptown. The dome's origin as industrial housing and administrative offices for the mining corporations was writ large in the slab-gray architecture and ugly rows of cool white lights. The streets were clean, the people well-dressed. The veneer of class was thin at best, however. Though arranged neatly and kept free of grime, there was no style or artistry to the layout or the edifices themselves. It reminded Lucia of Enterprise Station, with every storefront looking more or less identical. There was no sky above, only a troffered ceiling housing the simple lights. There was no ground below, just metal decking arranged in a manner reminiscent of a city street. To her sides, illuminated signage on the front of gray metal walls indicated the goods and services available beyond the equally unimpressive doors. It felt to Lucia like a large indoor shopping mall constructed to be evocative of a bustling city, but it lacked the requisite charm of either.

All things considered, it was clean and it was comfortable. For this Lucia was eternally grateful. She could forgive the capital city virtually any sin because it was cool and the air did not smell of brimstone. She stepped from transit station into the first commercial area, and paused a moment to assess her surroundings with a more critical eye before stalking out into the street. She was surrounded by the bustle of a busy commercial sector, mostly people in varying states of obliviousness plodding to and from appointments, deliveries, and the other sundry tasks of a Venusian workday.

She quickly identified the local constabulary, conspicuous in bright red uniforms. The police in Caelestus wore light armor and carried small bullpup-style bead rifles in reasonable calibers. The frangible ceramic beads were an obvious choice for working in a crowded metal bowl filled with innocent bystanders. As dangerous as rebounding projectiles might be, overpenetration was even more frightening. When the air outside was doing its level best to kill you, wise municipalities took care not to use munitions that might punch holes in the skin of the dome. Manny had bet her a week's pay she would not see a single bead gun over 8mm and no flechettes of any kind in Caelestus. She was far too intelligent to take that bet.

Her route took her directly out of the mass transit zone and in short order brought her to a more sedate business district. The closer she walked to the center of the dome, the higher the building blocks could be stacked. The dull silver and slate gray towers of the central district rose almost to the top of the arc, daring the fiery acid tears of Venus to touch their roofs. The height gave each an oppressive, almost imperial aspect. They were no more ornate nor visually appealing than the smaller blocks, but they dwarfed the surrounding areas with a glowering superiority.

Shorter buildings competed for attention with these looming titans by adding garish multi-hued holographic displays and animated billboards. Turning a corner, Lucia found herself witness to a pitched battle between armature companies. Erberhaus and AutoCat jumbo displays squared off against each other in a wide quadrangle before her. Each well-lit sixty-foot panel showed competing scripted commercial propaganda at the mostly-uninterested men and women shuffling about. Unperturbed, the marketing battle played out in three startling dimensions with production values that would shame the big Holovid studios. Lucia still knew very little about armatures, but as far as she could tell the Erberhaus brand was promising to turn regular dim-witted laborers into towering steel super men who could outwork entire gangs of the competition. The AutoCat holo was more nuanced, bragging about how efficient and specialized their line of products was, and spending extra time lauding the modular nature of their frames.

While she may not have been an expert on cyborg armatures, Lucia was an expert on branding and marketing. She recognized the waltz both companies were dancing. Erberhaus was playing the low cost and good reliability of their products against the more expensive and more sophisticated products from AutoCat. AutoCat had obviously recognized that the declining economic fortunes of Venusian mining concerns favored the Erberhaus business model. Rather than give up, they either located or created a niche where their models were worth the increase in costs. She tipped an imaginary hat to the ingenuity and determination of AutoCat's local sales VP. She respected a good executive.

She passed through the wide square, otherwise ignoring the flashing holograms and the chattering people walking beneath them. She passed between the Erberhaus building and its neighbor. She did not bother to read what the animated sign had to say about what services were available within. On the other side, the alley opened up into another quadrangle. Here she found her destination. One whole side of the square was completely taken up by the lavish lobby of a luxury hotel. Where other buildings in Caelestus were formless gray blocks, this one broke the mold. The main frontage had been replaced with an elaborate glass foyer, trimmed in faux brass and gilt. The carpets, easily visible through the clear panels, was a rich wine red and (as far as Lucia could tell) spotless.

A doorman in archaic livery stood by the ornate sliding doors. His purpose all but superfluous in an age of automatic doors, the man stood as a stoic anachronism. A grim-faced callback to the opulence of a distant land and a bygone century. Lucia wrinkled her nose at the affront to her intelligence. It would be a sad person indeed who was impressed by such vulgar excess. It stank of Pops Winter and the Combine to her, and this was offensive on a very primal level.

That man is a message to everybody who sees him. The thought was derisive to the point of anger. *He exists to tell everyone walking by that this hotel can afford to arrange people like furniture.*

Uncharitable musings notwithstanding, Lucia had a job to do, so she put her irritation aside to do it. She walked past the doorman without looking at him, and clear door panel slid to the side on silent glides. The doorman never moved, and the tangible affirmation of how superfluous he was only added to her irritation.

She stalked across the lobby, making a conscious effort not to move so quickly as to call attention to herself. It could be difficult to manage her speed before, and the constant adjustments she had been undergoing made regulating even harder. This hotel did not have guests check in at the front desk. That would be far too plebeian. A concierge met her as she approached the impressive imitation-oak desk, and inquired politely about her stay and any business she might have had on the premises. Lucia met the blank-faced woman with her own measured stare.

"I have an appointment with a guest. The nature of which is private."

"Naturally." The blue-haired concierge's expression was cold. "If you tell me suite I will call ahead to tell your party that you have arrived."

"Eleven forty-one. Tell them Ms. Ribiero is on her way up." Lucia turned and walked past the concierge, who was momentarily surprised by her speed. The blue-haired woman recovered quickly though, and within a few steps caught up to her fleeing charge and blurted, "Wait! You can't just..."

Lucia whirled on the woman, who crashed into the athletic brunette and dropped her DataPad. Lucia was a veteran of thousand clashes with hotel concierges. Her battles also included pushy waiters, arrogant maître d's, snooty valets, and more than one power-mad hotel manager. Her tone cut through the veneer of authority worn by the concierge like a straight razor through whipped cream.

"I can 'just,' and I am going to 'just.' I did not ride in a shuttle for thirty hours to land on this shit-smelling hell-hole to discuss with *you* what I can and cannot do. Make your calls and run along. I have business here and I'd prefer to get it done before the stink of this planet attaches to me permanently and I have to burn my clothes." Again, she whipped around and stalked away from the sputtering woman.

Lucia knew she had left the concierge in an unwinnable position. If Lucia was lying about having an appointment, then she had to be stopped. On the other hand, if she did have an appointment then further harassing her might mean alienating a rich customer. The beleaguered employee rapidly dialed suite 1141 and waited for confirmation of the appointment with the kind of fear only middle managers can ever truly experience. The line crackled to life and the bored man at the other end confirmed that Ms. Ribiero did indeed have an appointment and to show her right up. Her sigh of relief was audible at ten paces and she clicked the line closed. She had no idea what business the bitchy woman had up in the penthouse level. Most of the women who went up there were a very different species of professional woman. Naturally, she did not care either. Now that her job was not on the line, she could go back to watching the lobby and intercepting paparazzi, con men, and other undesirables.

Lucia's indifference to the concierge mirrored the concierge's indifference to her. She had needed to clear the lobby fast, and that was the genesis of her brusque demeanor. Manny's camera blackout device had very limited range and duration, and she was certain she had made it across the lobby in time to avoid facial recognition. Choosing her for this part of the op had been a measured risk. This sort of infiltration was very much Manny's skill set. Caelestus was a modern city however, and the near ubiquity of cameras and facial recognition gear in the commercial zones made using him here very risky. If Lucia got scanned in this hotel, they would get the ID of a New Boston beverage company executive. They would rather not be

162

identified at all, but Lucia's face was the one least likely to generate undue suspicion.

When the elevator opened to the eleventh-floor lobby, Lucia stepped out onto smooth white tiles. A receptionist sat in bored belligerence at a white desk facing the elevators. Lucia walked up the bald man, who looked at her through the tops of his eyes and never paused in filing his nails.

When it became obvious that the beam of pure disdain he was sending her way was not going to unseat the woman, he sighed and droned, "Do you have an appointment?"

"Do I look like a walk-in?" Lucia beamed her own look back, a look that was both evocative and eloquent. The man, who Lucia could see from his name tag was called 'Rick,' seemed to accept this response as an indicator Lucia was a kindred soul.

Green eyes rolled. "Honey, we get all kinds up here. Who are you here to see?"

"Hardesty."

If possible, the eyes rolled even harder. "You're here for Link? Girl, your agency is in for some trouble now. Oh my god. You are so not his type."

In spite of herself, Lucia was starting to like this guy. His honesty was almost refreshing. Hanging out with Docksiders was definitely changing her. "It's not that kind of appointment."

"Oh? Good for you! Ol' Linky is going to try to make it one. Just warning you."

Lucia laughed. "I'm not worried. You've seen one horndog you've seen them all."

"Tell it," he said with exaggerated enthusiasm.

"Does Hardesty get a lot of female appointments?"

Manny had warned her that chatty employees were great sources of intel. She decided to invest a little time with Rick the receptionist just see what she could pull from him.

"Sure does. And don't get me wrong, miss, they are usually half your age and ah... twice your *size*, if you get me?" Rick's hands hovered over his chest, belaboring his obvious meaning.

Lucia sighed. "Ain't that always the way with men? Half your age and twice the rack."

"Trust me, girl, you're dodging a bullet. None of his other appointments ever leave happy."

"Well, I suppose I'll just have to muddle through without that experience." She gave Rick a warm look. "Want to tell him I'm here?"

"Still a chance to run, girl."

"I like you, Rick. How'd you get stuck with this gig?"

The man turned in his chair to get a better look at her. "None of the girls could stand working with him, and I don't get distracted by the endless parade of hot young prostitutes. It's a self-discipline thing, you know."

"I've known you two minutes and I can already tell you are a rock, Rick."

"Oh hush. Don't be catty. Anyway, I'll just go ahead and buzz you in. Head on over." He pointed to a door behind his kiosk. "He's waiting for you..."

Lucia rolled her eyes at the theatricality of his ominous tone. "Thank you, Rick."

"Don't thank me until you are out of here, miss."

Chapter Twenty-One

The door buzzer warned Hardesty that his appointment had arrived. He sighed and downed the last of his whiskey, then quickly popped a mint into his mouth to hide the smell of booze on his breath. It would not do to have a potential booze vendor catch him drinking this early in the day. The woman who walked into his office was rather good-looking. Not his usual preference, obviously, but she had a terrific body and that air of easy sophistication women get as they age and figure out exactly what they want and how to get it. This was a woman who got what she wanted, Hardesty would have bet his life on that. She was wearing black slacks, blue shirt, and a short black jacket. All were tailored to show off her shape without being tawdry. This did not stop Lincoln Hardesty from allowing his appreciation of such to delve deeply into the realm of the tawdry, anyway. That was just his nature and he was disinclined to change now. These were expensive clothes, yet sedate all the same. The long-faced man silently wished a little more skin was showing, but he supposed that this was not that kind of woman.

He took all of this in at a glance, and simply enjoyed watching her walk across his office. He liked what he saw. She was graceful, athletic. Her walk was a cross between a panther stalking its prey and a gazelle poised to leap. Something about it was strange, though. It had a bounce, a twitch in the stride that put him off. It was not a skip or a problem with the gait itself, rather it was almost too fast and too light to be human. It bothered him that he could not place it. It did not appear likely he would ever figure it out, either. Focusing on her walk was difficult, because so many other more interesting things in those pants kept interrupting his observations.

"Mr. Hardesty," she opened with a smile as she reached his desk, "thank you for seeing me today."

He stood and shook the proffered hand. It was small and warm, though in no way delicate. Her grip was firm and strong, and she met his gaze evenly. *This is one tough broad.* The thought was complimentary. *I bet she doesn't take shit from anybody in the boardroom.* Lincoln liked toughness in people. Not so much in women, but he could make an exception in this case. *Or the bedroom, either, I'd bet.*

He leered back at her. "My pleasure, Ms. Ribiero. Please, have a seat." The woman slid over to a chair in front of his desk and descended into it. Again, Hardesty was disconcerted by the way she moved. It was both fast and precise, yet natural and graceful as well. He wondered if she was a dancer. "Now what can me and my people do for you today? It's not every day that Earthside vendors come out to Venus. We haven't been that interesting a marketplace since the gates opened up."

This was an understatement. With far more attractive planets available for mining on the other sides of Anson Gates, the Venusian economy was not exactly booming.

The woman's face never lost its composure, "Well, Mr. Hardesty, I must admit that I am here on a completely different piece of business."

"Really? I had assumed this was about beverage distribution contracts." Hardesty's people had done their level best to discern the woman's origins when she had requested the meeting. He was not embarrassed to admit being somewhat pleased to find out she had ties to alcohol distribution. Quality booze was nearly nonexistent on Venus. Now he was just concerned.

"I'm afraid not, Mr. Hardesty." She shifted in her chair to lean forward. "I am currently retained by the Dockside Trade Association. I wanted to talk to you about the relationship between the Dockside operations and your operations here on Venus."

The man leaned back at this, and he allowed a long pause before responding. "I see. I don't really believe in coincidence, Ms. Ribiero, and there seems to be quite a few Dockside professionals crawling around Venus these days."

"Well, Mr. Hardesty. There have been quite a few Venusians in Dockside lately. Some of the guilds are nervous about that. I'm here to help facilitate our various interactions in a manner the benefits both."

Hardesty did not like this conversation. He elected to deflect, if only to buy some time to sort it all out. "I don't currently have any interactions with New Boston, Ms. Ribiero. I'm a little confused as to why you are here to talk to me."

The woman's face took on a condescending, almost maternal, expression. "Oh. Lincoln, I think we are well beyond that part of the dance. We can try to impress each other with how much we do and do not know, or we can skip it and get right to business. I'm fine either way."

His long face twisted into a scowl, Hardesty conceded the point. "Fine, then, Lucia. Let's talk business, then. Let me kill the cameras first." He reached for a remote on his desk, then frowned when he saw the display.

The woman sighed, "They are off already, Lincoln."

Hardesty blinked at his remote, not quite understanding. He poked it with a long finger, grimacing in confusion, then finally comprehending. His eyes went back to the woman seated across from him. "Nice trick, lady. Got any more?"

"I don't do tricks, Lincoln."

"Me neither. Let's keep it that way, okay? A guy could get ideas about your intentions if you start jamming his security measures."

A delicate finger moved a magenta lock of hair off her forehead. "What security measures?"

Hardesty looked back down at the remote again, and this time a touch of panic strained the lines of his face. He swiped through screens, poked angrily at buttons, then threw the device into a waiting recycler in disgust. His gaze returned to the woman, and it took all of his self-control not to punch her right in her pretty mouth. Then he relaxed, and let a genuine chuckle burble past his lips.

"All right, Lucia. Your point is well taken. I get it: you got some slick shit going on."

"A girl can never be too careful," she replied, letting sarcasm color her words. "A man in your position might think ringing for some goons would improve their position in negotiations. I'd rather the conversation be kept civil and private. This way it will be."

"Right," Hardesty sighed. He decided this was the time to assert himself. It was probably a good idea to establish his stance before this chick pulled any more stunts. He reached into his desk and pulled out a large bead pistol. He slapped it down on the desk with a thud, and leaned forward to give Lucia a glare. "How's my position look now?"

The woman did not flinch. Her eyes darted to it for an instant, flicking across the weapon in an appraising look and nothing more. "If it makes you feel better, I am okay with that," she said with a dismissive wave of her hand for the gun.

"Well, aren't you ever the magnanimous one?" Lincoln leaned back, leaving the gun atop his desk in front of him. "So what do we have here? A big goon from Dockside slapping around Craddock's boys over at The Colander, and a pretty lady in my office with a bunch of high-tech jamming gear. What's a guy supposed to make of that scene?"

"Well, Lincoln," she began, "The Dockside crews are somewhat perturbed at the indiscriminate nature of Venusian operations in their territory. You and I may be businessmen, Lincoln, but these are not. Six months ago they were all just hoods and mobsters. It's the sort of thing the crews take very personally."

"That's what the other guy told Craddock, too. At least your message is consistent."

"Mr. Craddock was not receptive to that discussion, as I'm sure you know."

Hardesty guffawed. "Craddock is not the kind of guy who responds well to being told what to do." Hardesty raised an eyebrow, "Can I assume you understand the nature of Craddock's problem?"

Lucia nodded. "You don't have to be coy. The Red Hats have a runaway, and they went after him."

Hardesty ducked his head in affirmation. "That's about the size of it. I assume you already know that while I am sympathetic to their cause, I am not a Red Hat myself."

"I do. I also know that Craddock receives most of his materiel support through you. Obviously, no one in Dockside has any interest in your smuggling operations here on Venus. However it seems there is a lot of concern that perhaps Craddock's zeal to bring this runner in is the result of pressure from you."

The air in the room, already strained, began to thicken with tension. Lucia was dancing very close to the heart of the matter, and Hardesty was not foolish enough to underestimate her. The tall man folded his hands on his desk, fingers laced to keep them from

168

shaking or balling into fists. His response was measured, cordial even. "Now why would anyone think that?"

It was a loaded question. Her answer would reveal much about how well she understood the situation and how badly this ship was leaking. Her response was every bit as cordial as his question had been. "Because Manuel Richardson works for me, Lincoln."

The tall, long-faced man seated at the desk felt his stomach lurch. If Manny worked for her, and she worked with the big hitter that was bothering Craddock, then he was in a very precarious situation, indeed.

"So that little piece of shit works for you, huh?"

"He does."

"That feels real damn convenient. I guess the big fucker is the one who put Grimes into a shipping container and sent him back?" he did not wait for an answer. "Pissing off Grimes was a bad call, Lucia. He is a bad, bad, man." He continued, uninterested in her response. "What you and I have here is an impasse, then. Manny betrayed the Red Hats. They have rules about that."

"He also has extensive knowledge of your dealings with the Red Hats, Lincoln. Not to mention your other dealings." That was a shot in the dark, but it must have landed close to the mark. Hardesty's frown deepened.

"This is starting to feel like less of a negotiation and more like shakedown, Lucia. I don't respond well to threats."

"What do you respond to then? I am here to fix the issue, not pick a fight." There was no lie in her voice. Hardesty was confident that this part was actually true. All the same, he could not afford to move on this.

"We need that kid."

"You can't have him."

In that moment a thing occurred to Lincoln Hardesty. *If she knew what it was Manny has on me, then she'd already know I can't afford to let him go, and why.* A slow, ursine grin began to crease his face. *She doesn't know, and that means Manny doesn't know.*

He was safe, for the moment. The relief at this revelation washed over him like a cool summer breeze. After it passed, he turned his attention back to dealing with the pushy woman across from him.

"Then we need to find a way to ensure he is otherwise—" Hardesty stumbled here, words escaping him, "—rendered harmless." It was weak, but he needed her to believe there was a chance to win this.

"He's already harmless, Lincoln. He has had no interest or involvement in Venus or anything that goes on here for some time."

Hardesty tried to point her suspicions away from himself. "I could be convinced of that. We both know the kid can probably cause a lot of problems for me." He shrugged. "As long as he is quiet I suppose I can be reasonable. Unfortunately, Craddock doesn't see it that way. And Al calls all the shots from the Red Hats' standpoint." He felt the faintest pang of guilt for throwing his oldest friend under the bus, even though none of this would matter in three weeks either way. He just needed to buy some time.

Her disdain for his attempt at subterfuge was rather apparent in her reply. "I am not here to talk to Craddock. I'm here talking to you. I am trying to help you understand that we know your stake in this fight is larger than you are pretending it is. Please try to work with me, here. Before something gets out that could damage your interests."

Hardesty switched tactics, his voice going rough with malice. "Lady, if you knew shit about my stake in this, then you wouldn't be here talking to me. You'd have dumped it on me and had me by the balls. But you don't have me by the balls, do you?" He instantly regretted saying this. It gave too much away. He indulged a desperate hope the woman had not picked up on that. Then his hope died.

"Maybe I don't. Yet. At least now I know where to look, though." She winked at him. "Thanks for that."

In a flash, anger overtook Hardesty's better judgment. His hand went to the gun still sitting on his desk, a mute witness to the drama playing out above. The weapon came up and he leveled it at her face. "I told you I could be reasonable. I told you to deal with Craddock. Instead of working with me, you want to sit here and bandy veiled threats around? What? You've got some nice tech so you think you can fuck with me? Bad call. You are not on Earth, Ms. Ribiero. This is Venus. This is my town and my planet. Nobody fucks with me here. You hear me?"

"Oh, I hear you, Lincoln." Her voice was cold, passionless. It was neither angry nor afraid. "How is Grimes doing, by the way?"

The question confused Hardesty. "What?"

170

A starburst of agony exploded in the bones of his hand. The gun tumbled from limp fingers even as he opened his mouth to yelp in pain. The weapon never landed, for the woman who had been quietly seated only a fraction of a second earlier caught it easily in her right hand as it fell. Her left hand locked onto the lapel of Hardesty's suit and dragged his body halfway across the shining surface of his desk. In front of his face, she flipped his gun to her palm and dropped the magazine to the desk with a clatter. Then, still using only one hand, she turned the weapon on its side and released the receiver from the frame. What had once been an expensive handgun tumbled to the floor as three separate pieces. She dragged the man forward to growl into his ear.

"I'm the one who put Grimes in the box, Lincoln."

That started to make a lot of sense in his mind as Hardesty felt the sickening weightlessness of his feet leaving the floor. With terrifying strength, Lucia secured a grip on both his lapels and hauled him the rest of the way over his desk. The one-hundred and seventy-pound man had just enough time for a grunt of surprise before crashing to the carpet of his office in a tangle of limbs and tailored linen.

He was not stupid, and he determined within the opening seconds of this exchange that he was completely outmatched. He rolled to his back with hands outstretched, waving a transparent gesture of surrender.

"Holy shit, Lady! Okay! Okay! I'm done!"

The woman seemed satisfied with this, and her assault ceased. Cradling his bruised hand and bleeding dignity, Hardesty clambered to his feet and burned Lucia with an angry glare. She ignored it.

"I think we are done for today, Lincoln. Think about what I've said and we can talk again. Soon."

"Oh yeah. I'll be seeing you around, Ms. Ribiero." There was an obvious threat in his tone, and he did not care if she caught it or not. "Now why don't you go ahead and get the fuck out of my office?"

She laughed at him. It was a musical and lyrical sound, flush with sincerity and good humor. "Don't be such a grouch, Lincoln. At least you aren't dealing with my partner." With a sarcastic wave, she turned her back on him and walked to the door.

The view of her posterior, which had so delighted him earlier, was   suddenly   far   less   appealing   now.

Chapter Twenty-Two

T he room was very dark.

There were noises in the room. The sound of monitors buzzing was a droning hum perforated by the rhythmic beeping of some obscure medical device. Killam Grimes knew he was in an infirmary. Even if it did not have all the right sounds and smells, he had woken briefly when they brought him in and he had seen it.

He hated infirmaries. Infirmaries were a place of weakness, and he refused to be weak.

He was not sleeping. He had slept enough in the packing crate. He sat on his bed in the dark, legs folded underneath him in the way of the old masters. His spine was erect, chin thrust forward, eyes closed. He concentrated on his breathing, crafting each inhalation until he was satisfied with its perfection and then working on the subsequent exhalation. It took far more focus to breathe correctly than most people ever realized, and the work of executing a perfect breath calmed and emptied his mind of extraneous thoughts.

And Killam Grimes had far too many of those to contend with.

His rage and despair at his failure was an all-consuming thing. The deaths of his brothers haunted him. Two whole teams gone, and the target still lived. It was unbearable. He knew why they had failed in intricate detail. He had cataloged every mistake, every act of hubris, every ill-conceived conceit. Most of the responsibility had fallen squarely on him, and he endeavored to bear the burden of this in a manner befitting his position. He was the ringer, the senior operative. The others had looked up to him and sought to imitate his example, and the template he had given them was deeply flawed. His sadness threatened the discipline of his craft, and thus it had to be expunged.

The masters taught that dwelling on mistakes was poison. To languish in self-reproach was a prophecy, a promise of future failure for those too weak to overcome it. There was no such thing as failure: you either succeeded or you learned something in the attempt. Such was the path to true mastery of craft. If he was to right this wrong, Killam Grimes would need to heed the lessons of history's greatest teacher, and learn from his mistakes.

When his mind was truly calm, he could achieve *mushin,* the state of "no mind." While often couched in mystical terms of vaguely romantic martial arts fantasy, to the experienced fighter it simply meant that Killam Grimes was attempting to divorce his perceptions from the contaminating influence of his own ego. Ego was the enemy of wisdom. Ego told you that it was it was not your fault you lost. Ego told you that the other guy cheated. Ego made excuses for your mistakes.

Without ego, Killam could approach the operations in Dockside objectively, like a machine. He would observe each step like a drone hovering over the action, a dead thing silently recording information for later review.

The first operation failed for two very important reasons. First, they had not properly reconnoitered the big fixer. This was a failure born of repetition. The Balisongs had killed so many people over the years that they had forgotten that battle is unpredictable. They should have stalked for much longer while they still had the element of surprise.

Second, they had targeted the fixer first. Assuming he would be the greater threat to the overall operation, a decision was made to bring him down prior to moving on Richardson. Grimes had not been present for that choice. It pleased him to know this particular fault was not his.

His master's words breached his mediations. *The fault for a mistake is irrelevant.*

He stopped. Relaxed. He returned his focus to breathing. He had lost his *mushin.* The lapse frustrated him. It had been too long since he had returned to his lessons. Ego was an insidious thing, indeed.

When he had found it again, he returned his thoughts to the mission. The second operation failed because of haste. Having been exposed by the first attempt, the pressure on the team to complete the objective and get out of increasingly hostile territory had been enormous. Operating in Dockside was more difficult than anything they had attempted in the past. The Docksiders were insular and tribal. The Balisongs were outsiders and enemies there, and simply surviving undetected was a trial. It forced the team into a level of haste that ended up being catastrophic. They substituted brute force for careful planning, and his brothers died as a result.

Both missions had one central theme in their respective failures. The Balisongs had lost their way. They had forgotten who and what they were. They had attacked the enemy like a small special forces unit. This was a failure caused by pride. The hubris was insidious because it was born in a very honest place. Their training was superb, their skills universally unmatched. There was no fault of ego in this assessment either. An objective observer would agree to that much without question. Where they had been led astray was quite obvious, though. The Balisongs were *assassins,* not soldiers. The mission was not to search and destroy, it was to eliminate one liability. Through the clear lens of hindsight, Killam Grimes could see several better ways to achieve mission success than what they had ultimately attempted. Haste and arrogance had blinded him to any of these paths. The fierce confidence of his brotherhood proved to be a double-edged sword, more dangerous to their own interests than their foes.

Grimes held his *mushin* as his ego thrashed against the internal rebuke it was receiving. He was merciless with it.

We failed because I wanted to fight. I thought I was unbeatable. I thought our team was unbeatable. I forgot the lessons of my teachers and I have shamed our brotherhood with my arrogance.

This was not a man who was going to let that stand.

I must kill this traitor, and I must do it like a Balisong. No fighting, no duels of honor. The Balisong is a hidden blade. It deceives before it cuts. The enemy is dead before it ever perceives the danger. That is our way, and I will not stray from the path again.

From *mushin,* Killam shifted to *zanshin,* the "final" or "remaining" mind. This was a state of relaxed awareness and singular focus. In *zanshin,* Killam could direct all his mental energies to the task at hand without any distractions. He closed his perceptions to anything that did not serve the goal of killing Manuel Richardson. It was the kind of commitment required to thrust a blade past another man's defenses. It was the focused intensity it took to squeeze off a rifle shot at something two miles away without missing. It was the pointed, steel-sharp resolve that allowed a man to receive a mortal blow, for no other reason than to give his own fatal stroke in return. *Mushin* was the soldier's mind, the calm detachment of the strategist. *Mushin* painted tactics in broad strokes and prevented mistakes of hubris and myopia. *Zanshin* was the single thrust, the drop of poison in afternoon tea, the beautiful woman who gets close to the enemy general.

Zanshin was the killer's mind.

Killam cultivated his *zanshin*. He cradled it and nurtured it. He let go of his sadness and shame, because they did nothing to further the goal of killing the traitor. *Zanshin* did not indulge distractions. It allowed for emotion if that emotion helped get the job done, so he kept his anger. When the time came to drive his blade home, anger would be helpful. First, he needed information and he needed out of this infirmary. His eyes snapped open, and he slid to the edge of his bed.

Sixty hours in a shipping container in a non-climate controlled cargo bay had been an ordeal. Lesser men may not have survived it, but Killam Grimes was hardened to such things. Hypothermia and dehydration were the worst of his problems, and judging by the tubes and hoses stuck to his arms, he could guess that those had been adequately managed. His feet touched the metal deck, slightly colder than the air around it yet still comfortably warm. Sliding his buttocks off the edge of his bed, he shifted his weight to his feet slowly, just to see what his legs could handle.

They seemed fine to him. Perhaps a little shaky, but that was to be expected. His knees protested with dull pain, likely due to the prolonged period of cramped quarters and near-zero temperatures. He stood all the way up and just waited to see what his body would do. Nothing untoward occurred. He stood, he wobbled for a moment, and then he was fine.

Satisfied, Grimes found the light switch on his bed and dialed up the illumination. The rising light revealed nothing he had not already determined about his surroundings. It helped him search for the button to call a nurse. The switch was not hard to find and he pressed it.

The nurse who appeared was a portly man and he was not happy to see Grimes standing up. Grimes did not care. He gave the man curt instructions to notify Craddock of his awakening, then cut any protestations short with a threat of violence so specific and gruesome that the nurse left the room red faced and spluttering.

Craddock appeared within fifteen minutes, pushing his stocky bulk through the infirmary door and huffing as if he had been running the whole way.

"Grimes," he wheezed when he had managed to get all the way inside. "How the hell are you feeling?"

"Focused."

Craddock shook his head. "No. I meant physically."

"I'm fine. A little stiff, a little sore. No permanent harm was done."

This seemed to placate Craddock. "Good. Glad to hear it. We got a serious fucking situation here and we need you in the game."

"Tell me everything."

Craddock brought the assassin up to date on everything they knew about the situation with Manuel Richardson and Dockside with a highly abbreviated sixty-second briefing.

None of the information seemed to surprise Grimes at all. "Richardson works for the fixer. The big one is not human, and there are two women who work with them as well. One is the famed assassin, Mindy. The other is an unknown. She defeated me in hand-to-hand combat, so she is not to be taken lightly. If they are here, that means Richardson is here, too."

"That's what we were afraid of," Craddock replied. "We had eyes on the big one for a while but he burned his tails. We are pretty sure that this Mindy chick was the one who did that part. She came through intake as a military contractor. The other woman just paid Hardesty a visit. He's pretty shaken up by it. They claim they are here in official capacity, but something don't feel right about it."

"We have offended them in their home. We reached out and cut their noses where they work and sleep. The big one especially will not tolerate that. I know his type. Worse, Manuel has befriended them. They probably feel some sort of filial obligation to protect him."

"So they ain't really here to negotiate, you think?"

"Only if they think we can be convinced to let the turncoat go. Since we cannot allow that..."

Craddock sighed and wiped a hand down his face, "Right. It's gonna be a fight then."

"Perhaps not, Craddock." Killam spoke without inflection. "I will kill Richardson while he is here. I know how to do it, now. Keep the charade going while I hunt him down. When he is dead, there will be no reason for the others to stay."

Craddock gave his assassin a sideways look. "Except maybe revenge?"

Killam tilted his head to acknowledge the point. "Perhaps. But these are Dockside criminals. How far will they really pursue vengeance, when they are so very far from home?"

"You may have a point there, Grimes. You need another team to get started?"

"No!" Grimes was startled by his own vehemence. "No more teams. No more guns. No more trips in space ships. We failed before because I forgot the old ways. The correct ways. This time I will hunt alone."

Staring for a moment at his best assassin, Alasdair Craddock suppressed a brusque retort. He had long since gotten used to the melodrama of the Balisongs. He understood why they were the way they were and accepted it.

Establishing a deep commitment to an obscure warrior mythos was an important step in fabricating killers who did not ask uncomfortable questions. When a young person was selected for the program, the indoctrination began immediately and it was quite thorough. This universally resulted in a fanatical killer wholly devoted to an aesthetic that had been rendered obsolete eight centuries prior. That the system was effective was not in question. Grimes was a perfect example of this. He stood before Craddock wearing nothing but white hospital briefs. His body was perfectly medium in height and width, yet every muscle stood out in three-dimensional perfection, chiseled from white flesh like an alabaster anatomy chart. Sixty hours in a packing crate had done little more than make the man uncomfortable, such was his mental discipline and physical conditioning. Craddock had witnessed Grimes doing things that should not have been possible for an un-augmented human, and the man had made them look like parlor tricks at the time. He was the best hand-to-hand fighter on the planet, and had mastered virtually every weapon available on Venus as well as several that were not. Grimes was exceptional even among other exceptional people, a living testimony to the effectiveness of the Balisong program and its anachronistic methods.

The drawbacks of employing such a system in the modern world were non-negotiable, though. One of those drawbacks was how annoying to work with a Balisong could be. Their success rate was high, so he had learned to live with this.

Craddock sighed. "Okay then. What do you need?"

"I need a blade that will cut through armor."

"You need a fucking magic sword?" Craddock was equal parts sarcastic and annoyed. "Is that all?"

Grimes did not look like he was joking. "The big one has thick armor. We shot him with a Bozar and it did not penetrate. Right now he walks without worry. I need a blade that will make him fear."

The stocky man ground his teeth. "Yeah well, he jacked up two Stahlies without sweating much, too. I have no idea what we can do about that, but I'll make some calls."

"I'll also need information. I will need to know where they have been, who they have seen, how they are moving around. Can you get me this?"

"Hardesty is already digging all of that up. You'll get every bit of it. Let's be real, Killam. This is Manny we are talking about. He won't fuck up and do anything obvious."

"I know. We must get to his associates if we want to draw him out."

Craddock toyed with the thought of telling Grimes that they suspected Manny would try to break into Hardesty's records. It would give the assassin something to work with. He could set a trap there, if he wanted to. However, it also might expose Grimes to whatever it was Hardesty was so keen to keep hidden. Hardesty's secrecy on this point was maddening and counterproductive. Nevertheless, the Red Hats needed this shot at the pylons, and Craddock intended to protect Hardesty long enough to get it. This did nothing to change the fact he was not happy about being kept in the dark. He bit his tongue.

"Which one you thinking of hitting?"

"The woman. Not Mindy. The other one."

"Not interested in taking a shot at Mindy?" Craddock found this interesting. Grimes would normally leap at the chance to compete with a peer.

The assassin shook his head slowly. "The mission is to kill Richardson, not dance with other killers. My desire to test myself against Mindy is merely ego, and has no place in this mission. The other woman is a weak link. She will be easier to take than the big man or the killer."

"Didn't she beat you up pretty good last time?"

Grimes let that stand. *Zanshin* did not tolerate ego any more than *mushin* did. "She did. That is why I do not intend to fight her."

"Suit yourself, then. Make a list of what you need and give it to Sully. He'll get you sorted out."

"Thank you, Craddock." Grimes tilted his head, indicating that the conversation was over.

Craddock scowled at the disrespect, then stifled his retort and left the   room.

Chapter Twenty-Three

Manny met Roland in the secret room behind Ellie's bar. It was hard to tell just by looking whether or not Roland's glowering façade was worse than usual, since he wore frowns with the same frequency Manny wore socks.

"Learn anything?"

"Too much," Roland harrumphed. "Goddamn RUC is as bad a racket as any other under this goddamn bowl."

This amused the scout. "You expected different?"

"I hoped for better."

"Hope is always the first thing to grow old and die on Venus, Mr. Tankowicz."

"You are way too young to say old-man shit like that, Manny."

"The Venusian year is short. Technically speaking, I'm forty years old here."

Roland grunted in response as he sat down heavily on the floor. "Well ain't that just a damned convenient metaphor."

Manny's face cracked into a thin expression of sardonic amusement. "Just about the only convenient thing here."

Ellie Connelly swept into the room, her lined face a mask of tired indignation. "Little Manny has grown into melancholy Manny, I guess. Some of us like it here just fine, boy. Those of us who have enough sense to avoid trouble, that is." Her smoldering glare established with great clarity exactly who she might be excluding when she referenced that group. Her vulture's gaze swept over to the large man in the corner. "And who is this? Is this the fixer who crushes metal men for fun?"

Roland, suddenly embarrassed, lurched to his feet. With his head a few scant inches from the ceiling, the cyborg blocked the light and loomed over the smaller woman like a tree shading a child. His mass filled the corner and cast the fierce older woman in splotches of inky darkness. It should have been an intimidating presence, but the twin pinpricks of Ellie Connelly's eyes burned from within the shadow he cast and transfixed the war machine like targeting lasers. Roland knew that look and knew it well. It was the look of a mother bear when she thought her cub was in danger. Ellie was not looking at a big scary fixer from New Boston. She was staring down a threat to her child and she stood ready to kill it if she had to. It was a look all old soldiers learned to respect. No matter how overmatched, a committed opponent was always a dangerous one.

Unsure what to do under the baleful glare of this terrifying woman, he elected to extend his hand. "Pleased to meet you ma'am."

Ellie stared at the oversized paw as if it held a glob of rotting meat and feces. Roland left it hanging for far too long before letting it fall to his side.

The woman simply stared at Roland for a long minute, taking it all in. Then she sniffed and looked back to Manny. "He is a big one, now isn't he?"

Manny could not contain his laughter. It burbled forth and past his lips before he could stop it. It was not often someone so thoroughly dismissed Roland.

Roland shrugged and let her have that one. "Mom said I'm just big-boned."

Ellie turned her attention back to the big man. "Your mother was right." Her expression softened perhaps one or two percent, but it was noticeable and Roland took comfort in that. She was not done dressing him down however. "Well, Mr. 'Big-Boned,' what exactly does the guy who punches Stahlkorpers around want with little old me? Your Lucia has already warned me about how clever you are, so I expect you do not have a complicated stratagem in place. That means you two probably want me to do something risky and stupid to help you with your dumb plan to ruin my life. How close am I?"

"Close enough." Roland saw no point in lying to her. He was no kind of salesman and he felt certain she was no fool.

"Close enough?" Ellie stomped closer and peered up at the towering cyborg. Her eyes narrowed and her lips twisted into a sneer. "You really are a terrible negotiator, aren't you? What makes either of you two idiots think that I am going to stick my neck out for one wayward boy and his big robot friend?"

Roland, initially taken aback by the fearsome woman, was recovering himself. "Lady, I don't expect you to do shit for me. Manny says you care about the people here. Do it for them."

"And what the fuck does a New Boston thug know about the people here? Huh? You don't know shit, Mr. Fixer-man. You know how to hurt people and take what you want from those who can't defend themselves. You are no better than Craddock. You know nothing."

She reached up and grabbed the collar of her simple green blouse. Jerking it down, the woman tore the garment free of her shoulder revealing an amorphous blotch of scar tissue just above her right clavicle. "Do you know what that is, Fixer-man?" She did not wait for his answer. "Sulfuric acid burns are what Venus gives back to its people. We call them Aphrodite's Tears to make it sound pretty, and we wear the scars like a badge of honor because our own planet tries to kill us every damn day." With a yank, the shirt was returned to its proper place. "So don't you dare tell me what to do 'for my people.' As if this planet does not demand enough of us already, you of all people would tell me how I must help them? Where are your scars, Fixer? What do you know of Venus?"

"You know, Ellie." Roland's voice was quiet. This was different. Normally his voice was a booming rumbling bass that could rattle windows and rolled through the air like approaching thunder. Now it was soft, and Manny could not help but think it sounded just a touch dangerous. "You might be on to something. I definitely don't have any scars." He straightened and dropped his jacket to the floor with a toss of his shoulders. "I don't have scars because I can't get them, you see. You're also right that I don't have any stake here." His hands, working with superhuman celerity found the buttons of his shirt. In a moment, it too was on the floor.

Ellie's eyes widened slightly. Roland stood before her bare-chested. His skin was flat matte black, with a dull waxy sheen. His muscles, swollen and exaggerated, sat under the thick synthetic armor of that skin in grotesque slabs, a misshapen caricature of Da Vinci's ideal man. It was an ugly, alien body. Evocative of humanity but bearing no real resemblance to the template. Roland ignored her surprise and kept talking. "But if you head out to an old mining station about twenty miles from here, and check around back to where the cooling station was, you might find an abandoned supply dome. It used to house the helium tanks for the nearby work camps, keeping the miners from being boiled alive under their little temporary domes." He stretched his arms out wide, and the color of his skin began to shift from black, to brown, to green and through all the various colors of the rainbow before settling into an ambiguous Caucasian hue that matched his head and face.

Ellie stood transfixed, her ferocious demeanor slowly melting away to reveal a face both scared and confused.

"If you wander around that old supply depot, Ellie, you will find a large hole in the side. It's been a lot of years, so maybe the acid rain has scrubbed the scorch marks clean by now. Anyway, if you get a few friends and look around on the ground near that gap..." Roland's voice took on a growl that chilled Manny's blood and tore a squeak of surprise from Ellie Connelly. "...you just might find the body parts your fucking Red Hats blew off of a twenty-three-year-old kid who was trying to save a few miner's lives that day. If you do?" Beady black eyes blazed outward from under heavy brows, and he whispered, "I'd really like them back."

Manny was frozen by Roland's intensity, and even Ellie Connelly seemed at a loss for words.

"The last time I was here I lost two thirds of my fucking body, lady. So, you'll have to forgive me if your little scar doesn't impress me much. I'd had worse boo-boos before I ever set foot on your planet. Boo. Fucking. Hoo." The big man sneered at the old woman. "Life is hard here? Well, life is hard everywhere, lady, and nobody gives a shit about Venus because they all have their own problems. That's how it works everywhere. Get over yourself."

He pointed to Manuel. "That guy brought us back here to help out, and we are doing it because Manny is a good kid and I owe him. But I gotta say, I don't think Venus deserves his help. From what I can see, everybody on this ugly yellow rock seems to like being miserable. From the Red Hats to the RUC, and even you morlocks."

Manny winced at the ugly epithet, and Ellie's rage returned. She flew on Roland spitting words laced with venom. "You fucking piece of shit! Don't you ever call us that!" She moved to hit the big man, but paused, thinking better of it when she saw his posture and the expanse of lumpy armored muscle. Their eyes locked and they held each other with fixed glares, connected by an invisible rope of pure tension.

183

Roland's growl was almost intelligible. "Why not? Does it make you angry?" The big bald head swept back and a guffaw of pure derision burst from bionic lungs. "Hah! You live down here under Craddock's boot while Hardesty robs you all blind. The RUC treats you like subhumans because the Red Hats can't be bothered to stop bombing hospitals and schools. You spend every miserable day wondering when the next crack in the dome will leak pure acid onto your body..." Roland stopped to wipe his eyes with a hand. "...but being called a mean name is where you want to draw the line?"

"Easy for you to say," a sob choked the anger from her retort, "with your guns and muscles and metal parts. What do the rest of us have?"

"The first time I came here all I had was a uniform and the desire to help."

"And being so ill-prepared cost you your body."

"And now I'm back. Still want to help."

"What if we aren't prepared to sacrifice our bodies?"

"Then you don't deserve our help. Stay weak and scared and die here on Venus with your sad little scars, then. Grow old and sick, weeping great big Aphrodite's Tears while you lament just how bad you have it. Do nothing. Change nothing." He waved a hand rudely, dismissing Ellie's objections with contempt. "Fuck it, I don't care either way. But what the hell is the point getting all pissed off over being called a Morlock if you can't even be bothered to help yourselves when you have the chance?"

He gestured to Manny again, pointing to his bionic arm. "Manny was shot helping me. He lost that arm taking fire meant for Lucia. Fire from a man I should have killed years ago, I might add. He deserves my help because he's earned it. You? Not so much. Now, if Manny tells me to tear down this dome and kill every Red Hat on Venus, I'll take a crack at it." He looked down on the woman with a feral grin. "And believe me, I just might be able to do it." Then he sighed, "But Manny doesn't want that. He wants me to help you guys beat Craddock and Hardesty so you can have a better life. He seems to think that you want that too."

"We do want a better life—" Ellie tried to say more, but Roland cut her off.

"I remain unconvinced."

At this point Ellie turned away from Roland, her long skirt twirling angrily as she showed the big man her back. She looked to Manuel, and her eyes no longer betrayed her scolding maternal nature. "Manny," she breathed, "what are we to do? We're not weak and we're not cowards. You know this! Tell him!"

The next words from Manny's mouth were the hardest he had ever spoken. He was going to hurt the woman who spent most of his youth trying to help him. This was the woman who had given him the help and money he needed to flee Venus when he left the Red Hats. For these reasons and more, he loved her too much to let her lie to him and lie to herself.

"I remain unconvinced."

Ellie stopped, frozen at his cold tone.

"Roland is right, Ellie. Craddock and Hardesty do these things because people like you and me let them do it. All of this..." his organic hand flicked in a frustrated circle that enveloped their surroundings, "... is the way it is because everybody here is too scared, too tired, and too weak to do anything to change it. I've seen things, Ellie. I know it doesn't have to be like this. I just watched a bunch of criminals band together and kick the shit out a troop of Galapagos mercs and send both the Combine and The Brokerage packing."

"Venus is not Earth!" Ellie protested.

This time it was Manny who scowled at her. "I know, Ellie. But I've been as far as Thorgrimm, and I can promise you, people are people wherever you go. It's time to stop making excuses for how we behave."

"People will die. Good people, Manny. My friends. Our friends will die."

"Probably." His tone was merciless. "But is this what you call living?"

"You don't have the right to make that choice for them!"

"That has not stopped the Red Hats from making your homes their hiding places. It hasn't stopped Hardesty from exploiting their loyalty to expand his businesses. Businesses, I might add, that actively hurt everyone in The Colander..." Manny's voice trailed off, as if the train of thought he was on had suddenly jumped its tracks and careened into a new landscape of ideas.

Manuel sat down. "Aw crap."

185

"What?" Roland grumbled.

"I think I just figured out why they want me dead."

Ellie scowled. "You left them. They want you dead because they think you are a traitor."

"I've been hanging around in Dockside too much." This fact did not sound like it made him happy. "I'd have believed that before, but working with Billy McGinty has opened my eyes to what happens at the higher levels of these things. Nobody that high up actually cares about the occasional runaway, Ellie. Yet they have spent a lot of resources chasing me across a hundred light years and seven stations. Ever wonder why?"

"Because Craddock is an ass?"

"While that's true, it was never about what I did. It's about what I've seen." Manuel Richardson did not sound like a scared twenty-four-year-old. He sounded like a tired old man. "Gods, it's all so goddamn simple when I look at it! Moron!" He punctuated his self-rebuke with a bionic fist to the tabletop. "It's about Hardesty getting off of Venus rich and powerful. Here's how he's going to do it, too." He shifted forward, face intense. "It's so stinking obvious! OmniCorp has been trying to break the Venusian Laborer Conclave for years. With iron prices dropping, Venusian labor is getting too expensive to be competitive. OmniCorp wants to bring in cheaper labor and more machines to keep Venusian mining viable. The Union doesn't want that because it means lower wages and fewer jobs."

"We know that, Manny. It's one of the main reason we tolerate the Red Hats. They keep OmniCorp out." Ellie, for her part, was sounding far more nervous than her words might imply.

"Yeah, but Hardesty is a consultant for OmniCorp. He's at every meeting and involved with every transaction."

Ellie's voice lost some of its confidence. "We know that, too. He's the president of the whole damn union. Naturally he would be working at the same table as OmniCorp, if only to protect our interests. OmniCorp wants to bring in an entirely new labor force. It would ruin us all. Craddock keeps him there to spy and placate and ultimately hinder them."

A deep, rumbling chuckle began to emanate from Roland's chest at this. Ellie rewarded him with a frown that could freeze a Venusian sunset.

186

Manny's reply was less rude, though no more agreeable than the big cyborg's. "Yeah. I thought that, too. On one of my last missions, I found out that Hardesty was helping OmniCorp get more security into the domes." He held up a hand to stop Ellie's protestations. "I know. He could just be playing his role. But now I don't think so. I should have looked closer at the time, but like you I figured it was just Hardesty doing his thing, right?"

Ellie and Roland just looked at him.

"What if he's not just playing a role? Because if memory serves me, he was working on bringing in a whole army's worth of private professional security. More than enough to secure a beachhead for OmniCorp scab labor."

Roland chimed in, "The RUC has been letting communications and construction equipment slip through the checkpoints as well. They have no idea where it's coming from or what it's for, though."

"But I think I do," Manny said, his tone matching his heavy heart.

"Yup," Roland agreed. "OmniCorp is going to flood this place with cheap labor and equipment. That company is going to break the union and Hardesty is helping them do it."

Ellie's lower lip quivered, and her eyes grew wide at the implications. "He would not do that. That would be..."

Roland, ever the pragmatist, finished her thought for her. "A complete and utter betrayal? He would. He totally would, and I am pretty sure he did."

Ellie Connelly was having a moment. A big, scary, heart-wrenching moment. Her body swayed in undisguised conflict as she tried desperately and without success to convince herself that what she was hearing meant something completely different from what she knew it must.

Manny drove the knife home. "Hardesty has betrayed us all to OmniCorp."

Ellie was defeated. Resignation drove her shoulders into a tired slump. "No one will believe you."

Manny barked a short laugh at this. It sounded suspiciously like Roland's own derisive snort. "You forget who you are talking to, Ellie. Proof I can get."

"Can we count on you, Ms. Connelly?" Roland asked.

The older woman's reply was short. "I do not like you, Mr. Fixer. You reek of death and I can't tell the difference between you and all the other killers walking around The Colander." She straightened, putting her shoulders back into the haughty posture she had begun with. "Manny can count on me. As he always could. You can go and die for all I care."

"Good   enough,   Lady."

Chapter Twenty-Four

The information from Sergeant Cummings confirmed their suspicions on several fronts. The first item confirmed was that Cummings had very little idea at exactly how much contraband had been smuggled through the intake. Far more than some construction and communications equipment had been finding its way past the watchful eyes of the RUC. The manifests included high-end communications gear, complex electronics, sophisticated AI cores, and enough construction gear to build a small dome.

This dovetailed into the next confirmed suspicion. Namely that somebody was, in fact, building a dome. Roland had been a combat engineer and he knew how to build things in bad environments. There was no doubt in his mind about what all the equipment was for.

The final thing confirmed by Cummings' intel was the most obvious. Nestled in an addendum to a manifest was a late addition to an otherwise nondescript shipment of toiletries. Three crates, seven-by-four-by-four feet, weighing seven hundred-and-twenty pounds each. The manifest called them 'spare parts.' However, the checkpoint scans told a very different story. The scanner images, which Cummings had made sure went missing before anyone saw them, showed the distinctive shape and configuration of Shikomi Heavy Industries Kano-style armatures. None of their information indicated who the originator may have been, but the smart money was on OmniCorp.

"So those three are OmniCorp spies, then?" Mindy asked as the team compared notes in their sweltering storage unit.

"Seems like it," Roland affirmed. "Slid them in right under Craddock's nose."

"But why guys as conspicuous as Kanos? They stick out like sore thumbs down there."

189

Manny answered this one. "Because they could only get three in. They needed to make sure their operatives could handle Craddock's metal men if it came to that. Kanos will outclass Stahlkorpers, and even the BobCats won't match up well. A Kano can also mount more comms gear and better electronics overall. As for getting noticed?" Manny threw out a dismissive hand wave. "Folks here see so many armatures that Kanos are just a curiosity to them. After a few weeks they probably stopped caring."

Lucia chimed in. "So we figure these Kanos are OmniCorp operators. I suppose we need to assume that they will not be laborers. Are we thinking mercs and security contractors?"

"Most likely," Roland concurred.

Manny pointed the conversation in a more productive direction. "We need to connect them to Hardesty and OmniCorp. Ellie may not be well-disposed toward us right now, but she is not wrong about where people's loyalties lie. If we can't show all this definitively, Hardesty will act like he was spying all along and skate through this looking like a hero of the people." He looked over to Lucia. "How long were you in his office?"

She returned a confident nod. "Long enough. I got the whole thing on Echo. Complete layout and security specs."

"Good work, Boss. I'll make an infiltrator out of you someday."

"I won't lie, it was kind of fun."

"Okay, I think it's time for me to make a run at Hardesty's records. How bad does the security look?"

Lucia gave the young man a sideways look. "I have no idea how to answer that question. I think it looks pretty damn tight. The building is high-tech, and the staff don't strike me as morons. I would not even know how to start sneaking in there. You'll probably find it adorable."

"I only make it *look* easy, Boss. It never really is. Like when Mr. Tankowicz punches something and it explodes. It only looks easy... but he's actually hitting very hard."

"It's totally easy," Roland interjected. "I don't even break a sweat."

"You can't sweat," Lucia laughed. "You don't get to brag about that part. Bu the way, Manny, I think I may have picked up some of that soft-intel you like to talk about."

"Really?" Manuel looked pleased with his protégé.

190

"This guy has a real thing for stacked blonds. Like, a regular and frequent thing."

All eyes turned to Mindy, who suddenly looked very apprehensive.

"And where, oh where, could we find one of those?" Manny let the words slide from his lips with saccharine glee.

Mindy sighed. It was an expressive, dramatic, and wholly theatrical sigh. "Fine. I'll shake my ass for the bastard. But I'm not letting him touch me. I'm not that kind of girl."

"Don't worry Mindy. We don't need you to do more than distract him. Honestly, once I'm into his system I don't care what you do with him." Mindy's eyes lit up at this, and Manny shut her idea down in its infancy. "But try not to kill him," he added quickly. "If we kill him right before we expose him, it will look very suspicious. We need him to hang publicly, so the Hats will turn on him."

"All right then," Lucia said. "What's the plan?"

The plan was fairly straightforward, which is how Roland liked it. Ellie Connelly arranged for Hardesty's next 'appointment' with the local madame to be handled by Mindy. This required little more than the exchange of a modest sum of credits from Lucia and some of the local barter currency from Ellie. The madame did not seem to be overly distraught over losing the custom of Hardesty, since acquiring young girls that suited his tastes had become problematic. Most women who spent an evening with Lincoln Hardesty were disinclined to repeat the ordeal for any price.

Mindy had dolled herself up to play her part. It was a suitably staggering display of improbable proportions and a solid façade of overt sexuality so blatant it could actually deflect gunfire. Her chosen attire appeared to be some kind of latex applied to her body with a thin brush and judicious attention to detail. Patches of glitter and iridescent sequins were strewn about in artful patterns designed to accentuate certain regions. Roland was no physicist, but he had passed his engineering courses with strong Cs. He could not figure out how certain parts of her seemed to be defying gravity. There were no visible support structures, and certainly nowhere to hide any. It was Lucia who best expressed their collective opinions on her get-up.

"God DAMN it, Mindy!"

Manny just gulped and developed a morbid fascination with the tops of his shoes. That felt safest. Roland was predictably unimpressed. "Nice," he rumbled sarcastically.

"What? This old thing?" Mindy said with a slow turn. "I just had it laying around."

"Let's get you a coat. You can't walk through the lobby looking like that."

Roland was right, and a coat was secured so Mindy cold traverse the lobby without causing any cardiac issues amongst the patrons. Manny went along as her driver and handler. With his features altered enough to fool facial recognition software, the real risk was scanners picking up Mindy's augmentations. Manny was going to spoof the scanners with more mundane readings from a device in his satchel, but its range was limited and its success would be most dependent on how diligent the staff were about checking up on system anomalies. Dedicated personnel might notice issues with the scanners as they walked past and investigate potential sources. Lax employees would run the diagnostics, tap on the screen a few times, and then shrug when everything looked to be working fine. They hoped for the latter, but they could always abort if they felt compromised.

Lucia situated herself in the lobby, taking a seat on one of the red couches and fiddling with her handheld as if working on something deeply important. This was not entirely subterfuge, as she was busy patching into the building's security channel to facilitate eavesdropping. The concierge recognized her, and immediately found some other task to attend to rather than deal with the rude woman from Earth.

Roland sat on a bench across the street and grumped about his secondary role in the operation. The hotel had active bio-scanners, and there was just not possible to spoof his litany of modifications without making it obvious trickery was afoot. One did not need sophisticated sensors to pick up on many of his alterations. A simple pressure plate would reveal his weight, and the cheapest handheld scanner in the world would detect the density of his skin. If the scale read nine-hundred pounds, and Manny's device was saying 'unmodified human,' even the dumbest security gargoyle would want an explanation for the obvious disconnect. While his military exemptions might keep him out trouble, his detection would render the operation impossible. Roland took solace in the fact that they were not in Uptown, where even the streets had active bioscanners and most buildings prohibited actively modified people from entering without a whole lot of extra scrutiny. Thus, he could at least wait across the street in relative comfort.

He watched as Manny and Mindy approached the main door to the lobby and slip through it unmolested. The doorman, still stoic and unmoving, let his eyes wander up and down Mindy's body as she passed. Her sleek black wrap blunted the effects of her ensemble, while doing little to disguise the architecture of the woman underneath it. Neither did it hide the brazen sway of her hips nor buttocks, which is what seemed to have broken the doorman's veneer of professional detachment.

Once the doors closed behind them, Roland lost sight of the pair.

"Comm check, Breach" he mumbled into his subvocal comm mic.

Lucia sounded off first. "Mama Bear."

Then Manny, "Lefty."

Mindy, "Honey Pot."

"Any chatter, Mama Bear?"

A pause while Lucia scanned the security network for any sign their comms had been detected. "No chatter, Breach." Her voice caught just a little. They had elected to use callsigns because both Roland and Manuel were known operators at this point. It made sense, but Lucia hated to call Roland 'Breach.' 'Breach' is what the Army had called him. 'Breach' is what they used to kill and destroy. There was a lot of emotional baggage that had to be carted along with that callsign, and Roland had been avoiding it for decades.

'Breach' had also been what his friends in his squad called him. It was the name used by his cybernetic siblings and represented his purpose and role within their group. They all had one. There had been 'Lead' 'Comms,' 'Sneak,' 'Scout,' and finally: 'Breach.' It was an identity, a place, and a mission. It had made him happy once. Then it became just another thing the army took from him. This was a loss he found difficult to live with, and now he had resolved to take it back. It was Roland's burden and not hers, and she respected what he was trying to do with it. She supported the effort as best she could, though she hated calling him that name.

Mindy and Manny did not notice her internal conflict. They were focused on moving across the lobby with minimal incident. As had happened to Lucia, the concierge intercepted them and inquired about their business. Eschewing Lucia's brusque rudeness, Manny spoke for the pair and had the woman with the blue hair call up to confirm their appointment. Surprising no one, Hardesty's people encouraged the woman to let them up with all due haste, and the pair of infiltrators swept past the ersatz gatekeeper to the lifts.

Once inside, Manny exhaled a sigh of relief. "So far, so good."

"Nervous?" Mindy asked.

"Everybody on this planet wants to kill me, and my solution is to deliver myself right into their stronghold." His smile was weak and unconvincing. "Feels risky."

"Honestly? That kind of ballsy move can work really well. Nobody ever looks for the target in their own house. Besides, if this goes south I'll take care of you. Ironsides is down there, too. If things go really bad he'll just knock the building over and pull us from the rubble."

"Our bodies, you mean." Manny's expression was more relaxed now.

Mindy curled a lip in his direction. "I'd survive it."

"Game face, blondie." The lift was slowing.

Mindy untied her wrap and threw it open, letting it hang off her shoulders and revealing the expanse of her chest. Glitter and sequins accented her curves in all the places that made young men hyperventilate, and Manny's reaction to it was predictable. Mindy teased him. "Snap out of it, boy. Pick up your jaw and look like a professional."

"I said 'game face,' Mindy. That..." he pointed to her chest, "... is not your face!"

"Nobody is going to be looking at my face, Manny." She put a finger under his chin and lifted his eyes from her chest, "Nobody ever does. Watch this."

The lift doors whooshed open and Mindy swept into the penthouse lobby. She slinked up to Rick the receptionist and bent at the waist to lean over his desk. There were rutting mandrills in Africa who presented themselves in less overt ways. "I'm here to see Mr. Hardesty." Her statement was a breathy, husky whisper, and her backwater accent was dialed as high as she could get it to go.

Rick was having none of it. His eyes gleamed with constrained laughter at Mindy's affected demeanor and his retort was merciful in its brevity.

Manicured fingers swiped some screens and he met Mindy's batting eyelashes with a look of pure amusement. "Honey, you are barking so far up the wrong tree with that approach." His gaze lifted heavenward. "Hooooo-weeeee, that is over-the-top!" With a chuckle Rick held his arms out to the side. "Child, here is where you are going oh-so-very wrong."

He pointed to Manny. "If you want me to go goo-goo eyed you'll have to bring about two more of those and a bottle of good rose. The fact that this was not obvious to you tells me that you are not a real hooker. Do you even like boys?"

Manny, after overcoming his initial discomfort, began to get apprehensive all over again. This was a very inconvenient place to have their cover blown. Rick picked up on the scout's change in mood and hushed him. "Oh settle down, Manny. Ms. Connelly is an old friend. I've rebooted the cameras in here so we have about four minutes to talk."

Mindy and Manny both sagged with relief. Mindy straightened and abandoned her seductive slink. "Do you have any idea how close you just got to dying, buddy?"

"I live on Venus and work for Lincoln Hardesty, sugar-tits. I almost-die three times before brunch most days."

Mindy gave a respectful nod to this. To Manny she said, "This shitty planet of yours sure breeds some hard-ass bastards, Manny."

"No place like home," he replied with a shrug.

"Now shut up and listen, kids. Ellie has made it very clear to me that you guys are about to do this all wrong and it's now my job to keep that from happening. First, sugar-tits?"

Mindy scowled, "That's Ms. Sugar-Tits to you."

"Link is an insecure little boy. The super-vamp thing intimidates him. He wants you young, dumb, slutty, and helpless."

"That'll be easy, then," Manny interrupted, earning a glare from Mindy and a snort from Rick, who wisely decided to move on.

"Lose the femme fatale bit and go full debutante. Look all scared and surprised and wide-eyed at his wealth and magnificence. Just like a cotillion back home."

Mindy pointed an accusing finger at him. "Wait a minute. Are you from Gethsemane?"

Rick titled his head in a non-committal response. "Who? Me? They don't let my kind live there, Mindy. I'm sure you know that."

Mindy returned a knowing nod of her own. "Right. Gotcha. Setting phasers to 'slutty teenager' then."

Rick looked to the scout. "Manny, Link is expecting you. You have no chance of fooling him if he sees you. I can help you get into the system from out here, but Miss Thing is going to need to keep him busy for a while because all his security is new and updated. My codes only go so deep these days." Eyes flicked over to Mindy. "You up for the real thing in there?"

"Not a chance."

"Good for you. That means getting the information will be easier, but getting out of here harder. Whatever you do, get him away from his comm and away from his desk. He can call security from either and the security here does not suck."

Manny agreed with the sentiment. "We can handle security if we have to, but we'd like to avoid that. If Mindy is just going to conk him on the head anyway, we can just have her extract the codes we need the easy way."

The blond assassin nodded approval. "It will make things interesting later, but it will get the immediate job done faster. I can keep him from calling security, and then I'll thump him on the head and tie him up or something," Mindy added. "We'll tie you up, too, Rick. Just so you can keep your job."

"Don't threaten me with a good time, honey. Thanks all the same."

Manny straightened and asked, "All right. Let's bring Roland and Lucia up to speed on this. You otherwise ready, Mindy?"

Mindy gave him a shockingly doe-eyed look. It managed to be half sultry, while also half bewildered. "Why Mr. Manny, sir, I do believe I am, thank you very much." Then she giggled girlishly, which caused her to jiggle girlishly.

Rick was impressed. "Damn, honey. You *are* good."

Chapter Twenty-Five

Mindy slipped into Hardesty's office, silently confirming where all the exits and comm terminals were located. She had memorized Lucia's scanned layout, and her bionic ears and nose soon confirmed the office was empty except for Hardesty himself. Satisfied, she stepped past the foyer and let her wrap fall back off her shoulders. She adopted a slightly bouncy, tiptoe step as she walked, flouncing into the main office with a vapid look of childlike wonder. This delighted gait set all sorts of things bouncing, swaying, and rippling. The symphony of motion had the obvious effect on Lincoln Hardesty who was seated behind his desk with his feet upon its surface. His glass of whiskey nearly tumbled from his fingertips at the sight of the blond apparition before him, and his neck muscles bulged and flexed as he attempted to control his expression.

"Hello, Mr. Hardesty," Mindy purred. "My name is Kitty, and I guess I am your date for the evening. Are we going out?" The question was pitched with a hint of apprehension, and layered with the confusion of a young girl who was in over her head and unsure how to proceed.

"Oh no, my little Kitty. You and I are definitely going to stay in tonight." Hardesty slid his feet from the desk, making sure Mindy got a good look at his expensive designer shoes. With the confidence of a Gascon the lanky man stepped over to an ornate faux-wood liquor cabinet. It opened to his touch with a slight hiss.

"Can I offer you a drink?" He posed the question with exaggerated innocence. He stood before a cabinet filled with liquor costing several lifetimes of a Venusian laborer's wages, backlit by the soft blue interior light that illuminated the various bottles and their kaleidoscope of colored liquids. This was a favorite play of his. A deft maneuver that had flabbergasted more than one pretty working girl. He waited for it, and a knowing smirk creased his features when he heard the small gasp of wonder behind him.

He turned his head to look over the shoulder of his tailored jacket. "Something bubbly perhaps?" Hardesty took it as known fact that country girls loved bubbly sweet wines. They had not developed a taste for the better things yet. Without waiting for her answer, he selected a bottle of what would be cheap champagne on Earth, yet cost a fortune on Venus. He grabbed two flutes and brought them over to the desk, where the absolutely gorgeous blond girl still stood. He took a good look at her as he poured, really drinking in her figure. She had doffed the wrap while his back was to her, and she had moved to lean on his desk, perhaps to get a better look into his cabinet of treasures.

On closer examination he realized she was probably a year or three older than he would have preferred. His gaze wandered over that body for a long time, navigating the curves and crevices as if each might hold the secret to immortality. He realized two things when his ocular circuit was complete. First was that her age was entirely inconsequential. Any man who stopped to check that woman's birth certificate before enjoying the delights of her body was a fool. The second was that he was spilling a lot of expensive champagne.

With a curse he stopped pouring the cascading bubbly all over his desk. The blond beamed a thousand-megawatt grin and dragged her finger through the puddle of champagne. Then she licked the digit clean with a snicker. "Oh my, that is delicious!"

Lincoln Hardesty had begun his drinking early today. This was not uncommon, and thus his wits were somewhat less keen than they might have been otherwise. It could be forgiven if the combination of strong booze, black-market virility pills, and a surge of testosterone the likes of which he had not known since adolescence had rendered his normally restrained manner noticeably absent.

Leering, he plucked Mindy's hand from the air. He pressed the delicate fingers to his lips and wrapped his mouth and tongue around her finger.

This club-footed attempt at seduction proved to be ill-advised. The finger, so slim and delicate, tasting vaguely of champagne, turned in his mouth and a grip like iron closed over his chin. Her finger and thumb had seized his lower jaw in a painful pinch grip. A soft gasp and moan escaped the man's lungs, pain and fear immediately supplanting the drunken lust so welcome just the previous second.

As his brain began to accept what was happening he inhaled sharply to scream for security, but all that air left as a strangled gurgle. Mindy forced the man's head down into his desk where his face splashed against the soaked laminate.

"Hush up, Hardesty."

In a moment of panicked clarity, Hardesty's hand snaked out to open a desk drawer, where both his gun and the alarm button could be found. Long before he found either, small furiously strong hands dragged him away from his desk and torqued him head over heels to the floor. He inhaled, again preparing to shout for help. The blond demon drove the wind from him with a brutal strike to his chest with the heel of her hand. Those tiny fingers next found his comm handheld inside his jacket pocket and hurled it across the room. He searched for an escape, and found none. The twenty feet of carpet between Hardesty and the door may as well have been twenty light years for all his chances of reaching it.

"God, you are just awful." The woman's undisguised disgust hurt almost as much as getting hit did. Her knee pressed into his gut and the weight of her body, feeling much too substantial for that little frame, pressed him into his own carpet like a hydraulic press. "If you had played this with even a little bit of goddamn class I'd have dragged the nice part out longer. You could have at least watched me for a few more minutes." The pressure increased, and the breath leaked from Hardesty like helium escaping a leaky dirigible. "But sucking a girl's finger? That's how you go for it? Ugh!"

"If you kill me you'll never get off Venus!" It was a croak, a sad little choking threat that neither intimidated nor impressed his captor.

"You don't even know I am, do you? I'm not here to kill you, asshole. Think real hard and then you tell me why I'm here."

Hardesty did think hard. Still, it took several interminable seconds before he made the connection. "You're with that bitch from Earth, aren't you? Shit. What the hell do you want from me?"

"Nothing, really. You and I are just going to sit here until Manny is done raiding your records."

Hardesty's heart leapt into his throat. He had always assumed Manuel would attempt to breach his records if he made it here, and he had hardened all his data storage in anticipation of this. He had not, however, taken Craddock's advice to delete anything that was very sensitive. Too much of that information was critical. The dirt he had on OmniCorp was his insurance against betrayal, and without a reserve of quality blackmail material he would be far too exposed for comfort. All he could do was hope that his data security was good enough to thwart Manny. He knew the young scout by reputation only, and that reputation made him very nervous.

Then another, far more terrifying thought occurred to the man currently pinioned to the floor by what he now suspected was not really a tiny blond prostitute.

Manny doesn't need to break my security. He just needs to have this bitch break me! Lincoln Hardesty was not a strong or tough man. He would not hold up for long under torture, and he was too intelligent to pretend otherwise.

Mindy seemed to be aware of his train of thought. "I get bored real fast, Lincoln. If it takes Manny too long to get what he needs, I might try to pass the time by hurting you. The longer we sit, the more parts of you I am going to break." She activated her sub-vocal mic. "How we doing, Lefty?"

"Slow going, Honey Pot. Rick's codes barely got me to the admin level."

Hardesty could not hear this response, so Mindy paraphrased for him. "Manny says this could take a while." She punctuated this by grabbing the downed man's left index finger and bending it against the knuckle until it folded flush the back of his hand. Hardesty's scream was shrill and ended with a pathetic sob.

Mindy spared little sympathy for the man. "Oh for crying out loud. Don't be such a baby. It's a teeny little broken finger, not a shattered femur." She let that hang for a dramatic moment then added a single ominous syllable. "Yet."

Hardesty had no plan for this. He had taken it as given that Manny would infiltrate silently and hack his way through the records. There were a dozen fail-safes and booby traps built into the database sufficient to frustrate the best slicers on Venus. If the pain in his hand was any indicator, then these protections were going to be superfluous. This style of strong-arm tactic had never been part of

Manny's repertoire. The boy simply did not have the stomach for it. Manuel Richardson had had changed, Hardesty realized, and not for the better.

A crisp blow to the back of his head sharpened his focus and accelerated his mounting panic. The voice, which had been so charming and seductive before, hit his ears like harsh static through his pain and fear. "I'm getting bored again, Lincoln! If only there was some way to get Manny done faster..."

Hardesty knew he had to give them something. He wracked his brain for a suitably demonstrative concession that did not also send his carefully constructed plans into the recycler. He gave up the sanctity of his database as lost and focused on the damage control that would be necessary in the aftermath. Like all cowards, Hardesty opened his gambit by bargaining for his life.

"I'm the president of the fucking union! You know you can't kill me, right?" he stammered.

"Do you have any idea how many things I can do to you that are worse than killing you, Link? I could have you begging for death in ninety seconds if I wanted to."

That took the man aback, and his tone adjusted itself accordingly. "I can give you what you want, but if I don't get assurances about what you are going to do with the data, I'm dead anyway. We need to make a deal."

Small fingers closed around his left pinky. He sucked sharply through gritted teeth as the tension on the tiny joint increased to a dangerous level. Mindy's soft words in his ear carried malice disproportionate to their benign tone, making her intentions clear. "You are not exactly dealing from a strong position, Lincoln."

"I know! But I'll play ball if I have to. OmniCorp is going to push the union out, and I gave up on trying to stop them! The union is fucked no matter what I do, anyway. Manny is the only one besides me who knows what OmniCorp is pulling, that's why I sent Craddock after him! I can call off the damn hunt if you guys promise not to spill!"

Mindy hit the sub-vocal to converse with the team. "Hardesty says he'll leave Manny alone if we promise to go away and not mention to anyone that he is double-crossing his own people. What do you guys think?"

Manny answered first. "He's lying. He'd have to tell Craddock why he suddenly wants to call it off, and Craddock is not dumb enough to believe his bullshit after all they've gone through to get me. Plus the Balisongs will not let it go now."

"Agreed," Roland chimed in. "We need to shut this down and end the threat. Permanently."

"Lie to him," Manny responded. "Tell him it's only a deal if we take the data with us. For insurance."

"I don't think he's going to like that," Mindy cooed, looking down at the man underneath her. He squirmed and shifted like a helpless child. Only hearing one side of the conversation was unnerving her prey, which had been Mindy's intention all along.

"Make the alternative worse," Manny said, the words frigid with unvarnished malice.

"You are going to make some lucky girl a fine husband someday, Lefty." Mindy killed the mic and turned back to Hardesty. "Okay, buddy. Manny says we got a deal as long as we get the database as insurance."

"I can't let you have that!" Hardesty sputtered. Too late he realized that this was a colossally stupid thing to say, considering his current position.

Mindy agreed with this assessment. "Manny thought you'd take that position..." She grabbed his arm and without a second thought tore his shoulder from its socket with a twisting, wrenching movement. The noise of ligaments tearing and bones being pulled against each other merged to form a single prolonged and sickening crunch, eclipsed only by her victim's howls of agony.

"Okay! Okay!" he shrieked. "You can have them! Take them, you fucking bitch! Goddammit!"

"Thought you might see it my way." She waited for the man's sobs to subside. "The codes, please?"

Utterly defeated, Hardesty handed over his passwords and Mindy relayed them to Manny. In seconds, the scout was pulling petabytes of data from Hardesty's personal databases. "This is way easier than trying to break the security!" Manny crowed as his portable drives filled with the information.

"You don't have the looks for it, kid." Mindy replied. "You got it all yet?"

"We're good. I have full access now, so I'll dump the security system into a reboot loop. That will give us a good twenty minutes to clear the building. You just need to lock down Hardesty so he can't raise the alarm the old-fashioned way."

"Roger that, Lefty."

Mindy stood and hauled the whimpering Hardesty to his feet. Almost a foot taller than she was, Hardesty looked like an oversized stuffed animal won at a carnival game as Mindy dragged him to a long couch against one wall of his office. "This probably wasn't what you had in mind when you first thought about getting me in here, Link, ol' buddy," she chuckled. Then she threw him on the cushions, forcing another shout of pain from the wounded man. "But it's about to get real kinky in here all the same."

The little blond killer tore the finely tailored jacket from Hardesty's back and began to rip it into long strips of cloth.

"How do you feel about bondage?"

"Not a fan?" the doomed man squeaked weakly.

"That's too bad, because I love it."

Then she started tying.

Three minutes later and the curvaceous assassin stepped out of Lincoln Hardesty's office and into the foyer where Rick and Manny were waiting with nervous faces.

"He'll be all tied up in there for a good long while, boys. You got what you need?"

Manny nodded his assent and they looked to Rick, who replied with a bored sigh. "Fine then. Tie me to the chair. Whatever."

They secured the receptionist loosely to his chair with some leftover cloth from Hardesty's suit. The expression of bland resignation never left his face while they did it. When a moderately convincing job of securing Rick had been achieved, Mindy gave him a pat on the cheek and said, "Sit tight now!"

"Don't take any chances," Manny advised. "If you think they suspect you, run to Ellie. She'll help."

"Don't you tell grandma how to suck eggs, boy," Rick admonished. "Now get out of here you two."

Manny grinned and opened the team channel on his comm and called it. "Breach! We have the package. Honey Pot and Lefty are on exfil now. Coming out the front door. Alarms in eight minutes."

Chapter Twenty-Six

F rom her vantage point in the lobby, Lucia heard Manny call for exfiltration. She kept her ear to the security channel just in case, and sure enough there was a lot of chatter about a system reboot on the penthouse level. Nothing too excited, no sense of alarm, just a general kind of confusion and a few recriminations directed at the maintenance people.

"Honey Pot and Lefty, advise you take elevator to second level and exfil by stairs after that. Security is agitated but not active. Let's not spook them."

"Copy that, Mama Bear," came Manny's voice.

Lucia did not hear the man approach her from behind. She was focused on her task, and that precluded a high level of situational awareness. She could be forgiven either way, because when Killam Grimes wanted to be silent and unseen, ghosts envied his skills. When he struck, it was the barest flicker of movement from his wrist and elbow. So fast and so light it invoked comparisons to the beat of a hummingbird's wing, his darting hand stuck Lucia in the neck with a small needle.

The fast-acting soporative agent quickly swam through her bloodstream to her brain, and by the time she had slapped at the unprovoked sting, her reflexes were already slowing. Whirling, she scanned for the source of the pain, and found no one. Killam Grimes had melded back into the milling crowds of the busy lobby to wait.

He knew what was happening, and thus patience came easily. The woman looked back and forth, her hand still pressed to the tiny wound on her neck. She was becoming confused, it was written in her furrowed brow and wrinkled nose. The toxin slowed her brain and rearranged her synapses. Sodium ion blocking prevented the exchange of electrons across her synapses, and the reduction in action potential dragged her neurological activity to a crawl.

Suddenly thinking was hard and reasoning impossible. The woman who was used to seeing her universe move at quarter-speed was now trying to make sense of a world that she could not keep up with. If Grimes had gotten the dosage right, her muscles would start to lose tone and strength next, making her slow and pliable without rendering her completely immobile.

Within a few seconds he knew he had gotten the dosage right. She stood and wobbled, still looking about and trying to force reason through the fog of her failing perceptions. Her vision would be narrowing at this point, shrinking to a tight tunnel revealing only what was directly in front of her. If she had the presence of mind, she might call for help, but such reactive reasoning was beyond her already. She could only stand there confused and swaying.

After nine seconds, Killam re-emerged from the crowd to sweep up behind the woman and secure her by the wrists. She twitched slightly at his touch. It was a brisk jerk, deeply honed instincts telling her to fight free of his grasp. The chemical soaking her brain prevented her mind from maintaining this helpful thought. The insidious toxin instead stifled her drive to flee and replaced it with confused compliance.

When he pulled, she followed like a drunk marionette helpless against the strings controlling her limbs. Grimes slipped an arm around her waist. His other hand found her comm and quickly switched it off with a deft flick of his thumb. Then he led her across the lobby to a side door, where a stolen keycard granted him access to the service entrance and the dim alley beyond it. Nobody noticed or cared as they made their bizarre transit. There was nothing to see, really. They were just a man and woman walking across a lobby arm-in-arm. There was nothing so interesting about this action that anyone was inclined to look up from their own affairs and take notice, so no one did.

The tactic required no jammers, scanners, or clandestine electronic countermeasures. Merely the judicious application of speed and sleight of hand. Such skills had always been the skilled assassin's trusted friends, and Grimes was better than most with them. These were the old and low-tech ways of the craft. They remained effective in a galaxy of dazzling technological wonder because they relied on the failings of human nature itself, which was a thing both reliably selfish and conveniently immutable.

This moment was no exception to the rule. A person aware of their surroundings, a bystander putting even a modicum of effort into understanding their own presence in space and time, might have noticed something off about the pair as they hurried along. Sadly, no such individuals were present in the lobby of that hotel, and Grimes made it to his goal with plenty of time to spare. A hundred people stayed glued to their tiny handhelds and the scrolling screens of AR glasses, oblivious while a professional assassin abducted a drugged woman right in front of their noses. After all, there were things to buy and net 'casts to watch. The activities of the real world were just too dull and unimportant to warrant more than cursory attention.

This was all as he planned it to be, and the timing worked very much in his favor. In just a few moments, the toxin would take away her ability to walk, and he intended to be well clear of the big fixer's bench before that happened. He dragged his captive along and maintained a brisk pace that was soon taxing Lucia's ability to keep up. He pulled harder and kept moving.

Once out of the alley the woman began to stumble, though she kept her feet. Grimes was impressed at her strength. It was strange she was still walking as well as she was, but nevertheless it was clear he had only a few more seconds before he would have to carry her. They made it to his stashed roller before she collapsed completely, though he still had to lift her bodily into the storage compartment. With the clumsy-looking vehicle secreted in a deep alcove behind a recycling station, the maneuver remained safely hidden from the potentially curious stares of passers-by.

As he arranged her deadened limbs to close the hatch, he noticed her eyes looking up at him, glassy and befuddled. She was still awake, and that bothered him. Even being as strong as she obviously was, she should have been nearly unconscious by now. Yet her rheumy gaze, while slack and confused, showed no signs of drowsiness yet. He frowned and considered administering another dose, but the stuff was so dangerous he could not risk it. She was supposed to be bait for Manuel Richardson, not the catalyst for a war with Dockside. Alive, she was leverage over the big fixer. Dead, she was simply a reason for the monster to run amok.

He secured the hatch and slid into the driver's seat. Rollers in Caelestus were not permitted to move independently of the city's grid, so as soon as he activated the machine the municipal traffic computer asserted control over it. He dialed in four separate destinations, and then sat back to ride. He fought endless waves of tension that attacked his composure, driven by a powerful surge of adrenaline. Searching hard, he again found his focus. *Zanshin* needed to be perfect or he invited another failure. Grimes could not afford to be elated at his success so far, nor could he permit his doubts about the drug dosage to dull his focus. *Zanshin* meant nothing was allowed to distract him from his next immediate goal and the flawless execution of his plan.

Before every stop, Grimes set a small jamming pod to briefly disable the roller's transponder. At the second destination, he quickly moved to the back and opened the hatch. If the roller stayed off the traffic grid for more than thirty seconds, the delay would trigger a response from the closest traffic cop. Thus, he needed to move with some speed, and the mechanics of extracting his captive looked well-rehearsed. He removed the woman and the transponder re-activated with four seconds to spare. Then Grimes sent the roller on its way to complete its meandering transit of Caelestus empty.

The chittering transport had brought them to a thin alley between two large dance clubs. It was still early enough in the evening that neither place was particularly crowded, but the music was already too loud for comfort and the dirty brown strip of no-man's-land between them was empty and dark.

To an unlit door deep inside this crevice he dragged the now-unconscious woman, and his foot sent it inward with a crash. He brought her to a small room with a single light strip and narrow cot. This is where he deposited her limp form. He took her comm from his jacket pocket and removed the backplate and battery, just to be safe. A quick search revealed her sub-vocal microphone and earpiece, and those were subsequently disabled as well.

Satisfied, Grimes left the room to secure the door to the alley and make a call to Craddock. The man on the other end of the line grunted in surprised approval at the success of the operation so far.

"You got her that easy, huh?"

"It was not easy, merely well-executed. There is a difference."

"Whatever. Either way this is good because Hardesty is probably losing his shit right now. I can only assume the others escaped with whatever bullshit he was trying to hide from them."

"I moved when I had the opportunity, no sooner. Preventing the theft was not my primary goal."

"I agree with your call, Grimes. It's not our job to protect Link's stuff. You did good work getting that girl. You may have just saved all our asses." There was a catch in this, an addendum left unsaid.

Grimes knew what it meant. "But now I have to kill the rest of them as well."

"Looks that way."

Grimes, fully enveloped in his *zanshin,* considered the new mission parameters before responding. "That changes nothing for the present. You need to arrange for a meeting with Richardson so I can kill him. Then we will direct our attention to the others. The woman will remain useful until then. So, she dies last."

"I'll pass that along. He's going to call me any damn minute now. It will be nice to have some good news to give him. I expect he's going to be all kinds of pissed off."

On the edge of his thoughts, a tiny doubt now lurked. Something about this conversation was not right. Parts of the equation were not adding up to a logical sum. He dismissed Craddock and returned to check on the woman, who should be completely unconscious for several hours. He found her asleep and he secured her to the cot with DentiKuffs, then retreated to a dark room to meditate. His mind must be clear of doubt if he was to maintain the focus he needed to complete his task. Doubt was a slow-acting poison, sapping the will and weakening resolve. It had to be purged.

He settled his breathing and released *zanshin*. The emotionless floating detachment of *mushin* was required now. To this end Grimes simply allowed his mind to sit a moment, unlocking the chains of *zanshin's* fervor and crystalline focus.

Hardesty wanted the foreigners all dead now because they had secured an item from him. Craddock had implied rather strongly that this item represented a threat to all of them, and Grimes had to assume this meant the Red Hats. However, the phrasing and the tone of Craddock's voice indicated that Craddock himself was ignorant of what it was they had stolen as well. Upon this thought, the apprehension reasserted itself. From within *mushin* it was a distant, detached thing, an impression more than an emotion. It was an effect to be observed and analyzed and Grimes seized upon this to determine the genesis of his doubts.

Killam Grimes was not a detective and solving mysteries was never his role within the Red Hats. Despite this, he found himself far too curious about Hardesty's secret to leave it alone. Hunting and killing was a game of instinct, and Grimes trusted his instincts implicitly. His instincts told him that the pilfered thing was too important. Too many people were taking too many risks over it. Richardson was a hunted man and a traitor. Yet he came directly into the lion's den to retrieve it. Craddock did not even know what the thing was, yet he felt enough apprehension over it to hurl entire teams of Balisongs at Manny from across the solar system. Hunting traitors was common enough, yet Grimes could not ever remember a time when two teams were sent as far, or when a hunt had gone for as many years as this one had.

The Balisong had never considered these things before. It had never occurred to him that they might matter. This was because he had forgotten the old ways, and he was not going to repeat those failures this time. He stretched his mind into the uncomfortable places, opened doors in his thoughts he had tried to forget had hinges. He moved past the 'how' of his missions and kills, and into the 'why' of them.

Why did Richardson need to die so badly? What could his people have taken from Hardesty that made their deaths imperative as well? Why would Craddock go along with it if he did not know what it was? Killam Grimes was gifted in many ways, but imagination was not one of them. Several times he had to stop and quell his frustration. The mind was supposed to be his greatest weapon, and his felt dull and unpracticed. His ineptitude shamed him, and that had to be moved past as well.

Grimes killed for the Red Hats and the future of a free Venus. He believed in his cause with a strength and conviction that was unbreakable. It was his armor against the squeamishness and uncertainty that plagued lesser, weaker, men. He used that to keep his mind calm and focused, and it was in the warmth and quiet of his convictions that a solution came to him. He did no need to deduce what had been stolen because he was currently in possession of one of the thieves. He could simply ask her in as convincing a manner as he knew how.

Action followed decision swiftly, and Grimes was back in his captive's room barely ten seconds later. She was still asleep, so he placed a stimulant patch against the skin of her neck, and removed it as soon as she started to stir. It was an old trick, giving just enough medicine to wake the prisoner without restoring her full faculties. She may not be entirely lucid, but now he expected her to be able to answer questions at the very least.

Brown eyes fluttered and opened, and her tongue flicked across dry lips. There was a languid shifting as she discovered her bonds and the dim light of realization washed slowly across her expression.

"Good evening, Ms. Ribiero," Grimes said.

"Hello." The response was neither completely flat nor overly hostile. Her brain was still incapable of summoning the requisite emotional intensity to truly express her feelings.

"I have a few questions for you. I understand you may not want to answer them. That is commendable. I would advise you that not answering them will change nothing of your situation and may actually make things worse, however. My interview will be brief, and I do not believe being truthful will cause you to violate any other trusts you hold. If you choose to be recalcitrant, I will have to hurt you, and I have no desire to do that. Do we understand each other?"

The woman nodded.

"Good. You and your associates stole something from Lincoln Hardesty tonight. I would like to know, with as much specificity as possible, what it was."

Chapter Twenty-Seven

Managing Roland's fury was not a simple thing. When Lucia failed to show up at the rented sleeping pod they had selected for a rally point, the big man's mood had deteriorated from mild concern to the sort of quiet homicidal seething that almost always resulted in multiple fatalities.

Lucia's disappearance was noticed almost immediately, yet by the time they had pinged for a location fix on her comm it was dead.

"She cannot be far," Manny surmised. "They haven't had that much time."

With a few seconds' worth of tapping on his DataPad, Manny was back into the hotel security net and tracing her movements from the security cameras. Roland watched gray-faced as they saw Killam Grimes sneak up on Lucia and hit her in the neck before leading her away.

"Drugged her," the grim cyborg rumbled.

Manny swiped through a few more camera angles. "I picked them up in the alley outside the service entrance. From there he takes her to a roller. I'm pulling its transponder now." Municipal traffic networks were not the sort of thing Manny had difficulty penetrating. In mere minutes, he had enough access to follow the vehicle's route.

"All right. The car's transponder cuts out for twenty-five seconds at four separate points in the next ten minutes."

"Four locations then. At one of those he jumped out with the boss." Mindy had changed into her armored blue jumpsuit, and was busy buckling belts pouches to it. As if she had never existed, the prostitute disappeared and in her place was a professional killer positively dripping with weapons and gear.

"How far can that thing cover in twenty-five seconds?" Manny asked, mostly to himself.

Roland answered. "Doesn't matter. It would take at least a couple of seconds for him to jump out, pull Lucia out, and then send the car off. If he bailed out with Lucia during one of those blackouts, the thing will have traveled less distance while hidden than the other times."

"Right!" Manny said. "Let's see. First blackout it went eight-hundred-and-sixty feet. Second blackout..." a pause while he scanned the data, "...we get six-hundred and forty."

"That's a lot lower," Mindy pointed out.

Roland was less sure. "Check the rest. He could have stopped it just to fuck with us."

"Number three is seven-hundred and eighty. Fourth was just over nine-hundred."

"Either two or three, then," Roland muttered. "Probably number two."

"Should we split up?" Manny asked.

"Yeah. I'll take number two. You guys take three. What's in those areas, Manny?"

"Second blackout covers a good chunk of an entertainment zone. Nightclubs, bars, vape dens, VR parlors and that sort of thing. Third blackout is not far away from that. It runs through a neighboring commercial zone. Tons of retail and food services."

Roland started barking orders. "Everyone pull the maps up on your comms. Cover the zones and look for hiding places. He'll want lots of noise, electromagnetic interference, things like that to cover him. He'll avoid areas with lots of cameras, too. Manny, when you get close, try to slice through any security nets and use what cameras there are to see if he fucks up."

"What about you?" Manny sounded concerned.

"I'll do this shit the old-fashioned way."

Manny shook his head. "Caelestus cops are not a racket, Mr. Tankowicz. You can't just tear up a nightclub and not expect to deal with them."

"I'll be discrete." His tone failed to convince either Mindy or Manny that such a thing was possible. However they both wisely let the matter drop. If the Caelestus constabulary wanted to duke it out with Roland Tankowicz, that would just have to be their lesson to learn.

"Stay on comms, and I want check-ins every fifteen minutes. We rendezvous back here in three hours unless the trail gets hot."

"Roger that," Mindy acknowledged. "Let's grab a car, Manny."

Roland took off at a loping jog. Once he had the room he stretched his stride and accelerated. The folks wandering through the evening streets of Venus Caelestus were thus treated to the sight of a towering cyborg in a casual suit hurtling through the traffic patterns at more than fifty miles per hour. He vaulted whole rows of vehicles with great leaps that shook the ground when he landed, and his pace never suffered for the distraction.

He arrived at the entertainment block in less than three minutes, where he checked his comm to see precisely where the roller had gone dark and where it had lit up again. He began by simply walking the six-hundred and eighty feet as directly as he could, searching for likely places to escape a car with a drugged woman in tow.

The first few buildings were obviously bad choices. Ritzy, glitzy gentleman's clubs festooned with cameras at street level sent a very clear message to anyone who cared to look that no sort of trouble was to be tolerated by the owners of these establishments. Another few hundred feet of pitted metal decking later and Roland was looking at an altogether more appetizing locale.

The first thing that hit him was the noise. A thumping, booming rumble in the pit of his stomach that seemed to cancel out all other sounds as it battered the inside of his skull with tuneless rhythm. Then there were the lights. Signage both holographic and neon washed the sidewalk with an unforgiving photonic noise to rival its oppressive sonic counterpart. Combined, the noise and the lights would confound the passive eavesdropping of any police drone that passed by. A final scan of the building confirmed Roland's other suspicions. Not a camera or door scanner was to be found for many feet in either direction. If he was a professional killer with a drugged prisoner, this is exactly the sort of place where he would unload her.

Grimes would not be stupid enough to bring Lucia through the front door. This place looked like a legitimately functioning entertainment venue. Somebody would notice something. There would be real live bouncers inside who would not take kindly to such shenanigans. He knew this because decades ago he had been one of those bouncers. Insurance premiums were as immutable as death and taxes, so respectable nightclub owners did not appreciate patrons in the grips of powerful pharmaceuticals. Certainly not if those pharmaceuticals had been purchased somewhere else.

Forcing an outward calm he did not feel, Roland stalked across the flashing façade. Between this building and the next was a narrow space, not even wide enough to be called a proper alley. It was nearly pitch dark because the dull featureless metal walls had no sheen and any light that found its way in the space died an unhappy death against those surfaces.

It was perfect.

The glacial rage inside the big man began to churn in his guts. His anger was almost never a hot thing. It did not burn brightly and manifest itself in agitation or bluster. It simply existed as a frigid determination to hurt and kill bolstered by an unshakable confidence that he possessed the skills and hardware to make that happen.

He feared for Lucia, but he knew he would find her one way or the other. It would be best for everyone if he found her the one way. For if he found her the other, he expected he would kill every Red Hat on Venus before he calmed down enough to be reasoned with. That would be a sub-optimal outcome for all involved. If he kept his thoughts logical, he understood that there was virtually no chance she was dead or seriously harmed. The meticulous extraction methods Grimes used to get her out of the hotel proved this. Great care was taken to remover her without harm, and that meant they wanted her alive and whole for something. Roland could not guess what that might be with any specificity, though in a general sense he knew it was to draw Manny out in a way that precluded Roland from interfering. He acknowledged that this was a good plan.

He stepped into the deep black of the alley, then waited for his eyes to adjust. There were times he envied Mindy her bionic eyes, and this was one of them. His organic eyes were as good as modern gene therapy could make them, and once acclimated to the reduced illumination he saw through the darkness as well as most folks could in bright moonlight.

The club owners were using the space to store their recyclers and a few refrigeration condensers thrummed noisily in the dark. Whole sections of the ground were just lightly vibrating grates that let extra steam and water vapor escape from unseen equipment below the street level. It was a great place to defend, and a perfect setting for booby traps.

The machines that lived in Roland's body were very similar to the ones in Lucia's. The United Earth Defense Force had been wise enough to ensure the brain chemistry of a high-tech super-soldier never got too far out of nice, safe, and "healthy" parameters. As such, Roland could not experience acute anxiety in the classic sense. If his amygdala became too active signaling for stress hormones, the little nanobots would scrub them from his system before the thousand-pound armored superhuman could do something untoward with all that impressive offensive might. Since Roland had never really had any issues with anxiety, this feature had never interfered with his personality the way it was affecting Lucia's.

However, in the narrow corridor between those two nightclubs, Roland Tankowicz experienced a very strange, very disconcerting feeling.

He was afraid.

Thirty years ago he had been here. A lone soldier standing a dark enclosed space not unlike this one. In a similar suffocating darkness, a hidden bomb had torn a hole in the side of a dome and ripped his body apart. The improvised explosive had hurled his pieces raw and bleeding onto the orange dirt of this burning hellscape. Where the blast had destroyed his exposure suit, his naked skin instantly burned black, and his lungs took a great gulp of superheated air through the cracked faceplate of his helmet. He could not even crawl back to the shelter of the shattered dome just a few dozen feet away, because he had no arms or legs with which to pull himself. He had tried to hold his breath, tried not to breathe the atmosphere that was burning him to death both inside and out. The young man had closed his eyes tightly, because they were boiling to steam inside his skull, and that twenty-three-year-old soldier had bitten down on to a silent scream of agony for the longest sixteen seconds in recorded history. Roland remembered every one of the endless heartbeats it took for his squad to rescue him. Time is very relative thing when you are roasting alive in your own skin.

Two days later and he wished they had not. Blind, crippled, breathing on a machine and shitting into a bag, Roland Tankowicz had begged for death like a mother mourning a lost child. He had lived entire lifetimes of terror and pain in this brief chunk of time, and he awoke from his resulting coma a broken old man. This is when a portly scientist named Warren Johnson had made him an offer no man in his condition could refuse, and the young pile of failing organs leapt at it. A golem was born that day. The horror that would become known as Breach was birthed on Venus in a dark hole just like this one. That monster had done a lot of killing, and all of it had started here and started with the Red Hats. All the nightmares Roland had been trying to avoid were abruptly before him.

This dark alley frightened him because it was all too close to that catalyzing event. He had put three decades and millions of miles between himself and that day, and somehow, he had convinced himself that was enough. If he had stayed away from this planet, it might have been. Yet he was here all the same, and he was afraid. This remained a distant and unpleasant feeling, but not entirely unfamiliar.

If not for Lucia, he might have forgotten fear altogether. The irony of this was not lost on him. Roland was a man made of armor, an invincible juggernaut. The universe held few things that scared him. The sad terrible coincidence of his current existence lived in the fact that one of those singular things was the love of a small woman from Uptown. Another was a head full of bad memories about a horrible thing that happened on Venus. Now fate had seen fit to seat these fears across from each other as dueling obstacles to goals Roland was unable to abandon. Roland hated fear. He had gone to great lengths to avoid and conquer it. He even thought for a while that he had succeeded.

He had charged heavy gun emplacements on exotic worlds without any problem. He had kicked through fortified bulkheads to battle cyborgs and robots inside spaceships without issue. He had happily hurled himself into a hundred battles against impossible odds with a smile on his lips and a song in his soldier's heart. This was his way and he loved it. Roland wore fear like cheap jewelry; it was an afterthought at best.

Staring into a black alleyway while his guts churned like green recruit reminded him that this was a childish conceit. The man who could lift sixty tons and run faster than a cheetah, the hero of a dozen wars and a hundred battles, the hardened armored super-soldier of nightmare and legend, was having trouble taking a single step forward.

If he was not trying so hard to understand and process a heap of unpleasant and unfamiliar emotions, Roland might have laughed at the perverse cruelty of an indifferent universe. In the end it was Lucia who saved him, because despite his own heap of insecurities, he feared losing that woman more than he feared anything else. More than any bomb, more than the loss of his own soul, the thought of not saving her filled him with a galvanizing dread sadly indistinguishable from actual courage. He suspected he was not the first person to experience this sensation. He had been in enough battles to suspect that some of the more courageous men running into the fight were doing it not because they were brave, but because some horrible thing inside their own minds was chasing them.

He had brought no sensors. No tracking devices. There was no way to tell what might be waiting for him when he ventured into the darkness. He did not care, and his first stride into the alley was long and bold. There was no sound, no explosion, and no attack from within. Just bleak shadows and the quiet of empty space. He scanned back and forth, eyes squinting to pick out details as he passed deeper inside. He found the door about forty feet down, nearly hidden by the shadowed bulk of a recycler.

He paused, not exactly sure how to proceed. Then, with a small mental shrug of dismissal, he punched the door off its hinges.

Chapter Twenty-Eight

Killam's question took Lucia by surprise.

"What?" she replied, almost forgetting to maintain her illusion of drowsiness. Whatever Grimes had dosed her with had been strong, but her internal machines had begun scrubbing it from her system almost immediately. This did not prevent her from experience intense dyskinesia and confusion for a while, but by the time Grimes had strapped her to the cot she was already nearly completely recovered. She spent the time while Grimes was gone working on the 'Kuffs, and she was nearly out of them when he returned. Only a few thin strands of polycarbonate held them together, and she left these now while Grimes questioned her.

"What did you steal from Hardesty tonight?"

"You don't know?" She was not sure why this surprised her. It made perfect sense for Hardesty to hide his indiscretions from his clan of brainwashed assassins. It would not serve the man's interests to have the Balisongs know their biggest booster was, in fact, betraying them. It just felt strange to be questioned this way under these circumstances.

Grimes kept his voice calm and level. "Humor me."

Lucia let her brain run a few dozen scenarios. The time Grimes spent in meditation had allowed her to reign her anxiety over being drugged and captured back to a tolerable level, so her analysis was not ruined by encroaching panic. In about one second, she made her choice.

"We stole his records. He has been dealing behind the scenes with OmniCorp to break the Union and revitalize Venusian mining with machines and off-world labor. Manuel knew this was going on, and it's why Hardesty wants him dead. If the Union finds out Hardesty is betraying them..." She let that part trail off. She wanted

Grimes to fill in the blanks on his own. His response would tell her how much he knew and understood. It might give her leverage.

She watched her captor intently, dilating her sense of time to catch the nuances of his facial expressions. She looked for tells in the arch of his brow, the curl of a lip, the barest twitch of his jaw. To his credit, Grimes was inscrutable.

"This does not seem plausible."

"Why not?" Lucia fired back. "Hardesty has been at this for decades. He's a tired, drunk, self-serving horndog who likes wearing fancy clothes and screwing young girls. He's just done with it all and cashing out. People do that all the time."

"You are either lying or missing something. Craddock would never go along with it."

"Manny said the same thing. We figure Hardesty has something Craddock wants. A carrot to dangle in front of his nose. Something so tempting that Craddock might forget to ask enough of the right questions before giving Hardesty what he wants. We assume we will find it in the records we stole."

There it was. A tic, the slightest tightening of a single cheek muscle. Lucia seized upon the opportunity. "Think about it, Grimes. Everyone knows that zealots are easy to manipulate. That's why despots and megalomaniacs like them." Her sneer was cruel. "You're a zealot, so I presume you get that. Right now you are trying very hard to not believe me, but you can't deny that what I am saying makes sense."

Grimes knew she was wrong. *Mushin* was ego-less, so the crippling doubts that wanted to erode his resolve were simply the buzzing of flies against a closed screen door. He was aware of them, yet they could not exert any influence over his thinking. His specific knowledge of Lincoln Hardesty had been limited for quite some time, though the preparation for this mission had required some research. Hardesty's proclivities were hardly private, and his flamboyant bias toward excess was not new information. It stood to reason that Hardesty enjoyed being rich, and that OmniCorp had the ability to make him more so by many degrees. On the other hand, Hardesty had always been a staunch and material booster for the Red Hats. To betray them now was a bizarre shift for a man with decades and millions of credits invested in the cause.

219

The Craddock angle required more thought as well. Grimes knew Craddock very well, and even the cold assassin had noted that when a goal looked like it was within his grasp, Craddock could develop tunnel vision sufficient to blind him to all sorts of iniquities.

Nothing the woman was saying was impossible, and only a few parts were improbable. His mind, detached and emotionless, demanded more information. No conclusions could be drawn from what he knew right now. Quality of judgment was directly proportionate to the quality of data, and his data was too scant for the quiet mind to trust any judgments based upon it. He decided to shift tactics and see if there was any way to shake the woman's story.

"You haven't really made your case very well."

"Once we go through those records, the case is going to make itself. What you do with that is up to you."

He tilted his head. "You assume you will survive this?"

"Yes. Eighty-five percent sure I survive this."

"That's oddly specific. Do you want to tell me why you picked that number?"

"Sure. You drugged me because you need me alive and can't beat me in a fight. You could not have taken me too far from the hotel because Manny will have traced your car. I'm certain you did something to hide where we stopped, because otherwise Roland would be cleaning your organs off of his boots by now."

Grimes let his eyebrows rise a touch. The woman continued. "You can't kill me yet because you haven't got Manny, so I'm safe until you do. That would mean that your people will be trying to set up a meet to discuss my release in exchange for Manny." She dismissed this with a huff. "We all know that will never work, but you don't care. You just need him out in the open so you can take your shot. By now Hardesty will have called for all of us to be killed because we now have evidence about what he's been doing." She paused for a breath. "So, you can't kill me yet, and every second that goes by is another second for the rest of my team to find me. They will find me." She raised her chin and shook her head to forestall his response. "No, no, no. That's not an expression of hope or faith, Grimes. That's just the truth. Roland has been doing 'search-and-destroy' work his whole life. Manny was your best infiltrator, and Mindy still holds the top seat on the Hunter's Lodge leader boards.

220

It's not a question of 'will they find me?' but rather a question of 'how quickly.'"

"But if not quickly enough? Or if they have already been handled?" Grimes pushed her. He was intrigued by her analysis. There was much more to this woman than mere wired reflexes.

"There's your fifteen percent uncertainty."

He almost laughed. "I would think there is a lot more than fifteen points' worth of variation to that!"

"There would be, except you have to balance that against me escaping, too. The chance of me extricating myself offsets the additional risks. The scenario trees get complicated fast, with lots of branches crossing each other."

"Even if you are right, that does not explain why a drugged woman tied to a bed thinks her chances are so good."

Her face broadcast confidence bordering upon conceit. "That's because your data is bad."

"Do tell."

Lucia's hand darted forward and struck Grimes under the chin. His head snapped back and his teeth clicked together. She followed with another blow that drove the assassin off the cot and sent him sprawling to the floor. She was upon him before he understood what was happening, and his hasty defense was batted aside with skill eclipsed only by the contempt served with it. She cinched a forearm across his throat and pinned him to the floor.

"You see, Grimes. I'm not drugged, and I'm not tied up."

On cue, a massive crash shook the building, and heavy rhythmic thuds vibrated the floors. Someone very heavy was stomping their way.

"You got lucky, Grimes," Lucia hissed into his ear. "I got to you before Roland did." Then louder, she called out, "In here, Roland!"

Killam Grimes did not feel lucky. The door to the cell first crumpled, then tore away from its moorings. The towering black shape of the fixer blocked any view of the hall beyond it. Lying on his back, Grimes was forced to look way up to see the man's face, and for an instant it looked as if the big thing might stomp on his head.

Instead, Tankowicz looked to the woman and spoke. "You okay?"

"Yeah," she replied. "Dad's bots handled whatever gunk he stuck me with. I played possum to see if I could get anything out of him."

This statement made the Balisong's heart sink. He did not even know at what point he had lost control of the operation, or if he ever had it. He put this out of his mind and focused on escaping before they got around to killing him.

"Did you?"

"Not really. He's clueless. They've been keeping him in the dark."

Roland huffed. "Of course they are. Can't have good little killers asking too many questions."

Lucia looked down to the pinned man, "See? Everybody knows about using zealots."

The words stung, but Grimes could not afford to dwell on it. He shifted just a touch, probing for flaws in the woman's balance and posture. This hideout had a dozen secret entrances and exits, and he did not need a large head start to make any of them.

Lucia continued to converse with her partner, and Grimes waited for her weight to change when she moved. His timing would need to be perfect, and that was fine. His timing was always perfect.

When Lucia moved to drag him up, he exploded. In her haste, she had failed to search him after bringing him down, and thus his escape was made. He burst forward to his feet, knowing full well he was not fast enough to evade the woman. A nimble arm flicked out, palm extended. A small round metal ball arced from his outstretched hand and bounced off the fixer's chest. It hit the floor with clunk and Grimes heard Tankowicz bark, "Shit!"

With speed that was difficult to imagine for one so large, the big man pushed the woman aside and fell on the device. Killam Grimes did not stop to evaluate all the things that happened next. He sped through the door like a jackrabbit and streaked down the hall toward the closest exit.

The explosion was not as loud as it should have been. Grimes attributed that to the giant's body muffling the blast. He still had little idea exactly what Tankowicz was, but he felt certain it would take more than a small grenade to stop such a thing. Grimes ran faster. He cleared the door to the alley and was on the street in just a few seconds. In an instant, he had disappeared into the knots of people and autonomous rolling carriages bustling both ways up and down the lane.

Clearing the block, he reached for his comm. The next logical step was to call Craddock. To apprise his leader of the situation was the natural follow-up to losing the girl. But something stayed his hand, and he simply looked at the small black handheld.

What if the woman had not been lying?

He could not fathom such a thing. It made no sense. Hardesty was an ally, a friend to the cause. He had been one for as long as Grimes had been alive. Craddock was no fool, either. If Hardesty was up to something, Craddock would know. Nevertheless, if he separated his prejudice from the information, none of what that woman had said was all that far-fetched.

Doubt was poison. His masters had drilled that into his head from birth. To doubt was to invite weakness. He walked on, passing the first of his potential hideouts in favor of more time to think. This was an uncharacteristic choice for the dedicated assassin. His *zanshin* was shattered, he knew, and *mushin* remained maddeningly elusive.

Even for one such as him, internal conflict was inevitable. This could be excused if he was not in the middle of an operation. This did not seem an opportune moment for introspection. The thought made Grimes scowl even more deeply. The old war-master who had mentored him in his youth would have laughed at this fallacy. The wizened fighter would have rebuked his student, telling him that this was *exactly* the correct time for introspection. A doubt, a conflict such as this one could not be ignored or put aside lightly. Left unresolved, it would grow and weaken him in a moment requiring strength. He had to explore it, to confront it so it could be expunged.

He walked on.

So much of what he knew to be true was telling him the woman was a liar. Yet everything he knew about the nature of human weakness said that she could very well be telling the truth. He trusted Hardesty with the same blind loyalty every member of the union and the Red Hats did. This should have been enough to convince him of Hardesty's innocence; however, he also knew better than anyone that men were innately weak. This was fundamental. Resolve and dedication could erode over time. The keen edges of a true believer often wore down to the shapeless malaise of a jaded cynic. How did the old poet put it? What happens to a dream deferred? Had the years of struggle without success eroded the support they all relied on so much? Had Lincoln Hardesty's dedication to Free Venus dried up like a raisin in the sun? The sun was very hot on Venus, and truly strong people were few and far between.

Grimes thought of everything he knew about Hardesty. He mentally played all the conversations he had ever had with Craddock in his mind as well. The mental exercise calmed him, and his mind finally grew clear enough to let go of the terror his doubts had birthed. Without fear, without prejudice or bias, Grimes at last grasped what he needed to do with crystal clarity.

He had to know. If he did not kill the seed of doubt in his mind it would grow into a mighty oak before long. He would prefer to die rather than crumble under such weight.

A decision made, he stopped walking. He found he needed to look around just to get his bearings. He had become so entrenched in his own ruminations he had lost track of where he was. He stifled another internal rebuke for the stupidity of his lapse, as it served no purpose. Then he looked back down at the comm in his hand.

Craddock would want an update soon. That meant he had very little time to do this. No one could know what he was about to do.

Killam Grimes needed answers, and he knew exactly where to find them.

Chapter Twenty-Nine

"Wat the hell is going on!"

Craddock was shouting into the connection at the bruised and ashen face of Lincoln Hardesty. Hardesty snarled back, no less vehement. "Where the fuck is Grimes? You said he was handling them!"

"Grimes got the woman. Last I heard he was holding her somewhere near you."

"Thank goodness for small fucking favors, then! Do you have a plan for retrieving what they took?"

"Link, I don't even *know* what they took, so how the fuck am I supposed to have a plan for getting it back?"

Hardesty wiped at his face furiously with a palm. "It just some records. Data. It's sensitive as all hell, so I gotta get it back before they give it to anybody who can use it to hurt us."

Craddock refused to let the matter go. "Hurt us? Or maybe what you mean is before it can hurt you? I told you before that if this starts to stink like shit you and I were going to have a reckoning. I'm starting to think that reckoning happens now, Link."

"Don't be like this, Al..."

"Like what? Like a guy burning resources to clean up a mess somebody else made? Or like a guy who is starting to think he is getting played like a fool? Let me lay it out for you, Link. Right now I am sitting in The Colander surrounded by loyal and dedicated soldiers for the cause. These boys trust me to lead them to a Free Venus. Now you want me to throw them at off-world hitters because they stole something from you that you are too fucking scared to tell us about? Do you know how that looks?"

"You have to trust me, Al..."

"You have to trust ME!" Craddock roared. "You have to trust me with your stupid little secret, because the fact that you don't is telling

225

me that whatever it is you've lost is going to piss me way the hell off. There are only two things that would piss me off enough to tell you to fuck off, Link. One of them is you asking to date my niece, the other is you selling the Red Hats out. You haven't asked about my niece since she turned eighteen, so I assume that one ain't the problem."

Hardesty watched that barrel chest heave as his friend's breath came in heavy waves. The pause in his rant was a test, a chance to see if anything said had struck a nerve. Hardesty's face was unliving stone, betraying nothing.

Craddock calmed his voice and continued. "I am not an unreasonable man, Link. You are old and tired, and maybe you are done fighting for our freedom. I can get that. Really, I can. If you've sold out the Hats, just say it now. You are too far away for me to get to you, so you'll have plenty of time to run away. I won't chase you. Tell me the truth, cancel your deal, and just run. That will be the end of this. I'll end this scrap with the fixer and I'll cut Manny loose. We can survive that. You and me both can survive that. But you gotta level with me right now."

With his plans in a very tenuous place, Hardesty actually considered just spilling his guts to Craddock. It would ruin him financially, but he would be safe. In the war between greed and cowardice, however, Lincoln Hardesty's avarice remained the undisputed victor. "I haven't sold out the Hats, Al. You know I'd never do that. They stole a bunch of union records and OmniCorp communications. If you look real close, you'll see that some money is missing, too. Quite a bit, really. I ain't proud of that, all right? I'm sorry."

Alasdair Craddock did not buy that for a picosecond. Hardesty had been skimming from everyone for so long it was a cliché. He did not need to call Hardesty out on his lie, either. The mere attempt at deception was all that was necessary to confirm Cradock's suspicions. "Fine, Link. You're a crook. We can handle that. Let me contact Grimes and we'll sort out the situation with Richardson."

"Thank you, Al." Hardesty's relief looked and sounded sincere, at least. He cut the connection before Craddock could badger him any further and dialed up another call. This one was to Earth, and thus had to be routed through an Anson relay lest each sentence be saddled with a fifty-second light-speed delay. There was the small consolation of light carrier-wave traffic this time of night, so at least he could enjoy clear sound and video.

The face that appeared on his screen was as lean as his own, with a pointed widow's peak and narrow black eyes. The proud red and white OmniCorp logo was glowing warmly on the wall behind his head. The man on the screen did not look pleased to be receiving a late-night call from Venus. His mood did not improve when Hardesty laid out the evening's events and how they might affect the future of his dealings with OmniCorp.

"So exactly how sensitive is this stolen information, Mr. Hardesty? OmniCorp has a large investment in you already. The board of directors will not appreciate this setback."

"It's not really a setback just yet," Hardesty replied calmly. "The data is still here on Venus, and they won't be able to access the dangerous stuff without breaking a hidden layer of encryption. That will take quite a while. If we can bring them in soon, there will be no issue. I need access to some of your assets here to make this happen is all I'm saying."

"Exactly what are you referring to when you mention 'assets,' Mr. Hardesty."

Lincoln had a chuckle at the question. A suit-wearing businessman trying to play coy with a career smuggler and power broker was highly amusing indeed. "In this case, I am referring to your three operatives in The Colander. The ones mounted to Kanos. I have already closed off the spaceport here in Caelestus to the thieves, so I am confident the data will be returned to The Colander for extraction. I would like for it to be intercepted there by your people. Oh, and one of the targets is a heavily augmented man, ex-military. If you can spare some scanning drones or other espionage assets, he should be easy to spot and follow. I am also moving Craddock's people to help, but in this case, I think a little redundancy is in order."

Hardesty was rewarded with a small twitch of the man's face. It betrayed obvious irritation with how poorly OmniCorp had hidden its movements. "Fine then. Though I am very dismayed that you felt compelled to compile such a large quantity of sensitive intelligence, I suppose I can understand why you thought it necessary. As long as the data stays secure this should not upset our relationship. We are aware of Mr. Tankowicz already, and I will have our operatives intercept him and his people as soon as they return to The Colander. Please don't make this worse by attempting anything while they are still in Caelestus."

"Don't be ridiculous," Hardesty dismissed the admonition. "I'm trying to get of this rock, not sit in one of its prisons for the rest of my life. It has taken a lot of effort to keep the union in the dark about how dire the economic situation here is. If the regular troops find out I've been fudging the numbers to prevent a panic?" He shrugged at the screen. "My life is over and your investment becomes worthless."

"It is not OmniCorp's fault that Venusian labor is too expensive to be competitive."

"Yeah, but it is your problem. If the union finds out you've been propping up exports to satisfy your investors, there will be panic and rioting. Nobody is going to invest in your contracts if you set up your autofactories in the middle of a civil war."

"That is already understood, Mr. Hardesty. Until this matter is resolved, you will need to stay in Caelestus. If any union feathers get ruffled by fallout from this mess, you will have to stay there to un-ruffle them. How about Craddock?"

"Craddock is becoming very suspicious. I told you he wasn't stupid. It's only a matter of time before he puts it all together."

"Will he need to be managed?"

Hardesty thought about that for a long moment. He did not like the answer, and he hated himself for giving it. "Yeah. I think it's about time to take him off the table. His boy Sully is well-liked and not-too-bright. He'll be a perfect replacement."

"Excellent. My people will make that happen. You cannot be connected in any way to that event. In the meantime, I suggest you put the rest of your house in order. Mistakes like this have ended profitable relationships more than once, Mr. Hardesty."

"Same to you, pal," Hardesty let his affected corporate demeanor slip, and the jaded Venusian laborer came through as he killed the connection. "Fuck you," he added as an unheard afterthought.

He leaned back in his chair, a maelstrom of emotions warring in his head. Betraying Craddock had been easy when all he was doing was taking bribes from OmniCorp. When he began to actively work with the enemy to weaken the union and mislead the Red Hats, he had felt a few pangs of guilt. Nothing too acute, just a sort of nagging shame that was easily stifled by expensive whores, exotic booze, and a lavish lifestyle.

But tonight he had called for the murder of his oldest friend, and that actually hurt. The pain was competing with elation, though. Soon he would be free of Venus and its orange sky and blistering heat. He would be free of the oppression, the politics, the demagoguery and the fighting, too. He had given up of freeing the domes, and now he just wanted to free himself. Abandoning the cause had been easy. Betraying his friend had been hard. He would get over it. In just a few short days, none of it would matter anyway.

Sully would replace Craddock, further weakening the Red Hats. Sully was a good man, but a flaccid leader. Without a strong union, the Red Hats under Sully would fragment into tiny cells of fanatics, good only for the occasional bombing or assassination. A strong union might have propped him up, but Hardesty had ensured the union would fall apart when he resigned. With the help of OmniCorp, he had systematically weakened the union leadership to the point that the whole group was run by a collection of rabid morons. Volatile personalities and terminally incompetent people had been moved into key roles over the years. The carefully crafted combination of patsies ensured the whole group would collapse under even minute pressure as soon as Hardesty was not there to manage them. A couple of OmniCorp agents filled those ranks as well, prepared to stir up chaos at just the right moment.

It was a good plan, years in the making. Yet because he had needed the insurance of potential blackmail, it was also all spelled out in black and white in those stolen data files. There were names, dates, and personnel dossiers in there. The data contained timetables, secret communiques, diagrams, meeting notes, and long lists of payouts. It was a devastating wealth of incriminating details, all sitting in electronic black and white just waiting for someone to expose the whole thing. Everything was so dammed precarious at this juncture, and Hardesty had just lost control of a serious monkey wrench.

Oblivious to unseen eyes watching his every move, the spare man leaned further back in his plush office chair to close his eyes and exhale a huge sigh.

From his vantage point deep within the shadowed corners of the office, Killam Grimes tried to make sense of everything he had just heard. Infiltrating the penthouse had been child's play for a senior Red Hat operative. He had all the necessary codes and passwords memorized. Hardesty had dismissed all his staff for the appointment with his hooker, so there was no one to sneak past by the time Grimes had returned to the scene. The assassin had quite simply taken the elevator straight to the penthouse, walked through the lobby, and slipped in quietly while Hardesty argued with Craddock.

It seemed to Grimes, now that he had arrived at this juncture, that this had always been coming. Before this instant, he could not have known it would be like this. Now that he was here and fully involved in the reality of the present, it should have been obvious. The contradictions created by the knowledge he now possessed threatened to break his sanity. He had come here to confront his doubts, to purge the poison and restore his resolve. Despite those efforts, the man trembling in the shadows now felt less resolved than ever. He had been taught from birth that doubt was weakness, yet it was doubt that had brought him here. Doubt had given him the truth.

Truth made a person strong. He had been taught that as well. The little lies people told themselves bred weakness and sloth. A man was fat because he ate too much and exercised too little, not because of the nefarious actions of food producers. People were ignorant because they did not study, not because the system held them back. A young Balisong was allowed no lies, and so they grew strong.

Mastering all the emotions clamoring around in his head took herculean effort, but logic prevailed in the killer's mind and the sequence of conclusions was undeniable. The woman had given him doubt. Doubt had brought him to the truth. The truth made him strong.

His teachers had been wrong. Doubt was not poison. Hardesty was. One greedy man had exploited the unwavering nature of their dedication for his own ends. Doubt might have stopped this from happening, had he just been willing to entertain it.

The woman had been right all along. Grimes was a zealot, and this had made him weak.

Whether or not he was still a zealot, Grimes could not say. What he knew for sure was that two teams of his brothers had died for that man's lies and his greed. Countless more would suffer under the bootheels of corporate oppressors and their fascist governmental lapdogs if Grimes did not put a stop to it.

Like oozing ink, the assassin detached from the shadows and slid behind the reclining Hardesty. For a minute, he simply looked down on the man's face as it lay in repose, eyes closed and chest rising and falling while he caught his breath. Killam Grimes tried to imagine what thoughts might be filling that head at this very moment. Was Hardesty happy? Was he afraid? Confident? Smug?

The killer had no concept of what made a man like Hardesty tick, and he abandoned speculating when the lean man's eyes fluttered open. Those eyes widened at the sight of the feared assassin standing over his seat, and the precariously leaning chair toppled over backwards when he jumped in surprise.

"Dammit, Grimes!" Hardesty grumbled. "What the hell are you doing here?" The injured shoulder made Hardesty slow to rise. Killam's boot across his jaw sent him crashing back to the floor when he had nearly succeeded in doing so.

When it came time to kill, Killam Grimes knew better than to hesitate. He had no speeches to give, and no desire to hear what Hardesty had to say. Part of Grimes acknowledged that he was not as detached from his emotions as he could have been. Killing a man like Hardesty should have been a very quick and clean process for a true professional.

In   this   case,   it   was   neither.

Chapter Thirty

Lucia's ears were ringing.

The grenade had not been a large one, but the blast was deafening all the same. Roland appeared none the worse for wear, and she was glad for this. The look of concern on his face told her she should probably reassure him that she, too, was fine.

"I'm all right, Roland." Her own voice sounded tinny and distant.

"You sure?" He asked the question as if she was incapable of determining her own condition.

She dismissed him with a scowl, and barked, "Yes! It was just loud. Now let's get back to Mindy and Manny. Hardesty, Craddock, and OmniCorp are about to come down hard now that the hot potato is in play."

Roland grunted his agreement and pinged Mindy and Manny on their comm channel.

"I've got her, team. She's okay. We need to bug out fast and hard. Hit rally point bravo and stay low. All players are in the game now. Shit's about to get kinetic."

"Roger, Breach," Mindy's voice came through, sounding very relieved. "RP bravo, copy. Running silent. See you there."

Roland's jacket and shirt had been ruined by the grenade, and this meant moving inconspicuously was going to be a problem. Fortunately, Roland's bulk and the noise from the nightclub above them had been sufficient to muffle the sound of the grenade's detonation. The big man stripped out of the rags covering his chest and dialed his skin as flat and dark as possible. The trick had worked often enough in the past. In bad lighting, this would look enough like a tight black shirt to prevent too much staring, though anyone who looked closely would find themselves very confused.

"Ready?" Lucia asked when he finished.

"Let's go."

They exited into the alley and made their way to the street. Roland's handheld had not survived the blast, and his internal comm had no retinal display. He was forced to navigate from memory, which was a daunting task in the unfamiliar city. His military training proved to be his savior, and when he applied the basic orienteering skills every good soldier learned, he was able to get them moving in the correct direction.

The big cyborg kept a wary eye out for Killam Grimes. The canny assassin could be anywhere, and he had already proved to be highly resourceful. If Grimes wanted to take another swipe a Lucia, this entertainment sector held any number of convenient ambush locations for him to try. If he looked at it logically, he would have understood that this was unlikely. Grimes was far too outmatched to take them when they were wary. But threats to Lucia's safety had a way of making Roland behave in a highly illogical manner. The part of him that understood tactics acknowledged that this was the weakness Grimes had been trying to exploit all along. If his intense desire to kill the man was not otherwise clouding his thoughts, he might have been impressed with that.

Meeting with the rest of the team went without incident. Manny checked the various security InfoNets to see who might be looking for them, and the results were predictable. No one was surprised to find that the spaceport was on high alert. Ground transport to the other domes was also looking for them. Pogo planes to The Colander were suspiciously quiet about the group, and this fooled absolutely no one.

"He wants us to go back to The Colander," Manny sighed.

Roland agreed. "Obviously. His supporters are there. We'll be waltzing right into Craddock's stronghold."

"What's the plan, then?" Lucia asked.

"They won't hit us in receiving. They'll want to tail us until we get to somewhere more private. They run the whole damn place, so I don't see how we can avoid that."

"Should we call the RUC?" Lucia suggested. "They may be inclined to help us."

Manny winced. "That could be a real disaster, Boss. Instead of a few guys trying to bring us down, we could end up with a full-scale riot if the RUC gets involved. Everyone in The Colander hates them. Even folks who don't like the Red Hats."

Lucia tried again. Her brain moved faster than anyone else's. "What about Ellie? Can she help?"

Manny gave that some thought. "She could get us to the same freight haulers we came in on. She really doesn't like Roland though."

"Woman has taste, then," Mindy quipped, unable to stop herself.

Roland ignored her. "Make the call, Manny. Tell her it's the best way to get rid of me and she'll probably jump at the chance."

The call was placed. While reluctant to do so, Ellie agreed to help them. This came only after some spirited cajoling from Manny. The opportunity to get Roland off Venus did prove to be a significant motivator, surprising no one. They booked passage on the next pogo plane and loaded up for the trip. There was no effort made toward hiding their preparations, either. The trap being set for them was obvious and there was no point in pretending otherwise. Thinking they were going to slip through it was a waste of time and wasting time was not their style. The team recovered their equipment without incident and boarded their flight unmolested. The four-hour ride back to The Colander was a tense one, if uneventful. Knowing you were going to be attacked ahead of time did not make waiting for the moment any easier.

The group disembarked in steel-faced silence. All vestiges of subterfuge were discarded and the quartet that exited the landing station were conspicuous for their warlike appearance.

Lucia was wearing a full set of level II plates over a black bodysuit similar to Mindy's, if not as technologically impressive. She had eschewed a full helmet, settling on a minimal tac visor equipped with a simple comms rig and tactical HUD. She lost some protection, but it kept her weight and bulk down while preserving her peripheral vision. Lucia wore her beloved CZ-105 pistol in a high thigh holster. This and her PC-10 gauntlets were her only offensive weapons. The loricated armored gloves lent an inhuman mechanical menace to her appearance that was only increased by her suit of laminated armor plates and the tense set of her jaw.

Manny preferred lighter armor. He wore a simple gray ballistic weave vest and an armored vambrace for his right arm. His left arm, being made of most of the same materials Roland was, needed no extra protection. He had the same model visor as Lucia, and his long hair was pulled back in a loose knot to keep it out of his face. His satchel rode across his back, filled with whatever nefarious devices the clever scout felt might be needed for a mad dash through hostile territory.

Mindy had her armored blue jumpsuit, and the various accoutrements of the assassin's trade belted to her body. Her long Sasori dagger was strapped to her thigh, its pommel swaying just below the level of her waist. The suit was zipped tightly all the way to her throat, a clear indication to those who knew her that Mindy was all about business right now.

The three of them thus assembled would have caught attention under the best of circumstances. Even without Roland, their appearance and demeanor were very clearly broadcasting violent intentions. If any of the bleary-eyed Venusian laborers consigned to the dull existence of toiling under the Colander remained obtuse to the naked menace of the group striding across the reception area, the looming presence of Roland Tankowicz corrected any confusion.

Seven-and-a-half feet tall and wide as a car, the big cyborg had not bothered with tac harness or a visor. He wore plain black fatigues and a plain black shirt. He left his skin its default matte black color, and the brown leather stripes of Durendal's holster was the only color visible below his neck. The denizens of The Colander had seen a lot of weird stuff, and though new and exciting, a big man with a big gun was not the craziest thing they would witness in their lives. What had folks gasping and scurrying away was the helmet.

Roland had no bionic sensory organs. If he wanted tactical displays, targeting assistance, internal damage reports, or any of the other bits of data that were germane to operating on the 25th-century battlefield, he needed to be wearing his helmet. The helmet came in three pieces. A gorget for his neck that cupped his chin, a black skull cap that connected to the back of the gorget to protect his head, and a silver-white faceplate in the shape of a stylized mouthless skull. When all three pieces were assembled, the effect was chilling. Against the ocean of black that was his skin and clothing, the bright death's head seemed to be floating, a disembodied wraithlike messenger from death himself. In the dark inconsistent light of the battlefield, the grim skull's face was often the only thing the enemy ever saw clearly. It was a look designed to terrify, and more often than not, it worked.

If the commotion in the receiving area was any indication, the effectiveness had not worn off over the years. In scant seconds, almost all foot traffic had cleared the formerly bustling area and the path through to security was laid bare for all to see. No exotic sensory technology was required for the first, most obvious, anomaly to present itself.

"RUC is missing," Manny hissed. They all saw it, even from a hundred yards away. The security checkpoint was deserted, and Roland's scans concurred that the checkpoint was clear of all biologicals. He looped the team's visors into his scanner feed so they could see it, too. Manny said what they were all thinking. "That doesn't make sense. There is no way the RUC would ever help the Hats. Especially against a guy like Roland."

Lucia provided the answer. "OmniCorp is here. They have enough money and political heft to do this."

"Makes sense," Manny agreed.

"Look for the Kanos," Roland advised. "Those are the corporate goons. Stahlkorpers and BobCats are Craddock's. Remember their weak points."

"The Kanos don't have weak points," Lucia reminded him.

"Leave those to me."

It was eerie to walk through the abandoned security checkpoint. Scanners and kiosks sat empty and silent, mute witnesses to their passing. Beyond there, the concourse leading deep into the bowels of The Colander stretched before them. The wide spaces of receiving and security narrowed here, choking many lanes of foot traffic into one wide thoroughfare. Like most places under the dome, it was dim. What had been a minor nuisance before was now an ominous harbinger of impending danger. Roland hated choke points like this.

It was very close to receiving, and that made it an unlikely place for Craddock to jump them. Even with this understanding, something did not smell right.

"I'm on point, team. Mindy, you take sweep. Manny and Lucia watch the flanks. Give me sixty seconds to clear this hall."

"Wait," Manny called. "Set your scanners for passive sonics."

"I can't echolocate past forty or fifty feet, Manny."

"You will in a minute."

Roland was confused, but he knew better than to ask questions he was unlikely to understand the answers to. Manny knelt down and placed his palm against the metal floor. "I'm going to pulse for five seconds along a range from 25 kHz to about 400. Keep your gain in that range and you should get very good resolution... I think." The last bit was a quiet afterthought.

"Roger."

"Pulsing."

The actual sound was well outside human auditory range. Mindy yelped, her bionic ears obviously not liking the hypersonic pulse. It was over in five seconds, and sure enough Roland's HUD superimposed a detailed view of what lay beyond in ghostly pale relief over his view.

"Did it work?" Manny asked.

"Very well, actually," Roland said. "We need to use that trick more often."

"Fucking OW!" Mindy added. "That hurt!"

"Sorry," the scout replied. "I didn't know you could hear into that range."

"Neither did I!"

"Eyes front, team," Roland barked. "We are clear for the next hundred yards or so, but there is an open space at the end of this hallway that accesses a bunch of branching sections. There are moving bogeys in there. Shit, wait." He stopped explaining and sent the map data over to their visors so they could see as well.

"Craddock's or OmniCorp?" Lucia asked.

"Can't tell. Resolution was not great at this range. I think I count at least four bogeys, though. Probably means Craddock. The plan doesn't change much. I'll hit the door and mix it up with whatever is on the other side. If you see Kanos, keep moving to exfil, I'll catch up. If it's Craddock's Stahlkorpers, then feel free to help out. They aren't too hard to take down, but my gut says he has a lot of them. I don't want to get dragged down by their numbers because I thought I could handle more than a few at a time. Everyone copy?"

They did. Roland inhaled deeply. "Give me one minute, then I'll see you down there."

"Go get 'em, big guy," said Lucia.

"Save some for me," Mindy admonished.

"Don't die," Manny added helpfully.

Roland did not acknowledge this. He unslung Durendal and checked the magazine. He made sure fifty-caliber beads were indexed. The Stahlkorpers were tough, yet not so hardened that armor-piercing flechettes should be necessary. This was a good thing, because it would not be decent to have tungsten-tipped spikes barreling through the thin metal walls of the dome at twenty times the speed of sound. Too many innocent people lived here. Beads might punch holes in one wall, but doing so would shatter them into harmless fragments. They were the safer choice if you wanted to avoid what the military called 'collateral damage.'

Satisfied, he dug his toes into the deck and launched himself into a dead run. The hallway evaporated into horizontal streaks, Roland hitting his top speed of almost sixty miles per hour in about four strides. The metal door loomed wide in his view and Roland almost considered slowing down to assess its strength before attempting to breach it. In a moment of pique, Roland decided he would not slow down. He was not currently in a judicious mood. He wanted to break something and he needed something big enough to be satisfying.

The door was big. It was made of thick metal and well-constructed. It was a good door. The kind of door a proper craftsman might have been proud to install. It was a door that little doors would want to grow up and become, if doors could engage in that sort of wishful thinking. The door may have stopped a wayward supply cart, or perhaps a fork truck driven by a tipsy laborer.

It did not stop Roland Tankowicz. With a lowered shoulder the hurtling war machine hit that door with as much energy as a high-speed car crash. The metal heaved inward and buckled with a roaring, tearing, crashing sound. It held for a moment, as if it might actually resist the headlong charge of the furious cyborg. Even as the metal barrier pushed back, Roland's feet never stopped driving forward. There was a pause, a moment of pure tension while the deformed barrier held its ground defiantly and Roland shoved onward. It felt like an eternity, yet it did not last more than a half second. The proud door's instant of resistance died with the inexorable strides of size twenty-one booted feet.

Two tons of molded steel tore free of its tracks and fell with a crash into the empty space beyond. Seven Stahlkorper armatures stared into the now-gaping aperture where a giant black monster with a skull's face stood. They were confused and frightened, as so

238

much of what had just happened made little sense. This was supposed to be a surprise attack, why did it suddenly feel like they were the ones being ambushed? What kind of monster tears a section hatch off its tracks with his bare hands?

The damn thing wasn't even locked.

Chapter Thirty-One

Alasdair Craddock was snarling.

Hardesty had sold them out, that team of hitters from New Boston was due any second now, and Grimes was radio silent. The latest bit of news, delivered by his lieutenant, confused things even further and magnified his frustrations a thousand-fold.

"Grimes did what?" For some reason, Craddock needed it repeated.

"Grimes, uh... killed Hardesty, Al. About four hours ago. Lost his shit or something."

"Or something," Craddock grumbled. This was not good. Then louder, "We know for sure it was him?"

"Confirmed. Used his own, uh... codes and stuff. It was real messy, too. Like he was mad."

"That goddamn assassin is going to fucking ruin us!" He should not have said it. A passing courier heard his outburst and squeaked away in mortal terror. "Dammit," he grumbled. This was not helpful, and it was not the sort of inspired leadership his people needed right now. He forced a calm detached tone into his voice that he did not feel.

"And what the hell did you mean there's no RUC at the checkpoints?"

Sully shrugged. There were only so many ways one could phrase a thing like that. "There's uh, no one there. They're uh... all gone."

"They just abandoned a whole fucking checkpoint? Where did they go?"

Craddock was not sure why he thought Sully would have this information. Shouting at the man seemed unfair in this case. He was in a shouting mood, however, and that meant the shouting was non-negotiable.

Sully, wiser than he often sounded, just stared back at him. Even Sully knew this was a stupid question.

"Gah!" Craddock bellowed his frustration to the ceiling. "Fine! I need all the lads out, then. We got what, seven of them waiting past security? Put the others between us and there, roving patrols."

"Uh... sure thing Al," Sully mumbled. Then, when he realized his leader was waiting for him to go, he left with a dejected shuffle. The stocky man let all the air out of his body when the door closed behind his trusted lieutenant. He craved one good moment's peace before hurling himself back into the tempest, yet even this was denied him. His comm chimed rudely, scattering his attention and tearing a grunt of frustration from his lungs before he squelched it. He looked to see whose timing could be so amazingly poor as to call him now and growled again when the name flashed across his display.

Craddock answered the call as soon as he saw who it was.

"Grimes," he boomed into the mic, "where the fuck are you! What the fuck is going on?"

"Did you know?" The voice of his best assassin sounded strange to Craddock. There was a tightness, an edge of uncertainty that might have sounded like fear if it had come from any other person. Grimes had never known fear, so this had to be some other emotion.

"Know what?" Craddock's confusion was not feigned. He had a lot on his mind and this was not the time for riddles.

"About Hardesty. About him and OmniCorp."

Craddock's face fell. "Oh goddammit, Grimes. What did you do?" Craddock already knew the answer to this.

"What had to be done. Did you know?"

Since Grimes was not going to stop asking it, Craddock answered the question. "Not until about eight hours ago. He tried to lie to me, but I know him too well for that crap. I figured he had sold us out, just not how or to who."

"It was OmniCorp. He's been helping them break the union and us. He gave them the order to kill you, Craddock."

That stung the man deep in his broad chest. He had known Lincoln Hardesty for decades. They had come up together. They had been friends. Knowing that Hardesty had lost his guts and betrayed them hurt, however it was a betrayal Craddock understood. Sometimes men grew tired, sometimes they took the easy money and

241

ran. Craddock could have gotten over that. Calling for his death, on the other hand? That was a real insult.

"He's dead?" It was a stupid question, but it had to be asked all the same. He needed to hear it from Grimes himself.

"You have to ask?"

There was nothing left to do but damage control. "Okay. Where are you now?"

"I took a tramp from Caelestus. I've just unloaded at the level nine dock."

"All right, get here fast. The RUC is sitting this one out for some reason, and that fixer will be tearing his way through our boys at security any second now."

Grimes sounded even tenser now. "OmniCorp must have bought off the RUC."

Craddock sounded as confused as he did annoyed, which was impressive. "They want to handle this in-house, huh? That means the files will hurt them as much as us."

"They will want those files as badly as we do, Alasdair. The things on there will ruin us all! You cannot let them escape Venus with that data! Hardesty made sure that the Red Hats will implode if anyone sees what's in those files."

"Relax, Grimes. It sounds like OmniCorp can't afford to let them get away either. We knew they had guys down here. Link always said it was better to let them think we didn't know." He scoffed at his own gullibility. "Fuck. I guess now we know that wasn't the real reason he wanted us to leave them alone, after all. Fuck it. At least the OmniCorp shills will have to help clean this mess up, too. We can deal with anyone left alive afterward, I guess."

"They will come for you, too. Hardesty said as much. This would be the perfect opportunity to kill you."

This did not seem to bother Craddock all that much. "Let them fucking come, then. I've got all the lads out patrolling. I'll put our boys against theirs any day of the week." He paused then, a moment of prudence peeking out through his bravado. "Then again, if OmniCorp is going to take a swipe at me I'd like you to be down here with me when it happens."

"The fixer is formidable, Craddock. If OmniCorp has people here, let them try to stop him. I'll be ready if he makes it to you."

"I appreciate that, Killam."

242

"Don't confuse it for kindness, Alasdair," Grimes warned. "I have many question for you, and I require honest answers for all of them."

Craddock sighed. "The answers won't make you any happier or less confused than you are now, Grimes."

"I assumed as much. I'll be there in twenty minutes."

Grimes closed the connection from his end. He was uninterested in Craddock's reply and did not care to hear it. *Zanshin* was lost to him, unrecoverable amid the swirling maelstrom of anger, fear, doubt, and confusion. Instead he clung to *mushin*. The detachment better suited him at this moment. It allowed him to observe his own turmoil without being consumed by it.

He had a stop to make before moving to Craddock's office. His first destination was his private dorm, comprised of little more than a bare metal cell under the refractory level. From his locker he retrieved a recently acquired thin metal box. It had taken all Hardesty's connections and cunning to retrieve what was inside. With his new understanding of the man's motives, Grimes had a far more nuanced grasp on exactly what it must have taken to retrieve this parcel. It would not help his state of mind to ponder exactly who Hardesty might have made deals with to retrieve such a thing, so he did not allow such questions to penetrate his *mushin*.

Nimble fingers worked the latch and opened the box to reveal a long dagger, nearly twenty inches long and jet black. Hardesty's smugglers had assured the assassin that no substance would resist this blade, and no armor would be proof against it. It was a weapon for killing monsters.

It was his magic sword.

Grimes withdrew the blade from its scabbard and hefted the weapon in his hand. Frowning, he spun it in deft twirls and lightning-quick arcs as he adjusted to the feel and weight of it. Grimes was a master of blades in virtually any style conceivable, and he immediately disliked this one. The balance was terrible. It was not heavy enough at the tip to chop and slash, nor was it balanced at the pommel for speedy thrusting. The weight was primarily at the hilt and through the forte, making the thing simultaneously slow and clumsy in the hand.

He thumbed the activator stud and jumped slightly as the weapon came to life with a soft humming sound and a wave of heat. In a fit of curiosity, the assassin swept the blade into the thin metal of his locker. The dagger passed through it as if nothing was there at all, leaving a watery horizontal gash all the way to the wall as it filled the air of his cell with the stench of ozone.

Satisfied that the device was as advertised, Grimes deactivated the knife and strapped it to his waist. Poor balance could be forgiven if the thing could carve the armor off his foes.

He took another moment to don some light armor of his own, then left his room. He moved quickly, yet did not rush or give into undue haste. He started to feel the familiar calm of *zanshin* as the doubts and contradictions of the last several hours were pushed back to make room for the more important tasks of the moment. The stalking and killing of dangerous prey required all his attention, and this unsullied focus came as a welcome balm for his abraded sense of self. There was no more room in his head for anything besides the hunt, and he threw himself into it like a man jumping into a river to escape a swarm of bees.

His internal crises settled in his mind as he grew closer to his destination. There were people he needed to kill, and no matter how strange and frightening the galaxy became, this was something he understood.

Chapter Thirty-Two

Guns were strictly regulated in The Colander, but this was not to say Red Hat enforcers went at their tasks unarmed. There was no shortage of clever tinkerers and competent smugglers under the dome, and this meant that Craddock's metal men were in possession of a dizzying array of armaments both mundane and improvised.

The first of the cyborg thugs to recover his senses charged Roland with some kind of powered saw. The unwieldy device had a long bar and hundreds of savage spinning teeth the size of guitar picks. It screamed a horrible keening whine as the toothy blades spun around the bar so fast their shapes dissolved into an amorphous gray blur.

Roland was very conversant in his own systems and capabilities. He knew to the fourth decimal point exactly how resistant his surface armor was to most forms of small, medium, and heavy weapons. There were some notable gaps in his knowledge, however. For instance, he did not know how it might fare against a weaponized industrial rock saw wielded by a powerful armature. It posed an interesting problem. His armor was as technologically advanced as bleeding edge military research could develop thirty years prior, but it had not been designed to resist the ripping and tearing nature of such an attack.

Curiosity was not one of his vices, so the big man declined to explore that question under the current conditions. Stahlkorpers were strong enough to warrant respect, yet they were neither fast nor graceful. Making an armature strong and tough was easy, making it move well was hard. The thrusting rock saw was easily dodged, and Roland shot the man in the chest at point-blank range.

Durendal was not like regular guns. Because Roland could handle so much heat, recoil, and weight, it was more akin to a small cannon than a machine pistol. The bead cracked the armature open like an egg, blasting metal shards and parts outward in a blinding orange corona and a hail of lethal shrapnel.

To the eternal credit of Erberhaus Industrial Systems, Incorporated, the man did not go down. Roland's beads delivered a serious kinetic and thermal payload, but they did not penetrate well. The energy of the shot had stayed close to the surface, the ceramic spheres shattering early after impact rather than punching though the thick metal of his enemy's carapace. Still, the quantity of energy contained in the projectile was prodigious, and since twenty-fifth century technology had yet to break the laws of thermodynamics, all that energy had to go somewhere. The exploding beads gave most of it to the armor itself.

Instead of punching through the man, Roland's gunshot had blown most of the chest plate and thoracic hardware off his frame. The man inside also suffered several grievous wounds, yet ignored them because the machine itself was designed to keep wounded people upright and moving. A testament to his dedication to the cause of a free Venus, the dying pilot and his steadfast armature shrugged off the gunshot and brought his saw blade around again. Roland stopped the swipe with a forearm, forcing the wailing teeth back and away from his face with mere inches to spare. Another blast from Durendal pulped the doomed pilot and blew the back out of his armature in a spray of fire and gore. The smoking hulk then toppled, and the gruesome death of their leader finally galvanized the remaining men into action.

Six cyborgs either charged or opened fire at once, and the resulting chaos was far less effective than the volume and fury of it would have implied. To the experienced soldier, the assault was both childish and amateur. The men were uncoordinated, and each attacked in their own manner with no thought to what the others were doing. A good small unit offensive would have each member supporting the others, making the whole group more effective than the sum of its parts. When these six thugs exploded into action, they harmed each other more than they did Roland.

Two of them opened up with old-style scatterguns, which were as dangerous as a soft rain to Roland. The pellets bounced and ricocheted around the fray, however, and several helium tanks were punctured as a result. White plumes of boiling helium billowed outward, obstructing sightlines and confusing the Red Hats further.

Helium evaporates at -451 degrees Fahrenheit, so the expanding gas extracted huge quantities of heat from the air. The damaged machine pilots screamed as their armatures suddenly plummeted in temperature, freezing skin to metal and seizing actuators into solid lumps of ice. These unfortunate men ended up locked in their icy frames, dangerously hypothermic and immobile until they could thaw themselves.

Roland simply overlaid infrared to his HUD and fought on. He holstered Durendal in a smooth motion, deciding not to give his enemies a way to find him among the obscuring clouds of helium vapor and condensate. The frozen men glowed deep blue on his display, making them easy to spot. Being the easiest to deal with because they were immobile, Roland killed the first with an overhand right that collapsed both the helmet and the skull within it. Eerily, the armature remained upright and still, frozen joints and sturdy construction holding the dead man erect in his macabre metal sarcophagus. Then he ducked low and swept through the cloud of cavorting opponents to dispatch the other seized cyborg with a similar blow.

Something hit him from behind. The impact was severe enough to hurl him sideways and send him into a wall at speed. No serious damage was caused by this, and the old soldier swept the dissipating clouds with eyes and scanners both to find the source of the impact. Two cyborgs were closing in on him with improvised clubs, and he could only assume one of these had been what had struck him. He pushed off the wall and met them halfway.

The attackers seemed to be taken aback by this. Roland assumed they had overestimated the effectiveness of their blows. This was understandable since a hit like that would have been catastrophic for just about any light cyborg.

Roland was not any light cyborg. Roland was a Golem. He had survived trading punches with heavy armatures, and he had torn medium frames apart with his bare hands. The hit stung, but it would take many more like that one to bring him down.

As he closed on the pair, one of them recovered enough to get his club moving. His counterpart followed with the same strategy. Catching the heavy metal rod in his left hand, he leaned back and pulled the first attacker off balance just as his partner's looping swing would have landed. It was a brutally impressive hit, designed for murder and delivered with as much fury as possible. Yet his target had moved, and instead of smashing Roland's skull, he only succeeded in bashing the other Stahlkorper's arm from its shoulder. Roland subsequently employed the liberated joint as a club against his undamaged opponent.

For a second the two men danced in the galaxy's most bizarre fencing match. Roland, using a severed cyborg arm, parried two swings from the club before sending a chopping smash across the faceplate of his opponent. It was not a hard hit, and Roland did not expect it to do much more than step his opponent back. As expected, the goon staggered ever so slightly. Roland exploited the break in his rhythm to bring the arm down as hard as he could in a savage overhand strike. This sent the Red Hat stumbling backward to trip over some unseen obstruction. Any attempt to follow up and finish the man was forestalled by another scattergun blast and the untimely interruption of being tackled.

Somehow, Roland kept his feet while two cyborgs tried to drag him to the floor. While skidding about, he focused his attention on punching heads as much as possible. His feet were not properly planted, and the constant work of staying upright robbed his blows of their power. This kept both sturdy Stahlkorpers gamely in the fight for far too long. The last one with the shotgun soon realized his weapon was causing more harm than good, and in the first good tactical decision of the day, he abandoned his weapon to join the dogpile. Combined, the three cyborgs finally succeeded in hurling their enemy back and almost brought him to the ground. Under most circumstances, Roland did not fear going to the ground, he was a great wrestler and was as comfortable on the deck as he was on his feet.

This confidence did not extend into the realm of stupidity, though. Fighting three tough cyborgs at once meant the very real risk of getting stomped to death if he went down, so he worked hard to stay upright. The awkward mass of mechanical fury careened around the room, smashing consoles and colliding with walls like a protracted and meandering car accident.

The grit and tenacity of these men surprised Roland. They were not giving up, and showed no signs of fear or weakness. The reason was obvious, and Roland began to regret trying seven of them at once. Dismissing such thoughts as counter-productive, Roland dropped his hips, tucked his chin, and just kept swinging at all those gray metal heads. It was only a matter of time before he either went down, or got a good shot in. He would deal with each as it happened.

Snarling, Roland finally landed a clean hit to one of his antagonists, loosening the man's hold and breaking his balance. He lurched forward to exploit the gap, dragging the other two men with him and shoving the skidding one back with as much force as he could. This sent the Stahlkorper tumbling head over heels to strike the far wall with loud crunch. He whirled, an explosive twist of the hips that yanked another from his feet. Two thundering body-blows mangled that one's torso, and the clunky gray armature went stiff and ataxic as redundant control systems attempted to compensate for the structural damage. Roland kicked him across the room to land in a crumpled heap next to his compatriot.

That left one still clinging to his back, clawing and punching at his head. Roland's mood had descended into a very grim place, and the big man was all done putting up with that. He reached over his own shoulder to grip this nuisance by the helium harness. Dropping his hips and pulling hard, Roland sent the man flying into his comrades, just now clambering to their feet. They all went down like tenpins, and the old veteran spat a curse at his own lapse in judgment.

He had underestimated these men. He had been the biggest dog in the yard for so long he had forgotten what dedicated fighters with grit and courage could accomplish, even when technologically outclassed. History was replete with examples of smart, tough, resourceful forces bringing down powerful militaries. He was dangerously close to becoming one such example himself. It occurred to Roland that perhaps he spent too much time dealing with street muscle and professional hitters. These were zealots. They would not go down easily and working with hand-me-down equipment was all they had ever known. He was in their house, and playing by their rules. More caution would have been warranted if he had taken the time to think about it that way.

It was not so much that Roland respected these Red Hats. He did not and could not because these men were not warriors. They were terrorists and murderers and Roland had nothing but contempt for their methods. But they were also undeniably brave in their own foolish way. Pretending otherwise was an egregious tactical error.

Fortunately, Roland was highly dedicated to his cause as well, and his momentary lapse in judgment was now corrected.

"Enough fucking around, boys," he growled. Durendal leapt back into his hand. "I don't want to kill you if I don't have to. Give it up or die here." The four cyborgs stood as one, even the one-armed man. One spoke, and his tone was not that of a person ready to surrender.

"We will not let you pass, fascist. Run and tell your corporate overseers that the men of the Red Hats will not be—"

Durendal roared in a full-auto wave of incandescent wind. Roland's offer of quarter had merely been a ruse to buy time for his press-point system to paint the power cell housings of each armature with a laser-designated targeting reticle. The computers in his helmet and the computers in his weapon did the rest. Having used two beads already, eighteen remained indexed and ready to go. Sixteen beads were distributed evenly between the four Stahlkorpers, leaving two in reserve. This might have been excessive, but Roland had new respect for the sturdy chassis and he decided to be thorough.

The power cell of a Stahlkorper was located in the abdomen of each armature. This was a practical consideration. The gut was a central location, easy to keep cooled, and had plenty of room for reinforcement. While modified to tolerate the rigors of the Venusian environment, this hardening was insufficient for protection against hypersonic ceramic projectiles the size of gobstoppers. The first beads shattered the metal skin and ruptured the housings. The following projectiles blasted the power cells into scrap. When the cells lost containment, they exploded in spectacular forks of eldritch blue fire and dancing electrical arcs. The whole process took less than two and a half seconds, and left four sets of torso-less armored legs upright, still and alone. They wafted smoke from mangled hip linkages and stood like Stonehenge amid the scorched detritus of their top halves.

"I knew you'd say that," Roland grumbled to no one in particular.   Then   he   reloaded.

Chapter Thirty-Three

Lucia, Manny, and Mindy caught up to Roland just as he finished reloading and re-holstering his weapon. Manny looked at the deformed pieces of destroyed door, then looked at Roland in confusion.

"I do not believe the door was locked, Mr. Tankowicz. I'm pretty sure it does not even *have* a lock."

"Really?" Roland grunted back, indifferent. "Huh."

Lucia waggled her head in disbelief. "What is it with you and doors?"

Roland shrugged. "Programmed to hate them, I guess. Let's move on. I'd like to avoid a running gun battle all the way to The Quad, if possible."

Manny checked his handheld before responding. "The direct route is probably full of Craddock's men. We still haven't seen the OmniCorp guys yet, either. Hold on while I check the security net."

"If OmniCorp hasn't shut that down already," Lucia added.

Manny fiddled with something from his satchel before replying. "No. It's up. Thank goodness The Colander only gets shit hardware. A child could piggyback onto their security."

Roland suspected that the security net here was probably adequate for their needs, just not good enough to slow down a kid like Manuel. He did not argue the point, though.

"It's up, and active. And..." he paused, frowning into his screen, "...ohhhhh, clever! They've added a bunch of peripherals to the regular 'net. Scanners, drones, everything. They are looking for you, Mr. Tankowicz."

"Have they found me?"

"Easily. You couldn't hide from them if you wanted to. A lot of high-end comm and scanning gear is using the SecNet right now.

You light up like a nuclear blast. Mindy's not so hard to spot, either. All those augmentations."

"Great. I'm like a big cybernetic beacon. Perfect."

"We need to split up," Lucia said out of the blue. She did not sound pleased with this.

"Yup." Roland agreed. "Can they follow you, Manny? You've got that arm..."

"Three percent of the people down here have some sort of prosthesis, and my arm isn't even metal. Compared to the stuff walking around here? It's a pretty minor thing. If they knew exactly what to look for, they might find it. But since they don't?" He shrugged. "Just another walking wounded."

"Okay, then. Manny and Lucia, get to The Quad and get this data to Ellie. Try not to be seen. Mindy and I will draw fire and lead pursuit away from you guys. Once you have delivered the package and we have managed Craddock and OmniCorp, we'll rendezvous at the cargo bay. Got it?"

"Got it," they all said in unison.

With that, Manny and Lucia darted off into one of the corridors, leaving Mindy and Roland standing in the center of the wrecked Stahlkorpers and their dead pilots.

"Well, Ironsides," Mindy offered. "Where are we off to then? What merry chase shall we lead our foes on?"

"Might as well head straight to Craddock's office, I figure. We need to lead them somewhere."

Mindy titled her head. "And closing in on the leader ought to focus their attention real good. I approve."

"Thank you."

"Don't let it go to your head, Ironsides. Rules of engagement?"

Mindy could not see the grin behind his faceplate, but she could hear it clearly in his words. "Mind the civilians, kill anything that looks hostile. This is not a stealth run. We want them to come for us."

"Thank the gods. After that mess with Hardesty I am so ready to do this shit the hard way. If you were a girl I'd kiss you."

"If I were a girl you'd die trying."

Mindy ignored that and pulled her Sasori blade from its sheath. She flipped it around her palm a few times to settle it. "I'll take point. I know the way better than you, and I'm the only one who brought a can opener. Also, if anyone sneaks behind us I'll have your bullet-proof ass to cover mine."

"Using the knife? Feels risky."

"I couldn't smuggle anything in here big enough to bring down an armature."

"Can you handle Durendal?" It occurred to him that she might be strong enough to make it work, and he could manage without it if he had to.

Mindy gasped. "Me? Use that thing? Are you nuts? Lucia would kill me! That'd be like me wearing your varsity jacket or something!"

Roland did not think that this was a fair comparison. They were not in high school and guns were not clothing. "It's a gun, Mindy, not an offer to go steady."

"As if!" The little blond harrumphed. "Either way, I don't think this is a good time for me to start practicing with a new weapon. I'll mange with the knife."

"It is a good knife," Roland concurred. The weapon had been recovered from the body of her former partner and best friend, and had belonged to a new model of assassin android. Its monomolecular edge oscillated at hypersonic speeds and a plasma conduit in the spine heated the cutting surfaces like the photosphere of a white dwarf star. Dense metal and thick armor alike parted like wet tissue paper before the humming black blade.

"Ready?" Mindy asked.

"Lead on."

At a jog, Mindy darted off into a dark corridor. The walls immediately narrowed, and the ceiling descended to within a few inches of Roland's head as the little blond led him further from the more open corridors of the concourse and deeper into the dark heart of The Colander. In a few short minutes, the pair was moving through tight passages far below the main decks. Mindy called for a halt.

"I'm trying to keep out of wide open spaces, to force them to come at us one at time. As you can see, they aren't hitting us yet, which means they are waiting for us to get to a more open area."

"Is that what you would do?"

"If I had the numbers, yeah. Choke points favor the defender, not the attacker."

Roland sighed. "And we've stopped because?"

"There's a big ol' depot ahead, if I remember right. I figure if they haven't come at us yet, then it's because they want to take their shot over there or somewhere like it."

Roland cranked his scanners as high as they could go, but the maze of metal and machinery that was The Colander was impossible to penetrate using only his helmet's meager power. "I'll need to get closer to scan for hostiles."

"I was afraid of that. Okay. Let's move really careful, though."

Roland's attempt at stealth was a fairly comical thing. He was probably lighting up half a dozen scanner drones, which only made him feel more foolish for trying. In a few hundred yards, the two bumped up against a small man door. Roland aimed his suite of sensors at it and set them to as strong a pulse as possible. It would reveal them to anyone inside, but since they probably knew he was there anyway, he did not care.

"You want the good news or the bad news first?"

Mindy cocked an eyebrow. "The bad."

"There is a shit-ton of bad guys in there. Looks like all three Kanos and a couple dozen armed biologicals. They know we are here, and they are just waiting for us to come through this door so they can kill us."

"Well, shit. What's the good news?"

"No heavy weapons that I can see. Some old bead guns and lots of improvised stuff. The Kanos appear unmodified and unarmed."

"Okay," Mindy breathed. "That's not so bad. You got a plan?"

"I'm going to smash through this door and hit everyone as hard as I can. You wait here until they're all shooting at me. Then come on in and help."

The little assassin scowled. "That was your plan the last time!"

"I'm not a creative man. You got a better one?"

Her lips twisted into a pout. "I suppose not. Let me back up a bit first." Mindy moved about thirty feet down the hall, safely out of harm's way and waited. Roland backed up to get a running start.

"Here we go," Roland growled. Then he charged.

This door was much lighter than the previous one had been. When the onyx giant struck it with his shoulder, the metal panel did not merely buckle, it exploded into the depot beyond. The one-hundred-pound steel rectangle spun off into the dimness beyond like it was made of so much cardboard. It bisected a glowering man who had posted up across from it to get a clean shot at his prey when it passed through the opening. The flying door sent parts of his body spinning in all directions and threw his old UEDF-surplus bead rifle clattering to the floor.

The explosive noise and the dramatic vivisection of their compatriot stunned the assembled men into shocked paralysis for a fraction of a second, and this was how Roland got among them without taking a single hit.

The sprinting cyborg sprayed automatic gunfire as he beelined for the first Kano his HUD identified. The unarmored men scattered for cover from the fusillade and this opened a clear path to Roland's target. Lining up a big punch, Roland very nearly scored a free hit on the corporate cyborg. His fist sailed past the sleek blue helmet of his target, missing by a few inches at most. Stomping his right boot to the deck as a brake, Roland pivoted to send another strike at the whirling man. This too was barely dodged and Roland got a sinking feeling in his gut.

The chattering of gunfire began to echo across the depot, and the first dull stings of bead strikes prickled and danced along his back. The men recovering from his initial barrage and he was still dancing with an armature. Missing twice was a problem. Roland was very fast, and the only opponents who ever dodged his punches were the ones who were similarly quick, and that was not humanly possible. A Kano was expensive, and putting a pilot with augmented reflexes in one was even more extravagant. Such fighters did not come cheap and they were never easy to put down.

The man in the blue armature swung something heavy and sharp at his face, forcing Roland to duck. The blue cyborg was not as fast as Roland, but he was too fast for comfort nonetheless. The improvised weapon sliced through the air above his head, and Roland rocked back on his heels to evade the following backhand. Not just mounted to an expensive armature, not just augmented, the man was a trained fighter, to boot. Making things more interesting, his HUD chose that moment to chime a warning that the other two cyborgs were closing fast. There was no reason for Roland to hope that these were not similarly dangerous opponents. His tussle with the Stahlkorpers was still fresh in his mind, and the implications were not lost on him.

There was nothing he could do about any of it, so he let loose with another burst of beads from Durendal. The range was less than six feet, and the projectiles exploded against his enemy's chest like firecrackers. The blue cyborg staggered backward and lost his footing. The damage to the downed man looked bad, but Roland could see that it was mostly superficial. As with shooting the Stahlkorpers, the beads ruined the surface armor yet failed to penetrate.

Just as he lined up a follow-up burst, one of the other Kanos struck him from behind and spoiled his aim. His HUD blared alarms in his ears when something big and heavy crashed into his extended arm. Durendal spun away from his fingers and he lurched to one side, driven several yards away by the impact. Damage reports cycled through his field of vision and they were suitably dire.

As was so often his way, Roland ignored them and lunged. He had fought many cyborgs in his time, and he knew how to beat them. When a pilot sent a command to the chassis, the machine executed it instantly. Because the Kanos were not limited by human anatomy, they could technically move with as much speed or more than Roland could. The catch was that the machine was always faster than the brain of the operator, even augmented operators. A good armature like a Kano could move and act every bit as fast as Roland could, but it would never re-act with the same speed because it had to wait for the brain inside to issue a command.

This saddled Roland with the not-so-simple task of making sure his three high-tech, highly-trained opponents were always on their heels and reacting. He only knew only one way of doing this, and it was no more sophisticated a strategy than the one he had used to breach the room.

The black giant rained blows on the red Kano as fast as he could cycle his arms. His foe was no fool and backed away to create distance and keep Roland's focus while his teammates flanked. He suffered several murderous hits in the process, though he managed to stay upright and in the fight. A final left hook from Roland sent that one skidding across the floor, but gave time for the mangled blue Kano to dig his crude axe into Roland's guts.

His armor held, though the impact caused Roland to stumble. The third Kano, this one bright green, then caught him in the shoulder with some kind of metal club. Now it was Roland who staggered backward, reeling before the onslaught of three trained opponents working as a cohesive unit. He had lost initiative, and was forced to counter and surrender his advantage. Taking the time to snag the haft of the incoming axe created an opportunity for a club to find his back. Roland released the axe to hit the green one, and this allowed the red one smash him behind the knee. Punching the red one let the blue one bring the axe around again, missing Roland's neck by no more than a few inches. Dodging this decapitating strike got him hit in the side by Green again.

So it went, for a very long minute. Roland had more than ten times the strength of a Kano. He was faster and more skilled, too. Against any one of these men, his victory was assured. Against three, nothing was certain. The faceless, inexorable team of Kanos took careful turns drawing out and then scoring hits on the big black Golem. They fought as a perfect team. Never rushed, never reckless. It was a dance of silent terror for all involved. A violent, rhythmless waltz, where each blank-faced dancer was committed to part only at death. Every move was improvised yet critical, as a single misstep meant surrendering initiative to the other side.

Damage to all combatants began to accumulate. The brightly painted Kanos lost their sheen as heavy punches soon had them scratched and dented. Meanwhile, Roland's clothes were in rags and his own matte black armor showed the scuffs and streaks of numerous surface injuries. As the battle wore on it became obvious that unless the stalemate was broken, attrition would decide the victor of the bout.

This was not a fight between men, or even a war of machines. Roland's impressions were wry and bleak.

It's like a pack of starving wolves trying to drag down a grizzly bear.

A right hook landed on the green Kano, sending it skidding away. His reward for this success came in the form of a staggering impact to his shoulder courtesy of the red one. It sent the big man stumbling back to smash into a support column. A thought occurred to him as he righted himself and leapt back into the melee.

The   wolves   are   winning.

Chapter Thirty-Four

Lucia had to make a conscious effort to move slowly. Manny had no prayer of ever matching her speed, and her sense of urgency would have her outrunning the poor boy if she let it. The pace probably felt excessive to him, while to Lucia it seemed positively glacial.

Once below the main deck, they began to run into people. The upper levels of Colander residents had known to steer clear of their group, while Craddock and OmniCorp's efforts to avoid exposure had emptied the checkpoints of RUC. This was not the case in the lower decks. It was just not possible to avoid the everyday movement of laborers and other folk as they went about their daily tasks. Still, they made good time because the run to The Quad was not terribly long and Roland was drawing most of the heat from their path.

Both had hoped that they would not encounter any of Craddock's spies. This proved to be too much to ask for. It was unclear exactly when they were spotted, but in a dark and winding stairwell the first of the Red Hats ambushed them.

Lucia spotted the group of men first. They were little more than lumpy shadows on a landing beneath them when she recognized the silhouette of a man trying to crouch behind a railing. Her perception of time had stretched to a languid crawl and this proved fortunate. It allowed her what felt like several seconds to go through the steps of seeing the strange shapes, recognizing they were crouched men, and then finally acknowledging they were a threat.

In reality, this process took place in the span of one twelfth of one second. Knowing she did not have time to warn Manny, the speeding woman drew her pistol mid-stride and started peppering the landing with flechettes. Muzzle flashes and orange streaks of burning air sent brightly-hued spots dancing across her vision while her CZ-105 spat tungsten-tipped needles through the massed shadows. Screams of pain and terror responded, and the men below her scattered like cockroaches at the sudden explosion of violence. Manny yelped in surprise and fumbled to a confused stop. Lucia could not afford to wait for him and she leapt over a railing to drop to the landing below.

She whirled as she landed, picking targets that looked like deeper black shapes against the orange dimness of the stairwell walls. Her pistol barked three more times, and two shadows fell to the floor and were still. It was easier to hear than it was to see, and Lucia paused for a fifth of a second to listen for movement. There was metallic scurrying coming from the edge of the landing. Lucia surmised that the remaining ambushers were trying to regroup on the next level down. She posted up against the wall and tried to get a better look down the stairs. She was certain she counted at least four men still moving down there. They looked to be taking advantage of the twists in the staircase to find cover. Many finally sidled up behind her.

"How's it look, Boss?"

"At least four, maybe one more than that, still down there. Small arms only." Her hands slipped to her belt and back so fast Manny could not see what she had done, but the clattering of a dropped magazine informed him that she had been reloading. Absently, she pointed out, "They are just sitting there for now."

Manny stated the obvious. "They'll be calling for back-up. They don't have to shoot it out with us, all they have to do is hold us here."

"Should we go back up?"

"I suppose we could," Manny offered, though the hint of a chuckle tinged his answer. "But I'd prefer to keep going." Manny reached around to hand Lucia a small plastic ball.

"What is this?" she asked.

"It's a grenade," he answered, as if such a thing should be obvious.

Lucia spun to look at him. "How the hell did you get a grenade in here?"

"I made it. This place refines VOCs by the ton. There is a lot of really nasty stuff just lying around down here."

"Is it going to blow up the stairs? We need those!" Lucia's brain was running through a lot of scenarios, and many of them were not good.

"It's not that kind of grenade," was the cryptic answer.

"What does it do?" It felt like a silly question, but Lucia had a lot of reservations about the nature and capabilities of Manny's homemade munitions.

"Push the button on top. That starts the timer. Three seconds after that and you won't want to be within fifteen feet of this thing." Seeing her fearful expression, he sighed and took it back from her. "Just be ready to charge, and oh yeah... hold your breath."

He pressed a black button on the little sphere and sent it down the stairs with a gentle underhand toss. It pinged and clunked to the center of the landing and sat there.

It was the longest three seconds of Lucia's life waiting for the modest device to reveal its nature. With a bright flash and a loud pop, the plastic ball disappeared into an expanding cloud of white gas. In an instant, the entire landing was ensconced in a thick miasma of cloying vapor. Gasps, coughs, and screams of "My eyes!" started within a second of the explosion. These expletives increased in volume and fervor quickly. After only a second or two the screams of agony from below were chilling Lucia's blood.

"Go!" Manny gave her a shove, and the pair darted down the stairs. Lucia remembered to hold her breath as she raced through the fog. The sight of their attackers gasping and retching was all the motivation she needed to keep her lips pressed tight and her pace brisk. One man staggered out of the haze to try and stop them. He failed because a bionic left hook from Manny sent him spinning into the darkness and out of sight.

The pair cleared the landing without further incident, and were exiting the stairwell three levels down while their foes still gagged and sobbed above them.

"What the hell was that?" Lucia asked when they were well into the warren of refractory level tunnels.

"Mostly toluene, sulfuric acid, chlorine, and ammonia. I used a compressed helium charge to aerosolize it all and make sure I get good distribution."

"Are they going to die?"

260

Manny shrugged. "Toluene will screw up your nervous system bad in high doses. It's heavier than air, so if they pass out inside the cloud?" He winced, "Yeah. They'll die from it. The ammonia and chlorine give off chloramine vapor when you mix them, and that stuff is really unpleasant, but not *usually* fatal." Then, as an afterthought, "Some of the other stuff I used is really corrosive. A couple of those guys will go blind, I think."

"Jesus, Manny! We ran through that stuff!"

"We had visors. You might get a skin rash on your face, though. Sorry. Oh yeah, and your hair may change color."

"Arrgh!" Lucia did not have time to berate the boy, and his plan had worked so she could only fault him so much for exposing her to dangerous chemicals.

They moved on, trying to keep a brisk pace. Increased foot traffic in the lower levels slowed them down before long. There was small solace in that Lucia's armor and visible sidearm kept people from hanging out in their way any longer than necessary.

Just as they stepped into The Quad, Manny grabbed Lucia's wrist and hissed, "We just picked up a tail, Boss." He gestured to two otherwise uninteresting people staring into a junk vendor's stall and doing an extremely poor job of looking nonchalant.

Lucia was not sure what to do with the information. "We had to know that would happen. We are kind of conspicuous."

"We need to lose them before getting to Ellie. Can't bring Craddock's thugs down on her."

"Crap. Right." She huffed. "Gang wars are way less complicated than this urban espionage stuff, you know."

"Tell me about it. How do you want to deal with these guys?"

"The Tankowicz method."

Manny beamed. "I have just the thing! Come on!" He dragged her down the narrow pathway of vendors and hawkers. Lucia did not dare to look back and see if their followers were still with them. She had to assume they would keep up. Several twists and turns through gaudy strips of commerce, Manny beckoned her into a gap between larger permanent structures. It was much darker in here, and Lucia was grateful for a reprieve from all the noise and flashing colored lights.

Further inside what could only be described as an alley, though it really bore no resemblance to any alley Lucia had ever been in,

261

Manny pulled her behind a piece of derelict machinery that had been left there to rot.

A few seconds later, the two men following them appeared as garishly back-lit silhouettes framed by the narrow gap between the structures. They paused and looked at each other. Lucia imagined that some small part of them recognized that this was a strange place for their quarry to go. Perhaps a modicum of caution stayed their feet, and a brief argument ensued about how best to proceed. Lucia could not hear what was said. It did not matter, either way. Eventually, either a sense of duty or the fear of Craddock drove the men forward and into the deep shadows of the skinny metal canyon.

The men moved with an abundance of caution. Each stayed pressed to a wall and walked as if there might be land mines under their feet. The hunk of scrapped equipment that served as Manny and Lucia's cover gave them pause when they saw it. Recognizing the potential danger, the follower's eyes flicked back and forth from each other to the junk pile. Lucia decided that this was her moment and flew into action before their courage had the chance to falter.

Twelve feet separated the two pursuers from Lucia's hiding place. It may as well have been twelve inches with her speed. The first man caught only a glimpse of a darting black shadow before Lucia's right gauntlet spun his head in a sharp arc traced by a spray of teeth and blood. The glove gave a snappy 'pop!', and an electrical discharge rendered the man unconscious instantly. This saved him from the pain of his shattered mouth, yet also prevented him from arresting his fall. His head bounced off the wall and he flopped to the ground like a dropped sandbag.

She turned to the other, prepared to do the same to him. She saw Manny engage the man with a stiff jab from his prosthetic arm. She was startled and amazed to note that his blow serviced the thug in exactly the same manner as her own gauntlets. There was a pop and a small blue flash before the man slumped across his downed partner with the same slack jaw and glassy eyes.

Manny turned to look at her, a lopsided grin on his face. Lucia tilted her head and raised an eyebrow. "I thought Dad wasn't doing weapons?"

His grin widened. "I installed that one. It works so well for you, I just had to have it. The worst part was not having the electrical shock feed back into the arm's other systems." Manny shrugged. "I figured it out eventually."

"And Dad had nothing to do with it?"

"He may have consulted a little on the design..."

Lucia sighed in resignation. "He really does miss his work, I guess. Let's go."

Manny led her out of the alley and back into the noisy maze of The Quad.

"We need to get to Ellie's place without picking up another tail. This is going to be tricky." Manny sounded frustrated. "Craddock must be desperate if he is running guys through The Quad. So much for speed. Come on, I have an idea."

Manny proceeded to drag Lucia across The Quad in a winding and nonsensical path. They passed through stalls, moved through the back rooms of restaurants, slid down alleys, and generally avoided any open spaces. What should have taken about five minutes, Manny dragged out for close to an hour. Finally, Lucia recognized the alley where Ellie's back door was hidden, though they had accessed it from a thin gap at the other end. The pair slipped inside to find Ellie Connelly awaiting them.

The woman looked ten years older. Her hair was tied in an unkempt knot at the back of her head and she did not look like she had slept much the night before. Her greeting, such as it was, was bereft of warmth.

"Do you imbeciles know what you have done? What you have started? What the hell were you thinking?"

Manny looked hurt by her tone, but Lucia was far too frazzled to acknowledge it. "We did what we said we would. We have all the proof we need to fry Hardesty. No one will ever follow him again once this gets out. Hell, The Red Hats may never recover from this scandal. You should thank us."

"Thank you?" Ellie gave Lucia a look that conveyed very clearly exactly how much gratitude was felt. "For what? Killing Hardesty just put Craddock on the goddamn warpath! The RUC has disappeared, and we can only assume that is so something horrible can happen without them noticing! Once that information trickles down there will be riots! I would never have agreed to help you if I knew that's what you were up to!"

263

"Whoa!" Manny interrupted. "Hardesty's dead?" He looked to Lucia, "Do you think Mindy..." the words trailed off, leaving the obvious question unasked.

"No," Lucia responded emphatically. "She doesn't kill for fun or sport. It's not how she operates." Lucia turned to Ellie. "Hardesty was alive when we left his building. We got the data and his promise to let Manny go. Killing him would only make our lives harder at that point."

Manny nodded his agreement. "It does explain why Craddock has so many men canvassing The Quad for us, though."

Ellie's frown deepened. "You did not kill Hardesty? Then who did? The rumor is an assassin snuck into his penthouse and killed him. Your blond slut is the only assassin around here these days, and it happened just as you were there!"

Manny asked, "Is someone trying to frame us?"

They both looked at Ellie, who was suddenly very defensive. "Don't look at me! Hardesty's death is a bad thing right now. I hate him, but I certainly don't want rioting and an RUC crackdown."

"No one does," Lucia added. "That's why this makes no sense. Hardesty falling from grace served us way better than his death and possible martyrdom ever could." She paused, a faraway look in her eyes as she let her brain play with all the possible ways Hardesty could have been killed by an assassin. "Ellie, you are sure he was killed by an assassin? Not a thug, not an angry prostitute, not a disgruntled associate? Definitely an 'assassin?'"

"I have a source in Craddock's office. The phrase used by Craddock himself was 'that goddamned assassin.' I just assumed he meant Mindy."

"He didn't." Lucia knew there was another assassin crawling around Caelestus. An assassin that would not have reacted well to knowing Hardesty's secrets. "I think Killam Grimes has gone off the reservation."

Chapter Thirty-Five

Roland leapt back to dodge the swinging axe. This sent him into the path of a club, which he took across the forearms without injury. Taking the time to kick that foe away got him bludgeoned in the back.

Roland did not get physically tired, but the aggregate damage his muscles were taking was starting to affect his output. If he did not shut this fight down eventually, he would end up beaten to death. He accepted that his opponents were too well coordinated to give him any opportunities. In recognition of this bleak truth, he set about trying to fabricate some.

He dove at the blue cyborg, trying to tackle it to the ground. The operator's boosted reflexes and the speed of his armature made him slippery. Instead of a double-leg takedown, Roland only managed to grab with one hand. Switching to an ankle pick, the black giant suffered several crushing blows from the other two while he wrenched the blue foot from the floor.

A mounted Kano barely weighed six-hundred pounds. Even with bad balance and taking sustained hits, Roland had no trouble dragging his captured opponent from the floor and swinging him like a club at the other two. He missed the yellow one, but Red took the full mass and fury of the swing. The impact wrenched the man free of Roland's grip and both Kanos tumbled away in a rolling and scrambling mass.

Yellow hit him behind the knees in that instant and Roland felt himself falling. As soon as his back hit the floor Yellow was leaping on and bringing the club down in big overhand swings. Roland gripped the falling club and twisted it backward against the wrist joint. Then he swept the man off his chest and rolled on top. Gripping the club in his left hand, the old soldier punched once, twice, three times directly into the faceplate.

Firmly braced and with his full weight atop the yellow armature, those punches landed like jet-black piledrivers. On the second hit, Roland knew he had killed the man. The third was just to make sure. Accepting that he had spent far too much time with Yellow for this victory to be without cost, Roland dived off the corpse. It was certain Blue and Red would be on him in a fraction of a second. Roland simply leapt without looking, hoping he guessed correctly which direction to flee.

He struck the floor with a shoulder and rolled to his feet with balled fists up, poised to engage the fury he knew had to be coming. To his brief confusion, it never came. The blue and Yellow armatures were delayed by a tiny blond woman wielding a humming dagger and flitting about like a rabid hummingbird. She was doing well. Blue was venting coolant from a hip joint while Red staggered away from the darting needle, spraying sparks from a shrieking shoulder servo.

It was in that moment Roland realized that he heard no gunfire, no shouts from the men around them. He invested a quarter second in checking out his surroundings. What he saw was a charnel house of mangled corpses strewn about in gory disarray.

Mindy had been busy while he took his beating. His superficial antipathy for the killer could not overcome a sense of professional approval at her handiwork. It was not everyone who could take on a few dozen armed men with a knife. For Mindy that was just another Tuesday at the office.

Now that the larger fight had transitioned from three-on-one to two-on-two, Roland resumed his attacks with gusto. He bull-rushed into the fray with renewed vigor, scattering the remaining pair of cyborgs with his charge. This bought Mindy a second to breathe, and as one they whirled back-to-back and faced the Kanos.

Roland took Red, and without his teammates to provide timely distractions, the single Kano was woefully outmatched. His club was swatted away, and the crimson armature was forced into grappling range by his relentless opponent. The doomed cyborg thug gamely attempted to extricate himself, but Roland bent his limbs into deformed parodies of their former configurations. Spraying fluids and smoking from a dozen destroyed motors, the thug finally met his end when Roland twisted his helmet one-hundred-and-eighty degrees. Though his spine was shattered, the armature tried to keep the dead man upright for several long, horrifying seconds before all signals from the brain ceased. Whereupon the expensive cyborg crumpled to the deck and went limp with a long mechanical sigh.

Mindy's dance partner fared no better. All advantages of armor and strength were nullified by her speed, skill, and that unstoppable Sasori blade. It flicked and darted like a lizard's tongue, opening his armor or severing pieces from the whole with each lighting slash. Like his partners, Blue was neither unskilled nor a coward. Yet his efforts to stay in the fight came off as more clumsy and ill-informed with each harrowing pass. If the man in the blue armor knew this, it did not show, and he died still fighting when the tiny blond killer managed to slip her narrow knife under his armpit and deep into his thoracic cavity.

With two hands, Mindy yanked the embedded blade horizontally, dragging it across the ruined blue breastplate without withdrawing it. The armature went stiff and the man's screams, though muffled by his helmet, were clearly heard and understood by those nearby. Another twist, another shove. The knife turned and carved down to finally exit with a torrent of mixed blood and cooling fluid. Mindy flicked the smoking weapon to remove the ichor and turned away to let the dead man fall.

Tiny shoulders rose and fell as she panted and caught her breath. Her chest heaved like a great bellows while she snorted and sucked air. Blue eyes smoldered with a primal predatory fire that Roland recognized quite well. Both killers had enormous reserves of rage. Roland understood the fury and the hate he saw in the little assassin. He had it too, in his own way. He could never indulge it the way she did, but he did not begrudge her that.

"You all right?"

Mindy looked up, and flashed her irreverent smile. She held up her arms, bloodied to the elbows, and squeaked, "Peachy."

"Good. Let's keep moving before another round of goons shows up."

"Right," she answered. Then she bent down to grab a discarded bead rifle from the cooling hands of a nearby corpse. Rummaging through its pockets, she found a few extra magazines for it and tucked them into a pouch at her waist. "No sense leaving these laying around." She examined the weapon, cleared the chamber and reloaded it. "Damn, this thing's an antique!"

"Hey!" Roland sounded insulted. "We used those back in my EF days. It's a good reliable rifle. Lots of power, good range, takes a beating."

"Sits like shit in the hands," she replied, shouldering it while they walked. "Sights are crap. Rattles like sewing machine."

"The Army wasn't big on ergonomics. It will shoot when you pull the trigger and it will shoot straight. What more can you ask for?"

"Sights that aren't crap."

Roland grumbled a response less irritated than it sounded. "Kids these days are spoiled rotten."

Mindy selected a tunnel and they headed off at a brisk double-time. Roland's scanners and Mindy's bionic eyes strained into the yellowing gloom as their path took them deeper into The Colander and away from the surface levels. The halls grew narrower, and the ceilings dropped lower as they descended. Roland thought he might recognize some of the spaces and intersections from his meeting with Craddock, but it was hard to say. Everything under The Colander looked the same to him. Mindy seemed confident in the route, leading him around corners and through empty warehouses with singular focus.

Twice, they encountered squads of Stahlkorpers arrayed to intercept them. However, these ambushes played out very differently their predecessors. The subsequent roving groups of armatures lacked the coordination of the attack from the Kanos. In the first encounter, the six gray cyborgs seemed as surprised to see Roland and Mindy as Roland and Mindy were to see them.

Mindy's dagger and a merciless barrage from Durendal made fairly short work of the startled Red Hats. Roland again found himself impressed with the Erberhaus machines. It took a lot more fire to put one of those down than he would have thought. He adjusted his estimation of their quality upward and resolved himself to never refer to them as 'cheap' again.

Mindy postulated a theory. "I think their ability to track us is either going or gone, Ironsides."

Roland could not fault that assessment. "I'm with you on that. These guys almost tripped over us. Either OmniCorp has pulled their gear or we are down too deep."

"Think like a corporate espionage asset, Corporal." Mindy grunted at how obtuse Roland could be sometimes. "Craddock doesn't work for OmniCorp. I think OmniCorp threw everything they had at us already, and now they've pulled back. The Red Hat boys are running blind."

"You figure Craddock is on his own?" He ducked his head. "Makes sense, I guess."

This understanding had the pair alter their pace and route somewhat. While constantly exposed to surveillance, shock and awe was the more practical strategy. Now that they felt more hidden, the two could invest in a subtler approach. Roland's scanners thus managed to pick out the second group of patrolling cyborgs before he and Mindy blundered into them.

These six died as quickly as the last, though with less noise and destruction. Carefully placed shots and the quiet efficiency of Mindy's blade work put them down in short order. The pair worked in silence like two cogs in a well-oiled machine. When they had finished dispatching their prey, Mindy rewarded Roland with a rare compliment.

"Working with you is a lot like working with Mack, you know."

"High praise, indeed," Roland replied. "Mack was the best."

"I'm not talking about the rough stuff. Don't get me wrong, you're really good at that, too. But I'm talking about being in the field with you." She stopped and turned to look him in the faceplate. "I'm not always right in the head, you know? It's not always pretty what I do, and I don't always feel very pretty doing it. Sometimes I think I'm really ugly. On the inside, I mean."

Roland was not quite sure what she was getting at. "We are what we are. Is being pretty that important?"

"It shouldn't be, I suppose. But it's how I got by for a long time. I mean, it's no secret I use my looks to make stuff happen. Where I grew up, little girls were expected to be sweet and docile and most of all, pretty. They'd put me in pageants when I was a teenager and parade me around so whole bunches of creepy bastards could evaluate and grade my appearance. I'm pretty sure it fucked me up because I knew I was lying. I hated the dresses, the make-up. I hated the looks and the judging. Every fucker who thought I was attractive would have shit their pants if they knew what I was like on the inside. When it came out that I liked girls, well, let's just say I was

269

dead right about all of them." She sighed, and made a show of checking her confiscated bead rifle for damage or dirt before continuing. "Now I hate myself for being pretty, but I hate myself even more for not being pretty."

"That is pretty fucked up," Roland concurred with a sage nod of his head.

"Right? I liked Mack because he didn't care if I was pretty or not. He noticed my looks, but he never cared. You're the same way."

"I really can't say if you are pretty or not, Mindy. Honestly, I don't care. We're a team, you pull your weight and then some. You annoy the shit out of me, but I respect you anyway. Everything else is stupid."

"That sounds a lot like something Mack would say."

Roland thought about it. "We came up very differently, yet we ended up in the same places. Being permanently mounted to a machine gives you a unique perspective I guess."

The little blond killer nodded back. "I suppose it would have to, huh? Anyway, I guess I'm just glad that I can be ugly around you without worrying about it."

"You wanna talk ugly some time?" Roland asked as they began to walk on again. "We are about twenty miles from the place where I lost my body. My ugliness was born here. I thought I was past it, but every second I'm in this shithole brings it all right back. Every goddamn shadow makes me jump. I'm fucking scared, Mindy. Me! It takes a tank to scratch my paint, and suddenly I'm scared to walk into a dark alley here." He did not know why he was suddenly telling her this, but he was powerless to stop the tirade now. "I hate it so much and it's all I can do not to just rage and kill everything until I can escape. I hate myself for not knowing how to fix a problem without killing it. A million veterans deal with this every day without devolving into temper tantrums, why am I having such a hard time? It's weakness and I fucking hate myself for it. You want ugly, Mindy? I can do ugly. Ugly is the only thing I know."

"Let's not make this a contest, Ironsides."

It was good advice, and Roland said as much. "Good call."

Mindy, sounding more relaxed, offered him a deal. "Well, if we are fixing to get ugly, at least we are in the right place for it. You just go ahead and do whatever you need to do. You know I won't judge you if you promise not judge me."

270

"Deal." Roland had a sadistic, evil, delicious thought in that moment. "When we get to Craddock, I think we should have our own little beauty pageant. It'll be therapeutic for both of us."

"I think what you mean is an 'ugly pageant,' Ironsides."

"Yeah. I really do."

She laughed heartily. "I am so going to kill it during the talent competition."

Chapter Thirty-Six

Ellie Connelly's network of informants was a thing of beauty.

"Grimes came in on level nine. He stopped at his quarters to pick something up first. He is heading to Craddock's office now." It took the woman less than three minutes to secure this intelligence.

"Should we try to stop him?" Manny asked. "There's no telling what he is going to do."

"What did he stop to get?" Lucia thought this might be important.

Ellie scowled into her DataPad before responding. "Some kind of... knife? One of my people smuggled it in. They figured it was some stupid Balisong ceremonial blade or something. Very expensive, specially ordered from a robotics company on Wayfair."

Manny sighed, "Is it black? About eighteen inches long?"

"How the hell should I know?" Ellie grouched back. "Let me make a call."

Sixty seconds later she had the information they needed. "It's a black knife as long as you say. Do you know what it is?"

"It's the only thing on Venus that can punch a hole in Roland Tankowicz," Lucia said, her tone dangerous.

"And it's in the hands of a master assassin," Manny added.

"We need to know where Grimes is right now," Lucia barked at the woman.

Ellie looked like she wanted to spit a harsh retort, but then thought better of it and started to make calls instead. Lucia's eyes were flashing with the promise of extreme violence for anyone who stood in her way. It was a look Ellie Connelly had much experience with, and she was uninterested in the horrible consequences resistance might bring down upon her.

Soon, she had the answers. "Okay. Your big friend is smashing his way across the old supply depots, and Grimes is moving up through the refractory level, over by the old sulfur tanks. You remember those, Manny?"

The young man nodded.

"He's using the back stairs. Looks like he is trying to get to Craddock before your friends do. You have about ten minutes to catch him. You will have to run."

"Let's go," Manny said to Lucia. "Follow me."

The pair streaked off into the chaos of The Quad. Their flight was more or less headlong, and neither cared if Craddock's people picked up their trail or not. Even the densest Red Hat in The Colander would figure out where they were going easily enough. Lucia's speed was limited by her need to be led by Manny. He was not slow, but even his best pace was a fraction of Lucia's potential.

Her sense of dread was peculiar. Roland was easily a match for Grimes, the presence of a Sasori dagger notwithstanding. Roland could pluck the thing from the assassin at will if Grimes came straight at him. Lucia's brain, so wonderful, so powerful, was not returning a whole of scenarios where Grimes came straight at Roland. Grimes was going to emerge from the darkness to land a single blow. It was the only thing that made sense. He had seen enough of Roland to avoid a frontal assault or attacking his more armored areas. The strike would be to the back of the neck or under the chin. Possibly through the sternum if nothing else presented itself. Grimes would not care if he survived the attack, only that the blade went in deep.

Lucia was scared because she knew, far better than Grimes did, that such a blow could very well kill Roland. The single blade, wielded by a skilled hand, just might succeed where so many others had failed. This thought drove the frantic woman onward. It drove her to push Manny until his breath came in tortured wheezes.

She could not even warn Roland of what was coming. Encrypted comms were useless this far below the surface because so much metal and machinery stymied transceivers and killed signal fidelity. She dismissed using the local ComNet to get a call through out of hand. It would work, but that would be broadcasting her plan to anyone with the skills to hack a low-security telecom network. There was a chance that as they all converged on Craddock's office the shorter range might allow a call to make it through, and so she kept trying.

273

At last, Manny and Lucia burst through a hatch to find themselves in a long winding corridor on Craddock's office level. If Ellie's informants were correct, Roland would come in smashing from the other side to deal with Craddock. Grimes would be coming from this direction to stop him. The stairs Grimes was reportedly using led to a door at the end of the path about forty feet away. The duo had no way of knowing in real time exactly where their target was or when he would arrive. There was none of the usual signs that Roland was operating in the area yet, either. His ministrations were usually accompanied by explosions, the screams of wounded men, and the general destruction of the surrounding environment. It was hard to miss.

Grimes, on the other hand could be right behind you and you would never know it. He could be there and poised to strike already for all they knew, and this set Lucia's anxieties buzzing around her skull like a swarm of angry bees.

"Manny!" she hissed. "Do you have anything in that bag we can use to look for him?"

"Sorry Boss, no. These visors don't have the resolution for a hypersonic pulse, either."

"We need a plan!" She tried to keep her voice calm, but failed miserably.

"I'm going to rig the door," he advised the agitated woman. "If he comes through there, he'll get a rude surprise."

"Do it."

Manny set to work on the door. He attached small devices to each corner and wired them together. Then his hands returned to his satchel and emerged with a black tube the size of his forearm. Lucia squinted. "What's that?"

"Monofilament. They braid this stuff into cables and then use them to tow asteroids out of orbit. A single strand is damn near invisible, but hundreds of times stronger than steel for its mass."

"What are you going to do with it?"

Manny pointed to the walls. "I'm going to string it across this hallway. If Mr. Grimes comes down here too fast..."

"Ew, gross," Lucia remarked when she realized what that would engender. "I guess there's nothing to do but get back and wait for him to come, then."

"Keep trying Roland on the comms, too," Manny suggested. "His helmet comm has got to be better than these shitty handhelds."

"I have been. I'm hoping he can at least hear me."

He could not.

It wasn't until Mindy and Roland emerged from a parts depot into the same long corridor that he began to hear the first garbled messages from Lucia.

"Lucia?" He growled into the fuzzy static of the open channel. "Say again, Lucia!"

"What's up, Ironsides?" Mindy halted.

"Lucia is trying to send a message. It's too weak to punch through all this metal and machinery, though."

"Bad?"

"Not sure. I think she is heading our way for some reason."

Mindy grimaced, "She'd have to be fairly close already for a signal to get through at all."

"Let's keep going then. Maybe the signal will improve."

"Craddock's office is down here about fifty yards. You got any tangos on scan? My visor can't pick up shit in this."

"Other than the eight or nine guys around that corner waiting for us, screens are clear until we hit his door. After that I can't see much."

Mindy hefted her rifle. "You breach, I'll sweep, Ironsides."

"Roger that," he grunted in return.

With nothing else to do, the pair hit Craddock's men like the wrath of God itself. Roland rounded the corner and opened up with a long full-auto rip from Durendal. The hall was ten feet wide at most, and the massed men in Stahlkorper armatures may as well have been lethargic fish in a narrow barrel.

Forty beads, massive fifty-caliber ceramic spheres, broke across the first row of cyborgs like a burning wave. The three men in front died in the first quarter second. Heads exploded, breastplates shattered, and power cells ruptured in a brilliant cacophony of gory explosions. Roland did not wait for the men to fall. Even as the bolt slammed home on an empty chamber, he was charging. At nearly full speed he hit the second row of cyborgs, still reeling from the shock and awe of his fusillade.

A half ton of military hardware hit them at sixty miles per hour and the impact was suitably impressive. The unfortunate man who took the brunt of his charge did not die easily. His sturdy armature absorbed the hit with as much grace as could be expected, yet lost its feet under the sheer kinetic energy of it. Roland rode the man down, counting on Mindy to keep the others off his back. His punches started before they had come to a stop and he was leaping off the dead man while they were still sliding across the metal deck plates.

His feet found purchase on the floor and he whirled to face the rest. Among them Mindy was a cavorting blond phantom, carving pieces of the clumsy cyborgs from their frames with every pass. Her dagger leapt and swept about like a thing alive and Mindy was merely a puppet attached to its hilt. Roland threw himself back into the melee, and Mindy danced away to let his bull rush do its work unimpeded by the need to avoid her. The big black cyborg yanked another foe from the pack and put it bodily through the wall. The gray behemoth got wedged in the buckling bulkhead, and Roland tore its arms off trying to pull it free. Snarling, he settled for pulping the man's face with an obsidian fist and moving back to the center of the brawl.

Mindy had managed two more of the enemy with deft strokes from her Sasori dagger, and the final Stahlkorper was backing away from the tiny blond with hands raised. It was very clear to Roland that Mindy was not interested in taking prisoners or leaving live enemies behind her. She ran the man down in four strides and fell upon him. The black dagger rose and fell like a sewing machine needle, cycling dozens of times in just a few seconds and rendering the Red Hat thug inert like a fleshy pincushion.

Roland had no sympathy for the man. He was a terrorist and a murderer. The thug would have happily killed either of them, and wanting out of an attempted murder just because you were outclassed by your intended victims did not excuse that behavior in Roland's mind.

"You all right, Mindy?" He asked.

"Fighting guys your size is fucking brutal on the shoulders, Roland," she griped in reply. She spun her arms in wide circles to loosen the sore joints. "It's like running in wet sand."

"You get used to it." Let's go see Craddock."

"If he hasn't run away already..." Mindy admonished.

Roland reloaded Durendal and checked it for damage. "He's not the type."

Roland sidled up to the door and pulsed his helmet scanners at maximum. Sure enough, there were two men on the other side. Both were armed with large rifles of indeterminate configuration. He informed Mindy of this and she replied with a curt nod.

"You first, Ironsides."

"Story of my life, kid."

The metal hatch flew from its hinges like a dried leaf in a hurricane and a shower of sparks and metal fragments rained across the anteroom.

"Knock, knock!" Roland bellowed through the carnage.

Chapter Thirty-Seven

Killam Grimes heard the uproar on the hallway and knew he had lost his race with Tankowicz. His only hope was that Craddock's guards could hold the big fixer for a few more seconds. If he was lucky, he could use the confusion of a fight to time his killing stroke. He was only going to get the one shot, and the chaos of a pitched battle was as good a place as any to take it.

He shoved the stairwell hatch roughly and burst into the corridor leading to Craddock's office. As his feet cleared the threshold, his vision went white and his whole body was jolted by a wall of pure force. He could not hear anything through a loud ringing in his ears. Unable to arrest his momentum, the blind, deaf, and disoriented man crashed into the panel across from the door like a child tripping over shoelaces.

Grimes was far too smart to waste time wondering what had happened, and his training had included plenty of sensory deprivation exercises. The hows and whys of a booby-trapped hatch were unimportant and such questions could wait until he had recovered his faculties. He focused on the floor, keeping it as a reference point for all other directions and vaulted to his feet. Immediately, he spun to the side and slipped behind the open hatch for cover.

The incoming flechettes missed him by less than a foot and he swore in frustration. His vision was still blurry, but this hearing was returning quickly and he recognized the sound of the 5mm tungsten-tipped needles as they carved neat little holes in the metal walls. *That would be the Ribiero woman's CZ,* he realized. Her presence complicated things more than enough to infuriate him, but he could not assume she had come alone.

His door was made of thicker stuff than the walls, and the next impacts failed to penetrate his improvised cover. Without looking, the assassin returned fire from behind the door with his own bead pistol. He did not care if he hit anything, he just needed them to know he was armed so the enemy would not charge his position.

With his vision still spotty, he called out to his attackers to buy time.

"Ribiero!" he yelled. "I know everything now! You were right about Hardesty!"

Her voice came back strong and clear. "I knew that already, Grimes. I also know you killed him. So why are you here defending Craddock?"

"The Red Hats won't survive if that information gets out. It has to be stopped. Craddock is the only one who can keep us together. I can't let you kill him."

"Perhaps he should not have sent a bunch of guys in armatures to kill us first, then."

"Let me talk to Craddock. We can settle this."

"With your new knife?" Lucia replied, perhaps a touch more smug than strictly necessary.

Grimes stifled a wince. These people knew too much. "A precaution, Ribiero. Nothing more."

Manuel Richardson replied this time, "Okay. Toss it out, then, Grimes."

Grimes had to concede that the boy was clever. Relinquishing the dagger eliminated any chance of him killing Roland. He decided to change the subject.

"Where is the data you stole?"

The Ribiero woman laughed, clearly indicating his ploy had not gone unnoticed. "It's already in the wind, Grimes. There is nothing you can do, now."

"No, it is not. You have not had enough time to break the encryption. Your lie proves that there is still time to prevent a disaster. What are your terms?"

It was Manuel who responded to this. "No terms, Grimes." He did not sound as young as Grimes had thought him to be. "This is over. The Red Hats are over. If you've really seen what Hardesty did, then you already know I'm right. Just turn around and go. Become someone else, or something else. Grow past this, Killam. Or it will kill you."

"Don't you patronize me, turncoat," Grimes yelled back, his anger getting the better of him. "Venus deserves its freedom! The people demand it!"

"The people have not demanded anything, Grimes. They are just angry, which is how the Red Hats like them. You're angry right now, and that's how Craddock likes *you*. An angry man is a zealous man, and zealots don't ask uncomfortable questions."

Lucia chimed in, "Hear that? Sounds like the fighting has stopped down the hall. That means Roland is done with Craddock's guards." She paused for effect. "And no, there is no chance they brought him down. I think we all understand that, right? I figure you have about ten seconds to get past us before Roland does whatever it is he is going to do with Craddock."

Manny added, "I think you mean 'to' Craddock, Boss."

"Right," she replied. "'To' Craddock is much more likely."

Killam Grimes leapt from his hiding place. He understood he had little to no chance of outfighting the woman, but he only needed to get past her. He emptied his bead pistol magazine in her direction and was rewarded with the sight of her diving for the limited cover of an alcove. Richardson fell back, obviously surprised by the speed and ferocity of his sudden charge. For a brief, beautiful moment the assassin had a clear lane down the hallway. He stretched his stride and powered forward, determined not to let the opportunity pass.

His light ballistic vest saved his life. The first string of taut monofilament creased the garment and bit deeply into the reinforced weave. He felt the string just start to cut into his flesh and he let his legs buckle in response. As he fell, the line snapped over his chest and took a chunk of his right ear off. He hit the floor in a heap, but slid nimbly to his belly, then scuttled forward in a spastic low crawl.

After a few yards of low-crawling, he surged to his feet and started to spring again. Grimes was familiar with this kind of trap so the whole exercise took mere fractions of second. On his second stride, something knocked his feet out from underneath him and he went down hard. Roaring in frustration, he rolled to his back, spraying beads with his pistol and slashing wildly with his dagger.

Killam Grimes no longer had any *mushin* or *zanshin*. He was angry and scared and frustrated all at once. Hardesty was a lying traitor. His chance to save the Red Hats was slipping away. Everything he knew and understood about his universe was either a lie or about to change. He was not fighting for Venus any more. He was not fighting for his comrades. He was fighting to preserve a place and a time. If he could just stop this fixer and Hardesty's lies nothing would have to change. If he succeeded, it could all go back to the way it was before.

He rose again, and a fist struck him in the back of his thigh. A searing electric fire locked the limb and sent him back to the floor. He spun and sent the humming edge of his black blade arcing at the booted ankles of the Ribiero woman. Her boot rose and fell so quickly that the sole crushed his wrist to the floor and sent the blade spinning off into orange shadows.

He raised his gun hand to shoot her but a grip like a thousand vises closed over it. Both the weapon and the hand gripping it were then crushed, bones and gun parts breaking in the pale heart of Manny's mechanical fist.

Killam Grimes cried out, and this was no war cry. It was a wailing sob of pain, mixed with despair and defeat. He was not just losing a fight. He was losing everything he had ever known. Every friend, every brother, every belief and conceit he had ever held was dying in front of his eyes. He did not want them to die. He did not want them to die because it meant that he would not exist anymore, either. More terrifying, it meant that he had never really existed in the first place.

This was the worst of it. The pinned assassin knew that if he sought out *mushin* right now he would come to the one inescapable conclusion that he feared more than anything else.

It had all been a lie.

It had not been a lie at first. Like all the best lies there was a grain of truth at the center. The Planetary Council did treat them poorly, and the incompetence and corruption of the RUC was not in question.

But what the Red Hats has done, the things Hardesty had made happen, they were all suspect now. Grimes had done such horrible things, buoyed by the unshakable faith that his actions served a greater good. Now he did not know what purpose his crimes had served. Venus was no more free now than it was thirty years ago, though Hardesty was much richer. This no longer felt like coincidence. So many things that should have been obvious to Grimes had gone unexplored. Doubt was weakness after all.

If he failed now, and all those ignored doubts turned out to be valid, then Grimes was a hideous inhuman monster. No more than a pawn, a mindless zealot wielded like a prized blade by his betters.

Just like that, there was *mushin*. No mind, no ego, no self. The truth of his existence came into stark relief, and he examined his life without judgment. He was fighting a losing battle to preserve an illusion, and this was stupid. It was all an ugly fiction carefully constructed to keep him angry and obedient. With the shroud of fanaticism stripped from his eyes, the answers were all so painfully obvious.

He spoke four words aloud to his captors, and they came without the inflection of ego or shame.

"You must kill me."

His body collapsed, and he stopped fighting the grip of his opponents.

Neither Lucia nor Manny relaxed, and after a long pause Lucia spoke. "We don't do it that way, Grimes."

"I am a lie," the assassin whispered quietly. "Let me die with the other lies."

Manny sighed, "Oh, grow up. You aren't going through anything I haven't, or a dozen others like us. My life was a lie, too. I've got a ton of blood on my hands, too. We were lied to. Get over it."

Crying was a stoning offense among the Balisongs, but Killam Grimes no longer understood why that mattered. Tears filled his eyes, and he did not fight them. "I don't want to live."

"Good," Manny huffed. "You don't deserve to live. But don't make ending your life our problem."

Lucia's boot shifted, and Manny's bionic arm shifted to the assassin's neck. Grimes was hauled to his feet and shoved roughly against the warm metal bulkhead. He met the intense brown eyes of Manuel Richardson. "You don't want to live? Good. Killam Grimes is now dead. Go be someone else. I recommend you travel a bit. The universe is a huge place. Maybe you can find out who you really are out there." Then a weird look twisted his features and he added, "But since I can't have you following us..."

A powerful electric shock from Manny's hand passed through the killers' brain and rendered the man unconscious.

"Sorry," he added, though it did not sound sincere at all.

Chapter Thirty-Eight

T he gunfire coming from Craddock and Sully was reasonably accurate and suitably voluminous. It was also conspicuous for its uselessness. The beads exploded across Roland's chest in a miniature firework show and sent fragments pinwheeling around the office like a ceramic dust storm.

Roland was content to stand there and take the hits. Ammunition was a finite quantity and dealing with these two would be easier once their weapons ran dry. This took about five seconds. When the roar of hypersonic projectiles shattering against techno-organic armor subsided, Roland spared a moment to brush the last shredded dregs of his shirt away from his chest.

"Feel better?" His inquiry was delivered through the still roiling haze of smoke, so Roland took a single step forward to let Craddock see him more clearly. The silver death's head emerged from the cloud like the prow of a pirate ship and the movement of all that bulk sent the last wisps of gunsmoke swirling off into oblivion.

"Fuck me," Craddock responded eloquently.

"Not likely," was the growled retort. "Take a seat, Craddock." Roland gestured to a chair.

Craddock looked at Roland with a wary eye. "Maybe I'd rather stand."

"Maybe this is not a negotiation."

"Right," Craddock exhaled. "Guess I'll take a seat, then." He settled into his office chair and motioned for Sully to find one of his own. "So, what happens now, Fixer?"

"Terms."

"I'm listening."

"The Red Hats are over. You are to leave Venus and head for the frontier. If you ever come back, you're dead."

Craddock barked an ugly derisive laugh. "Bullshit. Those ain't terms. Here's my counteroffer. You all leave and take the Richardson brat with you. Fuck him. We don't need the hassle. You leave the shit you stole from Hardesty with us and you fuck off Venus forever. You stay out of our shit and we'll stay out of yours. How's that sound?"

"We are way past Richardson, Craddock. Do you know what is in the files we took?"

"Yeah. Hardesty sold us out to OmniCorp."

"Do you know why?"

Craddock sneered. "He got old and tired. He wanted to cash out."

"No, you uneducated fanatic, Hardesty knew the truth. Venusian mining is dying, and with it the Venusian labor economy. Just maintaining life support here is pricey, let alone using union members for labor. There's enough iron, sulfur and VOCs on other planets that don't have your problems to handle the demand. Everyone except OmniCorp is going to drop this place soon. Then OmniCorp and their automated facilities can scoop up all the contracts dirt cheap. It's all a hustle, Craddock. Everybody knows it." Roland reached up and removed his helmet before continuing. "You Red Hats have been fighting tooth and nail to defend a system that actively hurts the rest of the planet, and you idiots can't figure out why you don't have more support?"

"You a fucking economist, now? We'd get by just fine if we didn't have the council and the RUC fucking with us."

"Christ, you really believe that, don't you? Well, your pal Hardesty didn't. He figured OmniCorp would at least keep the industry afloat for another few decades. If they cut out the union there is a solid chance they can do it, too. For all his graft and bullshit, Hardesty really did want to help. He just knew you guys over here were going to be too dumb to realize it." Then, as an afterthought, "also he was a greedy prick."

"You got a point?"

"Yeah. The point is that the files we stole are going public soon. Period. You misunderstood my terms. I'm not saying you need to leave because I give a shit where you are or what you do. It's because once all the shifty crap Hardesty was up to gets out, this whole place is going to turn on the Red Hats. You will want to be as far from here as possible before that happens."

Hardesty's death at the hands of Killam Grimes cemented the truth of that statement in Craddock's mind. He refused to give the fixer the satisfaction of acknowledging this. "You don't know any better than me what's in those files, pal. You're bluffing." Craddock sounded pleased with himself. Roland disabused him of this.

"I never bluff. I don't need to get into them to know what they'll show." He began to tick items off on his fingers, "It'll be price fixing, bribes, sabotaging both the union leadership and the RUC. OmniCorp wants to buy these mining contracts cheap, but they also want them to look viable to attract investors. This is a real old con, Craddock. I am busting it wide open."

Craddock was not sure how much he believed the big man, but what he said had the disconcerting ring of truth to it. He did not have it in him to back down, though. "I don't give a shit either way, Fixer. I stand by my terms. You go fuck off, and leave Venus to the Venusians."

Roland chuckled, appreciating the irony of it all. "That's exactly what I am doing, Craddock. I'm leaving Venus to the Venusians, not a bunch of murdering terrorists."

"I have seventy guys in armatures between you and the exits, tough guy." Craddock leaned forward in his chair. "You might want to think real hard about your next moves."

"More like forty-seven, actually," said Roland with a grunt. "We got twenty-three on the way here."

"Twenty-seven," a squeaky voice corrected from behind Roland. "Plus, those three OmniCorp Kanos."

Craddock stifled a wince. Losing twenty-seven guys in a day was an unprecedented event. He felt sweat run down the back of his neck that was not attributable to the poor air conditioning. A busty blond woman who Craddock assumed had to be Mindy stepped around the big fixer and looked at the terrorist leader. She wore a bloodstained blue jumpsuit and carried an old bead rifle. Ever smiling, she pointed her weapon at his forehead.

"Why are we talking to these guys? Shouldn't we just kill them and go?"

Craddock decided that he did not like the little blond.

Roland's eyes never left Craddock. "I'd rather not have to fight my way out of here, and I'd just as soon spare the folks here all the chaos. It's like demo-ing a building, Mindy. A few carefully placed charges are neater and easier than just nuking it from orbit."

"Right," Mindy agreed, but she did not sound convinced.

"So, Craddock, are we being reasonable enough? Or do you have more threats you want to try out before you go?"

Alasdair Craddock was at a crossroads. He cast a quick furtive glance to Sully, and the look in his friend's eyes told him that Sully would back whatever play Craddock made. Strangely, this calmed him. Sully believed in the same dream Craddock did. Even more, Sully believed in Craddock. Hundreds of young Red Hats in The Colander were counting on him to lead them to freedom. He was not a sentimental man, nor was he prone to fits of nationalistic pride. He had been raised to hate the Planetary Council and the RUC, however, and it was in moments like this that his hate sustained him. A wiser man might take Roland's advice. A better strategist might try to turn the situation to his advantage. A weaker man might break and run. A Red Hat would fight to the death.

Craddock was unready to do this, either. Glorious death in battle was fine for the regular Red Hats, but Alasdair knew he had to survive this. No matter what Hardesty had done, and no matter what Roland had done, he would never fail the cause. The cause needed him. He was much too important to be killed.

For the dream of a free Venus, he could not die here. Sully knew that. Sully was loyal.

Sully died a loyal Red Hat to the last.

Sully opened fire on the little blond with a hidden pistol. The beads caved little dimples into the blue fabric of her jumpsuit without punching through it, though the woman yelped all the same. Craddock dove from his chair as the big fixer moved to cover the little assassin with his body. He was not a fast man, but fear drove him to speeds he did not think were possible. He heard the crack of a single bead from Mindy's rifle and he knew Sully was gone. He could not spare any thoughts for his friend, so focused was he on his own escape.

If Alasdair Craddock was thinking clearly, he might have acknowledged that his desire to live was not entirely altruistic. This might have made him sad, because it meant he had just sacrificed his best friend out of cowardice. Alasdair Craddock was not thinking clearly, he was thinking about running and about whether or not he had enough of a head start to escape.

He nearly crashed into Manuel Richardson and Lucia Ribiero as he ran, shoving the young man rudely out of the way. If he had been thinking clearly, he might have wondered why they made no move stop him. He was not thinking clearly, though. He was wondering if the unmoving form of Killam Grimes in his path was dead or alive. Then he was leaping over the body to keep running.

Alasdair Craddock was a full head shorter than Killam Grimes, which was the sort of useless trivia that had no real value to anyone barring certain very unique circumstances. Even if he had been thinking clearly, there was no way a reasonable person could have expected him to realize ahead of time that his height compared to Grimes' would ever be relevant to his escape.

In this unique circumstance, it was quite relevant. A monofilament line that had caught Killam Grimes across his chest was thus at the perfect height to decapitate a fleeing Alasdair Craddock.

Roland and his team came upon the headless corpse just a few seconds later. Lucia took one look and felt her gorge rise while the rest of them just looked disgusted. Manny broke the silence.

"What a colossal waste."

"Of what?" Mindy sounded incredulous.

"Potential. He was a good leader. There are probably a million ways he could have helped the people here that didn't involve killing innocent civilians or brainwashing children."

Roland was more to the point. "He lacked imagination. Let's hope his type of thinking is on the way out. This place doesn't need any more of the Red Hats."

"Or us," Lucia added. "We need to go. Anyone have a plan for getting us out of here?"

They all looked to Manny, who sighed theatrically. "Ellie is going   to   kill   us   all."

Chapter Thirty-Nine

Getting clear of The Colander proved a very complicated task. Gangs of roving Stahlkorpers still executing Craddock's final orders were hard to avoid. Those that could not be avoided proved to be no match for the four fixers from Dockside. The Red Hat metal men were well below half strength before the team finally made it to the relative safety of The Quad.

Further exacerbating their woes, the exit of OmniCorp assets had the RUC attempting to reassert itself as well. The acute lack of subtlety with which the group had managed their exodus did not go unnoticed. The swath of destruction in their wake left the Corps with many uncomfortable questions for Roland's team.

Thankfully, there was enough incriminating information on the RUC in Hardesty's files to put the whole garrison on its heels. Some firm words from Roland to Sergeant Cummings put most of that right, but it was with very narrow eyes indeed that the officers of the Republic Unification Corps escorted the four fixers to their shuttle.

Ellie Connelly saw them off. Whether this was to say good-bye to Manny, or to ensure that Roland actually left, no one could say. She hugged the boy tightly and kissed him on each cheek, then warned him to never come back with tears in her eyes.

Roland thought it was all very sweet until she stomped over to him and tugged his lapel in manner not at all friendly. He was tired and grouchy, and he did not suffer this gladly.

"What, lady? I'm leaving. You should be happy."

"I am not happy. You come here and kill fifty people, then you leave. How does that make me happy?"

"They were all bad people?"

"No!" She pointed to Manny. "They were stupid boys like that one. Lied to. Stolen when they were too young to know better by old men with too many wars to fight and too little balls to do it themselves."

Roland did not like Ellie, but she was not wrong about that part. He shrugged off her grip. "I was in good company, then. Try singing a song I haven't heard before."

She eyed him coldly. "You are a very dangerous person, Roland Tehn-KO-visch. Dangerous to your enemies, and to your friends. I love that stupid boy, and I can see him follow you like a lost puppy. I am frightened for him, because he is not frightened of you. At least not as much as he should be."

"Is this where you threaten me?" Roland's patience was beginning to wear very thin, and a dangerous edge crept into his voice.

"No. This is where I warn you. I watched Craddock for forty years. I watched you for four days. You may have been different men, but your methods looked very similar to my old eyes. If you would think of yourself as better than Craddock, just look at that stupid boy and remember what old Ellie said to you."

Roland had had just about enough of this. "Oh, cry me a river, Lady. If you had stepped up and led when these folks needed you to, maybe I wouldn't have had to come out here and do shit the hard way. I am so goddamn sick of hearing you bitch about how hard everything is, and how no one understands your problems. Well, where the fuck were you? Where the hell were Ellie's wise words of wisdom when Manny was ten? Who stood up to Craddock and Hardesty when they were still two-bit bullshit artists slinging sulfur in the refractories? It sure as fuck wasn't you. But who did show up to set it all right? Well, Ms. Connelly, it was that brave young man over there. He did more for The Colander in four days than you have in four decades. You're worried about what I might do? Hell, I'm terrified of all the crap you *won't* do." Roland turned his back on her, leaving her quivering with rage. Then he stopped and whipped back around, putting his nose an inch from hers. "One more thing. I swear to God, woman, if you call him 'stupid boy' just one more time I will stuff you into a recycler. That is a fine young man and a valued member of my team. You call him 'Manny' or 'Mr. Richardson' or 'sir.' We clear?"

The woman just stared at him, eyes brimming with the bitter tears of hate and shame. She wanted to slap him across the face, he

289

could see that much clearly. He did not care. He was leaving and if he had his way he would never see her or this orange hellhole ever again.

Ever astute, Lucia got wind of their interaction and swooped in to save them both.

"Thank you for all your help, Ellie. Roland? Why don't you help Mindy get our stuff stowed?"

"Good idea, Boss." Roland's words were only just intelligible under the rumbling growl. He stalked off on heavy feet to disappear into the cargo area of their shuttle.

"That man is..." Ellie's sentence faded away her brain unable to find the right combination of insulting words to convey her roiling antipathy.

"Right," Lucia finished. "He is right a lot of the time. He's just really bad at communicating."

"He is a monster," Ellie said with finality.

"That he is. Worse, he's the monster that other monsters check their closets for at night. Best of all? He's our monster."

"You are welcome to him, then." Ellie shuddered. "Venus has enough monsters to go around."

"You really are way too dramatic, Ellie. If there is one thing that I have learned from Roland, it's that people like to make their problems more complicated than they need to be. It gives us an excuse for not solving them on our own."

The older woman gave Lucia a sideways look. "Easy for you to say."

"I suppose it is." Lucia turned briskly and extended her hand to the older woman. "Thank you again for your help. Best of luck to you."

Ellie grasped the hand and shook it. "You too, Lucia Ribiero. Good luck."

Once they were safely in transit, Manny, Lucia, and Mindy trekked down to the cargo area of their ferry to check on Roland, who was once again riding as freight.

They found him seated comfortably in a pile of crates artfully arranged in a chair-like configuration. Lucia handed him a beer when they got to him.

"Everybody feel good about this run?" He asked after a long sip.

"Define 'good,' Mr. Tankowicz," Manny said.

"Objectives completed? This was your mission, Manny."

The young man sat heavily on a crate. "I guess so. I don't see us having any issues with the Red Hats now. And we didn't start a civil war, either. That's pretty good I think."

Mindy asked the question on all of their minds. "So what's bothering you, Manny-boy?"

He held his hands up in a defeated gesture. "I suppose I was hoping for more... I don't know, satisfaction?"

"Ahhhh." Lucia nodded her head sagely. "You want closure."

"I guess."

"That's a myth," Roland laughed. "Nobody gets closure. It was made up by twentieth-century quacks. You just learn how to be okay with the things that happen to you. When you figure out how to move on, they say you found 'closure.'"

Lucia rolled her eyes. "It's not a myth, Roland." Then she turned to Manny. "He's not wrong about how you get it, though. It's not something that happens, it's something you do."

"Shooting up a bunch of terrorist bastards helps." This was Mindy's contribution, and it earned her a six-eyed scowl from the rest of them. "What? What'd I say?"

"And they say I'm insensitive," Roland laughed.

Mindy barreled on. "Hey, Manny, I meant to ask you this before. Everybody in The Colander seemed so proud of those burn scars they get from the leaky dome. Do you have any?"

He shook his head, "No, I don't. The whole thing with Aphrodite's Tears is weird to me. It's not very hard to avoid the leaks, even when you work on the dome itself. Lots of the boys in my dorm would actually wander around the skin looking for cracks so they could finally get a scar."

Roland looked aghast. "What? Ellie was so proud of her scars. It's like they're some kind of merit badge or membership card."

Manny nodded. "People on Venus have been miserable for so long. The misery becomes an identity unto itself. The scars are a visible indicator of that misery. The scars tell other people that they have endured."

"But you never got any?" Mindy was still confused by this.

Manny looked at her through raised brows. "I never saw the point. I wasn't miserable. I liked my childhood, for the most part. I didn't know that it was all a lie until it was too late."

Roland chuckled. "So even the stupid acid scars are bullshit?"

Manny smiled, and it was a strange, satisfied little grin. "Everything on Venus is bullshit, Mr. Tankowicz."

"Let's never go back," Roland suggested.

"Seconded," Manny said with raised hand.

Lucia slapped the top of a crate with a laugh. "Motion carries."

Mindy had her own motion to pose. "And now that the business part of this trip is concluded, who thinks we should go grab a shit-ton of beers and spend the next thirty hours getting stupid drunk in this cargo hold?"

"Seconded," Roland growled.

And   that   was   exactly   what   they   did.

About the Author

Andrew Vaillencourt would like you to believe he is a writer. But that is probably not the best place to start. He *is* a former MMA competitor, bouncer, gym teacher, exotic dancer wrangler, and engineer.

He wrote his first novel, 'Ordnance,' on a dare from his father and has no intention of stopping now. Drawing on far too many bad influences including comic books, action movies, pulp sci-fi and his own upbringing as one of twelve children, Andrew is committed to filling the heads of readers with hard-boiled action and vivid worlds in which to set it. His work pulls characters and voices born from his time throwing drunks out of a KC biker bar, fighting in the Midwest amateur MMA circuit, or teaching kindergarteners how to do a proper push-up.

He currently lives in Connecticut with his lovely wife, three decent children, and a very lazy ball python named Max.

Read more at <u>Andrew Vaillencourt's site</u>.

Made in the USA
San Bernardino, CA
18 September 2018